W9-DDB-624

About Adam

About Adam

Stella Cameron

Thorndike Press   Chivers Press
Waterville, Maine USA   Bath, England

SOMERSET COUNTY LIBRARY
BRIDGEWATER, N. J. 08807

This Large Print edition is published by Thorndike Press®, USA and by Chivers Press, England.

Published in 2003 in the U.S. by arrangement with Harlequin Books S.A.

Published in 2003 in the U.K. by arrangement with Harlequin Enterprises II, B.V.

U.S. Hardcover 0-7862-5519-6 (Basic Series)
U.K. Hardcover 0-7540-1991-8 (Windsor Large Print)

Copyright © 2003 by Stella Cameron.

All rights reserved.

All characters in this book have no existence outside the imagination of the author and have no relation whatsoever to anyone bearing the same name or names. They are not even distantly inspired by any individual known or unknown to the author, and all incidents are pure invention.

The text of this Large Print edition is unabridged.
Other aspects of the book may vary from the original edition.

Set in 16 pt. Plantin by Elena Picard.

Printed in the United States on permanent paper.

British Library Cataloguing-in-Publication Data available

Library of Congress Cataloging-in-Publication Data

Cameron, Stella.
    About Adam / Stella Cameron.
      p. cm.
    ISBN 0-7862-5519-6 (lg. print : hc : alk. paper)
    1. Mayfair (London, England) — Fiction. 2. Portrait painters — Fiction. 3. Princesses — Fiction. 4. Large type books. I. Title.
PS3553.A4345A63 2003
813´.54—dc21   2003046698

SOMERSET COUNTY LIBRARY
BRIDGEWATER, N. J. 08807

For
Barbara Hicks
The Junkies, RBR, READ
And those wonderful people at
www.stellacameron.com

Prologue

Mayfair Square
London
January 1824

The trouble with the people at 7 Mayfair Square is that they are alive.

There is no doubt that bodies — the bones and blood, the mortal mind, the so-called heart and other various bits and pieces — get in the way of good, solidly disconnected logic. It's all that and the wretched feelings they swear by that may scuttle the sensible plans of a superior being like yours truly. Nevertheless, I must say that being a ghost can be more than it is cracked up to be.

My word, I almost forgot to tell you that I am the late Sir Septimus Spivey, esteemed architect knighted for his worldly accomplishments, the crowning glory of which was my family home at Number 7 Mayfair Square.

Desperation at the possible misuse of my

masterpiece forced me to hang around in mortal form until I was 102! 102, I tell you, when I was perfectly ready to commence my path to heaven a good ten years earlier. If my family hadn't shown themselves incapable of keeping my house in the manner to which it deserved to be accustomed, I should not have wasted those extra years trying to guide my ungrateful progeny. I rarely complain, but this delay put me considerably behind in angel school and it has only been through diligent work that I have made sterling progress — much to the annoyance of my "friend," William Shakespeare and one or two others I won't bore you with now.

That's history and I only mention it to let you know that since you will be supporting me in my current endeavor, you are on the side of right.

You'll be meeting the former Misses Smiles who used to rent 7B Mayfair Square — the second floor. Below the Smiles, Latimer More and his sister, Finch, had 7A — the first floor. And the third floor — for reasons only my granddaughter Lady Hester Bingham could explain — became her home and known as 7. Hunter Lloyd, her nephew, lived on the same floor. And that oaf of a painter, Adam Chillworth was, and is, in residence at 7C as they call the attic, and that's where that frequently silent, oppressive north countryman continues to live.

I had no intention of boring you with too much information, but why not bring you up-to-date on the happenings of recent years within the walls of my house.

As I planned, Finch More married Ross, Viscount Kilrood, a Scotsman who owns Number 8 Mayfair Square, in addition to considerable Scottish holdings. They divide their time between the London house and the Scottish estate.

Meg Smiles of 7B designed an audacious plan and snared Jean-Marc, Count Etranger, the vulgarly wealthy son of Prince Georges, ruler of Mont Nuages, a principality on the border between France and Germany. They own Number 17 Mayfair Square and a home at Windsor. That little arrangement wasn't quite what I had in mind but it worked well enough.

Meg's sister, Sybil, was as besotted with Hester's nephew, Hunter Lloyd, as he was with her and since their marriage this has remained sickeningly true. Hunter, a barrister, was knighted for services to George IV — that almost came to a nasty pass. A Cornish holding and considerable money came with the knighthood. The holding is small but nice enough. However, the boy insists on spending a good deal of time at Number 7 and Sibyl is as attached to Lady Hester as he is. Their little boy doesn't lessen the confusion about the place, even if more rooms have been made over for the family.

Drat, I knew I should get a headache — an ache in the region where my head once was, that is — if I tried to make you aware of the way things are and how they became so.

That leaves Latimer More, Finch's, now Viscountess Kilrood's, brother. I got lucky there. The unthinkable actually worked out and he settled on a pauper, an orphan from the most degrading beginnings, as his wife. Jenny O'Brien was . . . well, I must be charitable. Jenny knew she had no rightful place in the polite world and did her best to make that rattle Latimer see the truth. He didn't and they're married. The only good part of that arrangement is that they now live at Number 8, Ross and Finch's house, where they have a handsome suite of rooms and seem ridiculously happy each time Ross and Finch and their offspring arrive to crowd the place.

A moment please, I must rest after all that.

Did I tell you that one of the flawlessly carved newel posts in the foyer at Number 7 is my retreat? Well, it is. From here, at the base of my miraculous staircase, I observe all comings and goings. I admit that since my wings have matured from buds and are growing a little every day, I am not quite as comfortable as I used to be; the space inside the post has become somewhat snug. Yes, yes, of course I know I should be able to deal with this problem but I can't ask help in finding out how to make the change and I have had rather a lot of other things to learn.

By gad I forgot Birdie, that wretched, wispy little creature Hester insisted on adopting. The child is audacious but Hester dotes upon her and I suppose the girl dotes upon her, but she makes entirely too much noise. Fortunately she also dotes on Hunter and Sibyl and spends a goodly amount of time with them.

Toby! I can't be blamed if some of these people slip my mind. Toby is Jenny More's tatty young friend from her days of living in Whitechapel and, yet again, Hester took pity on the clumsy creature. He now lives in the best room in servants' quarters and is treated like a particularly intelligent pet.

Never mind all that. Forget about it unless one or two of them show up while I'm cleaning up the mess they've all made at Number 7. And they have made a mess. Almost nothing is simple.

But I have a plan, the Perfect Plan. My previous attempts to rid the house of Hester's unbearable lodgers (protégées as she pretends they are) were fraught with obstacles because I had not seen the obvious. Lady Hester Bingham must become a celebrity hostess and patroness in her own right. For this she will need her home to be serene and impeccable. There she will welcome literary gatherings, guide silly girls toward fine matches, and have the ear of every important member of the ton.

There are one or two problems to overcome — when haven't there been problems to overcome in this house? But getting rid of Adam Chillworth is my essential goal now, and since the only woman he believes he can love (as if love had anything to do with these matters) is Jean-Marc, Count Etranger's sister, Princess Desirée of Mont Nuages, then that must be arranged.

Since the attic at 7 Mayfair Square would hardly make an adequate home for a princess, I'm sure the girl's brother — once he stops trying to oppose the marriage, as he most certainly will — I'm sure Jean-Marc will provide a suitably splendid abode and, after all, the Princess herself is to come into a fortune. And if that dolt Chillworth climbs on his high horse and talks about not being prepared to live on his wife, well then, there are ways to force his hand.

I do foresee a nasty conundrum in Hester's

plans to renovate the house. Hunter and Sybil encourage all this, but from what I've heard of those plans, well, they must not be carried out and I shall rely upon your eyes and ears and, where necessary, your hands to help me scuttle their vulgar ideas.

The usual rule applies — your mouths are no good to me and should be kept shut.

I'm off to meet someone who will be my right hand in all of this, my earthly helper. In the past my error has been to seek the assistance of empty minds I assumed would be simple to control and guide. Never again. This time I have realized where I went wrong. This time a busy mind will be the weapon against any resistance. After all, doesn't it make sense that the busy mind of a self-centered person will clamor and scheme with such deafening vigor that my instructions, so craftily introduced, will go unnoticed in the din. Before this indispensable helper realizes what's happened, the deeds I order will be performed and even then, and with any luck, the arrogant prancer will still be too involved with other matters to notice mine.

It is time to set my plans in motion. Await my dispatches and be ready to act. Soon.

1

On a bitterly cold January afternoon, Adam Chillworth of 7C Mayfair Square wanted to be alone in his attic. No, not exactly true — he wanted to be with someone he must avoid at all costs, but if he couldn't be with her, his own company was all he could stand. In truth he couldn't stand that, either, but at least when he was alone he had no need to pretend he wasn't the most miserable man in London.

Having continued to pound on Adam's door until he let him in, Latimer More, former tenant of 7A, but now residing at Number 8 Mayfair Square, prowled about the place, examining everything from Adam's large but simple bed with its lumpy patchwork quilt, to the new green and gold velvet sofa beneath a narrow, dormer window. The largest portion of the attic, in the center and beneath a skylight, was filled with Adam's painting paraphernalia since producing portraits of the rich and famous, or the rich and infamous, was his life's work. Latimer stopped close to the shrouded easel as if Adam might whip off the covering and reveal his current work in progress.

That would not happen unless he was in the mood. He was not in the mood.

Adam made much of unfolding a handsome chinoiserie screen to shield his sleeping quarters from the rest of his home.

"Look at you, Chillworth," Latimer said suddenly, his chin thrust forward and his black eyes hard. "I'm dashed if you aren't the most irritating fellow. Quarrelsome. Moping around up here. Pining for —"

"Be quiet." Adam glared back with a forefinger touching his lips. He had another caller, this one tapping softly at his door. "If you find me so irritating, More, take yourself off. Aye, you do that. Take yourself off."

Latimer's smile infuriated Adam and the repeated tapping at the door didn't help. He strode to see who else was determined to pester him.

"Halibut?" he said. A young woman with specks of a February snow clinging to her shoulders, held the large, gray cat in her arms. Adam took his old feline friend from her and his stomach dipped unpleasantly. Halibut had only left Adam's care a few days previous. The cat belonged to she who must be avoided, the only woman he could ever love, the girl cruel fate had chosen to make a princess and out of the reach of a simple artist. Besides, she was far too young for him.

"Desirée . . . I mean, Princess Desirée," Adam said, trying but failing to sound calm. "Something's wrong with her? I knew it, I just knew it. Why else would she come back from the Continent in little more than six months when she said she didn't think she would ever return?"

"I'm Anne Williams, Mr. Chillworth — Princess Desirée's companion. I traveled with her from Mont Nuages. I'm worried about her, sir, most worried. She gave me permission to come over from Number 17."

"Come in, Miss Williams," Latimer said, taking her elbow and guiding her inside while he shook his head in exasperation at Adam.

Adam's skin felt too small for his body. He must tread carefully or his passion for Desirée would cause him to act foolishly. "Aye, well, would you be calm and tell me what's amiss? I'd intended to call at Number 17 —"

"Instead he persuaded my wife to deliver Halibut there," Latimer said, no longer looking at Adam. "He was too upset at losing his fat cat friend. Inseparable they've been during Desirée's absence, I can tell you."

Adam longed to tell Latimer he could stop prattling and return to his beloved wife, Jenny. "Miss Williams," he said instead, "please explain your concern for your mistress." He noted that the woman seemed too subdued in her heavy, brown wool cloak with the hood pushed down to reveal neat blond hair beneath a pleated brown bonnet.

She sighed and looked at the floor. Her voice was clear but soft, "It's been terrible. Oh, dear, Her Highness would not want me to say such things. I am only to ask you to accept Halibut for a time until Count Etranger's anger subsides. She is afraid so many raised voices will upset his delicate constitution."

Adam looked at Halibut who overflowed his arms and contentedly blinked golden eyes. The animal ate anything that wasn't hidden from him and weighed more than some two-year-old children. "Delicate, yes," Adam said and felt lame. "He isn't as young as he used to be, either." Halibut was five or so.

"I think it's the Princess who needs sanctuary," Latimer said, with the mischievous smirk that made the interfering devil even more handsome. "Please tell her you talked with Adam and myself and that she must never forget she has the best of friends at Number 7. She must come here — to Adam — whenever she needs support."

Subtlety had never been Latimer's particular talent, unless he needed it to be so for his own purposes. "I'm sure it would be acceptable for you to *mention* what is troubling the Princess," Adam said.

Moisture welled in Miss Williams's pretty brown eyes and she shook her head.

"Quite so," Latimer told her. "A faithful companion is a treasure. Please go quietly back to Number 17 and give Adam's message to Desirée." He ushered her out and closed the door softly behind her.

"*My* message?" Adam said the instant they were alone. "I didn't send any message. *You* did. You've dispatched that woman back to Desirée with an invitation to come here."

Latimer puffed up his cheeks and managed a bemused expression.

"You said *we* were her friends —" Adam

pointed out "— then made sure you talked about me and Number 7."

"You would have liked me to suggest she come to Number 8 instead? Jenny and I would be only too happy to entertain Desirée. We love her."

Adam wouldn't be further baited. "Jean-Marc can be an intractable hard nose," he said of Count Etranger, Princess Desirée's half brother and her guardian. "He continues to treat her like a child."

"I thought you said she is still a child. Isn't that supposed to be the reason you won't encourage the girl's adoration? If it's not, you'd better come up with another excuse for making the pair of you miserable."

Adam draped Halibut over his shoulder and went to sit in a worn, extremely comfortable brown leather chair by the fire. He had filled this place with oddities from his travels, and with some excellent pieces he'd vaguely thought might grace a more elegant home one day.

"She went away because she gave up on you," Latimer said. "Four years she's been in love with you and four years you've found pathetic reasons not to be open with your feelings for her. Don't you think she knows you want her? Don't you think she lies awake imagining she is in your arms —

19

even in that monstrous bed of yours? I'd suggest you have similar thoughts to keep you warm at night, only you're a man of the world, of course, with other diversions on your mind."

"That's enough," Adam said. He crossed his legs. Better to put up with the discomfort than give Latimer the pleasure of commenting on what happened to a part of Adam's anatomy at the thought of Desirée in bed . . . with a white sheet drawn to her chin . . . and a thin, lawn night rail, dampened by her unrequited ardor, clinging to her lovely body beneath that sheet.

"You don't take your late night excursions at present, do you?" Latimer asked. "A man might wonder if you had, er, suffered a loss of your former lusty inclinations."

Adam stretched out his long legs. Let Latimer see just how "lost" his "lusty inclinations" were.

Latimer raised his eyebrows. "You appear to be in pain, old man," he said, and the smirk returned, "but that's no affair of mine. Desirée's been back in London for over a week and you haven't seen her."

"She hasn't seen me, either."

"Good grief," Latimer said. "Is a gentle lady, a princess, or any other decent woman supposed to chase after *you?*"

"She was the one who left," Adam said, disliking his almost petulant tone. "Barstow told me Verbeux accompanied her back. Now the man's returned to Jean-Marc's service. Any idea why? I thought he and Lady Upchurch planned to marry and remain in Mont Nuages. It's true he re-deemed himself, but in a manner of speaking he had betrayed Jean-Marc. He was supposed to go back into Prince Georges's employ." Prince Georges, who ruled the little principality of Mont Nuages, was Jean-Marc and Desirée's father, a hard man who cared little for his daughter.

"Don't have a clue," Latimer said. "We'll get him around to the King's Fool for a drink. He won't say no to that and he may have become less tight-lipped than he was when he had a good deal to hide."

"I don't pry," Adam said. "If Verbeux's got something to tell us, he'll let us know."

Latimer sat on the green sofa and laced his hands behind his head. "She's come back because she can't stay away from you, y'know."

"Rubbish." He imagined her in his bed again. Beneath the damp lawn of her night rail, Desirée's body would flush. Sexual ex-citement was pretty on fair skin.

"I think she's decided to have you at any cost," Latimer murmured, his eyes closed. "Don't be surprised if she all but ravishes you the instant she gets you alone."

"Damn you, Latimer."

"You don't mean that." Another set of knuckles assaulted the door. "You'd better answer that. I don't know how you stand all these callers."

Adam almost mentioned that Latimer was one of the callers but thought better of it. "Keep quiet," he whispered. "Whoever it is will go away."

Latimer laughed loudly. "Everyone in the house — and elsewhere — knows you're in. You may be an unpleasant chap but you've got better manners than to keep someone waiting outside."

"Don't you have work to do?" Adam asked. "Shouldn't you be in Whitechapel seeing to your business?" Latimer dealt in oddities and rarities, which were primarily imported to his warehouses.

The door flew open.

Desirée rushed into the attic and flung herself down on the sofa beside Latimer without saying a word. She looked at Adam, then turned and buried her head in his shoulder.

Very comfortably, Latimer patted her

shoulder. "There, there, little one, there, there," he all but sang to her.

Adam put Halibut on the floor and stood up. He rested one hand at his waist, beneath his coat, and rubbed the other over the back of his neck. What he wanted to do was out of the question and he'd best keep his hands where they couldn't get him into trouble.

She made him tremble. In just six months she had become older in some indefinable way, older in spirit perhaps, and her face, the gray eyes filled with frustration, had lost any last traces of girlishness. Desirée was a woman and she shook Adam as no woman had shaken him before.

He was seeing her for the first time since she came home and the suffocating desire he'd felt for her before paled beside this bewitchment.

Latimer looked at him over Desirée's head. "Your Anne Williams said things weren't as they should be at Number 17 but she didn't explain why." He contrived to point at Adam, then at the Princess.

Adam opened his mouth to breathe. Latimer wanted him to take his place with Desirée on the couch. He crossed his arms instead.

"Hush," Latimer said, "surely Meg is on

your side in whatever is troubling you. She will help you."

Desirée shook her head and said in a choked voice, "Meg is a dear, but she's Jean-Marc's wife and you know how close they are."

"As they should be," Adam said. His voice sounded unused.

"Of course," Desirée said. "I know that. And I know that you, the most honorable man I know, Adam, would be the first to say so."

Honorable? He would hope she never had a chance to hear what certain members of his family thought about that.

"You are both right," Latimer said, easing Desirée from him and standing up. She promptly pulled her knees onto the sofa, modestly spreading the skirts of her simple, mauve velvet dress, and hid her face in the sofa back.

"Jenny is so anxious to have you visit," Latimer said. "She has missed you, as we all have. Marriage has made her bloom, Your Highness. I am the most fortunate of men to have such a wife, such a brave and beautiful wife. She has brought new meaning to my life, I can tell you. I am a changed man, a man with purpose. Every man needs a wife, just as every woman needs a husband to protect and adore her."

It was probably just as well that Latimer would not meet Adam's eyes. The rattle was making an ass of himself and didn't care because he intended to attempt, by any means available, to bring about a match between Adam and the Princess.

"Jenny has completed me, hasn't she?" Latimer asked him. "How many times have you mentioned your own longing for a good woman to anchor your life?"

Adam said nothing. He pressed his lips together and gritted his teeth until his jaw ached.

Desirée sniffed and her back shook. A mauve velvet ribbon threaded through her softly curled coiffeur had slipped undone and trailed from thick, light brown hair that shone in wintry light through the dormer window.

"I'll be off then," Latimer said, lifting his greatcoat from a hook on the dark green wall near the door. He swung the coat around broad shoulders and swept up his hat. His white linen sparkled against a dark coat and he cut quite the figure — and probably knew it. "Princess, I am concerned for you," he said. "You have been through a great deal and must settle down with a man who can be all you need in a husband."

Abruptly, Desirée sobbed and made fists beside her face.

Adam took a step toward her, but hesitated while he waved Latimer toward the door.

"Yes, well," Latimer said. "I'll leave you in good hands. Adam has a heart of gold and there is no more gentle soul. Allow him to comfort you."

Adam made a move toward Latimer who said, "Remember, love cures all ills," and let himself out.

The moment they were alone, Desirée raised her great, soft gray eyes to Adam's face. "I shall collect myself," she told him. "I have been overwhelmed and when Anne told me of your invitation to come to you, I was so touched, and so grateful. Then I became overwrought again. I'm sorry, Adam."

Looking away was impossible. He stared at her, silently cursing his pathetic inadequacies when it came to talking with such a tender creature. "You have nothing to thank me for," he said. "It was Latimer who thought to suggest you come." He screwed up his eyes and would have exclaimed at his stupidity — if he'd been alone.

Desirée didn't appear to actually hear his gaffe.

He cleared his throat. "Where is your chaperon?" It was only appropriate that he be concerned for her reputation.

"Anne is with Lady Hester, who gave her permission for me to come to you alone. I met Anne in Mont Nuages. She'd lost her place as a governess and needed another position. I needed a companion so we made a perfect arrangement. She is discussing tutoring Toby, Jenny More's little orphan friend. Lady Hester wants to better him, and Anne loves to teach." Once more tears welled and she bowed her head, rested her cheek against the sofa again. "You mustn't mind me. I shall deal with my brother and have my way, even though he cannot imagine that I will defy him."

Adam could no longer bear the slump of Desirée's narrow shoulders, or the vulnerable curve of her neck, her dejection. "May I sit with you?" Damn Latimer's hide. "The presence of a friend can be helpful in these matters, or so I'm told."

She nodded and he placed himself carefully beside her drawn up knees. He took one of her hands between his own and smoothed her skin.

"There cannot be anything so terrible as to bring you so low," he told her, wishing she'd decide to throw herself against his chest.

"You know Jean-Marc and you know how determined and unapproachable he can be. Once he makes up his mind, he is almost impossible to dissuade."

Her wrist was smooth below a gathered lace cuff. Adam studied her carefully. "I haven't seen you for so long and I think you are changed. You are more mature." This was why he should never try to make small talk with women, he was hopeless at it.

"I'm older," she said. "Twenty."

"That is not old," he told her hurriedly. *Say she is beautiful. Tell her you've missed her so much that you've felt your heart almost forget to beat.* "You've got several years before you're considered on the shelf."

Desirée's lips parted and her expression became distant. She cocked her head as if listening to a voice Adam couldn't hear.

He heard her swallow. Then, amazingly, she smiled at him with so much sweetness he bent toward her and would have kissed her had reason not returned at once.

"We both know that can never be," she said, confusing him. "Much as you want it, some things are best resisted."

Adam stared into her face but she might

have been alone for all the notice she took of him.

"Desirée? What do you mean?"

"Oh . . . Don't mind me, sometimes my mind wanders." She blushed, swung her feet to the floor and smoothed her skirts. "I have a question for you, Adam. We have been friends in the past and I'd like to know if we can be friends again."

"Of course." What else would he say?

"Good. Thank you." When she straightened her back he couldn't quite ignore her pretty breasts, their tops visible beneath a lace fichu. She had a small waist but her hips, like her breasts, were rounded and . . . thought provoking.

"Are you going to give me a hint of what's troubling you?" he asked, emboldened by his official classification as "friend." He barely stopped a groan. Friendship was all very well, but he would prefer an entirely different role.

"It's as simple as it is awful," Desirée told him. She offered her hand and, when he held it, pulled as if she could do anything about hauling up a powerfully built man of well over six feet. He sprang to his feet and made no attempt to release her hand.

"Jean-Marc is as convinced as you are

that I am doomed to be a spinster and spend my days doing needlepoint in the corners of his rooms."

"That's —"

"That is a reasonable assumption," she said with her irresistible French accent. "But he wants the unthinkable. He wants, he has *decided* that I must endure another London Season."

"Refuse!" Adam closed his mouth. He must have better control over his tongue. "I mean, you made a Season and didn't enjoy the process. Why would Jean-Marc want you to repeat such a thing?"

"You know why. He wants to marry me off to someone suitable. And Meg wants it, too. They're already planning things. There are modistes coming, and shoe-makers, and the parties we shall give are being discussed, although not by me."

He had an urge that shook him. If he made love to her, here and now, and then went to Jean-Marc to confess his sins and ask for her hand . . . Forcing himself on Desirée was an idea that repulsed him. He dropped her hand and put distance be-tween them. "You must obey your brother. He is your guardian."

Now her eyes glittered. She raised her pointed chin and crossed her arms tightly at her waist. "That will not be possible," she said. "A man may become a good friend, as you are my friend. That is all the male attention I shall ever require and I would trust you with my life, Adam. But I don't believe in marriage — for me."

2

If only Adam were not the most dear, the most kind, the most handsome, the most *wonderful* man in the world.

If only the mere sight of him didn't start a wobbly feeling in her legs and clenching inside her body.

And if only she could turn into the sort of woman he might think of as more than a pesky nuisance — an unremarkable nuisance.

Oh, it was too bad. Certainly she wasn't the kind of beautiful creature she had no doubt Adam could have whenever he chose. But what she lacked in classical beauty, she made up for in having a certain, *interesting* appeal, or so she'd been told.

She had shocked herself when she spoke aloud, rebuffing an advance he had only made in her imagination. Since she'd left for Mont Nuages Adam had never been far from her mind. Many times she had cheered and excited herself thinking of him making advances, which she was forced to turn aside. Of course, there were also dream moments when she gave in to him. All of that must stop now that she faced reality.

How long would he just stand there, staring at her as if she were beyond his understanding?

Oh, fie. She'd known her announcement that she never intended to marry was a risk, but Adam might at least have argued against her decision — even if he didn't insist that she marry him at once.

Impossible dreams showed an optimistic spirit and she should not feel foolish for having them. In truth, she did believe he might be more than a little enamored of her, but he allowed completely silly things to stand between them.

Could she help it that she was considerably younger than he, or that she had been inconveniently born a princess?

He simply stood and stared at her. And she had no idea what he was thinking. Her breath stuck in her throat. Why didn't he say something?

He gave a great sigh. "Foolishness. Of course you will marry, and marry very well. You will be a good wife and mother."

Desirée watched his mouth as he spoke and her own lips parted. Adam had a mouth intended to mesmerize women — or at least, one woman, herself.

"Desirée? Did you hear me?"

Desirée, will you have me?

She copied the way he pressed the tip of his tongue against the edges of his upper teeth. "Yes, Adam, of course."

"Good, then you will stop this nonsense and be agreeable about making this Season. After all, you were a child the last time."

She felt *much* too warm. Perhaps she was feverish. That would account for her continuing to pretend he said things she knew he had not. She must be careful, concentrate hard so that her longing for him didn't make her hear what she wanted to hear.

"Desirée?"

Adam's eyes were a dark gray, his hair black, curly, and as overlong as it had been when she'd last seen him months ago.

He was waiting for her to respond. "I cannot go through all that foolishness again," she told him. "Even as a child I rarely giggled and I have no interest in simpering for the benefit of gentlemen who are of no interest to me."

"When you meet the right man, he will be of interest to you." Adam turned his back on her and added coals to the fire.

Only Adam interested her.

He had a fine, straight back. Jean-Marc had called Adam raffish on occasion. Desirée thought her brother must envy a man who could be such a presence, so commanding and nonchalantly elegant when he clearly had little interest in fashion.

Adam was simply . . . a man. There was nothing vain in him and why should there be? Tall, well over six foot, strongly built — oh, he was so strongly built as to make her shiver at the thought of being in his arms. He had an air of quiet power, why would he ever need to posture?

He remained before the fire with one hand on the mantel and his head bowed.

"Is it so wrong to want to amount to more than a twittering thing who cares only for expensive frocks and gossip?"

"You fret too much for one so young," Adam said. "This is your time for enjoying yourself. Be carefree, Desirée, learn to giggle and have fun. You are little more than a child."

There it was again — she was little more

than a child because as long as he pretended he thought so, there could be no question of his treating her like a woman.

"Don't concern yourself with my little problems," she told him, pleased with her steady voice. "I'm capable of dealing with them myself. Anyway, I have a plan."

He faced her at once. "What plan?"

She drew up her shoulders and avoided looking at him. "I won't bore you with it. How is Lady Hester? I should see if she'd like another visitor."

Adam stared at her with narrowed eyes. He clasped his hands behind his back and approached her slowly, even ominously? She barely swallowed the squeak that reached her throat.

"I've missed . . ." Adam frowned. "I've missed your dratted cat. He's a rogue and a beggar, but he is good company."

"He has only been with me again for a few days."

"A cat requires nothing of one but food and a stroke — and a place in one's bed on a cold night."

A cat, Desirée thought, almost wanted more of him than she did. She cared nothing for being fed as long as she was stroked, she hoped many more times than once, and as long as she might curl up in

Adam's warm bed — with him.

She blinked. Her final attempt to make him see she was the woman for him, was about to be launched. Her opportunity to woo him until he knew he must have her might be short, too short, but she would do her best.

It was time to begin. "You like a simple life, Adam," she said. "And you have found one. Your paintings are a success. In London you are one of the most sought-after portrait artists, yet you don't change."

Adam held a hand toward her and Desirée rested her palm on his. His very white cuff had been laundered too many times, so why did it draw attention to the manliness of his broad, long-fingered hand?

He was smiling. "You don't sound as if you mind counting a simple man as your friend."

"Oh, but I don't. I love it that you don't have the airs so many gentlemen affect. You are — well, you're just who you are, you're Adam." She was babbling. "And that's quite comforting."

The smile broadened into a grin that made her feel she stood in the sun. "Thank you," he said. "Friends should comfort one another."

His fingers curled around hers and he held on firmly.

"Why do you live here?"

"I beg your pardon?"

Adam's startled response unnerved Desirée but she would not shrink away from what must be said. "I simply meant that you are a man of means and have no need to live in a rented attic. You could have a lovely house of your own if you wanted to." *And Jean-Marc might be more kindly disposed toward him then.*

"I am a simple painter."

"A painter who paints some of the richest people in England. Surely they pay you well."

"You," Adam said, "are impertinent."

"I'm honest. If you have no money it's either because you give it away or because you gamble — or perhaps you have great debts you must pay to people who are never satisfied."

Her stomach turned over. His eyes had become darker, as they did when he was angry, and he held her hand so tightly it hurt.

"Don't look so cross," she said in a rush. "I'm sure you know absolutely everything about me, yet you are secretive. That's not the way you should treat a friend."

He released her hand and gripped her shoulder instead, and pulled her so close she had to arch her neck to look into his face.

"I am not afraid of you, Adam Chillworth," she told him while she quaked in her half-boots. "But I am disappointed that just because I asked a question you don't want to answer, you speak unkindly and bully me."

"Bully? I would never bully you."

"You're pinching my shoulder. What's that if it isn't bullying? You're not at all like your brother."

Adam dropped his hand. He looked shocked; there was no other suitable description.

"How do you know I have a brother?"

She had not dealt with this at all well, probably because she had no experience of such things. "I met him." She waved a hand airily. "He was looking for you but mistakenly thought you lived at Number 17 rather than Number 7. We set him straight and he said he would find you here instead."

"When was that?"

"What a funny question. Yesterday, of course. Your secret is out, so don't keep pretending you have no family. Mr. Lucas

Chillworth was coming to you directly after leaving us."

Adam hesitated before saying, "Of course. Thank you for giving him directions."

"It was nothing. Adam, I don't like my life as it is. I am considering entering a nunnery."

Adam pushed the fingers of both hands through his hair. "Of course you are. Very appropriate, too. A contemplative life, absolutely. Silent prayer, now that will suit you since you have so little to say."

"I'm glad you agree." She would not allow him to goad her. "Will you help me find out what I must do?"

"No." His voice was suddenly thunderous. "No, I will not, and I don't know why you're trying to drive me mad but you should be pleased with the progress you're making. I'm going to talk to Meg and Jean-Marc. You must be protected from self-destruction."

"I must be protected? Of course, *you* aren't even a little self-destructive. That's why you have estranged yourself from a fine and influential family."

"You, Your Highness, don't know what you're talking about. You have spent too little time with people of your own age and have not learned that it is unattractive to challenge your elders on topics you cannot possibly understand."

Ooh, he knew how easily he could annoy her. And, he hoped that by making her cross, she would become too agitated to defend her opinions. Hah, his trouble was that he was male and therefore *he* rarely sensed the danger in belittling female intelligence — and determination.

He actually smiled at her, condescendingly, and now he clasped her arms and . . . kissed . . . her forehead.

She would not swoon. Desirée rose involuntarily to her toes, encouraging the pressure of his lips on her brow — oh, sweet ecstasy. Then she grimaced and planted her heels firmly on the floor.

"How kind of you to comfort me, Adam. I feel inspired to be as demure, malleable, and mindless as any man could wish me to be."

"Your High—"

"How dare you!" She stepped away from him. "You and I have shared too much for you to use my title in order to put me in my place. We have been on a first name basis for years and for you to Your Highness me now is disrespectful, not respectful. It is an attempt to make me less

41

familiar." She gave his chest a good poke but was immediately certain her finger suffered more than his hard chest. "It is too late. We have shared too much to turn back now. If we are friends there will be no more attempts to censure what I say."

Adam slumped onto his couch and his expression became morose.

"Don't sulk," she told him. "Such a good-looking man shouldn't spoil his face with scowls. Jenny More was remarking on how handsome you are, and that it was time you married and had your own children."

Adam dropped his head against the back of the couch and closed his eyes. "Jenny is so besotted with Latimer that she thinks everyone who is not happily married is deprived."

"And what do you think about that, Adam." She threaded her fingers tightly together. "Do you believe in marriage?"

He rolled his face away from her. "For some. A lucky few who find the person they need and who are able to pursue their ideals. For myself, I'd prefer never to marry rather than to consign myself to a passionless liaison. I should rather be alone."

Desirée could not restrain herself. She

sat beside him and settled a cheek on his arm. "You are not meant to be alone," she told him, and put a hand on his chest, beneath his coat. His heart beat hard, and steady.

Adam lowered his eyelids to look at her and he smiled. He stroked the backs of his fingers across her cheek and his eyelids sank even lower.

Desirée never wanted to move again. She snuggled closer. Her breast tingled against his arm. Poor, poor Adam, he had a great deal on his mind, of that she was certain, and he was tired by it all.

"Rest," she told him quietly.

He turned his face from her again and remained absolutely still with his hands relaxed in his lap.

If they need never move again, never speak again, or have a need to consider the world outside Adam's attic, she would be content — almost. Perhaps not *forever*, but at least for an hour or two.

She peeked at his hands and frowned. They weren't relaxed at all. In fact they were curled into serious-looking fists and the knuckles were white.

"You are troubled," she told him, continuing to lean against him. "Angry, even?"

His eyes, she noted, were completely

closed and he appeared to breathe evenly. And he was a bad actor.

"Why didn't you tell me you have a brother?"

He compressed his lips and his nostrils flared.

"Lucas is delightful, and he cuts quite a figure. Good-looking, too. He looks nothing like you."

Slitted eyes glittered speculatively at her. "You consider me ugly, Desirée?"

The question puzzled her but only for a moment. "Oh, Adam, you know that's not what I meant. Your brother is good-looking in a different way from you. That's what I meant."

"Hmph." He didn't sound convinced. "I don't understand how you came to meet him."

"I told you he went to Number 17."

"And is Jean-Marc becoming frugal?" Adam said. He still hadn't moved away from her and she had no intention of parting her body from his until she must. "Fired the household staff, has he? And now you are the butler who answers the door?"

"No, silly. You are being deliberately difficult. Verbeux heard Lucas's name and took him to Jean-Marc and Meg. I was also there. Naturally, since he is your brother, Jean-Marc insisted he lift a glass with him."

Adam groaned and scrubbed at his eyes.

"You are estranged from your entire family because you have disappointed them. Lucas seems very unhappy about that. He said he intends to mend the rift between the two of you and draw you back into the bosom of your family. He thinks you should live at Manthy House — with your grandmother, Lady Manthy, and your mother who sounds quite lovely. Lucas said —"

"What Lucas did or did not say is of no interest to me." Adam sprang to his feet. "I have not set eyes on him in several years and intend to keep it that way, although I shall know his motives for sneaking around here behind my back."

Desirée was indignant. "Sneaking, Adam? Of course he hasn't been sneaking. I told you exactly what happened."

The lines of his face had grown sharp and she was glad she knew the real man behind the flashing eyes and restlessly pacing body. The air about him seemed to crackle.

"You told me," he said, "that my brother told you he would come here directly upon leaving Number 17. So why didn't he come? Why has he still not come?"

The question puzzled Desirée. "I'm sure I don't know. Perhaps he became too shy to approach you when he must know you care nothing for him."

Adam pointed a long, blunt forefinger at her. "You are making assumptions about matters that are none of your affair."

"I see." She also stood up. "It is perfectly in order for you to ask any question you please about me, but you don't trust me to know anything about you."

When he didn't answer, she continued, "Thinking about your family saddens you, doesn't it? I can see it in your eyes."

"I will carry Halibut and see you across the Square."

"If you care for Halibut as you say you do, you will agree to keep him here. There is too much confusion at home." And she didn't care if Adam knew that she had in the past, and continued to use his care of her pet as an excuse to visit him.

"Where is your cloak?"

Let him be mean and break her heart. "Coot hung it downstairs for me."

Adam awaited her in the open doorway. "Halibut shall stay with me. I thank you because I am fond of the nuisance." He puffed out a breath and planted his fists on his hips. "Do not look petulant, Desirée. It doesn't suit you. When you least expect it, a man will come into your life and you'll know he is the one for you."

He already had, and she had no interest in another. "Laugh at me if it brings you pleasure, but I shall not find a husband during the coming Season. If I must, I'll go through the charade to please Jean-Marc and dear Meg, but it would be wrong not to be true to the vocation of my heart."

"And become a nun?"

And become my wife?

"Yes, absolutely. I shall make you so happy." Desirée snapped her mouth shut. It was his fault if she heard things.

Adam grimaced and said, "It would not make me at all happy but fortunately I know this is part of some game you play."

Tears sprang into her eyes and she bowed her head. He should not see how little control she had over her emotions.

"You are the one playing a game," she told him, although she shouldn't have.

"Why not say what you mean?" Adam spoke quietly again.

"I don't have to, you already know. And you know there are some things about which a woman can do little

47

without the help of a man."

Their gazes met and held. Desirée looked away first. He would do nothing against his will and he'd decided he wouldn't, or couldn't, consider anything more than a harmless companionship between them.

She smiled brightly and stepped past him, popping up to kiss him on the jaw as she passed. He would find out how difficult it would be to rebuff her.

"Damn you." He caught her elbow and jerked her back into the room. "Don't press for what can never be."

His rigid face stole her breath. She could not be afraid, not of Adam, yet blood pounded in her ears.

"Do you hear me?" He laced his fingers at the back of her neck, pushed her face up with his thumbs. *"Answer me."*

"Why can't it be?"

"It can't, that is all. You know perfectly well why."

She had already shed too many tears. Why did her throat make it so hard to speak? "I know I shall always feel the same."

"And I . . . I will not be a stain on any woman's life." Pained emotion passed over his features. He caressed her neck.

She was afraid for him, afraid of whatever terrible thoughts oppressed him. "How could you be a *stain* on a woman's life? What is it, Adam? Please tell me." She hesitated, then placed her hands on his chest.

"You should leave me," Adam said. *"Now."*

"So, if we ever speak of this again, it will be as if we are talking about strangers — just as you insist on doing now?"

"Desirée!" He bent over her, pulled her to him and trapped her hands between them. "You will drive me mad."

"You never have to see me again," she whispered. "You can go away from your attic and forget me."

He shook her. "You don't know then, do you? You don't know why I stay in *my* attic."

Before she could answer, his mouth covered hers and if he weren't holding her she would have fallen.

The kiss wasn't gentle or restrained. It was nothing she'd imagined in the hours, days, years she'd waited for Adam to do this. So quickly his mouth opened hers. The sound of his breathing, and hers, whipped like battling winds in her head. The only sensation was the pressure on her lips, the way he shifted his face, found another angle, and another, and pressed his tongue into her mouth until she touched the tip of hers to his, then grew bolder and reached, fusing them as tight together as it must be possible for a man and a woman to be.

Drawing back, he seemed ready to stop, but instead he pulled her top lip between his, lightly sucked her tongue, nibbled at her bottom lip.

He made a sound deep in his throat.

Desirée managed to slide her arms around his neck and pull him even tighter to her.

The feelings were much more than she had dreamed of in the lonely hours of wanting him. Her belly melted and liquid heat seared into her legs. The tips of her breasts felt as if they had hardened and they stung so that she rubbed against him to incite a tension she wanted to go on forever.

"You are irresistible," he said when at last he raised his face. "But I must resist you."

Resisting her meant that he touched her face as if committing it to memory. His fingertips on her mouth, her nose, her closed eyelids, her brow, were almost more than she could bear when she feared she might never feel his touch again.

She had to. "Kiss me again," she said softly. "I liked it."

His tight smile didn't soften his eyes. "You liked it, hmm? Well, you have no idea how I liked it. If you did, you would run."

There was the thud of feet at the bottom of the attic stairs. Adam and Desirée stared at each other, unmoving.

"Mr. Chillworth?" It was Mrs. Barstow, Lady Hester Bingham's companion and housekeeper.

Desirée put a finger on Adam's mouth. He shuddered and she lowered her eyes.

"Adam Chillworth? Mr. Coot says there's someone here to see you."

He drew a big breath. "Yes, Mrs. Barstow. I hear you. I'll be right down."

"Coot can't climb all these stairs anymore," Barstow bellowed, referring to the ancient butler. "And I'm not coming all the way up there if I don't have to."

Desirée had an urge to chuckle and promptly found her face clamped against Adam's shoulder.

"Right away, Mrs. Barstow," he said. "The guest sitting room?"

"Lady Hester's boudoir," Mrs. Barstow said.

Footsteps moved away.

"Who can it be?" Desirée murmured. "And why would they be with Lady H.?"

"There may be ice beneath the snow so walk carefully on your way to Number 17," Adam said, and tugged on his waistcoat. He made as if to touch her face again, but dropped his hand. He said, "Forgive me," and left her standing there, alone.

3

"There you are, you naughty boy." Blond, blue-eyed, pleasantly plump and fifty-something, Lady Hester Bingham reclined against pillows heaped on her purple and gold daybed. The sumptuous fabrics, also purple, showed off her lowcut green silk gown and pale, smooth skin.

"Come and see me at once," she said, offering Adam a beringed hand. "How could you keep secrets from your patroness and friend? You have a brother? A very beautiful brother, I might add, and you've never mentioned him? I might almost think you didn't consider me a friend worthy of sharing in those things dearest to your heart."

For the first time in three years, Adam looked into the face of his brother, Lucas. "Lucas," he said formally. And, turning to the elegant man who had been Lucas's friend since Eton, "Rolly Spade-Filbert. I wish you'd sent word that the two of you intended to visit." So that Adam might have been sure to be out.

In appearance Lucas Chillworth favored their gentleman farmer father. Dashing, blond, sinuously elegant of build, Lucas's wit and intellect sharpened his deepset brown eyes.

"If I had announced my intention to come, you would not have been here," Lucas said, unsmiling.

Adam didn't protest. His brother was no fool and he knew Adam well. Lucas approached him. "It has been too long, brother. You are changed and so am I."

This was not a conversation Adam wished to have in the presence of Lady H. or the hovering Barstow, or even Rolly Spade-Filbert. Perhaps least of all the latter, who had never missed an opportunity to treat Lucas's younger brother with contempt.

"I was on my way out," Adam said.

"You are Countess Manthy's grandson," Lady H. said. "Lady Elspeth is your mother. I knew her slightly when we were girls. Then, of course, she married . . . Well, our lives took us in different directions but I understand she's back at Manthy House." Absently she fingered the rows of pearls draping her admirable décolletage.

"How is Gilbert Chillworth?" She looked up at Lucas through long lashes. "I recall your father when he swept your mother off her feet, young man. Your manner reminds me of him. A heart-stealer — and determined to boot. He adored Elspeth. And, Adam, I do believe I see his face in yours. Can't think why I didn't connect the names. Actually, of course I can. What are you doing apparently so estranged from your family?"

Adam met Lucas's eyes and was relieved to see his slight shake of the head and the tightening of his mouth. Neither of them had reason to want their family history aired.

A movement behind him caused him to look over his shoulder. Anne Williams sat on the very edge of a damask chair, her back absolutely straight. An attractive creature, the high color in her cheeks suggested she was embarrassed to be present.

"That's Anne Williams," Lady H. said. "But of course you know she's Desirée's companion from Mont Nuages.

"Did you know that rogue Verbeux accompanied the two of them back to England. One wonders what happened to

Lady Upworth after the two of them left the country together. Miss Williams insists she doesn't know. I shall simply have to ask Desirée herself, or better yet, I'll speak with Jean-Marc and Meg."

Lady Hester looked up at auburn-haired Rolly Spade-Filbert, then indicated a plush stool near her side. Adam compressed his lips to stop himself from smiling. Rolly wasn't the kind of man to relish being ushered into a subservient position by anyone — least of all a female in whom he had no interest.

Rolly confounded Adam by pulling the stool even closer to the daybed and sitting down.

Lady Hester dimpled and flipped open a mother-of-pearl fan. "Thank you, dear boy. When those you have considered closest to you let you down, the comfort of a strong man can be a boon."

"Something you said reminded me of a conversation I had at Holland House," he said. "A very careful conversation, of course. The subject was our great patronesses at a certain club and the frightful power they exert over all the young ladies who come to London for their Seasons — and the men who wish to meet them. And there was talk of a certain dulling of the luster on their holy of holies."

"Really?" Lady Hester bent closer to Rolly. "You're referring to Almacks. Who were you talking to?" she whispered.

Rolly waved a hand in front of his face and plentiful lace flapped gracefully at his cuff. "Everyone says of me Rolly Spade-Filbert is to be trusted with anyone's confidence. He might as well be a stone statue, no word told him in confidence passes his lips."

"But surely —"

Rolly tapped her ladyship's arm with what Adam considered unsuitable familiarity. From the way she giggled and swept the back of his hand with her fan, the lady loved it.

For all the world, Rolly's smile suggested he was enjoying himself. When Adam had last seen him, his sharp-featured face had been clean-shaven; now he managed to make a well-trimmed beard and mustache appear all the crack. They certainly lent him a jaunty air.

"You mentioned being a patroness yourself," he said to Lady Hester. "You have a fabulous home and although I can't imagine why, I understand you are undertaking impressive improvements. I know the difficulty you've had dealing with the death of your dear, departed husband, but you are blooming again. Why not amuse yourself by developing an alternative to that dreadfully boring Almacks? Revive the art of innovative conversation, rapier wit — encourage daring fashions and capture all the *right* people. This would be where *trends* were set. Think how invigorating it could be — for the chosen ones."

"I do believe you read my mind," Lady Hester said. "We have a most elegant little ballroom here and it should be used. It must be completely made over. There isn't enough gold leaf and I rather think that I may have purple and violet striped silk on the walls. *That* would make tongues wag in admiration and we'd soon see the angling for invitations."

Frowning, Lucas cleared his throat. "When can we talk?" he asked Adam quietly. "Our mother misses you. She is a sad woman, in fact you may find her very changed."

Adam's heart slammed so hard it shortened his breath. "I must leave now. I have a sitting."

"The painting is going well?" Lucas asked, amazing Adam, who had never known his brother to show much interest in art, particularly Adam's.

"I have been fortunate enough to make a place for myself in the ranks of portrait painters," he said, determined that the rest of the audience should not hear more reasons for conjecture about his private business. "You're right, we are long overdue to become reacquainted. Accompany me downstairs and we'll arrange a meeting."

Rolly and Lady Hester continued to speak in low tones while Barstow settled her solid, gray-clad frame in a chair by the fire and picked up her needlework. Anne Williams went to the housekeeper and said, "I shall return to you tomorrow, then, and we'll see how Master Toby and I suit."

Barstow gave one of her rare smiles and Anne tripped from the room.

Adam wished he was sure Desirée had left for Number 17. He had made a terrible mistake in kissing her. Now it would be even harder to accept the inevitable, that he would never be considered good enough for her. That kiss might even cost him the pleasure of seeing her at all.

"Lead the way," Lucas said and looked to Rolly, who ignored him.

Adam studied this stranger-brother of his. When he'd said he was changed, he spoke the truth — from what Adam could tell. Lucas's coat was dark blue and of a conservative cut while he wore unremarkable buff breeches and top boots. A well turned out figure and not at all the dandy Adam recalled.

The two of them took their leave of Lady Hester, at which time Rolly said he'd be along shortly. Side by side Adam and Lucas went downstairs to the foyer.

"Are you sure there isn't somewhere we could talk now?" Lucas said. "I'm afraid I'll lose my nerve if I let you send me off."

There was — a humbleness in the man? Could there be? Had the bullying, underhanded youth who became a swaggering young buck found something deeper within himself?

"Wait for me in here." Adam strode to open the door to the red sitting room.

Given the identity of the lady whose portrait he was painting, sending apologies for being late was outrageous, but Adam could not believe his brother would come to him unless he was in trouble.

Lucas gave him the closest thing to a warm smile in Adam's memory and went inside the overwhelmingly red room.

Adam ran below stairs, calling for Toby, the formerly homeless boy who had arrived in Mayfair Square with Jenny O'Brien, as

Latimer's wife had been before their marriage.

The boy, who had become a favorite in the household, staggered from the pantry with a tarnished silver candelabra of massive proportions in his arms. "Mr. Chillworth, sir?" he said, finding space on the woodblock in the scullery to set down the heavy piece.

"Do you suppose Masters would allow you to deliver a message for me? To a lady at Apsley House in Piccadilly?"

"Run along," the under butler, Masters, said, arriving behind Toby. "But you don't go to your bed until this silver sparkles, mind." He rubbed a plump cherub on the piece and glanced at his blackened fingers with disdain.

Adam thanked the man and followed Toby to the first floor. Lady H. must be serious about her social plans or there would be no reason why the silver must be polished so promptly.

"Go to the tradesmen's entrance and request that my note be given to the Duchess of Wellington." Adam took a card from his pocket and went into the sitting room to use the writing desk.

Lucas had been leafing through a book but looked up when Adam entered, looked up with such a hesitant expression that Adam wondered if there was indeed dreadful news to be delivered.

He wrote on the back of the card and gave it to Toby, together with a coin for his trouble.

Now eleven, Toby had grown taller and more substantial in his months at Number 7. He bowed his towhead, cast Lucas a curious stare and made off.

"So," Lucas said. "I must say I had no idea your skills were sought after in such high places." His clear voice bore no suggestion of the north country beginnings he and Adam shared and which lingered faintly in Adam's speech.

"I've been blessed with loyal patrons who have recommended me to others."

"Such commissions must pay a pretty penny." Lucas didn't attempt to appear other than curious.

"Well enough," Adam said, and stopped himself from pointing out that since their father subscribed to the notion that to the elder son went most of the spoils, the younger son had better be able to make his own way.

Lucas put down the book and stood up. He clasped his hands behind his back, beneath his blue coat. He wore a handsome fob watch, its heavy chain shown off to advantage against a flat middle.

"You recognize the watch?" Lucas asked and Adam started. "It belonged to Grandfather Manthy. Our grandmother, mother's mother, gave it to me only recently. A sop, I suppose. A guilt gift because the old man made no provision for me."

"It's a handsome piece." Adam smiled faintly. "It becomes you." The old Lucas was present again. He knew a significant trust had been set up for Adam by their dead grandfather, but not its actual extent. Adam had not accepted the bequest and had no intention of doing so.

"Our mother pines for you, Adam."

The announcement was unwelcome. The fact that Lucas had been the one to tell him amazed Adam, who had lived with the knowledge that Lucas resented Lady Elspeth Chillworth's affection for her younger son.

"Is she well?" He cared about her, even as he detested the decision she had made when he was fourteen and she had left her husband and two sons in order to return to her parents' home.

Lucas watched his face intently. "Mother looks frail and tired but she is as beautiful as ever. She is even more remote. Poor papa, what a burden to love a woman with the countenance of a nun."

Adam gritted his teeth. He had heard enough of nuns for one day. Foolhardy it might be, but when he returned from Apsley House he would make an excuse to visit the Etrangers and try to smooth the waters with Desirée. He would learn from his lapse in common sense and, since he knew she enjoyed their companionship as much as he did, he had to believe there must be a way for them to remain close.

"You continue to blame our mother, don't you?" Lucas asked.

"I can't speak of it." He was still unready to examine all of his feelings about Gilbert Chillworth and his decision to take a wife so much above his station. Similarly, Mama's acceptance of Gilbert's suit remained a mystery.

"I understand." Lucas did what he'd never done before and threw his arms around Adam. He slapped his back and, slowly, Adam returned the embrace. "I've been a bad brother to you," Lucas said.

What was he to do, argue against the truth? "Ours was not an easy childhood."

"I made yours more difficult." Lucas had been and remained their father's favorite.

Gilbert had no time for a "feckless, daubing son."

"Say something," Lucas demanded. "I take it the old man remains determined to keep your portion outrageously small?"

"I need nothing from him, or from anyone. I have made my own way." Adam removed himself from the other's arms and held his shoulders instead. "Do you want us to be friends? Truly?"

"I do, very much. Coming to you has taken longer than it should have. I knew months ago that I wanted to become a true brother to you if you would let me."

Adam believed him and the sensation of warmth was extraordinary. "Then let it be so and we'll put the past behind us. My home is simple, but it's yours whenever you choose to come."

"And my home is yours." Lucas looked away. "I am living at Manthy House. Please don't say anything. Just think about it and keep an open mind. One day you will be ready to go to mother — and to grandmother who doesn't grow younger. Although I may not be able to remain there much longer."

"Why?" Adam frowned and tried to read Lucas's expression. His older brother looked at the ground, and sweat had broken out on his forehead. "Lucas, *why?* Don't evade the question. There is something wrong, isn't there — with you?"

"No." Lucas shook his head and gave a bright smile that didn't fool Adam. Some personal need had driven Lucas to him and unless he was mistaken, whatever it was frightened the man.

"Lucas, please —"

"You were always too delicate in your sensibilities. I imagine that comes of being an artist. My only concern is that you visit mother. Will you?"

"Perhaps." Adam doubted that. "You went to Number 17 yesterday."

Lucas threw up his hands. "I felt an idiot. Getting your address was a feat and even then the number wasn't quite right."

"You said you were coming to me when you left the Etrangers."

"Who told you?" Lucas asked, his brows drawn together.

"Princess Desirée," Adam told him and grinned. "She seems very taken with you. Thinks you handsome and charming. Don't worry, I didn't tell her the truth of your nature."

Lucas laughed. "Thank you for that. The reason I didn't come over yesterday was because I'd used up all my nerve for the day. If Rolly hadn't insisted on coming with me today I might not have seen you yet. You don't like him, do you?"

"I don't know him."

"You knew him as a bit of a bully," Lucas said. "That was all bravado because he wasn't sure of himself. He's a good fellow and the best of comrades to me. If you give him a chance you'll appreciate him, too."

Adam had already opened his heart dangerously wide. Any change in his opinion of Rolly Spade-Filbert would have to wait.

"The Princess seemed to know all about you," Lucas said. He looked about and said, "Any chance of a brandy?"

"Excuse me." Feeling remiss, Adam went to the vast and vastly ornate — and ugly — sideboard Lady Hester had installed. "Brandy? Or something else?"

"Brandy, please."

Adam poured two glasses and handed one to Lucas. "Rolly seems bent on mesmerizing Lady Hester."

"He enjoys mature women. And they like him."

Adam wasn't sure how to respond to that. He shouldn't care to have the likes of Spade-Filbert toy with Her Ladyship's feelings.

"The Princess spoke of you . . . almost with familiarity. I thought I saw more than polite interest in those lovely gray eyes of hers. Is there something going on I should know about?"

Adam drank some brandy. "The girl, as you've noted, is of royal blood. It's one thing for a man to take a wife of a lesser station — my good friend Latimer More married an orphan girl who had lived in poverty, and a wonder match it is. It doesn't work when it's the female who has the money, and in this case, the rank while the man is an obscure commoner."

"The Princess is well-fixed, then."

"Incredibly wealthy."

Lucas raised an eyebrow. "I understand. We know the problems that can cause. Too bad because she's an engaging little thing."

"Engaging enough, I suppose," Adam agreed, displeased to hear his brother assessing Desirée. "If you like women who appear undernourished. I prefer more meat on my females. Y'know I hate to do this, but I should start out for Piccadilly."

"I wish you needn't go," Lucas said. "May I visit you again soon?"

"Aye." Adam could scarcely believe he was pleased to agree.

"Tomorrow? Perhaps we could go to

my club for a meal."

Tomorrow Adam needed to paint without interruption. "Perhaps in a day or so. I'll get word to you."

"Will you?"

"My word is good. I'm a working man, remember, and not always free."

If Lucas was cut by the mild rebuke, he covered it well.

The front doorbell jangled and shortly there was a commotion in the foyer. Old Coot's voice was raised when he said, "He's left, I tell you, Your Highness."

Desirée responded in breathless tones, "He can't have. If Adam had gone out the event would have been reported to me."

"Worthy or not," Lucas whispered, "the lady spies on you."

"Don't close this door in my face, Coot." Meg, Countess Etranger's voice was unmistakable. One of the former tenants at Number 7 until her marriage to Desirée's brother, Jean-Marc, she'd lived in 7B with her sister, Sibyl Smiles.

"Didn't see you there, Miss Smiles — I mean, Countess," Coot said. "What can you expect of a man in charge of a lending library."

"I beg your pardon," Meg said. *"Lending library?"*

"So it feels, My Lady. Comings and goings. Up and down. Questions, questions. No peace and an old man needs some peace. No, Your Highness, Mr. Chillworth isn't up there. He's in there."

"You said he'd left," Desirée said in an outraged voice.

"I forgot," Old Coot said. "That's what comes of being in a lending library."

Adam closed his eyes and visualized Coot stumping up the stairs, leaving a princess and a countess unattended in the foyer.

Not for long.

"There you are," Desirée said, poking her head around the door. "Did you give instructions for Coot to pretend you weren't at home?"

"Females," Adam muttered. "Naturally suspicious. No, I did not do that. And I don't know why he suggested I'd left the house, although I'd intended to do so and must very shortly."

Meg slipped past Desirée and into the room. In a rich russet pelisse and a matching leghorn bonnet with dark, shiny feathers curving across the wide and rakish brim, she was lovely. The ruffled, beige silk cornet sewed inside the crown of the bonnet and tied with ribbons beneath the chin set off her heavy chestnut hair.

"Desirée, you are not to interrupt me. I have something to say to Adam and not much time to say it. I must return and help Nanny with Serena. Two is a most trying age." She noticed Lucas then, closed her mouth and frowned.

"My brother, Lucas," Adam said.

"We've met," Meg said, but didn't smile. Her mood put shadows into her brown eyes. "I need to talk to you, Adam."

"I'll be on my way." Lucas returned his glass to the sideboard. "Shall we say the day after tomorrow at about the same time?"

"Yes," Adam said, disquieted by Lucas's almost desperate request. "The day after tomorrow."

Lucas walked out, bowing briefly over Meg's hand, but giving Desirée a conspiratorial grin as he went. Desirée continued to stand in the foyer with only her head in the room.

"Really," Meg said, skimming off fine skin gloves, "this is too bad of you, Adam."

He raised his eyebrows.

"*Meg*," Desirée said, "I have already told you Adam has no part in this. You will mortify me. He doesn't care about these things, why should he? He's a busy man and doesn't have time for our little problems."

Gaping would be poor form. Adam had no idea what they were talking about and, therefore, had nothing to add to the exchange.

"Get in here," Meg ordered her sister-in-law.

Desirée hung her head and came slowly into the room, her feet dragging.

"Look at her," Meg said. "This is what Jean-Marc and I get for loving her and being concerned for her. She plots against us — plays silly games to make the task we must accomplish more difficult."

"What task is that?" Adam said, unable to look away from Desirée.

Meg slapped her gloves against a palm, then waved Desirée forward. "Come closer, ungrateful girl. And tell me you haven't discussed your feelings about coming out with Adam. Tell me he isn't encouraging you to be difficult and try to refuse a wonderful opportunity because he doesn't approve of what he probably calls *a silly fuss about nothing.* Ooh, you are naughty, Desirée."

Those wouldn't have been exactly his words, but close.

Gray from head to toe, gray, gray, gray,

Desirée was barely recognizable as the creature he'd held and kissed little more than an hour previous. She cocked her head and met his eyes squarely as if daring him to say anything about the ugly, flat gray hat she wore. Made of wool, it resembled a limp-edged plate tied beneath her chin with narrow gray ribbon. Her hair was dressed so severely it pulled at her hairline. He smiled at her, couldn't help it because she was his Desirée of the impish and irresistible face no matter what she did to herself.

"Don't you dare grin like the cake you are, Adam Chillworth," Meg said. "You have always been a difficult man but you don't have to encourage an impressionable young woman to be just like you."

Where would the Princess get such a hat, and the dowdy gray kerseymere dress and pelisse that were intended for a considerably more voluptuous person? They weren't hers, of that he was certain.

Screwing up her face, Desirée said, "Adam is no friend of mine in this and I could not be like him no matter how hard I tried. Don't be so silly as to suggest such a thing again. I want to go home."

"Meg," Adam said tentatively. He considered it best to treat angry women with caution. "I don't know what's going on here but I wish you'd sit down and let me arrange for you to have tea. I have to leave and —"

"Don't you attempt to slide away from this, you worm," Meg said, advancing with her pretty mouth pinched.

"He is certainly a worm," Desirée said. "I came to him for help. I asked him to suggest how I might make you and Jean-Marc see reason but he was useless. He is as bad as you, I say. Tell the truth, Adam. You're trying to persuade me to do this horrid thing, and Meg, I have already *come out,* to go through it all again would be embarrassing."

The manipulative chit had something planned, a strategy. Her comments were too glib to be spoken in true passion.

"Why didn't you tell me that before I rushed over here to make a fool of myself?" Meg asked. She passed a hand over her eyes. "Is it true, Adam? Did you advise Desirée to do as her brother has commanded?"

"Well . . . Yes, I did."

"She respects your opinions more than any other's, you know," Meg said, looking deeply thoughtful. She stood in front of him and regarded him seriously. "Why

74

didn't I think of this before? Be the friend you always have been to us and make her see that she is being unreasonable."

Adam glanced past her shoulder and caught the upward twist at the corners of Desirée's mouth before she could turn them down again. *Minx.*

"Say something," Meg demanded of him. "Will you be the counselor I know you can be? I know she can be irksome, but if you would find as much time as possible to be with her and use your very persuasive logic to show her the right path to take, we should be forever in your debt. Will you, Adam?"

What the devil was he supposed to say? "If you think I can help, then yes."

Meg's expression relaxed. "Thank you. I'll speak with you soon." She settled her notable bonnet more securely.

This time Desirée accomplished a most disagreeable pout and Meg caught the expression. "Behave yourself," she said. "Do exactly as you are told. Adam, she's all yours."

4

My ballroom!

Purple and violet striped? More gold leaf. If she starts on my Grendey japanned chairs I shall have to intervene.

There is nothing that need be done to the ballroom, I tell you, not one thing.

I must be calm. All this excitement over-whelmed me and then I may become distracted during flying lessons; not at all a good idea.

What do you think of Lucas, then? And Spade-Filbert? I only came across 'em because I was spy . . . I was looking into Adam Chillworth's secrets.

Now, now, no arguments on that score. He's a secretive one. Did you know he had a brother, or a titled mother, or that he was Countess Manthy's grandson and the late Count Manthy's favorite? And what about the trust, I ask you? I heard Lucas talking to Rolly about it and you may be sure I was shocked, both at the possible amount and at Adam's stupidity for leaving it unclaimed.

There's more there than has so far met the eye, but I have my ways and I'll know all there is to know about the man.

The main point is that with a tidy fortune at his disposal, and a fine family he may not have talked about, but which certainly will be talked about shortly — well, he becomes more eligible, doesn't he?

Well, you say, all well and good, then. This will go smoothly and be accomplished in no time.

Rubbish!

Everything else — no, there is one more development that's going just as planned, better than planned even. Hester. Did you see how her eyes sharpened when it was suggested she should pursue a certain social reputation. Purple and violet aside, this may prove a brilliant move. Actually, if there had been time I would have made sure Number 7 was The Invitation everyone pined for years ago. I considered it when I was . . . you know, present.

Nosy, aren't you? You want to know why I want Hester to turn into The New Hostess. Because, my addlepated friends, what could give Hester more reason to encourage Adam and Desirée to take themselves off — together — than her need to put this house in order. How would she explain to Princess Lieven, Lady Castlereagh, the Duke of Wellington . . . ah, yes, Wellington and all manner of other dukes and duchesses, statesmen, heads of state, veritable crowds of royalty — ahem, yes, well, how would Hester explain to the Right company that she had a lodger in the attic?

I shudder at the thought.

Protégé, you say? Hah, she would never be believed if she said she had a protégé in the attic and it turned out to be Adam Chillworth. Apparently that fellow has been painting the rich and famous all over London for several years. He'd be recognized and then what might they think of the arrangement. Most peculiar is what they would surmise. He'd embarrass her. No, she'll be kind to him but she'll be very helpful to us.

Clever of me to use Adam's own brother to introduce Rolly Spade-Filbert into the circle, wasn't it? The moment I saw him I knew he'd be useful. I'll admit it's a challenge to "guide" one with such a strong mind, but I trust my own ability. I knew he'd be interested in Adam's connections, y'know, that he'd see them as an opportunity to weasel himself into a new set (I mean the Etrangers) since he's outworn his welcome almost everywhere else.

Lucas is apparently a changed man, a gentler man. Rolly is already working on him to encourage Adam to court Princess Desirée.

But that is absolutely ALL that is going according to my plan.

Spade-Filbert all but drooled over Hester and if I didn't know it was impossible, I'd think he lusted after her. Pah, after her money, more like — and Number 7. We can't afford to leave anything to chance. Spade-Filbert must be closely watched. If you notice anything, ANYTHING that suggests he's too busy with some selfish little plan of his own to concentrate on mine, speak — no, just make a sign. Spade-Filbert must limit his activities to encouraging Hester to pursue a brilliant social future, and pushing Lucas to talk his brother into — running away with Desirée! Of course, that's just the thing. An elopement!

That's that for now, then.

Really, I wasn't going to say more, but after all, I am only someone who used to be human. You know it isn't like me to complain, but I am truly embarrassed by all this. Reverend Smiles (I already told you he's Meg and Sibyl's departed father) has become my loyal mentor. Now this is all very well and I admit the wings are growing in nicely, although there has been no discussion of my halo, but it does make for a frustrating situation when I know Smiles would rather I not interfere at Number 7. He is grateful for the help I gave his daughters but he would be annoyed if he should discover I'm still — well, guiding the living because they need my help.

Fie, I see uninvited trouble on the horizon and there's no place to escape without looking foolish. What's he doing here un-invited, anyway?

I must be polite. "What, ho, there, Will. Coming to admire my home?"

Look at the way he's turning his nose up at my fabulous swan ewer. "What's that, Will? Mr. Shakespeare to me, you say? What a sense of humor you have. After all we've shared you'll always be Will-the-Wit, Witty-Willy to me. And you know I'm delighted to have you call me Sir Septimus.

"No, of course I'm not joking. I never joke. I feel a true closeness to you, Will."

My, my, his writer's wrist must be stunting his humor. "Can't do that, Will. I'm not sure it's even possible, why don't you give it a try? Make sure you don't break something in the process.

"If you cannot appreciate the finer points of a Benjamin Heely longcase clock, that is a problem for you. It is not an overfussy mon-strosity. Your ignorance takes my breath away. The design is of brass on a black-japanned case and in case you didn't notice, the face is silvered."

Give me patience, my dear friends.

Let's see how he copes with meddling. "I wanted to talk to you about Mistress Hathaway's home in Stratford. It's as much my business as this house is yours so I'm going to offer my valuable help. That place must mortify you. It's SO rustic.

"Hah. When you criticize me, you are being helpful. When I offer you expert advice, I am interfering."

Oh, piffle, have you ever tried to clap your hands when . . . no, of course you haven't, yet. Take my word for it, one is never prepared for the sound of one hand clapping . . . Anyway, good old Will's gone off in a huff and good riddance. He's a spy you know, looking for ways to stunt my angelic advances.

I must get on, and so must you. Whether you realize it or not, we have a lot to accomplish in a little time. Adam and Desirée must be safely bedded and wedded, in whatever order proves most expedient, before the Count can start parading Desirée before every fortune hunter in the land.

Believe in me, my dear friends. I know you think me harsh, but I am as interested in the happiness of our young friends as I am in my own interests.

You don't believe me? Be cruel, if you must, but I have been known to be kind before — on more than one occasion.

Now, enough chatter. Meg has done us a great service. Desirée is "all Adam's." Indeed? A very convenient idea unless he takes Meg's trust in him seriously.

5

January was often London's most frigid month. This year the cold struck through boots to chill the very bones. Even late in the morning, as it was now, chimney smoke clung in gray wreaths about rooftops and frost painted fantastic pictures on the insides of windows.

Hunched in the warmest cloak she had found among the clothes she'd had Anne purchase from a modest establishment, Desirée pulled the hood lower over her face to keep out some of the snowflakes. And she shivered so hard her teeth clattered together.

White-dusted carriages with windows as frostily painted as those of the great houses in Piccadilly, moved more cautiously than usual over icy roads. Plumes of vaporous breath flew from horses' nostrils while top-hatted coachmen huddled low into their mufflers and pulled lap blankets beneath their arms. The world was muted and soft. Even the horses' tack and hoofs sounded as if they'd been wrapped in flannel.

Refusing to listen to Anne's pleading that she not come here today, Desirée had placed herself on the opposite side of the street with an excellent view of Apsley House. Adam had left Mayfair Square early that morning in his carriage. Determined to see him alone and away from prying eyes at Number 7, Desirée had already been prepared to leave, and had slipped from Number 17 with Anne. She couldn't risk leaving her companion behind in case she panicked and told Meg what Desirée had done. At this very moment, Anne was waiting inside Desirée's own coach in the yard of an inn around the corner.

A lady and gentleman, both exceedingly well-dressed, alighted from an elegant coach and walked past Desirée to enter a house behind her. She ducked her head but needn't have bothered. The couple had dined at Jean-Marc's and Meg's houses in Mayfair Square and at Windsor. They had sat at the same tables with Desirée but clearly they saw no further than the plain clothing, which would not be worn by Princess Desirée of Mont Nuages. She smiled and stamped her feet, did a little jig in place.

A band of high-spirited gentlemen who were loudly amused by their own wit strolled along. Some wore starched collars so high their chins were permanently raised. They dawdled and posed and pretended swordplay with their canes. Desirée felt nervous but she reminded herself that it was almost the middle of the day with plenty of people about.

The sight of Anne Williams hurrying in her direction wasn't welcome.

"Go back at once," Desirée told her when she got close enough. "If I miss . . . If my efforts are ruined because you distract me, then I shall be exceeding angry with you, Anne."

Anne's lips were blue. "Pray come with me, Your Highness. I cannot imagine your reason for being here like this, but it will not do. And even if you do not care, I must. Your brother would say I am neglecting my post and dismiss me at once. Then I shall be without a place." Anne slapped her woolen gloves together and stamped her feet. "Please forgive me for my outburst. You will become so cold you are bound to be ill. Let me take you home."

Desirée shook her head and turned back to watch the entrance to Apsley House.

"Your Highness. I regret bothering you with these things but have you noticed that M. Verbeux's humor grows worse? You are otherwise occupied, but I note how he is everywhere in the house. He watches us. Perhaps he watches us now and will tell the Count."

"Hush, Anne," Desirée said. "You imagine things. Verbeux suffered a great deal in Mont Nuages. Accompanying us back to England gave him a reason to put his own troubles behind him. I'm sure all you see is that he continues to be concerned for our welfare. He is a very kind man."

"That he is, Your Highness," Anne said in a rush. "Why I don't think I have ever met a kinder one, or a more thoughtful one. Why, when we were traveling I don't know what we should have done without him. There was nothing he would not do for us — for you, that is."

Anne stopped talking and forgot to close her mouth. Desirée regarded her thoughtfully. This was not the first time Anne had shown particular admiration for Verbeux and Desirée was not deceived by a flimsy excuse to talk about him.

"You worry too much." Impulsively, Desirée kissed Anne's cheek. "We shall look after each other and that means that you will not lose your place and I shall not become ill because of being a little cold. I find it exhilarating to be abroad on a day such as this." She caught sight of a tall man leaving Apsley House. "Anne — please return to the coach at once. Have Barnes bring you some warm food from the inn. And cover yourself with the rugs. I am safe and shall come to you soon. Be off with you. Quickly."

Still Anne hesitated, but Desirée shushed her and the young woman left, looking back every few feet before making a turn into an alley.

Adam, and there was no doubt it was he, had turned back to speak with someone at the front doors of Apsley House. Desirée calculated how she might encounter him "casually," where she should position herself to avoid missing him.

He walked toward the flagway.

" 'Ot pies," a ruddy-faced boy sang out, pushing forward the tray he wore suspended from a rope around his neck. "Warm yer up, miss, they will."

She dropped a shilling in the tray, declined the pie, and slipped around him.

Adam stood still, looking first in one direction and then in another as if deciding which way to go.

Breathing harder, Desirée threaded her way between the slow moving traffic to reach the other side of Piccadilly.

One coach drew to a halt a few feet distant and a lady lowered a window. She raised a quizzing glass to get a better look at Adam, who didn't appear to notice her at all. He had moved to the curb but seemed no more decided upon his direction.

Annoyed at the anonymous woman's frank interest in Adam, Desirée hurried toward him, drinking in the sensations she got simply from observing his tall, solidly built body in the black cloak he favored. His hat was lowered over his eyes in rakish manner. The cloak was of heavy, serviceable stuff. She would be warm inside it, with him.

"Desirée?" He saw her before she realized he'd looked her way. "Gad, girl, what are you doing here? It's bitter. Dash it all, that cloak is useless to keep you warm, and those boots? Where did you find the pathetic things? I don't know how you got here, but go home by the same means and at once."

She didn't miss how he looked at her, even while he spoke coldly like the nasty thing he could be. He looked at her with heat in his eyes. Such dark gray eyes, and so haunted. If she hadn't heard his angry voice she might think that, despite his words, he wanted to see her if only to be diverted from other, deeply troubling thoughts. Desirée drew closer and raised her face to his. "Please don't be cross with me, Adam. I swear I cannot bear more cruelty than I am already bearing. My family cares nothing for me and I have not one ally to turn to — except you."

Without warning, he caught hold of her left arm and pulled her so near she felt the tension in his body. "All you think of is your own petty affairs. Do you think you are the only one with concerns? You stand here on this street where the poor come and go doing their best to live, and you think only of yourself."

Tears sprang into her eyes and they burned. Desirée's throat hurt and she couldn't quite catch a breath. He was right, of course, but she was not untouched by the plights of others. "I cannot cure all the ills of the world," she told him. "I do what I can. No matter, you have no need to know what I do or do not do. I was wrong to come here. Forgive me."

He pressed his lips together so tightly they turned white at the edges. "Little fool," he whispered in a terrible hushed voice. "You have no idea the danger you court. You understand nothing of men or the animals that they are. If you did, you would not risk being alone on this very street. This is a man's world here, do you understand? Women do not come here un-accompanied."

She swallowed and said, "No, I see, I didn't know that. I should leave at once."

"You will not take one more step on your own. Do you hear me? Meg has entrusted your guidance to me so I shall guide you. I wager it won't be long before you wish your sister-in-law had not made such a rash request."

She hung her head. "Never," she told him. "Be angry, but please do not be cruel. What have I done to you for you to treat me so?"

The odd noise he made frightened her. For an instant his fingers dug even deeper into her arm. "I have told you that you are a babe playing with fire — or similar words. Believe me when I say you do not know me."

"But I do." Inside her body, she trem-

90

bled from shock, and from wanting him. "I thought I did. Let me go."

"I accepted a charge to take care of you. When I give my word it is a bond. Why are you dressed like a scullery maid?"

Would she ever do anything to satisfy him? "I thought you would prefer me to look ordinary. I think you are uncomfortable with useless, expensive fripperies."

"You mean that because I am a man who doesn't live as well as your cat, I am to be pitied? You want to make me feel more comfortable by dressing as badly as I do?"

"*No,*" she said, incensed. "How foolish and rude of you."

His gaze moved from her eyes to her mouth and his lips curled.

"You think that because I have been surrounded by men of privilege I admire them?" Heavens, she sounded like a child to her own ears. "Well then, yes, that's exactly right. Not that you dress badly — I like the way you dress, but I thought you might be more comfortable with me if I appeared like any other ordinary girl."

"You are *not* ordinary," he said, his tone still low, but softened. "You are lovely and regal. Even when you are incorrigible you are lovely. I'm sure a great many other men will think so when you come out."

"Adam?" A slender lady dressed in a simple but beautifully cut long black coat stepped hesitantly forward. Desirée had noticed her alighting from a grand town coach that remained a few yards distant. "Adam? May I speak with you?" Three sable-edged capes fell over her shoulders and her bonnet was similarly trimmed. She wore a veil but it didn't hide eyes the color of violets, or small, perfect features.

Desirée looked at Adam and might have cried out at the sight of his face if they had not been in a public place. He no longer saw her. Adam saw no one, of that she was certain. In his mind he had gone to a place where whatever visions he saw tore at him, sucked the color from his features and closed his expression.

"Here, girl," the tall lady said, looking at Desirée. With a shaky hand she found a sovereign in her reticule and pressed it on Desirée. "My son is the most generous of men but evidently you have caught him by surprise. I hope this will help you. God-speed."

With a heart that hammered in her breast, Desirée made to turn away. She would not embarrass Adam by trying to return the coin. But he would not let her go. Rather he loosened his grip a little and turned slowly to look at this woman who said she was his mother.

She whispered his name again and held out her hands to him, but if he noticed, he chose to ignore the gesture. "I have missed you," she told him.

"This lady," Adam said to her coldly, "is Princess Desirée of Mont Nuages, not a beggar."

"You could not know," Desirée said, narrowing her eyes at Adam. "I am not good at fashion, nor even particularly interested in it anymore. I didn't think I looked like a pauper but my dress is unpretentious. Thank you for your kindness." She returned the sovereign, smiling at the woman. "Adam and I have been friends for some years. I am so pleased to meet his mother at last." How she wished she might meet her own mother on the streets of London and see pleasure on her face, but she had never known how it would be to be loved as a daughter.

"I'm surprised to see you," Adam said finally. "I was told by some who are close to you that you rarely leave Manthy House." He emphasized, *some who are close to you,* and his mother's eyes glittered behind her veil. "One might think you knew I'd be here."

"Good day to both of you," Desirée said, feeling sick and almost light-headed. "I will leave you to your visit."

Still Adam did not release her.

"No, no, I'm so glad to meet any friend of Adam's. I'm Lady Elspeth Chillworth." She offered a hand and Desirée took it promptly. "I have my coach. Could I persuade the two of you to come home for lunch?"

"No," Adam said through his teeth.

"Your grandmother would be beside herself with happiness," Lady Elspeth said. "You know how she loves you."

"Yes, I do," Adam told her. "And I love her. Our positions are unfortunate."

"Because you blame me," Lady Elspeth said. She put a gloved hand to her mouth and glanced at Desirée. "Forgive my outburst."

Horrified at Adam's behavior, Desirée tugged at his sleeve until he gave her his attention. She caught at the collar of his cloak and pulled until he brought his ear to her mouth. "This is terrible," she whispered to him. "The lady is your mother. Whatever your differences, put them aside out of respect."

He straightened and said, "Her Highness pleads for me to show you respect as my mother. She knows nothing of my family and I hope she never will. It would have been better if you hadn't come upon me like this. Forget me again, as I shall forget you. Good day."

Lady Elspeth stepped back. "Yes," she said. "You are your father's son. What you decide to believe, you believe forever. So be it, my son, but unlike you, your brother does not have a strong will. He is in trouble, Adam, I'm sure of it and I don't think I can help him. He will not even tell me what brings him so low."

"This is unsuitable conversation in front of the Princess," Adam said.

Lady Elspeth raised her chin and in-clined her head. Desirée thought she must be about the same age as Lady Hester but she was much more finely built.

"You don't know how to trust, Adam," Lady Elspeth said. "If I didn't see the openness in Her Highness, I certainly should not speak in front of her, but if ever a man needed a friend, you do, and I see that you care about each other in some way. Is it safe for me to talk in front of you, Princess Desirée, or will you betray my son by making jest of what you witness here?"

Desirée tore her arm free of Adam's hand. "I would do anything for Adam. He is the best friend I have ever had. I confess that I am deeply shaken by the way he treats you, but I shall not reveal any of this to another."

Lost, that was how she saw him now. Adam Chillworth, that self-contained and powerful creature was lost for the moment. He concentrated not on his mother, but on Desirée.

"Ah," Lady Elspeth murmured. "I think I see well how it is here. I shall leave you now. Please consider helping Lucas. There is a strangeness in him which I have never seen before. You were not friends as boys, but I know he loves you — envies you even."

Adam continued to stare into Desirée's eyes and she felt as if he were clinging to her, begging her not to desert him.

"I've said enough." Lady Elspeth bowed her head. "I don't ask you to do it for me, but for your brother's sake — and your father who loves him so — intervene in whatever threatens him. I know you have also hardened your heart against Gilbert, but he loves you a great deal. It's just that love has always been difficult for him to demonstrate."

"Adam," Desirée said and slipped a hand into his, not caring how unsuitable it was. "Please don't harden your heart so."

"Thank you," Lady Elspeth told her and turned to hurry to her coach.

The maroon conveyance with the elegant coat of arms on its door swept Adam's mother away but Adam didn't move. He folded Desirée's hand in both of his and she saw him swallow repeatedly.

"There's no need to talk at all," she told him. "You should be at home where you can be alone."

He didn't answer her.

"My coach is in the yard at the King's Arms. Come back with me."

"Yes," he said, a wooden man.

"Come then."

He rubbed her hand. "I sent my own coach home. I was going to get a cab."

"Now you don't need one."

"I apologize for what you witnessed. The thought of it shames me."

"Then I am hurt, Adam Chillworth. You and I are companions, aren't we?"

Once more he studied her face before he said, "I think we are. Fate is a joker, isn't he?"

He puzzled her but she didn't ask what he meant. "Mock what I ask you — if you must — this may be a strange time for this, but let's deal with something right here and now. Do you intend to marry?"

His frown let her know just how odd he considered her timing. "I shouldn't think so," he told her at last.

"Good, then we have so much in common and there is no other I trust as much as you. Despite having family, you and I are alone. Let us make a pact to be friends forever, and to help each other forever. If you agree, let us shake hands on it."

Solemnly, he did as she suggested.

Friends forever. Yes, that's what she wanted, that and so much more, but declaring a bond of friendship was a good place to start.

He said, "God sent you to me," and carried her hand to his mouth. With his eyes shut, he kissed her cold fingers. "I am a hard man and I have been a careless man. But I can change. For you."

As she watched, he kissed her fingers again and she swayed nearer to him. Adam wanted to change, *for her?* "We can both change — for each other," she told him. He wanted to make her an intimate part of his life after all. She would have to be patient, prepared to wait until he was ready.

"Come," Adam said, "let us go to the

King's Arms. Neither of us wants to be here."

Oh, but she wanted to be here, as long as he was.

"I am blessed to know you," he said. "And we shall be partners of a sort, at least until you meet the man who will make you a suitable husband. I shall always love you, but I'll know and understand when we must be friends from afar."

6

"By now Meg and Jean-Marc will have missed you. I insist you return home and put their minds at ease." Also, Adam acknowledged, not a single feeling he had for Desirée was brotherly, or even *friendlike* at that moment. For both of their sakes he'd do well to separate himself from her before he lost his mind and did some of the things he wanted to do. "Take my arm at once. I'll accompany you to your carriage."

Desirée blinked and moisture glistened on her eyelashes. The odd snowflake settled on her nose and high cheekbones — and her mouth — like butterfly kisses.

"I'm sorry for annoying you, Adam," she said, bowing her head and slipping a hand beneath his elbow. "You know I would never wish to do so. I'm so impulsive, that's all."

He barely contained a groan. How was he supposed to concentrate on making her like him less — not much less, just a little — when she could be so adorable? And, even more so, how would he ever find a way to meet her, to smile at her and relish her company rather than seeing her, dancing naked, in his very soul? She thought she knew so much, yet she knew nothing, and this creature was not for the likes of him.

"Adam?"

He'd been staring toward Hyde Park Corner, looking at but not really seeing the tearing about of young bucks, their tomfoolery in the snow, the outrageous spectacle of a man swathed in white furs and whipping on the poor devil of a horse who pulled him in a canary yellow phaeton.

"I shall go to Hatchards and find a new novel I've heard a great deal about," Desirée said. "Don't trouble yourself further about me. I am quite safe, I assure you. Apparently my attempts to appear ordinary work well, even if they do offend you. I may even visit the Burlington Arcade — I have never been there. Later I shall bring some special treats for Halibut."

Something like traveling fire made a rapid path from his most sensitive places to his head and he felt himself color. "You could wear a coal sack, Your Highness, thrice used both right side and inside out and still you would turn the head of any man of taste." *Any man capable of seeing beauty within, as well as without — and intellect gentled by innocence Adam didn't believe even carnal knowledge would destroy.* "You are a gently bred girl and the Arcade is a . . . You will not go there and you will never mention it to me again."

She had begun to remove her hand from his arm. They frowned into each other's faces and he adjusted her fingers to curl inside his elbow once more. "Oh, very well, pout if you must. You think I have no right to tell you what to do and you are correct. So, a compromise? Can the novel wait another day or so? I will ask Jean-Marc and Meg if I can take you there when I have an errand of my own."

"Yes," she said, her voice breathy. "That would be kind, thank you."

"Good. Then let's away to the King's Arms at once."

"Of course, thank you, Adam."

Could being polite cause death? He almost smiled at the thought. "Be careful on the cobbles," he told her, leading her carefully into the street. Yes, dammit, one or two more "thank you's" and he might have to swallow his tongue to stop himself from howling with frustration. That would undoubtedly choke him.

"Hold on, tight," he said, grinning openly. He did believe he was losing his mind over a slip of a woman who should make him a better sister or cousin than . . . lover.

The grin felt fixed but wouldn't entirely die.

He handed her onto the opposite curb, touching her lightly at the waist as he did so. And muscles in his spine tightened. *I don't want to be polite, I want to take her to my bed.* The words cried out so loudly in his head they shook him for fear she must hear them.

"Good day to you, Mr. Chillworth."

A French accent; a man's deep voice addressing him familiarly, fleetingly disoriented Adam. M. Verbeux, who was settled at Number 17 Mayfair Square as Jean-Marc's valet and confidant once more and who was treated with respect in that household, stood in Adam and Desirée's path.

"Morning to you, Verbeux," Adam said. "Wretched weather."

"You forget that I have lived most of my life in Mont Nuages. We should all be bereft without our snow. Good morning, Princess."

Desirée's fingertips and thumb had come together on the underside of Adam's arm and even through the thick material of his coat he felt his skin pinched. She muttered something meaningless to Verbeux.

"But of course, Your Highness," the man said, "I happened to be in this area when I noticed you."

Adam felt sorry for the fellow. He was a poor liar — at least on this occasion.

"Has my brother asked you to spy on me?" Desirée demanded. "We both know you didn't simply *happen* to be here. You were following me."

Verbeux, lithe, his hair, mustache and beard dark, as were his arresting eyes behind small wire-rimmed spectacles, actually seemed uncomfortable, a rare occurrence in one who was supremely sure of himself.

"I take my responsibilities seriously," Verbeux said and Adam glanced at Desirée to gauge her reaction to this exceedingly handsome man.

"You have no responsibilities where I am concerned," she told him.

He inclined his head and smiled just a little. "Your father released me from his service so that I might protect you on the journey back to England. Now that I am once more in the Count's employ, it remains my responsibility to ensure that you are safe. Your brother cares deeply for you."

"Bosh," Desirée said without grace. "He doesn't want to be bothered with me so he has you follow me around and meddle in my business."

"Meddling has nothing to do with it," Verbeux said. "My task is to make sure that a vulnerable and unworldly young woman doesn't get into trouble from which she cannot easily be extricated. You do not need to be told that your impeccable reputation must be safeguarded at all costs. Soon you will be the center of attention among the most eligible men in England, and from elsewhere. There can be no question about your . . . no questions at all about you. Going about alone like this is out of the question."

"That is an *outrage!*" Desirée's face turned very pink. "You *have* been told to spy on me. Aren't you going to say anything, Adam? This is cruel, harsh, this attempt to curb my sense of adventure."

Adam felt obliged to speak even though he didn't consider it his place. "You are a special woman," he told Desirée. "And, contrary to your beliefs, wearing rude clothing makes you no less outstanding. I for one am grateful your impulsiveness is kept in check."

"*Are* you? What wrong have I ever done through being impulsive? None, I tell you. Goodbye, both of you, I must get back."

"I have a carriage," Verbeux said.

"So do I," Desirée told him.

Verbeux gave an extravagant shrug. "Then I'll have your carriage sent on."

"You will not send my carriage on without me," Desirée told Verbeux. "Even if I wanted to, I couldn't leave poor Anne to return alone."

Verbeux looked blank. "Where is Miss Williams, Chillworth?" he asked with an accusing note in his voice.

"How did you know to look for me here?" Desirée asked. "You didn't know I came by my own carriage and you didn't know Anne was with me, so you couldn't have followed me."

Adam regarded her with admiration. He'd been too preoccupied to think of the questions Desirée had been so quick to ask.

"I answer to the Count," Verbeux said. "How I knew to look for you here is of no consequence. No need to remain, Chillworth. I will accompany the Princess now."

Even if he were inclined to allow Verbeux to brush him off, which he was not, one desperate plea from Desirée's eyes was enough to make sure Adam refused to leave her.

"Desirée has kindly offered to give me a lift back to Mayfair Square. She has taken pity on me in this vicious weather. Excuse us, please, I'm sure you'll want to get on."

Verbeux's expression closed. He raised his hat to Desirée and turned expressionless eyes on Adam. "I will inform the Count that his sister is in safe hands." He turned on his heel and strode smoothly away.

"Odd fellow," Adam said and added without thinking, "Why did he really leave Mont Nuages?"

Desirée hesitated then said softly, "He did marry Lady Upworth."

It was impossible to listen to this girl, to watch the way she formed words, and not be mesmerized. "Aye, that's what we all expected. I don't see the connection to his coming back to England."

"Ila was increasing. She became ill during childbirth and did not recover. He really loved her." She tapped his chest absentmindedly. "It wouldn't do to mention Ila. He will not speak of her."

Adam breathed deeply and looked to the heavy sky, blinking against the snow. "Probably blames himself." This was an unsuitable direction in which to take the conversation. "Because she wasn't in England," he added, hoping to deflect more discussion of the responsibility some men felt when a woman died of some condition while carrying their children.

Desirée looked as if she saw something distressing in her mind. "I know a good deal about it all, you know," she told him. "Since a woman does not increase without a man's help, I suppose he could feel responsible. Imagine being loved that much."

"I find that easy to imagine." And even the thought of Desirée suffering, as Adam had seen women suffer in giving birth, with his child overwhelmed him with protective, with loving, with terrified feelings. "I should never recover from the tragedy."

Desirée bowed her head.

"I forget myself. You should not be burdened with such things. I will take you home."

Rather than start to move, Desirée raised her face and watched him with something approaching ecstasy. "What is it?" he asked her.

"You will take me at home, Adam?"

He frowned at her. Her English was perfect yet she sometimes constructed her sentences strangely. "Of course. You must be frozen and I am remiss. Quickly, let's go to your carriage."

She remained still, and she blushed furiously, laughed awkwardly. "Yes," she said. "Foolish of me. Perhaps I do not always hear well."

He didn't understand what she meant, but decided it didn't matter.

Side-by-side they hurried to the yard of the King's Arms where Desirée's carriage was the first they saw. Anne Williams sat inside, peering anxiously through a space she'd rubbed on the inside of a steamed window. The coachman, Barnes, stood with several other coachmen. They all stamped their feet and guffawed loudly.

Adam put an arm around Desirée and all but swept her off her feet in his haste.

"When will you visit Manthy House?" she asked when he least expected the question. "Your mother is a charming woman, generous and kind and she obviously loves you very much."

Beside the coach, Adam pulled her to a

stop and swung her to face him. Lowering his head he looked closely into her face and said, "You know nothing of my mother, or my life when I was growing up. Things are rarely as they appear to be."

"No." Her voice was high and her eyes wide.

"Remember that and never mention my mother to me again."

"Yes."

"Barnes," he called. "If you can be spared we should enjoy your services." He slammed the coach door open and didn't bother with the steps. Bundling Desirée inside and following her, he managed a smile for Anne whose surprise was obvious.

The instant Desirée landed on the seat beside her companion, she pulled herself into a corner, straightened her back, and told him, "Men have died for their pride. They have also broken hearts for the same silliness. You may be impressive with your brutish force and slicing tongue but I, for one, am unimpressed."

He opened his mouth to speak. "Do not argue with me, my good man," she cut him off. "Sit there quietly and consider your outrageous behavior — how you beat down your own mother with unkind words, meanly spoken."

"I have warned you," Adam said, his gut tight, "do not interfere. And unless my ears deceived me, only moments have passed since you agreed to do as I ask."

"I have changed my mind." Desirée shifted to the front of her seat and her knees touched his in the confines of the coach. "That would be since you threw me into my own coach. And if I do not obey you, what will you do to me?"

She had him there, dammit. But he would find a way to divert her.

"You will do nothing to me," she said and suddenly her eyes misted, "because . . . you know why, you foolish man. Remember one thing if you remember nothing else. Your decisions do not hurt only you, and the heart you break becomes yours to bear."

He glanced at Anne who was white-faced and evidently close to tears herself.

"Desirée," he said quietly. "Our fates are not in our own hands."

"Posh," she said without conviction. "Some may simply accept disappointment, I am not one of them. It will be my job to do all I can to make you see how love over-comes any barrier." She turned pink again. "I will do my best to help you put whatever you have against your mother behind you."

As soon as she finished speaking, she closed her eyes as if closing the conversation. Very well, let her use any trick that pleased her, and any attempt to cover the true meaning of what she'd said.

Adam did not believe this woman he'd loved for four years, and felt guilty for loving, spoke only of barriers to a love between mother and son.

God help him to do what ought to be done without crushing Desirée — or turning himself into a disappointed man doomed to hunger for her the rest of his life.

7

The expression on Adam's face when he saw her walking into the attic almost caused Desirée to flee. Either he was . . . no, he *was* devastated by something. She saw two envelopes and some sheets of paper in his hands.

He turned from her. "Please, if you know what's good for you, go away — quickly."

Only half an hour previous he'd left her carriage when Barnes pulled up in front of Number 17. With barely a nod and a muttered goodbye, he strode away through the gardens in the center of Mayfair Square to reach Number 7 on the other side.

Desirée had exchanged pleasant words with Meg and sworn Anne to unwilling silence about her mistress's plan to leave her brother's home again, immediately. Desirée had slipped out through the gardens at the back of the house in hopes of avoiding being seen by someone who might report to Jean-Marc.

Cautiously she closed Adam's door and advanced. He'd removed his cloak and thrown it across a chair. His hat rested on top and his hair was tousled.

Adam didn't face her. He stood like a man made of marble.

On tiptoe, Desirée approached until she stood immediately behind him. She settled her hands on his back and stroked him, bracing herself for him to shrug her away.

He didn't.

She didn't speak and neither did he, but he bowed his head.

Adam was deeply upset and Desirée couldn't bear it. How easy it was to push her hands beneath his arms and reach as far as possible around his chest. As easy as it was to rest her cheek on his back and just hold him.

She recalled with chagrin how before she had entered her carriage at the King's Arms she had misheard, or translated to her better liking, what he said to her yet again. Despite her best efforts, this continued to happen but usually she did not blurt out her reactions to the foolishness. *You will take me at home?* " Horrors.

Paper rustled and he pressed one of her hands tightly to him.

Desirée thought they stood there, exactly like that, for a long time before Adam said, "You have a kind heart, but you need to be at home now," in a strained voice that unnerved her. He moved out of her arms. "Off with you."

"Off with me?" she repeated. "No. No, absolutely not. You need me."

"I do *not* need you." And now his voice was terrible. He swung around. His flaring nostrils and tight lips caused her to take a step backward. "I don't need anyone. I never have. Need is a liability. The wise man is alone and I am wise."

She crossed her arms.

"You would be wise to leave me," Adam said. "This is no time to parade that stubborn will of yours."

"Tell me what is wrong."

"Don't you know when it's dangerous to be with someone?" He tossed the papers among paints and brushes, bottles and jars on a table. "Are you so sheltered that you don't imagine you could be harmed?"

"You would never harm me," she told him, but her throat was dry and her heart beat faster. "Stop being unreasonable and let me help you. Is it those papers? Are they a letter? Who are they from?"

"That is not your affair," he thundered.

"By God, must I be pestered even when I'm already desperate."

Desirée pressed her hands into the folds of her green striped kerseymere skirts. Her palms were moist. "If I were desperate, Adam," she said in barely more than a whisper, "would you abandon me because my pride would not allow me to accept your help?"

He drove the fingers of both hands into his hair. "I would not. But that would be different." He sank to sit on the sofa. "You have no idea what you're talking about. Your life and mine could not have been more different — could not be more different now."

"Because no one can have suffered as you have suffered?" Distracting herself by swinging the cloak from her shoulders and putting it with Adam's, she willed the beating at her temples to stop. "You have had a difficult life whereas mine has been simple?"

His response was to rest his elbows on his knees and shake his head, slowly, wearily.

Desirée heard Halibut complain for attention and saw him curled on Adam's bed. Should she try to persuade Adam to lie down?

"You deserve happiness," Adam said. "And you shall have it if only you will allow Jean-Marc to guide you. Stop rebelling and do as he tells you to do."

"And then I shall be happy?" She laughed when she felt like crying. "How does that happen? I attend all manner of boring, meaningless affairs and smile at prancing gentlemen as if I find them fascinating and desirable? Then from among those who ask for my hand, the one who is richest and has the most exalted title will be given permission to take possession of me?" The choked cry that escaped her throat didn't please her.

Adam looked up at her, his eyes shadowed. "Yes. That is the way of it and it is your duty to accept the wisdom of others more able than you to make such decisions."

"I see." Helplessness she could not accept stole her composure entirely. "But your lot is more difficult. Hmm, I see. And will you allow others to make *your* decisions, and tell *you* what must happen?"

"My dear girl, we are not helping each other. I need to think. Please leave me alone and when my head is clearer, I will ask if you would be kind enough to let me visit you."

"Ooh!" She made fists and whirled away, marched as far as the bed and back again. Bending over him, she said, "You know I cannot — and will not — leave you like this. I ask you again, what has happened?"

Adam fell against the back of the couch and looked at her directly. "I will never have what I truly want. It isn't possible." His throat moved sharply as he swallowed. "But I will do anything to make sure you find happiness."

"I asked you a question."

"Aye. And I should tell you that I have a note from my brother Lucas asking if you and Miss Williams will join us for luncheon tomorrow at the Clarendon Hotel in Albermarle Street. Naturally Jean-Marc will not agree, but I don't subscribe to the notion that a lady should be ignorant of her own affairs."

She did not believe that an invitation to luncheon with Lucas Chillworth was the reason for Adam's low mood. "I should like to go," she told him. "And I'm sure Jean-Marc will agree unless you tell him he should not."

Adam raised an eyebrow. He had placed his hands beneath his legs on the couch.

"You won't tell him I shouldn't go, will you? After all, Anne will chaperon me, and you will protect both of us."

He laughed and she did not at all like the way that sounded.

"You cannot know how bored I am," she told him, then closed her mouth and sat sideways on the couch where she could watch him closely. "No matter about my feelings — except I do want to go tomorrow. There were two envelopes. Was the other nothing more than a pleasant invitation?"

"You do not stop. You press and press as if you are certain you will have your own way in everything. Princess Desirée asks, and she must be told, and she must get whatever she wants."

For a moment words failed her. She glanced at his mouth and, angry as she was, recalled how heavenly it had felt against hers. His black hair, so unfashionably long and curling, had an effect on unmentionable places within her. She barely restrained herself from touching it, and from kissing that mouth of his.

"Good afternoon to you, Desirée," he said and rolled his face away.

Desirée abandoned caution and knelt on the sofa beside him. She observed him with narrowed eyes and resolved to be silent until he spoke again.

A pulse beat hard in his neck and a muscle beside his mouth twitched. He pulled his hands from beneath his legs and curled them on his thighs. Adam had the most beautiful hands she'd ever seen. Large hands, but so well shaped and with long fingers. A dusting of hairs showed dark against his white cuffs.

With one finger, Desirée touched each of the whitened knuckles on the hand nearest to her. She followed the raised bones all the way to his wrist. With the backs of her fingers, she stroked the hair to discover how it felt and was surprised to find it soft.

The sharpest tightening pulled between her legs. She ached and wanted the ache to stay forever.

With great care she pulled his fingers out straight and chafed skin that was too cold.

Still Adam didn't speak but the muscles in his face constricted harder. His eyes were not only closed, but squeezed tight shut.

"Let me help you," she murmured. "Perhaps you should rest on your bed. Yes, that is what you should do. I will help you get comfortable and then I will watch over you while you sleep. You are not alone, Adam, because you have me. You always will."

He drew his lips back from his teeth.

"You are suffering and I cannot bear it," she told him. "You have often looked after me, now I shall look after you." With that she loosened his neckcloth and undid the top button of his shirt. She found she shook terribly, and she knew she should not be so familiar, but he had no one else to do these things for him.

She saw him open his eyes and stare straight ahead as if he saw something she did not see.

"Take off your coat," she told him. "I will cover you with your quilt. Come, Adam, lean forward."

"Why must I be tortured?" He cried out so suddenly that Desirée started to tumble from the couch until he grabbed her by the shoulders and hauled her so close only inches separated their faces. "You will help me be more comfortable? You will have me rest on my bed while you watch over me?" His laughter was awful this time. "Your naiveté frightens me. You would be helpless in the hands of an unscrupulous man."

Oh, yes, you may be an unscrupulous man with me if you like. To be helpless with you would be heaven.

"Don't look at me like that," he roared. "What do you want of me?"

To be your love. To live with you for the rest

of my life. To have your children, to make you happy always.

"Desirée?"

If she told him her thoughts, she would lose him, lose what little she could share with him. "All I want is to ease your sadness." She lowered her voice. "And chase away your anger."

He moved and she could not have escaped even if she'd wanted to. With a strength that rendered her helpless, Adam got to his feet, hauling her with him. She was crushed against him, her breasts flattened to his chest, her shoulders raised by the force of his grip.

A rage in his eyes faded to hollowness, as if he was besieged by questions he either couldn't or wouldn't ask.

Slowly he took his hands from her shoulders, but only so that he could wrap her in his arms, wrap her in an embrace so wild she felt him shudder again and again.

Desirée slipped her hands about his waist and raised her face. She stood on tiptoe and settled her lips on the place where the pulse throbbed in his throat. She nuzzled him there, and held him tighter.

"No," Adam said. He set her feet flat again, but he didn't withdraw from her, rather he settled his chin on top of her head, and he used his palms to massage her back, jerky caresses from her neck to her waist, and the spreading of a hand over the back of her head, fleeting passes on her neck.

Adam pressed himself into her, into the cradle of her belly and she blazed when she felt That Part of him, the hardness of it, the way it pulsed — its size. Her face throbbed and her breasts prickled.

She wanted him to kiss her. "Kiss me, Adam. The way you did before."

Once more he studied her face, touched her face, but his kiss when it came was firm and closed, and delivered to her forehead. He rocked her, kept his lips on her brow, and each breath he took sounded labored.

From her face, to the sides of her neck, over her shoulders and to her elbows and, finally, at her waist, he stroked her, and when he held her waist, he urged her even more tightly to him. Desirée could not help but return his pressure with an urgent thrust of her hips.

Holding her beneath her arms, resting his thumbs beside her breasts, Adam pushed his face into the crook of her neck and Desirée laid her cheek against his hair.

His thumbs were beneath her breasts

then. She could think of nothing but how it might feel if she wore no clothes, if Adam wore no clothes, and they stood like this, and he covered her breasts completely, and she could feel That Part of him hot, heavy, seeking on her belly, between her legs.

She gasped aloud. She had pored over books not intended for her eyes, studied diagrams and explanations. Still she was not entirely certain what the details of the act of love might be, but she grew moist. The temptation was to part her legs against his thigh, to rock back and forth on the hard muscle there, but not even that would be enough. There was more and if she understood it correctly, as she thought she did, then he would put himself inside her.

Desirée kissed his cheek, did her best to reach his mouth only he did not help her. If he entered her body, they would be one, with no beginning and no end and she knew she would feel whole as she never had before.

"I am so wrong," Adam said against the skin of her neck. "I have made it impossible not to explain the cruel facts of our situation. And when I have finished, you will understand that we cannot be together again. My fault, not yours. I should have resisted — only I couldn't. It was impossible from the moment you returned and I could tell you felt at least some of what I feel."

Desirée kept her eyes closed. "I feel weak. It is from wanting you and I shall always want you. If you try to keep us apart — well, I shall not allow you to do that."

"Silly, passionate girl. You will do what's best. Don't tremble so. Desirée? Oh, I have done you damage. Don't faint. The emotion is too much for one who has no experience."

"I shall not faint," she told him, but her limbs didn't want to hold her and she sagged against him. "I do have experience. I have kissed and been kissed, and I have been held." She had been held so that she felt her womanhood flower yet it had not and never could quench her thirst for him.

Adam muttered something that sounded like a curse and picked her up. "I have failed your brother, and Meg. You are not for me yet I have . . . I have awakened you and that was not for me to do."

He took her to the bed and stretched her out on top of the quilt. She smiled up at him and moved away from the edge of the mattress.

"Do you have any idea how beautiful you are?" he asked her.

She lowered her eyelashes.

What she'd craved happened then. Adam sat beside her and settled his hands over her breasts. When she looked at him, he watched his fingers as he passed them back and forth over her flesh. Through her bodice, he squeezed the tip of each breast between finger and thumb. He grew pale then paler. The squeezes became a gentle pulling and her bottom arched from the bed. Adam pressed between her legs and even through her heavy skirts there was a raw and needy response, an ecstatic response.

"Why?" Adam said and the pallor had reached his lips. "You were made for me, but not meant for me."

Gathering her courage, Desirée caught him by the hair at his neck and pulled his face to her breast. And she reached between his big thighs to finally feel the true shape of him. Adam cried out and grew still. His body seemed to leap within her probing fingers and the heat in him amazed her. There he was like molten iron.

It was not enough. "Come to me," she

said. "Lie with me and show me every-thing." As she spoke, she urged him to climb on the mattress with her.

"God forgive me," he said in a strangled voice, and kissed her. He leaned on her and he was too heavy, but his weight thrilled her. He kissed her as he had the day before, but with more force. She could only respond as he allowed her to do so. The power and the control were his. Her mouth was forced wide open and filled with his tongue. His searching rocked her face and turned her head this way and that, and she continued to hold and stroke the evidence of his virility.

He paused to breathe, rested his head on the pillow beside her.

"Let's stay here," she told him. "There is plenty of room for two in this bed. We can hold each other until it grows late and I must return home. I will comfort you like this and you will comfort me. Lie down."

The only sound he made was a sort of moan that faded at once. He released her hold on him and stood up, taking her arms from around his neck.

"Adam?"

He stared at her while he backed away, didn't stop staring as he gathered up his cloak and threw it around his shoulders. "I must leave you because I don't trust myself to stay. I am only a man and I am already tried beyond endurance. We must talk so that I may explain what I can't expect you to know otherwise. After that, we must not be alone again."

Moving was out of the question. Desirée had turned cold and stiff. Even Halibut, who had roused himself to sniff her face, could not distract her or make her limbs work.

"If you wish, we shall have lunch with my brother tomorrow," Adam said. "Anne Williams must be there. And when I return you to Number 17, I will ask Jean-Marc's permission to visit with you there. Only in your home can it be safe. I will have to make you accept what I have been forced to accept."

He left her then.

8

Give the gentleman his wings at once. The Adam Chillworths of this world have no need of angel school in the world to come. Should think he might have to start wearing a hat at all times until he gets there — being that someone like the Reverend Smiles or even Thomas Moore himself will insist that a halo must be slapped on his head this very moment whether he wants it or not. He won't want one of those twinkling away above his manly head. Shouldn't think that would raise his stock with the ladies. Oh, but I forgot, he is a reformed man, no more lusty romps that last for hours in the cards for Mr. Chillworth.

Sickening. If it were still possible I'd cast up my accounts. It's not natural, y'know, walking away from a beautiful and willing girl who has begged for, ahem, attention. Suspicious that. And disturbing. You don't suppose — no, if he had plans to kidnap her and ransom her virginity, I would have had an inkling. Besides, a plot like that requires brilliant cunning and apart from myself I don't know of another who could plan well enough to carry out . . . Not, of course, that I would ever stoop to such a thing!

Look, this is a bit embarrassing, but I should like to ask your opinion on a matter of the highest importance and delicacy.

Do you think I could possibly be missing something here?

What? Well, I must say, there's no need to be rude! That's the last time I treat you as equals. My fault, I suppose, for thinking I could appeal to your higher sensibilities.

I was only testing you, anyway. Now you shan't know what's really on my mind . . . I'm not going to ask if you noticed what I noticed — you'll just have to work everything out from scratch like I do. Oh, all right, I'll give you a hint: When is a coincidence not a coincidence?

Hah, confounded you there. I was joking, I did notice a little oddity that puzzled me, though. Did you?

Oh, this is too entertaining . . .

Damn me, Will's heading this way. I must be quick or I'll have to talk to him and I'm not in the mood. My newel post awaits. Time to rest the memory of my bones in a good, solid place. And even that isn't so easy while I get the measure of these handsome wings.

"I was not speaking to you, Shakespeare. Now run along and find something useful to do. Sharpen a few quills, anything.

"No, I most certainly didn't call out to you. Well I'm blessed, you think the only reason I'd be guffawing and saying that something was too entertaining would be because I'd just seen one of your plays?

"If there's one thing I can't abide it's a self-centered man who can't see beyond his own selfish wants. Off with you, I say. And until we meet again, consider a question: With all the quite passable properties erected during your time, why was a pathetic little cottage the best you could do?"

That got rid of him. See him shambling off? He only has himself to blame if he doesn't have as much as a couple of pimple-sized wing buds to show for all the years he's been here. Yes, he does fly, you've seen him, more or less, but how would you like to have to abuse your elbows and shoulders like that. Besides, it looks too ungainly.

Piffle — no, I will not allow conscience to interfere with a perfectly good time. Get behind me, all of you. Leave me alone, I say. I am singular in purpose and will not be diverted. I AM NOT GROWING SOFT.

Ah, I cannot fight it. I admit that I admire —

to the smallest degree — Adam Chillworth. He may actually be a man of principle, but if he thinks I'll allow his standards to get in the way of my necessities, well, need I tell you which of us will be disappointed?

Stop detaining me. I have to make certain all is as it should be for our sojourn in Albermarle Street tomorrow.

9

"If Lady Hester finds out we've had a cozy gatherin' wi'out her, she'll, well, she'll no' show it in front o' us, but she'll be upset and I canna bear it."

"*Jenny.*"

Sibyl, Lady Lloyd, and Meg, Countess Etranger, cried out at Jenny More with such exasperation she cringed in her favorite amaranthus pink brocade chair.

Meg and Sibyl were sisters who had once lived at 7B Mayfair Square. The impoverished orphan daughters of the Reverend Smiles — late of Puckly Hinton in the Cotswolds — remained the unspoiled women their father brought them up to be, despite marrying well. Meg, chestnut-haired and with eyes her husband liked to tell her were the color of fine cognac, and blond, blue-eyed Sibyl, both mothers, continued to look for and often find the best in others. And they still laughed together as they had when they'd been girls in a country vicarage.

On this particularly cold morning, the sisters and Jenny sat close to a lively fire in Jenny's sitting room at Number 8 Mayfair Square. The house belonged to Finch, Viscountess Kilrood — Latimer More's sister — and her husband Ross, Viscount Kilrood. Latimer and Jenny were in permanent residence there. Ross and Finch moved in whenever they visited London from their Scottish estates and the two couples truly enjoyed sharing company.

Sibyl and Sir Hunter had arrived late on the day previous and had succumbed to Meg's repeated pleas that they stay with her and Jean-Marc rather than return at once to Number 7. The sisters' children were to spend time together like brother and sister.

"Lady Hester Bingham is a great lady," Jenny said when she found her voice. "She's also been a wonderful friend t'me, and she's takin' the best o' care o' my wee friend, Toby. She's given him the first real home he's ever known. She's even arrangin' for Princess Desirée's companion t'tutor him wi' Birdie and that little girl is her Ladyship's own."

"By adoption," Meg and Sibyl said in unison and Sibyl continued, "Lady H. is a peach. Of course she'll look after Toby. Mark my words, she'll adopt him, too, and she'll finally have both the daughter and the son she's always wanted."

Such an eventuality was Jenny's dream, but she would not be diverted from her present concerns. "We could send for Lady Hester now."

"No." Once more the sisters spoke together.

Meg said, "If I had a say in what is to be discussed at this gathering, which I don't, but if I did I would urge considerable caution in the pursuit of your goal."

"Pish posh," Sibyl said, wrinkling her fine little nose, "how very unlike you to shilly shally about, sister. We all want the same thing here."

Jenny sat very straight and arranged the skirts of her new pistachio day dress made of terry velvet. Latimer had chosen the material because he said the light green intensified the deep green of her eyes.

"Have a care," Meg said, "my husband is not a man who takes any disloyalty in his house lightly."

"Oh, Meg," Sibyl said, laughing, "Jean-Marc finds your spirit charming and you know it. Have some more chocolate and let's get down to the business at hand."

Jenny didn't make a move to pour the chocolate, even though she was the hostess this morning. "Verra well," she said sharply. "We'll consider this a preliminary meeting, but I'll no' have Lady Hester left out again."

"What if she doesn't agree with our plan?" Sibyl said. "Tell her, Meg. Tell her that if Lady Hester decided to be a priss and tell Jean-Marc, everything would be ruined."

"I shall *tell* Jenny nothing," Meg announced. "How can I when I don't know what the plans are. If Jean-Marc discovered I was going behind his back and attempting to defy his strategy to marry Desirée off to a wealthy, titled man who would form an advantageous alliance between two great families . . . Well, I don't know a thing about anything like that."

"Marryin' for love is the only way a man and woman can be truly happy," Jenny said. "And ye can fib a fib or fib straight out, m'Lady, but ye agree wi' that. Ye dinna want the Princess given to a bad man — I mean to a man who fancies her face and her body, but only because she's rich, and a man who doesna' as much want t'find out if she's a mind."

"Oh, Meg agrees," Sibyl said, all innocence. "Don't you, Meg? After all, *you* married for love. It just happened that your beloved was a very wealthy man. I also married for love."

"Indeed," Meg agreed, "and Sir Hunter is hardly a barrister of little repute."

"Let's no' argue," Jenny said crossly. "Before we know it, the Princess will be here and we've still t'make a single decision."

"Decision Number One," Sibyl said. "Desirée shall not marry a man to make a good family alliance, or a man who has a goodly portion but wants hers also and . . . well . . . sees her as a pretty enough bedfellow."

Jenny gasped, she couldn't help it. The three of them had once been part of a most entertaining club that explored the mysteries of the male in detail, but she continued to find it difficult to discuss such matters openly.

There was actually a blush on Sibyl's neck, but Meg smiled with what Jenny could only think was glee.

Sibyl cleared her throat. "I shall take it we're agreed on Decision Number One."

"Decision Number Two," Jenny said in a rush, anxious to finish their preparation. "Desirée shall marry —"

"Adam Chillworth," Meg declared and clapped a hand over her mouth. "Of course, I only anticipated what you were about to say, Jenny. I don't think for myself in these things."

"You do, too," Sibyl said. She got up from her chair and went to stand behind her sister's. "Adam was your friend when he was almost too shy to speak to the rest of us."

"He was your friend, too," Meg said. "And if I could say it, which I can't, I should mention what an upstanding man he was and is. The staunchest of friends, the kindest of acquaintances, an animal lover, absolutely sweet with children. In short, one would understand exactly why that minx of a sister-in-law of mine has mooned after him since she wasn't quite seventeen. One would understand if one could, but one obviously cannot."

The expression on Sibyl's ethereal face made Jenny want to giggle. In azure gros de naples, her fairness seemed almost translucent. At the moment she glared down at Meg and tapped her repeatedly on the shoulder. "*Don't* persist with that nonsense. Not one of us wishes to bring Jean-Marc's fury on our heads."

Meg shrugged. "I'm sure you don't, and

I shall not reveal your meddlings. After all, as long as I am not a part —"

"Bah," Sibyl said, bending close to Meg's ear and speaking loudly enough to make that lady jump.

"Listen," Jenny said. "I'm sure ye're tired still from your journey, Sibyl. Let's make a pact to do whatever must be done to bring about the only possible match for Desirée and Adam. *Anythin'*, is what we'll do. And please remember that the great, glowering tower o' a man Adam is will fight us all the way because he thinks he ought to. Wee — I mean, great fool. Are we agreed?"

"Yes," the chorus said.

"I would agree," Meg amended hastily, "if I could, which I can't."

"Ignore her," Sibyl told Jenny. She went to stand with her back to the fire and massaged her waist. "I agree, of course. I wish I were as sure of how to give Desirée a little push without going too far."

"It's Adam —" Meg stopped.

"Who needs the big push," Jenny finished for her, but looked at Sibyl. Rather than show off her waist more or less at its real level as was the fashion, Sibyl's gown was quite high-waisted and Jenny was almost certain her svelte friend was increasing for the second time. Jenny settled a hand on her own stomach and felt a rush of happiness. Soon she would tell Latimer they were to have their first child.

Jenny glanced up to find both of her friends watching her curiously. "I think we know what we have to do," she said serenely. No one should know about the baby until she'd shared her joy with Latimer. "The challenge will be to make a good job of it. Hush, I hear footsteps in the foyer." They had sworn not to risk getting caught peeking from the windows, but the timing was right for Desirée to arrive.

Sibyl crossed her arms tightly and puffed out a breath. Her smile was completely artificial.

"Be calm," Meg told her. "You have your decisions ready. Just remember not to blurt them out. Subtlety is the thing. Try to buck Desirée up. Let her know — very carefully — that you support her. Better be roundabout in this instance. Don't actually mention the man's name — oblique, that's the thing."

"For someone who couldn't possibly say anything about all this, you have a great deal to say," Sibyl told her, bobbing on her toes as if her heels refused to remain on the carpet.

The door flew open and Lady Hester Bingham bustled in — with Desirée close behind.

"You must be so vexed with me, gels," Lady Hester said. Her lavender velvet carriage dress was trimmed with mounds of swansdown as was her bonnet, and she carried a muff, also swansdown, of huge proportions. "Oh, I must say I'm relieved to be out of the snow. But I plead ignorance as my defence for not being at home to receive your invitation. I had to go out — on a delicate mission." She tapped the side of her nose. "Can't share it with you yet, but the time may well come. Anyway, the dear Princess was on her way here when my carriage drew up at Number 7, so when she told me she was to meet with all of you I guessed what had happened and came at once. Isn't that grand?" She clapped her hands.

Jenny looked from Meg to Sibyl, and on to Desirée. The first two appeared embarrassed and apprehensive. Desirée seemed confused.

"It is grand," Sibyl said. "Come along and sit down. Be comfortable. We're having chocolate. Will you join us?"

"No time for that," Lady Hester said, taking Princess Desirée's elbow and guiding her to a seat on the sofa. "So, what did you decide before we arrived?"

Jenny felt like a statue made of ice. She couldn't utter a word.

"You are mysterious," Desirée said and chuckled.

Lady Hester wagged a finger at her. "This is not a matter for levity. The time has come to take matters into our own hands, as is usually the case when dealing with a male of the species, especially a particularly hard-headed specimen. I am not wrong, am I, Sibyl, Jenny, Meg? You have been thinking of a problem looming in the lives of two of our favorite people and have decided we must take drastic steps."

"So much for the subtle approach," Sibyl murmured.

Jenny widened her eyes at Sibyl and Meg. "You know the best way to deal with these matters. I leave it all to you."

"Oh, no," Sibyl said. "Not so fast, young Jenny. We're in this together."

Lady Hester made an exasperated noise. "Save your chatter for later. Now, we will not mince words. I have spoken to Hunter who is in agreement. He says he and Latimer have already spoken. What conclusions have you come to?"

If only the Polite World would be more

direct, Jenny thought. Lady Hester might be talking about almost anything, even if it did seem likely that Desirée and Adam were the focus of her attention. One thing was for certain, Latimer should suffer for having little chats with Hunter behind her back. If Latimer was concerned about a possible liaison between Desirée and Adam, he hadn't discussed it with her — or not in definite terms, anyway.

"Speak up," Lady Hester demanded.

Desirée squirmed. "Your invitation came rather suddenly," she said to Jenny. "Usually I should be delighted — and I am now, of course — but I'm in a bit of a rush. Anne is waiting for me."

"Why?" Lady Hester said, finally selecting a straight-back chair without arms that allowed her to sit and show off her beautiful skirts and the swansdown at their hems. "Desirée, I've been meaning to speak with you about the recent change in your wardrobe. Not, of course, that you don't look quite charming. But, really, sweetness, you are too subdued. That maroon is striking, but too old for you. And so plain, even if the fabric is good. I suppose we should be grateful you continue to make the best of that ridiculously small waist of yours. Good idea, of course, when you're somewhat lacking in . . . higher parts. Makes the best of the little things."

"Lady Hester," Sibyl said in horrified tones.

"Ye've a lovely figure," Jenny said, feeling quite cross with Lady Hester. "My Latimer always says it's the quality of the material that counts, not the quantity." She blushed furiously.

"Does he now," Meg said, smiling with mischief, "but then, he can afford to make such announcements when his wife has both quality and quantity."

Jenny found her handkerchief and dabbed at her brow.

"You have a marvelous figure," Meg said to Desirée, "but I must agree with Lady Hester's assessment of your clothing. I don't even know where it can have come from. And darling, not so much as an earbob or one of your beautiful necklaces? Oh, do promise me you'll allow me to pick a few things out for you — just now and again."

Mutiny narrowed Desirée's startling gray eyes, but she took a deep, calming breath. "Of course, Meg. Thank you very much. I shall appreciate your guidance."

Lady Hester gave a huge and very loud sigh. "Are you going to tell me why you have to dash away when we're having a perfectly lovely time."

Jenny leaned to pour more chocolate and glanced up at Desirée who, far from looking as if she was having a lovely time, appeared miserable.

"I am invited to lunch at the Clarendon Hotel in Albermarle Street. Naturally Anne will accompany me."

Meg frowned. "I wasn't aware of this."

"I asked Jean-Marc and he was pleased for me to go."

Meg subsided but her brows remained raised.

"With whom are you having lunch?" Lady Hester asked.

"Adam and his brother, Lucas," Desirée mumbled.

Lady Hester clapped her hands. "Capital! May I speak for all of us? Dispense with any foolish and false delicacy?" She directed the question to Jenny, Meg and Sibyl and immediately forged ahead without waiting for any response. "Desirée, are you in love with Adam Chillworth?"

Desirée turned pale and sputtered.

"Of course you are. I was merely trying to observe the niceties by asking you. You *are* in love with Adam and he's in love with you although I have never seen a man fight his natural feelings with such knuckle-headed determination. Hah, he has not reckoned with us."

"But —"

Lady Hester waved Desirée to silence. "These are the things you must do. Starting today. At the hotel, find an excuse to take Adam aside. Swoon. Trick him into kissing you, then tell him, 'Oh Adam, being with you makes me the most happy woman in the world.' "

Silence descended, heavy silence before Jenny asked meekly, "Ye dinna think that's a trifle hasty?"

"Not a bit of it. Fear not, Desirée, my little love, Lady Hester will guide you every step of the way — we all will."

Meg shook out her skirts. "Very admirable sentiments, I'm sure. If I were part of all this, which I'm not of course, I should consider the cause a noble one."

Lady Hester stared at Meg, found a lorgnette and took a closer look. "Hmph," she said. "Whatever you say, turncoat."

Meg opened and closed her mouth, but Lady Hester's attention had already left her.

"The only thing to fear, Desirée, is the wedding night. Bit of a shock, that. Terrible affair, in fact. But we'll teach you how to get through the ordeal and arrive at absolute bliss."

"Lady Hester," Sibyl said weakly, "don't you think this is unsuitable, especially given that we have other problems to surmount first?"

"Not at all. How will Adam's resistance hold up against our combined strength? Tell me that. He's as good as married already."

"Well," Meg said. "I don't think —"

"I do," Lady Hester broke in. "And in case you've forgotten, I'm senior here.

"I always think it's best to be the one to make an excuse to retire — at the wedding celebration, that is. Heats up a groom every time — not that I think this groom will need encouragement on that score. From what I've heard, he's more than ready for anything that arises."

The loud groan that met her announcement didn't deter Lady H.

"Yes, the bride should excuse herself and say she wants to go to bed. Makes the groom feel desired. Of course, that can turn him into a bit of an animal, but if he's ready to go, so to speak, it'll get the thing done quickly.

"By the way — never mind all that rubbish about keeping your body covered at all times. Flickering candles on flushed ivory skin — pert breasts formerly untouched by human hands, a waist waiting to be spanned — total submission. Hah, as long as the man thinks it, that's all that matters. Give in and enjoy yourself. Anyway, submit and voilà, heaven will soon be in your grasp . . . so to speak."

10

Try as he might, Adam could not contain the exhilaration he felt at being with Desirée again. Certainly, even as he assumed a serious countenance, aloof even, he pounded himself with reminders of all the reasons why he must not continue to desire this woman, not just as a lover, but as his wife. How hopeless it all was.

"How do you like the Clarendon?" Lucas asked Desirée. "And you, too, of course, Miss Williams?"

Anne Williams was pretty in silver gray with a paisley falling collar Adam was certain belonged to Desirée.

Before Anne or Desirée could respond, Rolly Spade-Filbert, who had accompanied Lucas as if everyone had expected him to be present at lunch, deliberately placed his forearm on the table so that the tips of his fingers touched Anne's. He looked into her blue eyes and said, "I can tell you like it. You glow and I can feel your happiness in your quiet dignity."

Desirée caught Adam's eye and raised a single brow. He returned the look of surprise at Rolly's public attention to a servant, behavior that was out of keeping with the man's nature.

A delicate oyster soup with eggs had been served. Adam thought it suitable for the ladies, but he preferred something with more substance. In truth he doubted anything would please his palate today. The second letter he'd received yesterday, the one he had not told Desirée about, had warned him — no, ordered him to move from Mayfair Square and never to see her again. She was, the anonymous writer warned him, not just a threat to his safety but a promise of death. *Abandon her at once or you will die.* Whoever sent the note assumed Adam could be frightened off. At first the idea had outraged him. Later he recognized that he had an enemy who valued his own life above all others, his own wants above all others, and he wanted Desirée for himself.

Desirée spoke. "This is a charming place." But she appeared anything but charmed. Anxious and uncomfortable would be a better description of her demeanor. She wore a plain maroon pelisse over a matching dress and the rich color showed off her fair hair and skin. Desirée only grew more lovely.

"You were in Mont Nuages," Rolly said to Anne Williams, who kept her eyes lowered and seemed as disinterested in the soup as Adam. "You are English. What took you there?"

Adam noted how Anne looked to Desirée in appeal.

"Anne went as a governess," Desirée said smoothly. "Unfortunately, or fortunately for me, her employers invited a sister to join them and the sister took Anne's place with the children. So she was free to come to me." Desirée's smile was bright but her eyes held no particular liking for Spade-Filbert.

Lucas also pushed his soup around in its bowl. His manner had been distracted since Adam had arrived at the Clarendon with Desirée and Anne. Adam stared until he caught his brother's eye, but Lucas looked quickly away again.

"Oh," Desirée said unexpectedly. "That gentleman over there, Anne. The one in black with his back to us."

Anne looked around a well-proportioned room where silver and crystal glinted on white linen at every table. Sounds were muted, the subtle hum of conversation punctuated by laughter. Waiters moved smoothly among potted palms, statuary, and the guests.

At last Anne said, "Who do you mean?"

"*There,*" Desirée whispered. "By the statue of — oh, I don't know, but it's a muscular statue of the male variety."

Adam smiled behind a hand.

"Do you see?" Desirée persisted.

"Oh." Anne's voice was small and she sat back in her chair. "It's M. Verbeux, isn't it? He's following us."

Rolly, handsome in a dark green coat and buff waistcoat, immediately turned around to look.

"I say, old chap," Lucas said. "Better not make a scene."

"There's nothing to make a scene about," Desirée told him. "It is M. Verbeux. I've heard he comes here for lunch every day but I was momentarily surprised to see him."

Anne opened her mouth but before she could speak, Desirée covered her companion's hand on the table and said, "I never thought to mention it. Now, let's finish this very good soup."

"I'm grateful you could all come," Lucas

said, as if he'd already forgotten Verbeux. "London can be so depressing at this time of year — if one has few diversions, that is."

"I should have thought you could have as many diversions as you please," Desirée said with her typical kindness. "Shouldn't you, Adam? After all, your brother is a handsome man. I've seen many a lady fluttering her eyelashes at him since we arrived."

"I am bored with the type of lady who flutters her eyelashes," Lucas said. "What I need is a woman with a mind who will stimulate, as well as amuse me. I am tired of the parade of artifice and the preoccupation with beauty. Beauty comes from within. And the shameless waste of money on fripperies? Some of these gowns must cost enough to feed a poor family for months."

If Adam could have found a thing to say he would have done so. This changed brother left him speechless.

"Give me modesty," Lucas continued. "Let me look upon a woman who can present her real face to the world and let the world admire her for what she is. Simplicity, I say. Simple gowns. Unadorned beauty. There are times when a man is so dazzled by jewels that he cannot quite remember the lady at all once he has left her."

To Adam's annoyance, Desirée smiled admiringly at Lucas.

"You've got a point there, old chap," Rolly said, regarding Anne Williams. "Blond hair, blue eyes, a flawless complexion — what more could a man ask for?"

Anne blinked several times before she relaxed a little and smiled back at him.

"Princess," Lucas said. "You don't seem like a woman interested only in the empty, elevated world of the privileged. You are lovely in the most natural way, and comfortable with yourself. No wonder you and my brother are friends. He is as genuine as I believe you to be."

If Desirée hadn't given him a look filled with sweetness, Adam wasn't sure what he would have said. As it was, she didn't wait for him to speak at all.

"I am most fond of my own brother," she told Lucas. "My half brother. Jean-Marc is considerably older than I — in fact he is my guardian — but I am never in doubt of his love for me, even if he is annoying sometimes. It pleases me so to see that you and Lucas share a similar closeness. Yes, Adam is genuine. He has custody of my cat Halibut most of the time and that traitorous feline adores him, so I know this man is good. And he is not only my friend, he is my *best* friend."

"Thank you," Adam said before the lump in his throat could render him speechless.

Rolly, who wasn't even pretending not to be enthralled by Anne, tugged at his auburn goatee and said, "The best of friends, hmm? You know what they say — the best of friends make the best of lovers."

"I say, Rolly," Lucas exclaimed. "Have a care."

Adam found his voice again. "I'm glad we are together again, Lucas. I'd doubted this would ever happen." And he wasn't entirely comfortable that it had — yet. He certainly didn't care for Rolly's company much more than he ever had and was suspicious of his attentions to Anne Williams.

The soup was removed and replaced with jellied pigeons, potted salmon and toast points. Rolly fell upon his plate with gusto and Adam felt obliged to show a healthier interest in his food.

"I like the salmon," Anne said. "But I don't like the look of the little bird."

"It tastes excellent," Lucas informed her,

drinking deeply of his wine. "Be daring and try it."

Desirée's attention had wandered to the table where Verbeux sat. Adam looked over his shoulder and found the man looking back at him. Verbeux had decided to be open in his observation of Desirée and Anne and had moved to the opposite side of the table so that he could face them. So much for the man simply eating his lunch there.

"I shall be bold," Lucas said. He drank more wine, cleared his throat and crossed his arms. "Could it be that you are in love, Adam?"

A club, walloped into his middle by a prize fighter, couldn't have shocked Adam much more. He opened and closed his mouth and didn't dare look at Desirée.

"Aha," Rolly said. "You have your answer there, Lucas. No laughter or loud denial. The man *is* in love. With whom, one wonders."

Adam felt Desirée's concentration on him and met her wide eyes direct. They had become moist and uncertain. A hint of tears shone and she held her bottom lip in her teeth. He smiled at her while he cursed his brother and his friend for their meddling.

He and Desirée remained like that, staring at each other, while he felt her softly reaching out for him and battled against wanting to announce to the world that it was she with whom he was in love, Princess Desirée who was the woman who had spoiled him for any other. He would like, then and there, to kneel before her and beg her to become his wife.

Her mouth trembled.

Muscles in his face became rigid.

Lucas and Rolly were not pressing anymore but Adam knew what they were thinking, and they were right. What they didn't know was that Desirée's brother would never consider him for her, not only because he was a commoner and considerably older than she, but because her family required her to form an advantageous alliance.

There would be nothing in a marriage between Adam and Desirée that would be advantageous to Jean-Marc's family.

Adam raised his glass to her alone and said, "To our friendship, may it flourish forever."

"And bear fruit," she murmured, to Adam's consternation. The poor girl was confused but fortunately the others made no comment.

A man's raised voice intruded, but Adam couldn't turn from Desirée. "I'm glad you trust me with that rascal, Halibut. He keeps me warm at night. Likes my bed."

"It's a lovely bed."

To Adam's enormous gratitude, when he looked around he discovered that their companions were staring at a waiter who approached with enough haste to show he was flustered. Someone followed him.

What could Desirée be thinking of to make such a careless remark? She continued to look into his eyes with an expression of adoration.

"Gad," Lucas said, not quite under his breath. "This is a pretty turn."

The waiter arrived at their table and stood aside.

Gilbert Chillworth, gentleman farmer of Northumberland, estranged husband of Lady Elspeth Chillworth and father of Lucas and Adam Chillworth, looked at Adam with cold disdain.

"Good to see you, father," Lucas said. "I didn't have any idea you were coming to Town."

Still a commanding figure, Gilbert said, "Why should you? I didn't inform you, did I? Why would I? It's Adam I've come t'see." His clothes were as expensively understated as ever and fitted his long, robust body perfectly. Like so many fair-haired people, he showed no sign of turning gray and his face was as firm and good-looking as ever. A vital man, Gilbert Chillworth, and as hard as any Adam had ever met.

Lucas signalled the waiter and said, "A place for my father, please. At once."

"Not necessary," Gilbert said. He motioned to Adam. "I'll see you now. Upstairs. I've secured a room for the purpose."

Adam didn't move.

"You'll do me the favor of showin' a little respect and doin' what I ask. You'll be back with this lot soon enough."

11

Gilbert Chillworth had not taken a room only to have a private place to converse with Adam. On the way across the black and white tiled lobby, Gilbert signalled to a clerk behind the glistening mahogany front desk and, by the time they reached the top of the first flight of stairs, a uniformed boy followed with two bags. Apparently Adam's father intended to take up residence, even if only for a short period.

On the third floor, the boy took the key from Gilbert's hand, unlocked a door and led the way into a comfortable sitting room where a fire already blazed in the fireplace. He carried the baggage into a bedroom Adam could see through an open door and lifted them onto the bed.

When Adam saw that his father had no intention of rewarding the boy for his labors, he gave him something himself. He loathed the moment when he and his parent — a stranger to him — were left alone.

"I hate this town," Gilbert said. He raised a lace curtain to look down on the icy street. "Corrupt to the core as is everyone who lives in it."

Adam waited.

"Pour me a drink," Gilbert said. "Have one yourself if you like."

Decanters stood on a gilt trolley and Adam poured a measure of Scotch into a glass. He handed this to his father who made no comment about Adam not joining him.

"How many years has it been?" The man sat in a deep chair and stretched out his booted feet. "Five? Seven?"

"Twelve," Adam said. "I was twenty-two."

"Of course. You look a lot older now. See your mother, do you?"

"Once, by accident. Apart from that, no."

"No," Gilbert echoed, dropping his chin to his chest and staring into the fire. "Shouldn't think you would, or not if she could avoid it."

The carpet was made of silk and the fire-light picked out threads of silver among deep blue scrolls. Rococo panels decorated pale blue walls and the furnishings were suitably sumptuous. Adam stuck his hands in his pockets and wandered about. He would not be drawn into one of the arguments his father had repeatedly instigated since Adam was a boy.

"What are you doing with Lucas?" Gilbert asked. "Trying to take lessons? You'll never be half the man he is, so give it up."

"If you hold Lucas in such high regard, why did you humiliate him in the dining room? It was despicable and I felt for him."

Gilbert smiled a little but his eyes remained cold. "My son understands me. He is no soft-handed whiner."

Unlike you. Adam had no doubt about what Gilbert had left unsaid. "If you've said what you brought me here to say, I must return to my luncheon companions."

Gilbert drained his Scotch and held out the glass. "Fill it up this time."

Adam took the decanter and set it on a table within his father's reach, and retreated again.

"Disappointment," Gilbert said, pouring his glass to the rim. "Always were, always will be. Useless dauber. Broke your mother's heart, that's what you did. Broke her heart and broke up my family."

Adam turned away quickly and the room seemed to move. He felt sick. From the day his mother left her family Gilbert had blamed his younger son.

"All you had to do was what you were told. Give your older brother the support he had a right to expect from you and let him get on with setting himself up in society. That's what his mother wanted for him. And she wanted you to learn how to take my place when the time came. You'd be there to run things after I was gone and make sure your brother had what he needed. And you'd have been taken care of for life."

Adam decided to sit down after all and chose a chair as far from Gilbert's as possible.

"If you'd been a different lad, your mother and I would still be together. You drove her away. She couldn't stand watching you make a fool of yourself with that namby-pamby painting nonsense. Don't think I don't know what your life is now. Living in some attic, scrabbling to keep yourself on nothing but the pittance you get from me."

Adam had rarely touched Gilbert's *pittance* except in his first years in London when he'd been scrambling to establish himself as a painter. For years now the money had been drawing interest in an account for which Adam had a specific purpose when the right time arose.

"What's Lucas been saying to you?" Gilbert demanded.

"That's between Lucas and myself."

"What my son says to you is *my* business and don't you forget it. What's he said, then?"

What the devil . . . Why not tell the truth? "Lucas and I have decided it's long past time for us to be brothers in the real sense."

"In the real sense." Gilbert laughed and sprayed his drink on his trousers, which he wiped at with no visible concern. "That's a good one. Brothers in the real sense. You aren't brothers in any sense — or almost no sense."

Adam grew cold. He sat quite still.

"Never mind that. I've come to give you some news. I hope it'll make a man of you. I'm cutting you out of my will. Should have done it years ago. From now on you won't get a penny from me and if you know what's good for you, you'll keep your own counsel about it. Tell your mother and she'll guess why I've done it. I wouldn't want to upset her like that."

"Damn you!" Adam shot to his feet. "I don't want your money. I don't want a thing from you. She shouldn't have left us alone with you, but you drove my mother away with your foul temper and your violence."

"I never set a hand on her," Gilbert said, sitting forward. "Not a hand. I loved her then and I love her now. She stood by you but you disappointed her and she couldn't tolerate being around you. Your brother was a man from the day he was born, not a milquetoast, but you had to embarrass us all. You couldn't even pull yourself together when you were grown. Oh, no, then you crawled away and disgraced your family by living however you could. I'd not have started the allowance if I hadn't wanted to save your mother from the shame. She's a lady and from a fine family. She never deserved a feckless son like you."

Adam genuinely feared he might do something he'd always regret. His father was a strong man but he was a good deal older and few could hold their own against Adam. "Are you finished?" he asked, determined to leave at once.

"Not quite," Gilbert said. "Stay away

from Lucas. If you don't, I'll make sure he suffers, too. And I'll tell him why, then we'll see how long he wants t'be a *real* brother t'you."

There was threat in those words. "Tell him. Tell both of us. You only have power over me if I give it to you. I don't."

Gilbert stood up and walked by Adam to lock the door. He spun around and removed a bulky envelope from a pocket inside his coat. "Sit down," he said, his voice softened. "There, where I was sitting. I have been torn about what I should do, but I think this is the only way and should be done for your own sake."

Torn between forcing his way out and doing as his father asked, Adam held his ground. Then he knew what he would do and went slowly to sit where Gilbert had suggested.

"This belongs to me," Gilbert said and gave the envelope to Adam. "I show it to you in hope that you will come to understand what you should do and be man enough to do it. If you do, in time I may find a way to change my heart toward you. God knows I have tried to do what is right."

The folded pages were thick and crackled when Adam smoothed them flat.

"You," Gilbert said with an emotion Adam had never heard in him before. "You are the embodiment of a dear woman's shame."

12

Adam had been gone so long. Lucas had said barely a word since his father had treated him shamefully in front of the others. Mr. Spade-Filbert chatted pleasantly, mostly to Anne, but frequently glanced at his friend with concern.

Desirée could think only of Adam and the anger — and the pain — she'd seen on his face when he left the room.

A commotion broke out near the door to the lobby. Desirée almost expected to see Adam there, but instead a young boy struggled with a waiter who sought to put him out. Meanly dressed, the boy seemed to be crying. The waiter spun him around, took him by the collar and marched him away.

"Excuse me," Desirée said, and got up.

"Princess?" Lucas said at once. "Are you unwell?"

"Quite the contrary," she said, forcing a

smile. "I merely want to go into the lobby for a little air. Anne will accompany me and we shall be quite safe."

To her annoyance, both men made to get up at once. "I said I do not need your attendance. Adam will return and you should be here." That Adam would see her in the foyer was obvious, but if they didn't make the connection she wouldn't point it out. "Come, Anne."

Anne knew her mistress well enough to recognize her urgency. The two of them walked across the room and Desirée struggled to keep her steps measured and her head held high as if she had nothing in particular on her mind.

Once in the lobby, she spied the distressed child once more. He continued to mumble at the waiter, who urged him toward the street.

"Your Highness," Anne said. "I know you too well. You are determined to champion that boy. He is a stranger and quite wild-looking and he could do you harm. I must suggest —"

"No, you must not," Desirée said, careful not to sound cross. "As you say, you know me well and you also know I will not be dissuaded at times such as this. I shall merely see that he is treated fairly."

Anne groaned but Desirée had set her course and had no intention of being diverted.

"One moment," she said, tapping the waiter firmly on the back. "What is troubling this boy?"

The man turned to see her but did not release the boy. "His type aren't to be trusted, miss. Coming in here with some story about being in a fix and needing help."

"It's my cat," the lad said with downcast eyes. " 'E's 'urt and I can't 'elp on account of I gets sick at the sight of blood."

Anne groaned afresh and Desirée shushed her. "Take us to the animal at once," she said, and to the waiter, "Let him go at once."

Reluctantly the man did as he was asked and, rather than flee, the ragged boy looked into Desirée's face with pleading brown eyes and tried to push dark, tangled hair away from his forehead. "Thank you, mum, but this ain't for the likes of you."

"Move," she told him. "Now." She took hold of his wrist and hurried with him to the slippery flagway.

"If only you weren't so impulsive," Anne said breathlessly. "Children, old people, poor people, and *animals*. You think you must save them all and you can't. Not that wanting to do so isn't admirable."

"Be careful you don't slip," Desirée told her companion. "This snow settles on top of the ice and walking is treacherous." The snow she spoke of had started falling while they were inside the hotel and had become a thick enough veil to obscure anything more than a few feet away.

"It was awful," the boy said. "Joe jumped out of my coat — 'e goes everywhere with me — and a man 'it 'im with the wheel of 'is cart. Joe was lyin' there whimperin' and 'e 'ad blood on his legs. The man just went on and I couldn't do nothing so I went for 'elp. 'E's down 'ere."

"What's your name?" Anne asked.

"I'm Ben." He led them down a winding alley lined on one side with a tiny terraced house and on the other by a wall where snow-dusted ivy clung. Ben stopped in front of a house with windows so dirty Desirée had the thought that it must always be dark inside. " 'E was 'ere," Ben said, getting down on his hands and knees and frantically digging in a drift of snow. "It can't 'ave covered 'im up. I ain't been gone that long."

"We must return to the hotel," Anne said. "We shall be missed by now. Oh, my goodness, M. Verbeux! There will be a terrible fuss and the Count will find out."

Ben had started to cry louder, and to fling the snow aside with desperation.

Desirée lowered her voice. "I fear this doesn't look good. But I agree with you that we'll be in trouble if they don't know where we are. Go back and tell them. I'll join you as soon as I've comforted Ben."

"I certainly shall not leave you alone here."

"You certainly shall."

Anne waved her arms. "Respectfully, Your Highness, you must return with me."

"If I were a conventional woman — and a coward — I might agree. I'm neither. Oh dear, look at him. He's mad with grief. Go, Anne, please. I'll try to bring him back with me to get warm."

Anne opened her mouth again but Desirée gave one of her most ferocious frowns and Anne rushed away, skirts flying, and passed from sight around the first bend. Soon she would return with the men who would feel quite entitled to be indignant with Desirée. The thought provoked her.

"Are you sure this was the spot, Ben?" she asked. "These houses all look the same. Perhaps it was down there." She pointed farther down the alley.

" 'E was 'ere. I know 'e was." Slowly Ben stood up and covered his face with his hands. " 'E's gone. Someone probably picked 'im up and threw 'im in some rubbish. 'E was the best friend I ever 'ad."

Desirée cried, too, she couldn't help it and when the grubby child drew close to her, she put her arms around him and drew him to the wall near the door to keep them both as much out of the falling snow as she could. "Don't you have a family?"

He shook his head.

"How do you live, then?"

She heard the door behind her open but before she could turn around, a strong arm caught her about the waist and pulled her inside the house. The door slammed shut and the bolt shot home. Heavy gloom and a stench that turned the stomach greeted her. She screamed, but not for long before a hand stifled the sound, and cloth of some kind was wrapped around her head.

Desirée feared she would vomit. With both hands she tore at the arm around her waist and kicked with her heels, connecting with the fronts of her assailant's legs. "Let me go," she cried, knowing the cloth muffled her voice. "If you don't let me go you will be in serious trouble."

The man who held her laughed and hauled her feet from the floor. Carrying her facedown, he walked with her, his boots thudding on hard floors. Her forehead slammed into a hard edge, a doorjamb she thought, and she was pushed, facedown, onto a piece of upholstered furniture so dusty that she coughed.

"Now you just listen to me," the man said. He pinned her down by the neck.

Desirée struggled with all the strength she had . . . and earned herself several punishing slaps to the backs of her thighs. The blows were so hard they brought tears to her eyes and she felt she would choke inside the head covering.

"Calm down and hear what you've got to know. It's for your own good. If you ever say I told you this, I'll find a way to kill you, so listen, do what I tell you, and forget you were ever here."

She held absolutely still and waited.

"I work for someone you think very highly of. We're more like partners, really. He's a bit sweet on you, too, but you're getting in our way, see? I can't have him wasting time on you and getting careless, not when we're so close to what we're after.

"Adam Chillworth's a clever man. He

isn't the man you think he is. He's dangerous and ruthless. He's filled a few graves in his time. You may think you can change him —"

"He's a painter," Desirée shouted as clearly as she could. "And he's gentle."

"I'm only telling you this once," the man said. "Then I'll leave you here. You'll be found — sooner or later. When you are, you just say you were attacked by a gent with designs on you. True enough. A pity we don't have longer to enjoy each other. That's all you say, but this is what you will remember. You're getting in my way by diverting Adam. I won't allow that. Stay away from him, or I'll make sure you do. And anyway, in the end, the *painter* you think you know always gets rid of anyone who becomes a threat to what matters to him most — and that isn't a particular pair of soft thighs. He can find more of those whenever the mood strikes him.

"Stay away from Adam Chillworth."

13

Adam started down the final flight of stairs to the foyer. He seethed behind the composed face he had put on for those who awaited him in the dining room.

He wanted to leave the Clarendon.

He wanted to be alone and try to forget that Gilbert Chillworth was his father.

In a pocket inside his coat he carried the papers entrusted to him, papers that explained Gilbert's motives for wronging him. They were twisted and cruel —

"Chillworth!" Verbeux's shout stopped Adam. "*Vite,*" Verbeux broke into a run. From his appearance he had been outside without his coat. Alarmed, Adam met the other man just as he was about to mount the staircase.

"Is she . . ." Verbeux looked toward the upper floors. "If only you tell me the Princess came to you and that she is in a room here, I will bless you and promise to keep your secret."

"Desirée? What are you saying about her, man?"

His eyes wild, Verbeux grabbed Adam by the neckcloth and he overbalanced on top of the frenchman. They sprawled together, scrabbled on cold tile and even as Adam pushed to leap up, Verbeux hit him. He might be much larger than Jean-Marc's henchman, and stronger, but the frenchman had surprise on his side. They struggled to their feet and Verbeux launched a second blow to Adam's jaw before he struck back, a punch to the gut delivered with mounting, black foreboding.

Women screamed and men shouted.

Several fellows with determination in their eyes threw themselves between Adam and Verbeux, and Adam stood off at once, raking his hair back from his face. "Get out of my way," he told the intruders through his teeth. "It's all over." Looking around at the gawking bystanders he said, "Away with you. The sideshow is closed."

Verbeux threw up his hands and nodded vehemently. "Yes, yes," he said, and people drew away, pretending to go about their business whilst keeping an eye on the two of them. "My apologies," Verbeux said, picking up his eyeglasses and replacing them, but his eyes were wild and his breathing hard. "I am beside myself. She isn't . . . ?" He inclined his head toward the staircase.

"No, she is not. No. In God's name, what has happened? Quick, man." Now was not the time to settle petty arguments.

Verbeux flung about, staring toward the door, then back at Adam. "*Mon Dieu,* I picked up the *Times.* I saw you leave with that rude man but your brother and the other one were still there and I saw no hint of danger. But I was checking the sailings. No more than a few minutes, I assure you."

"Where is she?" Adam shouted. What felt like an iron hand closed on his throat. "She left the dining room? Alone?"

"With Miss Williams. By the time I followed, the manager said they had gone outside with some ragged boy who was crying for help. I followed but there was no sign. I returned in hope there had been some mistake and it was an elaborate plan between you and . . . I hoped both women had reentered the building by another door. Forgive me."

"But the manager saw them go and did nothing?" Adam made a move toward the desk but Verbeux grabbed his arm. No man restrained Adam Chillworth. He wrenched his arm free. "My brother, and Spade-Filbert? Still in the dining room?"

"Spade-Filbert realized what had happened before I did and left. The other Mr. Chillworth waited for you. Now he's gone, too," Verbeux said. "But I have no faith —"

"Neither do I." Adam ran for the door, all but colliding with Anne Williams. Wet and crying, she stumbled into the foyer to be swept against Adam's chest. "What has happened? Where is Desirée? Take me to her now."

"Don't shout at her," Verbeux said, his usually pale face turning a dull red. With amazingly gentle hands, he took Anne from Adam, who did nothing to stop him. "Anne," Verbeux said quietly. "Hush, now, *ma petite,* and tell me what you know."

Adam thought he would explode in the seconds while he waited for the girl to respond. His temples pounded and he couldn't uncurl his fists.

"She's not there now," Anne said, choking on each word. "We went with a boy whose cat was hurt. We couldn't find the cat but the Princess wouldn't leave the boy. His name is Ben. She sent me back to let you know where we were.

"Then I couldn't bear to leave her there

alone so I disobeyed her and returned without coming here. She's gone and so has the boy. I saw Mr. Lucas Chillworth and showed him the alley. He is in a state."

"Please," Adam said, flexing his fingers, "take us to this place."

As Anne started to leave, Verbeux pulled up the hood that had slipped from her head and settled her hand beneath his arm. "Be calm. This is no fault of yours. If there is any fault, it is mine. I was careless."

Frigid air and snowflakes laced with biting ice hit Adam's face and he felt it as if his skin were Desirée's soft skin and it was pierced. If something had happened . . . it could not be that Desirée was harmed.

Anne sped along the flagway, her halfboots soaked. Verbeux supported her and talked too quietly for Adam to hear.

She reached the entrance to a tiny, curving alley and looked back to make sure he was there. Adam nodded once, grimly.

"The Princess was here with Ben when I left her," she said, and halted in front of a terraced hovel where snow piled against the walls. "The snow falls so fast it has filled in the hole she dug. You can't see where it was anymore."

"Dug?" Adam brought his face close to

Anne's. "What do you mean, *dug?*"

Anne trembled and her tears flowed freely. "Trying to find Joe, that's Ben's cat. It was hit by the wheel of a cart that passed and —"

"Yes, yes," Adam said, cutting her off. "Verbeux, please take Miss Anne back to the Clarendon and ask for assistance —"

"I don't need to be told how to look after this lady," Verbeux said. "I shall see she's cared for, but the Princess is my charge."

"She is *my* charge," Adam said, too reckless to temper himself. "Meg told me so, and so it is. I shall find her and if a finger has been set on her, I will kill the scoundrel who dared to touch the silly girl. Oh, how exasperating her sweet spontaneity can be. Go, go. And be on the lookout for the Princess. I shall go the other way. She cannot be far away."

He didn't wait for Verbeux to respond, but jogged on along the alley. All of it was the same, the same grimy houses on one side, the same sooty, ivy-draped wall on the other. If he had time he would be sick. If he couldn't calm himself at least a little, the pain in his head would overtake him entirely.

He wanted to hurt someone.

Nothing, no sign of a scuffle, no wheel tracks, not that anything larger than a small cart could pass this way. At the end there was only one way to turn, left, and he faced a warehouse yard. Retracing his steps, he searched the virgin snow for clues until he arrived at the place where Desirée had supposedly last been seen. At least Verbeux had taken Anne away. There was nothing more she could do here and she was not a robust creature.

Desirée and the boy could have been invited inside somewhere to get warm.

He stood back and surveyed the house in front of him. Black paint peeled from its front door and the windows wore thick masks of dust. He rapped on the door and frowned when it swung slowly open. From the interior he heard voices, one male and coaxing, the other distinctly that of Desirée who was refusing to "take another step without Adam."

Relief flooded blood back into his muscles. His calves, thighs, and shoulders ached. He didn't care that he was achingly erect.

Moving cautiously, he edged along a greasy wall and deeper into the place that smelled of rancid, fatty food and unwashed bodies. He located the room he looked for and recognized Lucas's voice at the same time. His brother was consoling Desirée. For a few moments, Adam hung his head forward and took deep breaths.

"Allow me to take you home," Lucas said.

"I want Adam."

Desirée's declaration made Adam feel he could wrestle dragons if necessary. He said, "Don't be afraid. It's just Adam," and walked in.

Her pelisse was torn. Her bonnet wasn't in sight and Desirée's light brown hair hung loose about her shoulders.

"Thank goodness you're here," Lucas said. "I got lucky. Kicked around in the snow a bit and heard a man shouting in here and a woman's scream. When I hammered on the door, the blighter opened it and just about ran me over getting away. Couldn't risk going after him when I had to see if Desirée was in here, her condition and so on. She won't tell me what happened."

Desirée watched Adam's face as if Lucas were not there. Adam wished that were the case. He took a step toward her, extending his arms, and she threw herself against him, touched his cheek, his jaw and neck, pressed her face into his chest and grasped handfuls of his coat. She made not a sound.

Over her head, Adam looked at Lucas, who showed no inclination to make himself scarce. He should, Adam thought, be ashamed of himself for being too impatient to be with this girl to treat his brother well.

Lucas screwed up his face and said in a low voice, "I don't think all is entirely well, if you know what I mean."

Adam frowned and shook his head, no.

"Not all men are civilized," Lucas said.

How well Adam knew this and how desperately he didn't want to consider that the woman he loved had been damaged in some irreparable manner. "Are you ready to talk to me?" he asked her quietly. "Whatever has happened, I will make sure you have nothing to fear in future."

"Not until we are alone," she said.

"You shake so, Desirée. I shall carry you to the hotel and call for the coach."

She gazed up at him, a little smile on her lips. "You may carry me anywhere," she said, "take me anywhere."

He felt his own smile fix and dared not check Lucas's expression. These outlandish little comments of Desirée's were becoming more frequent — or perhaps he was making much of nothing.

Desirée put her arms around his neck and sighed, gazed into his face with adoring eyes. When he picked her up she weighed too little. He must see what he could do to change that.

"You're on dangerous ground, brother," Lucas said evenly. "Have a care. I've heard that a certain gentleman is very protective and very conscientious about his responsibilities. If he were to discover —"

"There's nothing to discover," Adam told him sharply, grateful that Desirée seemed disposed to be quiet. At least, he hoped she was calming herself rather than about to faint. "I've known her since she was a child and she isn't so much more than a child now."

"Exactly," Lucas said, looking at Adam from beneath lowered eyelids. "A child from a different world."

"She is twenty," Adam said, growing angered again. "Don't persist with this."

A babble of voices erupted in the minuscule front hall. Adam heard Jean-Marc, Count Etranger, and steeled himself for war.

Wrapped in Rolly Spade-Filbert's arm, Anne came in first looking utterly miserable and frightened. A silent Verbeux followed closely and stood by, his hands loosely linked in front of him.

Jean-Marc, Latimer More, and Sir Hunter Lloyd jostled their way into the tiny room with the result that the group stood with only a foot or two between each of them. Argument ebbed and flowed, rushed and slowed, and Adam wanted only to make a path through the lot of them and get Desirée back to his attic. And to hell with what anyone thought about it. From now on he would find a way to know where she was at all times and be damned with some anonymous coward threatening him that she was a deadly menace.

Jean-Marc turned on him. "Why are you holding my sister like that?"

"She was faint," Adam said. "And there is nothing in this room that is clean enough for her to lie on."

"Put her down at once. A few words from me and she'll decide she hasn't the luxury of fainting. Do you hear me, young lady. On your feet at once."

Desirée opened the eye nearest to Adam and appeared to send him some sort of signal. The other eye was squeezed shut in the most obvious manner.

"Set her *down*," Jean-Marc demanded.

Hunter, blond and distinguished as ever, and as dashing, assumed what Adam took to be his barrister voice and said, "I say, Jean-Marc, easy does it. We all want what's best for Desirée, always have. What do you expect Adam to do, drop the girl?"

Adam grew warm inside his stiff collar. "Is your coach nearby, Jean-Marc? What are all of you doing here, anyway? How the devil did you know to come?"

"We were lunching at Hunter's club," Latimer said with far too much enjoyment in his smile. "Verbeux recalled we should be there and sent a message about —"

"Dammit, More," Jean-Marc said. "This ravager doesn't need another word of explanation for *our* actions."

"I say," Hunter murmured.

"I'm the one who should bloody well *say*," Adam snapped. He put Desirée down and wished he had the heart to stop her from leaning heavily on him. "Something happened to her here. Instead of leveling accusations — outrageous accusations — at me, why not help find out the truth of why your sister has been victimized by a scoundrel?"

Jean-Marc's dark eyes, as dark as his almost black hair, narrowed and his flaring brows gave him the devilish look, which, once seen, was never forgotten. His fine features grew sharp and Adam knew the exact moment when the other man feared the loss of all control. He pounded his right fist into his left palm and circumnavigated the boxy space with measured steps.

Verbeux moved closer to Anne who had separated herself from Rolly and who only had eyes for her mistress.

"Take me to Number 7," Desirée whispered. "I can't bear it here any longer."

"What did you say?" Jean-Marc asked. "Speak up, girl. And show some sense, and some respect. I have been entirely too lax with you and as of now, that is all over, all changed."

"Go away, Jean-Marc," Desirée said.

Latimer cleared his throat, coughed, cleared his throat again and simply convulsed with laughter. He bent over and slapped his knees and shortly Hunter's chuckles joined it.

"You think this is funny?" Jean-Marc pulled gloves from his pocket. "My sister is taken advantage of — and I'm not diverted by your story of some nameless, faceless stranger, Adam — she's taken advantage of, perhaps even ruined by, by, well perhaps ruined, and the best I get from my friends is laughter. You, sirs, are insolent and you're no friends of mine." He held the gloves in a threatening manner and

Adam wondered how many of them Jean-Marc intended to call out.

"I say," Hunter said.

"So far all you've done is promise to say something, Sir Hunter," Jean-Marc said. "One wonders how you fare at the bench."

Desirée let go of Adam and faced her half brother. "Listen to me." She leveled a finger at him. "You sound like a pompous, egotistical . . . *rattle*. If you had any consideration for me, you would make sure I wasn't exposed to more overtaxing emotion. You don't care for me at all. Come Anne, we shall leave these, these, *louts* to argue among themselves and go home."

"No!" Every man present joined the chorus.

Adam stuck his hands in his pockets and looked at the floor.

"Well," Jean-Marc said. He cast an apologetic glance at Adam and pulled on the gloves. "I'm thankful you're safe, Desirée, and you, Miss Williams. Let us go to Number 17. You will get the Princess to bed, Miss Williams, and we shall assess the situation, gentlemen. Assess and act. Desirée's reputation must be protected at all costs, and the villain must be found, of course. Since we have been in on this together, perhaps we should work together."

Male agreement followed.

"What a marvelous idea," Desirée said. She retrieved her mangled bonnet from behind a sofa of indeterminate color and from which tufts of its innards sprouted. She yawned elaborately. "I shall sleep for the rest of the day and through the night. I can feel that I shall.

"And I shall sleep peacefully knowing that you men will discuss what happened to me today, the manner of person who attacked me, what he did to me, what he said to me. How fortunate I am to have so many clairvoyant gentlemen to take care of me."

It was Adam's turn to feel like laughing. He swallowed the urge. "Correct me if I'm wrong," he said to her, "but I think you need to tell your story quietly, and to one person who doesn't make you feel threatened."

"Fair enough," Jean-Marc said, looking not a little chagrined. "We'll use my study, Desirée, and I'll make sure we aren't interrupted."

Desirée sniffed and shook her head.

"Dash it," Jean-Marc said.

Latimer flexed his broad shoulders. "Well, it isn't as if you've been really close, you two, is it?" he said with characteristic bluntness.

That bought him a Jean-Marc sized scowl.

"I'm the best equipped to watch over Desirée," Adam blurted out, instantly shocked that he'd said any such thing.

"Really?" Jean-Marc's silken smile wasn't pretty. "Why would that be?"

"Because I am lower profile than any of you, bigger than any of you, and can carry out my business wherever I please, whenever I please — including in Desirée's presence. Not one of you has the same luxury. And she is like a little sister to me, the sister I never had. I will defend her to the death."

"I accept your offer!" Planting her feet apart and raising her chin, Desirée looked upon Adam with triumph, perhaps with . . . pride? "You will make me feel safe — till death do us part!"

14

Spivey here:

What the devil . . . Oh, dear, I'm not myself, we never mention him around here.

What happened? Tell me who nobbled Princess Desirée. What? Oh, is that so, well I wouldn't tell you something if you were the last persons left alive, either . . . but surely you'll tell me since I'm not exactly viable?

Blast your hides. I shall not forget your uncivil behavior toward me.

Oh, I'll give you another chance. I was diverted, you see, took my eye off things because I had to "sit" through a lecture from Reverend Smiles. In front of my entire angel class, no less. All because I had a little collision. Not even a really disastrous one, just a lot of bouncing about and turning upside down, you know what I mean. No, I don't suppose you do.

I flew straight into King George III. No, I'm not joking. I looked at him, recognized him, and the sight of him shocked me so much I forgot to slow down. He hasn't changed. Not a bit of it. Looks a bit more pasty than the last time I saw him — that would be when he knighted me — but apart from that, and my never having seen him without his wig before (disturbing, that, seems too . . . intimate) and of course, he wasn't wearing the crown, but apart from those minor changes, he was his old puffed-up self. Slip of the tongue there, I meant he was very — royal.

Anyway, Reverend Smiles didn't care about my being surprised and couldn't give a fig about the King having knighted me. I saw the Reverend's little smile when he told me such trifles were not important around here. He just kept saying, "Chaos in class is not acceptable."

I digress . . . again. Back to the matter in hand. The Princess out and about on her own and getting into a pickle? How did that happen? What a slipup and who was responsible? Damn him whoever he is because we now have the entire Mayfair Square Militia mobilized to get in our way.

And would one of you tell me what that girl, Desirée, is thinking of? Don't answer that! She's a female — doesn't think. But if she continues making outrageous remarks to Adam in front of Jean-Marc, he'll lock her away until he marries her off — and that won't be to Adam Chillworth.

Also, I'm concerned about Rolly Spade-Filbert. I do have a definite plot in mind, y'know, and . . . no, I won't tell you about it. You don't help me so I will not share with you, either. Don't interrupt me again. I have a plan and I am still impressed with my brilliance in choosing a Busy rather than an Empty accomplice. The empty minds were an admirable idea since their owners could be so easily told what to do, even if they did get my instructions all wrong sometimes. But the busy mind is also, in most cases, a good mind and there should be no misunderstanding. The problem with Rolly Spade-Filbert is that I fear he may be too involved in his own selfish agenda to pay the necessary attention to mine. And all this chatter of his with the Williams girl — what does he think he's about there?

Fear not, I shall prevail.

I almost forgot to tell you what HRH said to me. He warned me about the evils of leeching, said the best thing is to keep one's blood to oneself and never to trust doctors. Really, he spoke as if I were his dear friend, most gratifying but, given my stature among architects at the time, not surprising.

I say — oh, it's nothing really, just a stray thought in passing, about keeping one's blood to oneself. If that were possible one might take the suggestion seriously. But there is certainly one heartening thing about being bloodless — one doesn't have to worry about leeches after all.

15

Jean-Marc propped his elbows on the mantel in what had once been his retreat — his library and study — and massaged his temples. He welcomed heat from the fire on his chilled legs.

Retreat? Hah. Not since Meg, Meg Smiles then, had first entered this room for an interview. Almost four years ago he'd retained her to guide Desirée through her Season (her first Season, that was) and from then on nothing had been the same in his life. Whenever possible she was with him. Into this masculine sanctuary appropriate but softer furnishings had gradually been added and he'd grown accustomed to working at his desk while his wife and daughter played on his favorite Aubusson carpet.

Praise be.

Now his happiest moments were spent with Meg in his arms, or just sleeping beside him, or when the two of them were with two-year-old Serena.

Well, he couldn't hide in comforting thoughts for long on this miserable afternoon. Behind him a giant flap raged and soon, after the chaotic comings and goings, the crying, pleading and ordering had subsided or at least lulled a little, then he must take charge as his position demanded and let all of them know how things would be handled.

A chaise covered with gold damask flanked the fireplace on one side and from the corner of his eye, Jean-Marc could see his wife's slippered feet there. If there was a choice, she invariably chose to be close to him. He doubted any of the rest of them sat. In fact he could hear and feel them moving about as they talked — or wept as was the case with Desirée. Damn their selfish father, the one parent they shared, for refusing to be interested in a female offspring, and damn the girl's pleasure-seeking mother who had all but abandoned her since birth.

He had been made Desirée's sole guardian and he was too young, or perhaps too impatient, to guide a woman of twenty who would not be guided. Not so far, but that would change.

"Jean-Marc," that lady said. "You are not listening to me. I am in my most desperate time of need and you ignore me. You don't love me, nobody does."

He raised his face to the ceiling and prayed for patience.

"Everyone loves you, Desirée," Meg said. "Do try not to sound like a petulant crone, you are annoying."

At a knock on the door Jean-Marc turned around. An under-butler entered with a large porcelain vase overflowing with cream roses. He went to Desirée who sniffed into a handkerchief and shook her head.

"Put them on the desk, please," Meg said and Jean-Marc hadn't the heart to point out that he didn't like his desk cluttered.

Latimer approached the flowers with comical haste and bent to examine the vase. He said, "Hmm," and "Hmm," again, then announced, "It's Ming, by jove. I know you don't want the gift, Desirée, but would you at least see who sent the vase?"

Jean-Marc smiled. Latimer was an importer of oddities and rarities and very successful. He'd become the man to see for authentication because his knowledge was impeccable.

"Look yourself," Desirée said. "No one I care for would send me roses."

Hunter leaned against a bookcase, one foot crossed over the other, lost in thought. Adam, damn his handsome hide, stood with his imposing legs braced apart and his hands linked behind his back. He stared at the roses.

A man ought to be grateful that at least Verbeux had gone about other business, that Miss Williams had taken to her bed, and Lucas Chillworth and his friend had been sensitive enough to excuse themselves on leaving that wretched hovel to which Desirée had been abducted. Not that Jean-Marc knew much more about that now than he had an hour ago.

Professional curiosity had overcome caution and Latimer held a small card in his hand.

"Well?" Desirée said, showing little sign of the collected young woman she'd become. "Go on, Latimer. You've taken out my card. You might as well read it to the whole room. Who knows, perhaps the flowers are from that unspeakable creature who handled me so . . . Read it, please."

"I say." Hunter roused himself and straightened away from the bookcase. "You did tell him to open the card, y'know, Your Highness."

"Desirée has had a shock," Adam said promptly. "Aye, a terrible shock and she's fragile. She's not to be held accountable for a small ill humor."

Jean-Marc considered the painter who had hidden his family and everything else about his personal life, and saw a formidable foe in the making. Whenever Adam looked at Desirée he guarded his expression — probably to hide the passion he knew he must not show — but tenderness, and at this moment protectiveness, were never far away.

"Thank you, Adam," Desirée said and continued to look at him with gentle eyes.

"You do know Meg's right, don't you," he said. "We love you and will always keep you safe."

"I know you will," Desirée said. "I love you, too."

Jean-Marc glanced at Meg. She gave the slightest of shrugs to let him know she'd had the same reaction as he to Desirée's response. In this instance Meg's support didn't make him feel better, not that they couldn't both be wrong and reading too much into a few chance words.

"Read the card then, More," Adam said

to Latimer with a heartiness that sounded forced. "Let's find out who our Princess's extravagant admirer is."

"Princess Desirée," Latimer read in deliberately sonorous tones. "I hope the little notes I have left in recent days are not annoying. It was and is my fervent hope that we might renew our acquaintance of several years ago. I shall never forget you at the costume ball when you wore pink sequins and net and pretended to me you were supposed to be a concubine! You were the sweetest girl even then."

"You've been getting notes?" Adam said with not even a shadow of a smile. Then he remembered himself and turned up the corners of his mouth. "I imagine there are so many notes of admiration delivered that you grow weary of them."

"I don't read them," Desirée said promptly. "Don't keep us in suspense, Latimer. Tell us who *this* admirer is."

Latimer turned the card over. "I beg to call on you again as I did on several occasions at Riverside in Windsor." He looked up. "I didn't know you had a beau following you around in the country."

"Continue," Desirée said.

"Of course." Latimer cleared his throat and read on, "Please consider allowing me to take you around the Park in my carriage. And perhaps when it grows a little warmer, we might ride there together. With deepest respect, Anthony FitzDuram."

"Who the hell is Anthony FitzDuram?" Adam and Hunter asked in unison.

"He's the son of Burris FitzDuram," Jean-Marc said, "The —"

"Judge," Hunter finished for him. "I'm dashed. They are also the FitzDuram single malt family and their pockets are so deep they drag on the ground. Burris is a good judge and a good man and I hear nothing but admiration for the entire family. Anthony's the brain of the group, so I recall being told. Oxford man. He's into politics now. They say he's got a brilliant career ahead of him."

"A nice boy," Meg said. She smiled at Desirée. "I also remember how naughty you were at the ball. You informed him that your gown was supposed to be bands of transparent stuff to show off your skin and flesh, only it was wasted on one with so little flesh — or something similar."

Desirée smiled at that. "I don't know why he continued to be interested in me after that. I'd have expected him to be married by now."

Adam laughed and said, "How could any

man not be entranced by you. You take the breath away."

"Yes, I understand. Take me away now?" she said. "My dear Adam, how impetuous you are." She paused, coughed, tried to pat her own back.

"Oh, we must make you happy again," Adam said. He went to her and smoothed her hunched and quaking shoulders. "If you agree, Jean-Marc and Meg, I will accompany the Princess to Number 7 where it is quiet and I can talk her through the unpleasant events of the day. Perhaps you agree that it will be more comfortable for her to talk to just one person?"

Perish Adam Chillworth's audacity. Jean-Marc seethed. The man openly comforted Desirée and talked about *accompanying her to Number 7 where it is quiet!* "I do agree that she should talk to one person rather than a crowd, sir, and that person shall be me," he said, more forcefully than he would have liked. He pretended not to see Meg's reproachful glances.

Again there was a tap on the door and the same under-butler — Thompson — put in another appearance. He threw wide the door and announced, "Lady Hester Bingham and Sir Robert Brodie to see you, m'lord."

Jean-Marc muttered under his breath. This was a plot, an evil attempt to get rid of him through driving him mad.

"Hello children," Lady Hester said, gliding into the room. Resplendent in a chic carriage outfit, silver shot with blue and trimmed with silver mink, she went directly to the center of the room where she pulled off her gloves and gave the impression of one in perpetual motion.

Jean-Marc was certain he had already met Sir Robert but couldn't recall where or when. Broad shoulders, powerful build, hair prematurely white but with eyebrows, mustache and beard that were all still red: He was a commanding figure.

"This is my very good friend, Sir Robert Brodie," Lady Hester said. "He's a surgeon here in London and a very sought after one, too. He was kind enough to accompany me this afternoon since I think he's convinced I'm overwrought."

"Are you?" Jean-Marc asked.

Lady Hester turned her blue eyes on him. "News travels, Jean-Marc. I've learned about Desirée's terrible experience." She went directly to Desirée and threw her arms around her neck. Her Ladyship's mouth brushed the side of Desirée's head and Jean-Marc could have sworn a message passed between them. *Women.* They were so devious. Give him a straightforward man any day — depending on the situation, of course.

"Good afternoon," Sir Robert — a Scotsman — said, offering his hand and shaking Jean-Marc's firmly. "In fact we've a'ready met. I was invited to a costume ball in this house about three years ago. I met your charmin' wife — you weren't married then, o'course, and she stole my heart, only to dash it within half an hour when I saw she only had eyes for you." He smiled, showing strong, square teeth. "But I'm a forgivin' man and a good loser. You're a lucky bounder, m'lord. And I'm a lucky man to have met Hester again. Isn't she extraordinary?"

Jean-Marc looked at Lady Hester, who continued to whisper with Desirée, and had to admit, "Yes, extraordinary. A pity she was widowed so young but I have felt that she would still like to experience the complete possibilities of life — you know — between a man and a woman and I don't think she mourns the loss of her husband nearly as much anymore."

"She's shared some o' that wi' me since I became her physician. Apparently she's been reprimanded by some of the influential hostesses for laughin' and havin' a pleasant time when —" he dropped his voice here "— her husband isn't cold in his grave t'hear them tell it. They don't acknowledge that she's been alone for years."

"And what does she say to that?" Jean-Marc asked.

Sir Robert's eyes crinkled at the corners. An appealing devil to the ladies, Jean-Marc decided. The surgeon's eyes twinkled. "I think ye can imagine the answer t'that."

Jean-Marc considered before saying, "I thought you were a surgeon, not a family physician."

The good doctor laughed at that. "A surgeon must first be a physician, no? And if he chooses to take on a personal patient, he's free to do so."

"As you say." Jean-Marc knew when he was beaten.

"Take a look at the Ming piece, Lady H.," Latimer said. Clearly his concentration had not left the beautiful vase. "It's a gift to Desirée from an admirer. So are the roses. What do you think of it?"

"Very nice," Lady Hester said but didn't sound interested.

The under-butler still hovered in the doorway and Jean-Marc frowned at him. "Was there something else, Thompson?"

"Ahem. Mr. FitzDuram, the gentleman who brought the roses, asked me to inquire whether Her Royal Highness might leave a response to his note, which he could pick up later."

"Oh, really," Desirée said and sighed. "I am tired yet I cannot have any rest until I have confronted what has happened to me, quietly, with Adam who is never judgmental and who doesn't interrupt every word I say."

A burning sensation attacked Jean-Marc's belly. This minx would not manipulate him into abandoning his responsibilities.

"Desirée." He hoped the way he looked at his sister warned her that he would have no nonsense. "FitzDuram is a polite young man with excellent prospects. And I think you like him, hmm?"

Desirée waggled her head. "Well enough."

"Good. It's important for you to be seen out and about. I shall have Meg write a note on your behalf inviting him to call around eleven on Wednesday morning. If you have no objection, I'll tell him we approve of your taking a drive with him."

"I don't want to go, but I will. And I'll make sure he doesn't ask again."

"You'll do no such thing," Jean-Marc informed her. "You will be the polite girl you know how to be. Give the man a chance, you may come to like him."

"I remember him and I already like him. That's all I feel about him. Now, I am so tired. Please be kind to me, brother."

Jean-Marc steeled himself for his sister's melodramatic arguments and said, "Of course I'll be kind to you, my dear. Why don't we go upstairs to my small study. I'll make sure there's a fire there and we can be comfortable — and quiet."

Desirée flopped into one of a pair of French fauteuils, grasped the gilt arms so tightly her knuckles shone and, at the same time, closed her eyes and wagged her head from side to side. "It is all too embarrassing. I don't want to talk to you about it."

"I am the one, the only one, you should wish to discuss this with."

"I love you, Jean-Marc," Desirée said, "but there are some things I'm not comfortable discussing with you. Please don't press me."

"Yet you are comfortable talking to Adam about them?"

"Yes." *Emphatic.*

Jean-Marc noted that Adam looked

pained and almost sympathized with the man's difficult position.

"Very well." Lady Hester chose to sit on a green silk covered couch facing the fire. She leaned back and made sounds that suggested she was making decisions. "Listen to me and remember that I have more experience in these matters than any of you. You in particular, Jean-Marc. Pay attention."

At any other time he would have laughed at this lady's audacity. "I'm listening, My Lady."

"Good, see that you continue to do so. There is a point at which dutiful concern spills over into possessiveness. I hope this is not the case here and now with your attitude toward your sister. What do you think, Meg."

He looked at his wife and she turned pink enough to worry him. She said, "I can only give my support to my husband's wishes. That is my responsibility and I happily perform it since Jean-Marc is the most reasonable of men."

The idea of Meg's unwavering loyalty was a rush in his veins. But she loved him and he wasn't sure she actually agreed with him. He looked at her and desire overtook him. How, he wondered, could he get the two of them out of here and into the bed-chamber they unfashionably shared at all times?

"I also trust Adam, of course," Meg continued. "And I consider him to have a gift shared by few, the gift of being able to listen and know the right, the most helpful thing to say afterward. We have long been friends and I could not bear to think of life without that friendship."

Jean-Marc flexed his fingers. Other than demanding Meg's silence — which he would not do — he had no choice but to allow her to extol Chillworth's virtues.

"You are," Meg said, looking at Adam with a sincere smile shining forth from her lovely face, "supportive and honorable — brave. You are a man who always puts himself last."

The room had grown quiet.

Murmurs of agreement followed and Jean-Marc's temper churned. He had been betrayed by his own wife's golden tongue. And he still wanted to bear her away and kiss every inch of her.

"Well said!" Lady Hester, her face flushed with emotion, clapped her hands and looked at Adam. "I think it would be most suitable for you to help Desirée in any way you can. Like Meg, I trust you implicitly. Jean-Marc, with your agreement, and since I know Anne Williams needs rest, I will chaperon the two young people myself. What do you say?"

What could he say? "Since Adam is hardly a *young person* I shall charge him with responsibility for my sister, as well, Lady Hester. Naturally, I cannot turn down your generous offer."

"Very wise," Lady Hester said, slipping a hand beneath Sir Robert's arm. "We will be in the foyer in case there are remarks that need to be made without our presence. Kindly don't keep me waiting long."

Latimer and Hunter drifted away at the same time.

"Run along," Jean-Marc told Desirée and to Adam he added, "My sister is headstrong, but you know this. Beware of any unsuitable demands she may make on you and encourage her to settle down and start preparing for the Season. You could be a helpful influence, Chillworth."

Adam's discomfort was palpable, even though he retained his formidable air. "Desirée will be in good hands," he said. "I hope to help with sorting out today's events."

Once Jean-Marc was alone with Meg, she got up from the chaise and stood before him. She rubbed his arms, and his resolve to remain aloof crumbled. He took her by the shoulders and drew her close. Her face was upturned and she ran her tongue over her lips, probably out of nervousness but for him the move was erotic.

"You, my darling," he said, "want the best for Desirée. And I do know I'm being manipulated by the one woman in the world who almost always has her way with me."

"That sounds exciting."

He pulled her against him. "Your fearlessness will get you into trouble — the best kind of trouble and quite shortly. But you worry me. I warn you that the match you have in mind cannot work — and I like the man you ladies have chosen for Desirée as much as you do. But he would not make her happy in the end. Forbidden love can be intoxicating, but when the wild passion of it wears off, a man such as Adam cannot keep a woman like Desirée happy. She would come to resent him.

"Still, it will do no harm for him to counsel her — particularly with Lady H. on guard."

Meg flattened her breasts to his chest and draped her arms around his neck. "Does that mean you are about to tire of me? After all, ours is not an equal match."

"My dearest witch, you are my equal in every way."

Meg ducked from his arms and ran to lock the library door. By the time she returned with her bodice already unbuttoned, her full breasts were all but naked in a flimsy chemise.

She came to him, pulling her arms from her sleeves, and by the time she stood in front of him again she had only to wriggle the chemise to her waist in order to be enchantingly half-dressed.

Meg's mouth trembled. She sought his hands and filled them with her breasts. Jean-Marc looked down as he fondled her, then stopped and tilted his head to one side. "You feel wonderful . . . but you feel different."

"I am different," she told him. "It's still early, but we are finally to have another child."

He swept her from her feet, knelt and stretched her on the carpet before the fire. Lying on his side, his head propped, he studied her before leaning slowly over her. "You are everything to me," he told her. "You make me alive and you make me more happy than I will ever be able to explain. Thank you, dearest wife."

Jean-Marc kissed her.

16

Rather than take them to her boudoir, Lady Hester surprised Desirée by leading the way to a drawing room just beyond 7A. On the door of what had been Latimer More's home before his marriage to Jenny was a sign Desirée hadn't noticed before: Vicar In Residence.

When she paused to stare, Adam looked at the door and said, "Gawd, the old phony's back. He's been on some sort of pilgrimage — but not for long enough as far as I'm concerned."

"A *minister* lives here?"

"Keep your voice down," Adam said, "or you may tread on a toe or two. I'm not sure you met the Reverend Larch Lumpit. Moved in last year when Lady H. took pity on him because he had no living. You were away by that time. We don't see much of him when he is here because he has become a contemplative — prays all the time except when he's eating what Barstow makes especially for him."

"I heard about him," Desirée said without adding that everything she'd heard had been awful. "Fancied himself heaven sent to take care of Jenny?"

"Mmm. Even managed to get himself moved from 7B to 7A after Latimer moved next door. Said the stairs were too much for him. Barstow dotes on him — only don't ever suggest she does. I think he takes her kindness as his due."

"Take me." Desirée blinked and clamped her mouth shut. *Tossed over his shoulder and carried swiftly to his rooms where he would close the door softly to avoid attracting attention. Kissed, again and again, perhaps standing just inside the door because he couldn't bear to wait another second, or stretched out on his couch . . . or slid beneath the quilt on his bed. He might take off his jacket and waistcoat, unbutton his shirt even. He might . . . touch her again while he kissed her . . .*

"Desirée! What is it? Are you ill."

Her beloved's voice. She smiled softly at him. Her beloved's voice *shouting* at her. "Oh, yes, yes, Adam dear. No, I mean no, there's nothing wrong and I couldn't feel better. I was lost in thought for a moment."

"I think I'd give you a penny for those thoughts," he said.

Desirée lowered her eyes. "Well, I believe I should expect a higher price than that."

"Children?" Lady Hester called from the drawing room.

"If I were forty, or fifty, she would still treat me like a child," Adam said in low tones, ushering Desirée ahead of him into a room with the palest of moss-green silk on the walls.

Desirée was grateful for Lady Hester's intrusion and looked about the room. So recently had it been redecorated that Desirée could smell paint. Striped cream and green draperies were drawn back from windows with a view on the small side garden between Number 7 and the tall fence that separated it from Number 6. Mounded snow covered every bush, clung to the top of the fence and covered the grass.

"Sit by the fire," Her Ladyship said. She tugged on an embroidered linen bellpull beside the fireplace and waved Desirée and Adam toward a small but plump sofa in plum-colored velvet. "Come along, come along. Barstow will see to it that we get some refreshments."

"It's very nice in here, Lady Hester," Adam said. "Tasteful. I had no idea it was being changed."

She fluttered the fingers of one hand. "It

was overdue and since I have new plans . . ." She let the sentence trail away and Adam didn't press the subject.

Sir Robert had walked as far as Number 7 with them before excusing himself. Desirée wanted to know more about Lady Hester's friendship with him, if that's what it was, and why she had failed to mention the man earlier. But first, and much more so, Desirée wanted to get away. She wanted, oh, how she wanted, to be alone with Adam. How long, she wondered, would they have together.

She sat where Lady Hester had told her to sit, but Adam remained standing. Why would that dreadful man who had accosted her say evil things about Adam? He stood with his arms crossed, his head slightly bowed, and she felt that his thoughts had taken him far away — not something she cared to contemplate.

"There you are, Barstow," Lady Hester said. She settled into a slipper chair. "What is that sour look for?"

Barstow's considerable bosom rose with an exasperated breath she made no attempt to suppress. "I thought you and that Sir Robert had taken yourselves off." A solidly built woman, she wore nothing but gray and her hair, uncompromisingly styled, was the same color. The effect was formidable, but Desirée knew how much kindness there was in this faithful servant.

"We were out," Lady Hester said. "Now I am back — with Adam and the Princess. We should like tea, please, and some of cook's delicious pastries." She glanced at Desirée and smiled. "I want you to help me put some meat on this girl's bones. She is much too nervous and has little appetite. And this is the time of her life when she must bloom."

Desirée thought better of asking why.

"Young things looking toward marriage and children are more sure of fulfillment if they are in robust health. Isn't that so, Barstow?"

"Yes, Milady."

The heat in Desirée's face annoyed her since Adam would see it. She would not look at him.

"Was there something else, Barstow?" Lady Hester asked.

"Yes, Milady. The Reverend Lumpit has come home."

Spivey here:
Look, I'll only take a moment of your time but surely you see how distraught I must be.

Just as I have success within my grasp. Just as I begin to believe that with the help of a few women who don't know what they're doing I will see Adam Chillworth married to Princess Desirée and safely installed — far away from here — Lumpit returns. I told him not to. The man is an Empty I once thought would help me — in getting rid of Latimer More to be precise.

A nightmare, I tell you. It was a nightmare. The wretch began to think for himself and ruined everything — almost.

And Barstow refers to Number 7 as his home!

Lumpit must and will go.

But I do think things may be shaping up rather well with Adam and Desirée, don't you? Now, nothing particularly interesting will happen between them today, so you can all just run along. I'll let you know when you're welcome around here again.

Oh drat, I am not to be given a moment's peace.

"Yes, sir, Reverend Smiles, sir. I hear you, sir. I'll be there at once. Goodness and mercy? That's the subject of the next class? I'll look forward to it. Show and tell? Show and tell what? Oh, yes, yes, of course."

An example of my own goodness and mercy? Why, there are so many that my only difficulty will be to choose just one.

"Au revoir."

"I noticed he had," Lady Hester said of Reverend Lumpit's homecoming. She untied her bonnet and gave it to Barstow. "The sign on his door? Necessary, you think?"

"Oh, yes, Milady. He's a man of God and it's important everyone knows 7A is a holy place now and not to be entered lightly. Reverend Lumpit doesn't like visitors. He prefers to go to those he helps."

"Is he in there now?" Lady Hester's soft mouth had drawn somewhat tight.

"He is, and resting after his journey. I'm making him a light snack right now."

"Half a dozen pasties, a pound or two of cheese, a loaf of bread, a bathtub of ale —"

"Enough, Adam," Lady Hester said, but her eyes crinkled. "Reverend Lumpit must wait until you have tended us, Barstow, and that may take some time."

Barstow left, her face like stone, and Lady Hester settled herself more comfortably. "So," she said, "When she returns you will have left. I will tell her you had to go and I will make sure she doesn't find out where you are — which will be in the attic, of course."

When the ensuing silence became unbearable, Desirée popped to her feet and went to the windows with unseemly haste. The pressure of the day had become more than she could bear. Adam had spoken out for them to be allowed to talk together — alone — yet he had made no further attempt to do so.

"I don't mean to upset you," Lady Hester said. She spoke in a soft tone. "Do you think I sometimes doubt myself and say the wrong things? If you do you are right. I want the best for you — I have wanted the best for all of you. This time, ah, yes, this time the task is great."

"What task would that be?" Adam asked with quiet fervor.

"I think you know," Lady Hester said. "May I be forgiven if I am wrong, but I will be an accessory to something I believe in and which I think you two believe in. I don't know, I just don't know, but I will take the chance with you. I will do what I can to help. All I will say as a warning is that if you betray my trust, you will break my heart."

Desirée trembled. She turned her back on the pristine beauty outside and regarded Adam, soundlessly appealed to him for his strength and wisdom.

Adam stared back at her. "What would be a betrayal of your trust, Lady Hester?" His eyes didn't as much as flicker.

"Squander love and you will betray me," she told them. Looking at Adam she added, "Take love lightly, use it to quiet your hunger then fall back when you confront the disapproval you know must come, and I shall know despair — as will you. Think with your heads as well as your bodies. If there is a way to have what others would deny you, find it, but do no harm. Now leave me."

Spivey here!
Now what do you have to say for yourselves, hmm? Embarrassed, aren't you? And you should be. You should have listened to me. I always told you Hester was a brilliant woman.

17

A hand covered Anne Williams's mouth and arched her neck back. She'd been sleeping in her small room next to Princess Desirée's dressing room. She awoke bathed in sweat, her body sodden inside her cotton night rail.

Her scream was only in her head.

Breathing. Harsh, excited breathing fanned her cheek.

She managed to open her mouth and bite his fingers. Her reward was a hard knee driven into her buttocks, against the tip of her spine, and the deep pain that shot to her belly.

Dusk came early in January. With the drapes closed, the room was so black that no hint of a shape showed no matter in which direction she rolled her eyes. Her heart smote at her breast, lodged in her throat.

Behind her in the narrow cot, one arm pushed beneath and around her, the other clamped over her mouth while the elbow trapped her arm to her side, lay a man, a naked man. She knew he had taken his clothes off because she could feel him swelling hard against her bottom, feel the hair on his heavy thigh where it rested over her hip. The night rail had twisted about her body and his hot, pulsing flesh prodded her bare skin.

Just like the other time. She screamed in her head again, and prayed to be saved.

"Don't struggle." A hoarse whisper against her ear. He nibbled at the lobe. "You want this. You like it — we both know that. I know everything about you. If you struggle, you'll get hurt, then it won't be so much fun — for you."

She forced her head from side to side, bucked with all her might.

"I'm going to take my hand away from your mouth. If you make a sound, I'll kill you. I'll break your neck so fast you'll hardly know you're dying. That'll shut you up. Will you be quiet?"

If she could reason with him, perhaps it wouldn't go so badly for her. Anne nodded. Bit by bit he eased the pressure on her face until she lay panting, and trying to pull her soaked gown over her body. He didn't make a sound, but he pulled the night rail over her head and threw it to the floor before falling on her neck. He kissed her long and slow while he left not an inch of her untouched. He caressed her, then covered her mouth once more and plunged the fingers of his other hand between her thighs.

First he stroked her tender flesh with unexpected finesse, isolated the center where she burned and, even as she tried to press her legs together and deny her response, an aching fire began to burn. Then Anne forgot to hold her legs together. He abandoned her mouth to weigh her breasts and lightly pinch her nipples. She turned her face into the pillow and jerked against his delving fingers, silently urged him to finish what he'd started.

He smelled of leather and, faintly, of fresh sweat and his hard body curved around hers, a strong, very masculine body. She wanted to see his face.

"You like this," he said. "Good, because I like it, too, and I shall come to you again, only next time I will expect answers from you."

His fingers moved faster and faster, and she strained to reach back and find his rod. As her fingers closed, she convulsed, tried to trap the exquisite awakening that blossomed out of control and keep it alive.

"Now you want something else, don't you." His rasping, anonymous voice frightened her even as it excited her. "Curl over your knees."

She shot her legs straight down and crossed her ankles.

"Don't fight me," he said and his fingers closed hard on her upper arm. "Do as you're told. It will bring us both pleasure."

With her eyes squeezed tightly shut, she willed herself to turn into stone.

"Very well. This will remind you who is master here." While he crushed her face into the pillow, he started to rake the nails of his other hand down her back, but stopped. He said nothing, but settled a hand lightly on the area instead.

They lay still like that until at last he said, "Your skin is soft, I didn't want to mar it. But you will remember this night. You will remember how I excited you, and you will do as I ask. If you don't, I will have to make sure you lose your place here. I know what happened in Mont Nuages."

Gritty tears forced themselves from the corners of her eyes. Only three other people were supposed to know what had really happened to her in that dreadful place and this could not be one of them —

yet he also knew her past. Who could she turn to when she didn't know her enemies?

"This is what you will find out." He spoke for only moments before sliding from the mattress and covering her with the bedding. "Don't attempt to move until I am gone. If anyone needed proof of what a passionate creature you are, they'd only have to see you as you were a few minutes ago. Pleading for it. Urging me to satisfy you."

She wanted to cry out that her body had only done what was to be expected, but if she spoke he might become angry again.

"I'll return soon and if you have defied me, the Count shall discover that his sister's companion is a whore."

Anne pushed her face into the pillows and pounded the soft bedding with her fists. What she had done, she had done, but her sentence had been too harsh.

The man covered both of her hands on the pillows. The mattress sank as he sat beside her hips and he leaned to settle his cheek on the back of her head.

Anne lay still, but her heart thundered while she waited for him to force himself on her again.

When he spoke it was even more insistent. "It is not my way to hurt women.

227

This has sickened me as much as it has sickened you, but it seems I have no choice if I am to survive. Perhaps you will come to welcome my attentions and miss me when I am not with you."

She shook her head.

"Don't be so sure." He slid a hand beneath the covers and played his fingers over the side of her naked breast, and Anne felt again the dart of hot pleasure. "I feel you react to me," he said. "You will not be the first woman to crave a man who has power over her."

18

The attic glowed by firelight. Desirée said, "When I'm here it feels like the safest place on earth." Her eyes were soft and shining. "With the draperies closed and candles alight, little wonder you don't want to move from Mayfair Square, I wouldn't, either."

How lightly she spoke, Adam thought, lightly about situations that would never become part of her own world. "I have been very happy at Number 7."

She touched the back of his hand and tilted her head. A little worry line formed between her eyebrows. "*Have been?* You say that as if you might go away. Adam, you won't go away, will you?"

"One day." He would have to one day, when the bells had rung for her wedding and she was borne away by a man judged more worthy than he.

Halibut, whose timing was often impeccable, wound his big, soft gray body around their legs. He purred loudly.

"Why would you leave at all?"

Why? "Nothing stays as it is, dear . . . Desirée. The time will come to move on. For you and for me and for others of our special friends."

"No," she said. "I cannot bear to think of it. Adam . . ." She seemed to consider before she slipped her hand into his and led him to the couch. "Sit down with me, please. There is something heavy on my heart. It feels strange because, in a way, it is a legacy of my birth, yet I have not lived as I was intended to live — my choice — and I do not take privilege for granted."

They sat, facing each other with Desirée still holding his hand while she stroked its back with soft fingers. Her hands were long and narrow, and unadorned. And she did not know what her touch made him feel.

Helpless longing.

"People born into luxury and destined to know nothing but luxury may be considered shallow. Sometimes they are dismissed as lacking intelligence and being absorbed with their comforts." Desirée gave a short laugh. "And sometimes they are shallow, empty-headed and self-centered."

He turned her hand, palm up, on top of his and covered it. If in touching her he took too great a liberty, so be it. There had already been extreme transgressions on his part and he didn't regret those, either. But he must not lose control again.

"Adam?" She looked at him in question.

"If you're speaking about yourself then I can tell you that no one would ever consider you as other than the intelligent woman you are. And, for my sins, I know you are not shallow."

"For your sins? What can you mean?"

He watched her lips move, the glimpses of small teeth. Deliberately looking away he said, "You were able to spar with me when you were seventeen. Since then you have only spread your wings. You are too curious for your own good — yet I wouldn't change you. And self-absorbed people are not concerned for others. Your kindness is something you cannot hide. And you are fearless, my silly, brave girl. Running about alone in places where women do not go. Dashing off to help a boy you did not know." He had already said too much, enough for any woman to guess he admired things other than her mind.

Desirée grew more somber. "You flatter

me and knowing you mean what you say only makes me feel that I have more to say. Adam, I know I am often petulant and demanding. I pursue what I want, often without stopping to make sure I could not hurt another if I got it. But I am changing. Every prize has its price and some prices are too high to bear. I am resolved never to exact too high a price for my friendship — or for my love."

Such a serious one for twenty years. Serious and irresistible. Why was he given such a dilemma — such an unbearable struggle, one he would not shift from his shoulders even if he had the chance?

He remembered to breathe and regretted the need to talk. "You are special. I am honored to have you as my friend. Now I must ask you about what happened earlier." Only a desperate man was grateful to speak of something he would rather not even think about. "I know what occurred with the boy, his story about a cat. Our villain knows you, that you adore cats, damn his hide — forgive me my strong language."

"The boy was sent deliberately with his story about a cat and it was a lie, wasn't it?" Desirée's face lost any trace of color. "Do you think that man who attacked me is someone I speak to, someone polite, even someone I think of as a friend?"

"I can't guess how well he knows you, but at the very least he knows of you." Frightening her badly might help him keep her safe but he could not bear to push too hard. "Did the boy try to follow when the man pulled you into the house?"

Her fingers curled into his palm and she leaned a little closer. "I don't know. I don't think so. I was . . . I was frightened."

Murderous thoughts did nothing to help a man think clearly. "He didn't beat on the door?"

She shook her head. "No, I'm sure he didn't. I screamed, but only once because the man covered my face and mouth with cloth."

Inside, he shook with rage but he kept his hands steady on hers. Her face showed the signs of how long this day had been.

"Please tell me everything that happened. Everything that was said."

Desirée looked anywhere but at him.

She no longer wore the cloak she'd used to come across the square with him. Her thick, straight hair shone in the candlelight and the pale skin at her throat and décolletage gleamed almost luminous. The gown she'd changed into was another of the plain affairs she'd taken to of late, this one dark blue with a tight bodice and soft skirt relieved only by a satin belt of the same color.

"The dress becomes you," he said. "Your eyes take on an even deeper hue." He squeezed her fingers and hoped to encourage her to be open with him.

"He lifted me up and carried me into that room where I was when you came. I fought with him, kicked him. All he did was laugh at me."

Adam prayed that he be allowed to meet this man — alone. "Go on," he said.

"He — he — he —" She swallowed and squeezed her eyes shut. "He turned me in his arms and carried me so that my face was down." Parting the hair on the left side of her head, she showed him a purple welt. "My head hit a doorjamb somewhere."

Before he could restrain himself, Adam released her hand and spread his fingers over her cheeks and neck while he gently rested his lips on the wound. He shifted and eased her close beside him, put an arm around her and rested her head in the hollow of his shoulder.

"You're too brave for your own good, Your Highness," he told her.

A fierce punch to his unprepared middle

made him gasp. "You will never call me that again. Do you understand?"

"You have a pointy little fist — Desirée. And of course, your command is my wish."

"You've got that wrong."

"I don't think so," he said, loving the way she felt, the way she smelled. "This isn't an easy question to ask, but did he touch you in any way you considered inappropriate?"

Her face turned up and she looked into his eyes.

And her lips were far too close, as were the rapidly rising and falling tops of her breasts.

Concentrate.

She whispered, "He held me tightly but I was not easy to manage and he threw me down on that horrid couch. He was angry and slapped my limbs, but I think he was running out of time. All he did after that was talk."

Adam stroked her hair and labored to calm himself. He would choose to be grateful that she had not collapsed from fear and he believed she would have if anything more intrusive had been done to her. "What did he talk about?"

She rested her forehead on his neck and fell silent.

"Please tell me."

"I can't."

Adam's heart thudded. "I assure you there is nothing you could say that would shock me."

"*I* was shocked and saying it all aloud again is . . . I am *not* a ninny." Her lids closed but her eyes moved beneath them and a little color returned to her cheeks. "I prefer not to dwell on unpleasant incidents but I must tell you this. He said he works for someone I admire. Then he told me he was really this other man's partner. And he said — it sounds silly — he said his partner is interested in me."

So, the attacker's partner wanted Desirée. "Why would this one who was with you behave as he did when it had to be against his friend's wishes?"

"I don't know if it was or not, but . . . Oh, Adam, he had a horrible, raspy voice as if he was talking through something. I can't pretend — I was sure I was going to die there. He said he couldn't have his friend wasting time on me, not when they were getting so close to what they want. Then he said things about you."

Adam held quite still. He had already heard more of his personal business discussed than had ever been his intention.

But what bearing could it have on Desirée?

"He said," Desirée mumbled, "that you have killed people. Or that's what he meant by filling graves, I think."

The hair on the back of Adam's neck rose.

"Adam," she said. "He said I was getting in his way by, well, by *diverting* you. This sounds silly, because I couldn't do it even if I wanted to. But he said if I didn't stay away from you I'd be in trouble. He told me to stay away from you." She sat up and bent forward. Halibut licked her fingers and she stroked him listlessly.

Fear smote at Adam. "Is that all?"

"Except that you get rid of anyone who becomes a nuisance to you."

"Desirée —"

"Don't say anything for a moment. Please don't or I will lose the courage to say what's on my mind. You are gentle and honorable." She shrugged and peered up at him, somewhat impishly he thought. "You do have unpleasant qualities, like being silent for long periods of time when you're displeased, and sometimes treating me as if I were too young to be told the truth, or trusted to be mature. I am very mature now, Adam. I am your good friend and you will always be my best friend.

I . . ." She looked into her lap again.

"Are you suggesting I pout?" he asked.

She giggled and said, "Yes, you pout. But I believe nothing that man said of you. He wants something from me and doesn't want me to have anyone to turn to."

"You already have Jean-Marc to look after you."

"I know, and he would fight to the death for me. But his work for my father takes him away often. You are a busy man with your painting but you are usually in London." She stood up, lifting Halibut as she did so. "Any enemy of mine does well to fear you. You are not any of the things that person suggested, but you would protect me and in doing so, others might get hurt. And you also need someone whose loyalty is beyond doubt to support you. I am and will be that person."

It was time to interfere with her innocence, Adam decided, just a little, or perhaps slightly more than just a little. Where love between men and women was concerned she lived in a fantasy world of kisses and touches she most probably thought were the whole cake rather than a slice of it. A little heavy breathing, resting her head on a man's chest — even feeling his hands on her breasts through the

238

bodice of her dress. He had not, never would forget how she had found the amazing boldness to reach between his thighs and fondle him, but such fumblings were a pale shadow of what could be.

"You look strange, Adam," she said. "And irritable. We must be harmonious, especially now when there is someone who wishes you harm — someone who will abuse me in order to draw you to them. Someone who may have come to hate me out of hate for you. We cannot pretend that these people don't want to get me out of the way. I don't know why I threaten them, but I do. Please don't waste time being angry with me."

Adam could not argue with her logic. He got up. "What do you really understand about how things go between men and women?"

Her trusting gaze all but undid him.

"Things go differently between different men and women," she said. "Every person is an individual. Their feelings and actions match who they really are."

"What do you know of instinct?"

"That which one is born with? Very difficult to change, I should imagine. Once a soggy pudding, always a soggy pudding, so to speak."

He smiled. Couldn't help himself. "So to speak," he agreed. "But what of those who are strong?"

"We need them. They get things done. They know what they want and pursue it. I think passion is strong in such people and it could get out of hand. I would always be cautious with the strong, silent sort of person in whom I feel a kind of fire. After all, the sort of passion that makes someone an ally, could also make him a dangerous foe. Anger and passion are one on occasion. I think."

She thought a deal too much and her ability to think things through prevented her from being an easy mark. Not that he wanted her to be an easy mark, just more easily molded and guided — by him — and kept at a distance that didn't encourage lascivious thoughts on his part.

"Don't you think I'm right?" she said. "At least in some parts of my theory."

Adam scratched Halibut between his ears, buying time to come up with an innocuous response.

The cat purred so hard, his eyes crossed and his claws stretched and curled in the air.

"Oh to feel such ecstasy," Adam said. "This cat knows what complete satisfaction feels like."

"I wish I did."

Adam ducked his head to look closely at Desirée's face. It was pink. Her eyes were lowered, her mouth turned down a little.

Halibut leaped from her arms with such force that she cried out.

"I agree with a good part of your theory," Adam said and gripped her shoulders with little finesse. "I seem to recall that you have called me silent and watchful on occasion. Have you ever thought I might be a passionate man?"

Her eyes grew huge and she nodded. "You have already shown that you are."

"Good, because I am. Most artists are passionate — or so I've been led to believe. So, if we persist with your theory, the fire inside, there should be heat. Touch me, Desirée. Touch me wherever you please."

She stared steadfastly into his face, slowly raised her hands and opened buttons on his shirt. She slipped her hands inside and rubbed the hair on his chest, pushed her fingers to his skin.

And he shuddered.

"You are indeed hot." Her voice was husky. "Do you feel hot? Where do you feel the most hot?"

Damn her. "Perhaps I feel a little warm

but not in one place more than another." He lied.

"So you are passionate, but I know you are also steadfast and protective. You would never hurt me, so your attempt to make me fear you has failed."

What had not failed was the ability of his mind and body to rush to readiness. His flesh pulsed. He was so hard he wondered if he would ever be soft again. With all that he was he wanted to be inside Desirée. He wanted to make her his and his alone — forever. The need raged within him. If he had any sense, he would march her from 7C this very moment because regardless of her clever mind and tongue, she was not ready for what he had in mind.

She walked away from him and made sure the door was locked.

Adam's pulse stampeded. He stood absolutely still, gauging how to hold himself back during approaches she most definitely intended to make.

Desirée strolled, her fingers trailing in the folds of her skirts, watching him by turning her head a little, and climbed up to sit on a high, round stool draped with white velvet where he sometimes posed a client who preferred to be painted in the studio. The stool was secured to a platform that placed the subject so that he or she seemed adrift above the floor.

When he could speak, he said, "Stay exactly where you are until I help you down. You'll hurt yourself if we aren't careful."

"I'm quite safe," she said. "I've always been agile. But kindly don't come any closer or you may cause an accident."

Adam frowned. "You cannot stay there."

"I can and I will — until I wish to go elsewhere and do otherwise. I liked the way your chest felt, Adam. Hot and hard, and dangerous. Dangerous because I think there is no part of you which doesn't feel exactly the same. Is that painful?"

"No," he told her and instantly wished he hadn't been so sharp.

She smiled. "That's wonderful. But you did just confess that you are hot, and hard, and dangerous all over." She closed her eyes and shuddered.

"I want you down from there," he told her.

In response, the naughty girl pulled her skirts above her knees, high above her knees, and crossed one leg over the other.

Adam all but swallowed his tongue.

Sweat broke out between his shoulder blades and he moved to stand behind his work table — in an attempt to hide a certain attribute that was given to making scenes.

"Well," Desirée said, "of all the reactions I might have anticipated, having you run from me wasn't one of them."

Fledgling hedonist behind an innocent face. Very well, he would see just how brave she was. He left the shield of the table, pushed back his jacket and placed his hands on his hips. Several paces placed him before her and he braced his feet apart. One glance should be enough to warn her she was playing a game for which she wasn't as prepared as she thought.

He stood so close he could see the smooth texture of the skin on her limbs all the way to . . . Lace underskirts made of some fine stuff frothed at the tops of her thighs, but they barely covered the essentials.

"My, my, Adam," she said. "You are so finely built. I always knew you were, but — to be perhaps overly frank — I have not yet had all the opportunity I need to peruse the dimensions and the agility of your, er, Male Carrier."

"Male Carrier."

"Well, from my reading it does carry things, although not for long before it gets rid of them." She shrugged, glanced down at her bosom, and undid the top two buttons on her bodice. "I find I have swelled somewhat myself and I think it helps if I make more room." She pointed at his *Male Carrier* and made vague circles with a forefinger. "In fact, feel free to make more room there if it would help. Loosen things up a bit, I know you'll feel ever so much better."

"Stop this at once," Adam told her. "I can't imagine what has got into you or what you hope to achieve by such behavior."

Once more she held onto her skirts, and uncrossed and recrossed her legs. She bent to pull off her slippers and Adam saw what happened when she made "more room" in her bodice. She did not have large breasts but they were large enough and when they fell forward his mouth dried out at the idea of pressing his face between them.

He sighed. "You truly are an innocent with too much courage. You don't have any idea what your actions may be doing to me."

"Of course I have an idea, you mutton head. I can see what's happening to you."

Adam sniffed at that. "I advise you not to call a man mutton head unless you are certain you will suffer no reprisal."

"Dimwit, that's what it means. And oh, please, do exact some sort of reprisal on me." She undid another button, and another. "If you aren't careful, you'll poke a hole in your trousers."

He took a step toward her and tripped over Halibut, who rushed away, wailing. "Drat. I'm sorry," he said to the cat who retreated beneath the bed.

"Now see what you've done," Desirée said. "Poor, poor, Halibut."

Adam turned back to her and shook his head. "You are determined to be ruined. Why?"

Her dress was about her elbows and hips and she had placed her hands on the stool behind her to brace herself — and to thrust the tilted tips of her breasts out to their best advantage.

Adam made the instant decision that any pose would show them off to magnificent advantage.

Her rib cage was small and her waist smaller. He could see her navel and the gentle swell of her hips. And . . . "I shall stand outside while you dress, then take you home." He was a man, only a man, and he wanted to take her. "*Desirée*, are you — aren't you wearing any intimate garments beneath that dress?"

"Not one." She smiled charmingly. "Why?"

"To make it easier to undress, so that I can offer myself to you." Holding up her skirts, she slid lightly to the platform and jumped to the floor. And she ran at him, pulling her arms from her sleeves as she went. In front of him, she stopped and she also stopped smiling. "Do I appeal to you? As a woman, I mean?"

Adam put his hands in his pockets and cursed, not quite quietly enough. She tossed her head and frowned at him.

"Of course you appeal to me as a woman. You didn't have to take most of your clothes off to prove that."

"Oh, but I did, I had to be sure I had the power to arouse you." She smiled again. "And I believe what you say. I do. I already thought so from what I saw. And from a certain small examination on a previous occasion. It's really most exciting." She was holding her dress to stop it from falling to the floor.

"Some of a man's reactions have little to do with affection. Do you understand that? Men are susceptible to the physical. I believe women are also, but to a lesser degree. A woman thinks first of attachments of the heart. Men are preoccupied with the body, with certain — certain acts."

"And that is how it is for you with me?" She pressed her lips together to stop them from quivering. "I knew some of this but still I feel foolish. You're right, I am a romantic."

"I didn't say that's how it is with me when I am with you," Adam said. "But I don't want you to elevate me to something more than human. I have cared about you from the day we met — as a dear and special woman who has blessed me with her trust. You have mine, too, Desirée, you always will."

Adam retrieved her belt, slung it quickly around her and fastened it. He waved a hand at her. "Now, put on the rest of this thing."

He heard her swallow before she said, "I want you to kiss me first."

"No."

"Please, Adam." Her eyebrows turned up in the middle and she looked tragic. "Just for me, will you do it? I have the most wonderful plan worked out. In fact, I have already made an important arrangement — or I've sent it on its way."

He stood with a shoulder to her.

"Ad-am. Please. Two kisses — no, three — and I shall not ask again. At least,

I'll try not to. And then we shall talk about how to make sure we can take care of each other while we track down the evil ones."

"No." The last thing he wanted was Desirée involving herself in his business. And what was going on was his business.

A thought, unexpected and horrifying, numbed Adam. He had a sickening notion that he knew why the unpleasantness of today had occurred, and who had instigated it. Every word her attacker had spoken to Desirée might have been an attempt to ensure that this idea would never come to him.

Gilbert had said, *"Stop mooning around after a woman so far above your own station. I believe you are only making such a public show with her now because you want your brother to be jealous."*

"Adam?" Desirée's voice had grown uncertain and soft. "You may not think you need me, but you do, and I certainly need you. I believe far worse things lay ahead than behind."

"Desirée," he said, stopping himself from looking at her with the greatest difficulty. "I will keep you safe or die in the attempt. But if you interfere with what I do, you could hurt both of us."

"I shall not do that. In fact, I believe . . .

no matter. I shall not press you for now."

"Thank you." The warning letter he'd received hadn't been written by Gilbert. His energy needed to be used in solving the mystery. "It's late, Desirée."

"You're right," she said. "And I should go, but first, my kisses please or I shall never sleep."

"I can't kiss you while you're like that."

She sighed. "Of course you can. Unfortunately you are a man of iron and I cannot move you at all. But the least you can do is allow me to pretend otherwise." He didn't hear her move before she stood in front of him. "Let me dream that you want me and cannot stop yourself from touching me."

"You are impossible," he told her. "You will have your own way no matter what you must do to get it." And under other circumstances she would have to do very little. As it was he must protect her virtue for another.

His temples thudded.

"Thank you, Adam," she said, closing her eyes and puckering her mouth.

For an instant he glanced downward, just an instant. He was no saint.

The next instant, she ran her fingers into his hair and pulled his face to a breast. She pressed the nipple to his mouth. "The first kiss," she said. "I must know how it feels."

Oh, drat, to fight her over this would be dastardly. He opened his mouth and sucked the nipple in, used the end of his tongue to tease the hard tip until she panted. His own eyes closed and he widened his lips, drawing as much of her inside as he could.

He heard her pant, but only at a distance.

Spanning her waist and feeling how she trembled, he nuzzled between her breasts and took the other nipple in his mouth. This he kissed and nipped until he feared he would disgrace himself, and he released her.

"Oh, Adam."

He straightened and looked down into her eyes, eyes that swam with tears. And the tears slid free to course down her cheeks.

"I've frightened you. I knew I would. I told you this was a terrible idea. I shall never forgive —"

"Now my mouth."

He drew in a breath. Desirée stood on her toes and offered him her parted lips. Their kiss went on and on and Adam couldn't keep himself from passing his hands over her naked flesh.

Damn his conscience. All he would get for being a responsible gentleman would be the honor of thinking about her in another man's arms. And what would that benefit him? Why not go ahead and force Jean-Marc's hand?

At last he took his mouth away and dropped his hands, and Desirée whispered, "I could not refuse you, could I, when I knew what you wanted and could give it to you?"

He shook his head and felt a little dizzy. She confused him, and so did the faraway expression in her eyes.

"Of course I am yours whenever you send for me. Yes, yes, I will come to your bed and do whatever you ask. I am ready for you to teach me how to be an exciting, imaginative lover."

This must be the aftermath of unaccustomed passion that muddled her thoughts and words. She'd suffered a shock.

A start, a faint blush and very quickly she replaced the bodice of her dress — and he watched as she covered each breast, did up the buttons, smoothed out wrinkles. She went to her cloak and removed a pair of fine, embroidered stockings from an inside pocket.

She sat on the couch and revealed first one limb, then the other, while she smoothed on the pretty lace things.

Adam caught sight of a flash of darkness between her thighs and turned away. He wanted no more glimpses of things forbidden to him.

"There," Desirée said, sounding pleased with herself. "Please sit with me again. I have to tell you something important and we may not have much more time since we have used up so much."

He didn't argue, didn't attempt to defend himself, just sat as far from her as possible on the couch.

"I hired a messenger with the very best of credentials," she said. "By now he will have been on the road for hours."

Puzzled, he looked sideways at her.

"He rides north, to Ross and Finch, with a plea for their help. He doesn't know the contents of my letter."

Adam rubbed his eyes. "Help with what? You need to sleep. When you wake up again you will be less disturbed."

Desirée slid closer.

Unless he got up, which he wasn't about to do, Adam had no place farther to slide.

She slid some more, and some more until her thigh pressed his and her weight rested against him. She put her head on his shoulder. "I have already explained what must be obvious to you. We have no choice but to be together at all times. I'll be on watch for you and you'll be on watch for me."

"Impossible. You have been warned that I am a danger to you."

"Possible," she said, all defiance. "I am not easily frightened by blowhards."

"You know you must marry appropriately. For that to happen you cannot be known to keep company with another man."

"You are appropriate for me. It doesn't matter what others think, I *know* that without you I have no . . . I tried to leave you and you see what happened?" She held up her palms. "I couldn't. There is a way for us, Adam. We will elope and get married."

He flinched. Each breath seared his throat. She was a princess and only twenty years old. He was a commoner, a painter making his own way and almost fifteen years her senior. Unlike many men his age, he did not think it was his due to take the flower of a girl's womanhood. He could not take his eyes from hers. Not lying with her — no matter the consequences —

made a farce of his honor because he wanted to, oh how he wanted to.

Desirée looked back at him with her soul in her eyes. "There will, of course, be nothing between us since you don't really want it," she said. "You came through the test with flying colors. You wanted me in *that* way but only with your body, not your mind. But you are too honorable to *do* it."

He was cursed. That was it, someone had put a curse on him. "You don't know how I feel . . . you don't know what you're talking about. This is all wild thinking, Desirée."

"Not wild, intelligent. The point is that Ross and Finch will witness the wedding — they'll do it for you because you want them to. I already know the high esteem in which they hold you. Then, as a married couple, we can spend all of our time together. Later, of course, we will explain the truth and, given the reason, Jean-Marc will forgive us. He will even think us daring and be grateful we have dealt with our troubles successfully."

"Look." He had to take command, to stop this ridiculousness before she managed to bear him away on her enthusiasm. "Even if we did this, we would have to return to London. I have work to do. In case you've forgotten, I've a living to make."

"Of course you do and that's as it should be," she said and got up. She swung her cloak around her shoulders, retrieved her slippers and marched to stand beside the bed. She studied it hard, then looked about the attic. "Cheerful. Very cheerful." Before he could marshal the wit to stop her, she rolled up the carpet she'd been standing on, hefted it onto the bed and arranged it down the middle. "There, that's perfect. We will be able to keep up appearances while preserving our reputations. A bundling board. Brilliant, don't you think?"

Spivey here!

Knowing you lot, you've been too busy bruising your eyeballs on unmentionable goings-on to notice what has happened. Bless my socks, they're going to do it, y'know. And I do believe I'm going to laugh. Yes. Tee-hee, they're going to do it.

19

Reverend Lumpit, pacing the foyer while he read a book, presumably of prayer, was an unwelcome sight to Desirée, and she could imagine how Adam felt about the situation.

After leaving the attic, they had stopped to speak with Desirée's "chaperon." Barstow, her demeanor pleasant, had informed them that since Lady Hester had an early morning appointment, she'd retired. Barstow did add, "Some hours ago," with a too-innocent expression.

They had reached the foot of the stairs, but Lumpit had stopped with his back to them while he carefully examined a man-sized wooden ewer carved in the shape of a swan and mounted on a plinth. The clergyman stroked the vessel and murmured to himself.

Desirée held onto the banister. Adam pulled her cloak closer about her neck and she leaned back against him. Happiness made her smile, probably foolishly if anyone were looking at her, but just to feel his touch was absurdly heady.

From her right and very close by came a sound. It wasn't like any sound Desirée had heard before. Unearthly, that's what it was. She looked over her shoulder at Adam, who watched Lumpit. "Adam," she whispered. "Did you hear that?"

"What?"

It happened again. "*That.* Someone laughing, but it's not normal."

"Your imagination is running away with you. Understandable after all you've been through. Come little one, I'll get you home."

A wheeze, a snort through a narrow nose, and, ever so softly, the rusty chortling — she heard them again. "Adam!" She turned and gripped his arm. "It's — it's right here." She slapped the top of the newel post with the flat of a hand. "Listen."

A mighty crash reverberated through the quiet house. Adam leaped around Desirée and ran to Lumpit who had dropped his book and stood, his fingers curled beneath his wobbling chins, staring at the frightful spectacle of Lady Hester's valuable ewer lying on the very hard stone tiles. The sculpture had been knocked from its plinth. A distressing scatter of wooden debris had slithered in all directions.

Reverend Lumpit — Desirée frowned when she recalled that the man had been referred to as a curate. Since he clearly had not gained a more elevated post in the church one wondered about his title. *Vicar in Residence.* No matter. Reverend Lumpit had faced Adam as he appeared and was, even now, babbling about the shock to his delicate constitution and how irresponsible it was to have such things as the oversized ewer so carelessly placed.

"It'll be all right," Adam said. "Aye, it'll be fine. Why not go into 7A and pour yourself a settling drink."

Lumpit frowned. His red lips pushed out in a pout and his shiny face registered deep disapproval. "Imbibing out of weakness is a poor idea, Mr. Chillworth. This must be cleaned up." He actually looked from the floor to Desirée with some hope.

The under-butler, Evans, arrived from below stairs with Toby in his nightshirt and trotting at his heels. Evans quickly assessed the damage. "We can put this fellow back in his place," he told Toby who, with Adam's assistance, immediately helped grapple the swan back onto its platform. Unfortunately the many missing parts were obvious. Tips of feathers were sadly lacking and the rather jaunty beak had lost an inch or so. "We'll find a box for all the pieces and wait until the morning to find out what Her Ladyship wishes to do."

Lumpit glared at Toby. "Boys rushing around. Bound to disturb things." He took a deep breath, straining his cassock until it gaped at each button. His childish blue eyes and the manner in which he combed his thin hair forward reminded Desirée of some refugee from the Roman Empire.

Evans looked at the clergyman with pure dislike. "I assure you, sir, that Toby had nothing to do with whatever happened here. Now, if you'll excuse us, we'll get what we need."

"Above his station," Lumpit said once Evans was out of earshot. Not a particularly tall man, Lumpit's girth was considerable and he gave off ire in waves that threatened to pop his buttons from their holes. He fastened his baby-blue eyes on Desirée. "Have you no sense, Princess Desirée — I know that's who you are because you've been pointed out to me. You didn't deign to meet me before you left for that horrid place where your father lives."

She said, "How do you do?" but didn't offer her hand.

"Adam Chillworth is a painter — of no particular worth as far as I know. You are a princess and you are also extremely young. Obviously you have sneaked away from your bed and your home to engage in a clandestine meeting with this one." He jerked his head at Adam. "Fortunately for you I am a man of God and not given to gossip. And I'll make sure the servants have nothing to say about any of this, either. But I shall have to speak to your brother, Your Highness. My conscience would never rest if I pretended I hadn't seen what I have seen."

"The Princess's brother is aware she's here," Adam said. "Lady Hester has been the chaperon while the Princess and I had a discussion."

"You need spiritual guidance." Lumpit indicated the battered swan. "I've always maintained that things, particularly unpleasant things, happen for a reason. Clearly I was intended to be delayed here so that I would see the two of you skulking around and immediately set about saving your souls — and other things."

Adam's face had reddened. "Good to talk to you, Lumpit. Hope I'll run into you another time. Now, if you'll excuse us."

Lumpit clasped his hands over his

stomach. "Can't do that, I'm afraid. I'll have to insist upon coming with you now."

Larch Lumpit took a step closer to Desirée and sent up a howl. For no apparent reason, his feet shot from beneath him and rose so high in the air that the first parts of him to hit the stones were his shoulders and the back of his head. A closet flew open and the coats and umbrellas inside flew into the foyer. The magnificent chandelier overhead swung and jingled like hundreds of tiny bells.

Desirée went to Adam's side and said, "How did that happen? One minute he was standing there, the next he was in the air."

"Most puzzling," Adam said, getting down to look closely into Lumpit's face. "He hit the floor hard enough to shake the house. Perhaps we'd better send for a doctor."

"I don't need a doctor," Lumpit thundered. "There is something amiss in this house. A reaction to sin, I should think. I shall hasten to play my part in putting it to rights. An exorcism may be in order."

Desirée was too annoyed by Lumpit's pompous attitude to inform the two men that the fall had nothing to do with chandeliers swinging, or cupboards flying open and all the clothes inside leaping out. She might also have pressed for intelligent considerations of the sounds she'd heard, sounds almost definitely coming from a wooden newel post!

There was a rap at the front door and it opened to admit Verbeux. The cold outside, and his warm breath, had fogged his glasses. He took them off and found a handkerchief. Desirée watched him with some trepidation. She had no doubt but that Jean-Marc had sent him to find her.

"You seem somewhat upset, sir," Verbeux said to Lumpit. "If there's something I can do to help you, all you have to do is ask. Surely it's cold on the floor. Let me help you up."

With an ill-humored scowl, Lumpit allowed himself to be hauled to his feet.

Verbeux puffed a bit. Desirée didn't recall seeing Jean-Marc's adviser and right-hand man without his spectacles and the fine quality of his dark, long-lashed eyes captured her attention. He wore his dark hair combed straight back but curls escaped his ministrations and one or two fell over his forehead, while others touched his collar. Since she'd first met him, he'd sported a mustache and goatee. She smiled, thinking that there seemed to be a rekindled interest in gentlemen having beards. Rolly Spade-Filbert did, too — and Sir Robert Brodie. But she stared at Verbeux, such a handsome, clever man, and so alone now that he had lost his wife, and she felt sad for him. His wife, Lady Upchurch, Ila, had been financially destitute and in search of a husband. She had chosen Jean-Marc, until she fell for the enigmatic Frenchman, and he for her. They had been very happy but for so short a time.

"Jean-Marc asked me to walk over and escort you," Verbeux said to Desirée. He looked at Adam. "Is it possible that we could talk before leaving? You, too, of course, Princess."

"Marvelous idea," Lumpit said, so loudly Desirée expected a frightened congregation in the foyer at any moment. Lumpit slapped his thighs. "Come on in to 7A. My home is your home and you can be comfortable there. I shall call to have the fire made up and hot chocolate brought for the Princess. I'm sure I can interest you fellows in a brandy."

Verbeux stared after Lumpit, then at Adam and Desirée who promptly looked at each other. "You are kind, sir," Verbeux said to Lumpit, who had already thrown his door open wide.

"Mr. Lumpit is always kind," Desirée said. "And we must get together soon — perhaps for tea at Number 17?"

Lumpit's suspiciously pinched little mouth parted in a self-deprecating smile. "I should be charmed." He executed a bobbing bow.

"Consider it arranged then," Verbeux said, not glancing at Desirée. Lumpit entered his rooms with a light step, apparently having already forgotten his invitation for them to join him there.

"Mon Dieu," Verbeux murmured. "That was dangerously close. The sitting room do you suppose?" He pointed to the red sitting room.

Adam nodded. He took off Desirée's cloak and held her elbow until she was settled in one of the room's three couches, and as close as possible to the dying fire. He put his own cloak aside with hers and Verbeux placed his on top.

Verbeux sat on the edge of one of the matching couches grouped before the fire. He was separated from Desirée by the portion of her own sofa she wasn't using. Adam promptly sat beside her and the three of them huddled forward, toward each other.

Desirée's stomach turned over slowly. Before they'd even left the attic Adam had resembled a human thunder cloud. His frown was deeper than ever now. Everything rested on his shoulders. He could give her plan away and it would be over — and he might come to rue his failure to see the danger she saw. Whatever his decision, the relationship they'd shared would never be the same.

She couldn't hold her tongue any longer. "What is it, Verbeux? Has something happened?"

Verbeux regarded them both. He seemed not even to blink but Desirée had known him long enough to see when he was troubled. He gripped his knees and continued to watch them.

"Adam," he said suddenly, "perhaps Princess Desirée would be less anxious if you held her hand."

She jumped and felt all color drain from her face. He did know more than he should.

Adam looked at her sideways and the corner of his mouth turned up. He offered her his hand and she put hers on top. He entwined their fingers.

"You are making plans to elope."

Desirée let out a small cry. She squeezed

Adam's hand tightly.

"How did you know that?" Adam asked and, disturbed as she was, Desirée noted he didn't deny it was true.

"Intelligence is my business," Verbeux said. "Finding things out has always been part of my duties."

"So Jean-Marc knows," Desirée said. She searched her mind for a way to leave with Adam before her brother could lock her in a room somewhere and keep her there until the morning of her marriage to a total stranger.

Hopeless.

"I am deeply afraid that I am not expressing myself well, but no, the Count doesn't know. And I shall not tell him. But it is essential for you to carry out your plan quickly. It's imperative. Telling the Count will be your responsibility once you return to London.

"You, Chillworth, are a man of honor, but that honor will be tested. The Princess must be, er, intact since there will be an annulment once it is safe.

"You both know that a marriage between you cannot work over time, but for a short while it will distract whoever is plotting to acquire the Princess. I intend to keep my eyes on you because I believe this villain will reveal himself and then we shall have him."

Desirée couldn't think of anything to say and apparently Adam was afflicted with the same condition.

"You are going to the care of Viscount Kilrood and his lady — good, responsible people. I have sent my own message of explanation to back up yours, Your Highness, and fully expect their cooperation. Naturally, when you have gone through this marriage, it will be necessary to confide in those closest to you, including Count Etranger. Everyone we know we can trust must draw close around you. They will understand, but not without a good deal of shouting and marching about on the Count's part. That can be handled. But my greater concern is making sure the threat has passed."

Adam said, "I continue to feel I am the problem here and Desirée is being used in some bizarre part of the plot."

"You cannot be sure," she told him. "I think we are both part of this plan."

"So do I," Verbeux said and she grew even more tense. "The Princess because someone has designs on her, and you, Chillworth, because you threaten those designs."

She had not had an easy life but tonight she knew the greatest fear of all: losing the man she loved. "Adam, I cannot bear to have you out of my sight."

Adam shocked her by putting an arm around her shoulders and pulling her against him. He kissed her forehead and shushed her. "How soon must we leave?" he asked Verbeux.

"I understand you have commitments to your work. If you go in, say, two nights, it will give me plenty of opportunity to arrange everything and you can inform your clients you will be gone a few days."

A few days? Desirée would have liked to have Adam to herself for much longer.

"I will take the Princess home and I must ask you to return to your rooms and lock the door. I will bring Desirée tomorrow and you can make your plans. By then I will have more to tell you. You do understand that you must keep this marriage as quiet as possible? It is for the Princess's protection. On the Count's behalf, I am putting her into your care — I have also given up fighting the impossible. She will come to you no matter how dire the warnings. As she has said, you will watch her back and she will watch yours."

"How do you know I said that?" Desirée

was outraged at the betrayal.

"It doesn't matter. In turn I shall watch both of your backs."

She caught at Adam's sleeve and held on. "You don't understand, either of you. I told only one person — besides you — and then I had no choice because I needed help with my plans. Now they are given away and that can only mean . . . We are trapped!"

Adam comforted her, but didn't take his eyes from Verbeux's face.

"You are not trapped because you are a fine judge of character and your confidence has been protected."

"But you know. You were told." The room might be chilly but Desirée's skin stung with heat all over.

"She had no one else to turn to," Verbeux said. "Remember, we have a history of sorts and that doesn't exist for her with anyone else."

"What are you talking about?" Adam asked.

"Anne Williams," Verbeux said, his expression troubled.

"She betrayed Desirée's confidences?" Adam said. "Yet you say she is trustworthy?"

Verbeux pointed a steady finger at

Desirée. "Listen quietly and do not cry out. Anne is your friend, but she has suffered terribly this day. If she were not so strong, she would have used her privileged knowledge in an attempt to save herself."

Desirée slapped her hands over her mouth.

"While she was sleeping, after the two of you had been through so much, she was assaulted by a man who crept into her bed."

Desirée shook her head repeatedly and cried.

"Poor Anne," Adam said, holding Desirée firmly.

Verbeux continued. "His behavior was unspeakable and I still don't know that he didn't . . . He told her she was to spy on the Princess and be ready to report what she'd found out by the next time he visits her. If she doesn't find answers to the questions he has asked, he suggests she will wish she had."

Spivey here again.

My ewer! That despicable Lumpit and his despicable poking and pushing have ruined it. A Joshua Barnsworthy carving — this is too much. I can only hope that Hester retains a worthy artisan to make a repair.

271

Oh, dash it all, it's only a ewer. In truth I am using it to divert myself from my feelings. What did you say? Yes, I do have feelings and I am cast down. What manner of animal posing as a man abuses a young woman like Anne Williams? He shall suffer. I shall seek him out and punish him. No, I am not becoming softer, but I am a gentleman — or was — still am in the ways that matter.

Do not presume to accuse me of putting on — what did you call them? — magic acts? Such insults. You may think whatever you wish to think. Should be able to control myself, you say? At least to keep my mouth shut in living company. Rot, that's what I say to you.

And don't think I won't watch over young Princess Desirée also. What a charming and unaffected woman she has grown to be. Too bad her brother is such a stuffy ass.

Excuse me. I was simply being honest.

It will be a grim day if Chillworth ever makes that sweet creature unhappy — in the house Jean-Marc will give them as a wedding present once he stops threatening to call his new brother-in-law out.

There is the matter of an annulment. Now Consummation is difficult to prove, my friends. In fact I shall not trouble myself about it too much. Let nature take its course.

20

The young soldier in his red jacket, sword at his hip, became more flushed as the hours went by. The attic wasn't particularly warm, but the uniform was. Adam pitied him, but he also respected him for refusing to pose amid furs, silks, famous family paintings and an overall vulgar display at his mother's excessive house.

Captain Lord Summerfield was young for his military rank but no doubt significant strings had been pulled. His rise to the top was likely to be extraordinary. A second son, he was following the arrangements made for him with grace.

"Would you like some water?" Adam asked. "This is really coming along well. Your mother will be pleased." He was pleased he'd used heavy black silk on the stool. "Not that a handsome subject is difficult to reproduce."

"Mother wants a painting of me in all

this paraphernalia to add to her gallery. She's in a hurry because she's afraid I'll get killed before the job can be finished."

"You are harsh on your parent, My Lord," Adam remarked, but couldn't help smiling.

Halibut had chosen to curl into the silk beside the boot Summerfield rested on the floor. His other knee was raised with the heel of the boot hooked against the silk and over a rung of the stool. The young man had endeared himself to Adam by insisting the cat be included in the portrait, and there on the canvas was a pleased-looking Halibut.

Arrangements for the cat's care would not be made until the last moment when, as Adam and Desirée had decided, they would ask Lady Hester to take him in. Apart from Anne and Verbeux, she would be the only one with knowledge of their plans. Adam knew she would be pleased.

Tonight they would leave. With the warnings he had received about how he was to behave toward Desirée, he should feel little excitement, yet he felt he might boil over with joy. Whatever the circumstances, he and Desirée would be together, at least for a while, and it was more than he had ever allowed himself to dream about. An arrangement made for the sake of expediency might not be the stuff of a great romance, but he wanted whatever he could have with Desirée.

Tonight. Yesterday, last night and this morning had been a nightmare of waiting.

"You become lost in your painting, Mr. Chillworth. You work in a fever," Lord Summerfield said.

Adam raised his brush from the canvas and said, "Passion causes a kind of fever in most of us, don't you think?"

Summerfield was still considering his answer when Old Coot opened the door without knocking and shuffled forward to present Adam with a card, which, at first, Adam couldn't seem to read.

Coot puffed quite alarmingly. "Can't ever find Evans, or anyone else useful, when they're needed. You can see why I had to come myself and at once. She would not take a seat in the sitting room and keeps saying she should probably leave since you must be working."

Adam's fingertips felt numb. He read his mother's name several times before the blood rushed back to his head.

"I say," Summerfield said and hopped down off the stool. "Sounds like my cue to get lost. I'll admit I'm a bit over warm, and

I'd like to be outside. All right with you if we stop?"

Adam admired him for his impeccable manners and easygoing personality. "Not at all. I leave London tonight but will return in a few days. Shall we say Friday morning of next week?" This was the message he'd intended to give the man anyway.

"Perfect." Summerfield gave Adam a mock salute and nodded at Coot when he passed him.

Coot waited until the soldier's boots made a distant thump on the stairs and said, "They don't make fighting men the way they used to." He didn't continue and Adam didn't press him for an explanation.

"You can't leave a lady —"

"No," Adam said. "The lady is my mother."

"Thought she might be. You look like her. Visiting from the country, is she? I've heard about your brother, but not your mother. Thought she must have died, like your father."

The blatant digging for information was obvious to Adam but he knew the best way to close this unfortunate subject. "My father, Mr. Gilbert Chillworth, is very much alive and farms up north. I think it would be better if my mother came up here.

Would you ask her to do so, please?"

Coot's incoherent mumblings accompanied the man on his mission.

Adam kept on his smock and left the paint on his hands. His family didn't want to accept what he was, but he had no intention of pretending to be something different.

What did his mother want? He hadn't seen her for several years but now he would meet her for the second time in days. Of course, by the time Coot finally reached the lobby, the lady might well have changed her mind and left.

The papers his father had given him to read were well hidden — his mother must never see them. He straightened the drape on the stool, then spied the carpet he'd left on the bed since Desirée put it there. He didn't know exactly why except that he was probably trying to become accustomed to the new situation that lay ahead.

Leaving the rolled up carpet on the bed — his mother could think what she wanted to think — he pounded on sofa cushions and straightened the table in front. He was grateful to have made such progress in turning his cramped space into what Desirée considered cozy.

He looked for somewhere to put away

his bucket filled with soaking dirty dishes bound for the scullery, but when he heard light steps approaching, dishes didn't seem to matter.

His mother had left her family more than half his lifetime ago. Why would she seek him out now, and why would he feel the same raw mix of love and betrayal as he had when a teenager? At least he now had some insight into why his parents had fought when he was a child. In his account, Gilbert wrote that his wife had tricked him into having another child. He had never wanted Adam but, nevertheless, it was disappointment in their younger son that drove the couple apart. Adam blamed his father, but his mother should not have left her children.

She was standing outside his door. Even if logic didn't tell him she'd reached the top of his stairs, he would feel her there.

She knocked. A single, uncertain knock.

Adam went at once to open the door and stand back, spreading an arm to welcome her into his home. The lady was about to suffer another shock about her daubing younger son.

"Good day to you, Mother. You've surprised me." He wanted to tell her how young she looked and how beautiful in a carriage dress of lavender gros de Naples and a pelisse with a short cape of India muslin. When he'd been a child he had found it impossible to look away from this ethereal woman, and today she cast a similar spell. Her Lyonese hat of plum-colored crepe with lavender and pink stripes under the brim delighted him, as did the pink gauze and roses on its crown. Her curly hair was as black as ever.

She stood before him, studying him, a faint but unmistakable quirk at the corners of her lovely mouth. Then she gave a small, unconvincing laugh. "I thought you might tell the butler to turn me away."

"You are the one who chose to do all the turning away."

"Perhaps."

Tears welled in her violet eyes and she averted her face. "This is a comfortable place and so like you," she said. "When you were little you always found a private nook for yourself where you could feel closed in and able to explore your thoughts alone. And read, of course. You have always been almost frighteningly intelligent."

Once he'd accepted that she knew his habits so well. Now he wondered if she ever did or if she was merely adept at sum-ming up a given situation and saying the right words.

"Too intelligent to waste my mind on painting?" He didn't like himself for his meanness.

Mama frowned in puzzlement. "Oh, no. It would not be possible to get the very essence of a subject onto a canvas if you weren't intelligent. And I have been told that you do exactly that."

He felt bemused. Why would she say such things now? "What brings you here?" He should want to become close to her again, but he wasn't sure that's what she wanted and wouldn't risk being hurt and embarrassed again. And she'd already let him know how unimportant he was to her by leaving him and never making contact.

"I have two reasons to be here," she said. "You, and Lucas."

She walked around him and studied the painting of the young soldier. It was far from finished but he was having a day when he thought the piece quite good.

"It's the man who passed me downstairs," she said. "You are so talented. Little wonder you are sought out all over London."

He looked at his hands and tried to collect himself. These didn't sound like words from the woman who considered his occupation degrading enough to leave her family and pretend he never existed.

"This has to be the younger Summerfield boy. I didn't study him downstairs but he is very much like his mother. A handsome woman. I saw the slightest sign of recognition when he looked at me but he was probably fifteen when last we met."

"He's a natural subject. Very straightforward. It always shows."

"You're right," she said, standing a little closer. "My favorites are the small studies you did of all the Blummidge grandchildren. So sweet. Is it true that you painted Lady Conygham —" she smiled behind a hand "— in nothing but her jewels?"

Her girlish curiosity amused him. "Not exactly."

Mama looked disappointed. "Well you should have heard that old Dowager Duchess of Franchot crowing about the portraits of her family.

"And I was amazed to learn that poor woman who married Lord Byron allowed their daughter to sit for you."

"Aye." He neither encouraged nor discouraged the line of conversation. "One feels a deep intelligence in that one. She may be destined for greatness."

"Isn't it true that Wellington had you copy a painting of Harriet Wilson and make her look a lot younger?"

"How do you know all these things, Mama?" He had an unsettled sensation that his well-connected mother and grandmother might have had something to do with helping his career to its current considerable success. The thought distressed him. After his father had threatened to throw him out if he didn't give up painting — because it had destroyed his parents' marriage — he left at once, asking nothing of his family and dreaming of showing them he didn't need their help.

Lady Elspeth pretended she hadn't heard Adam's question. "How sweet to have a cat in the picture of Summerfield," she said.

There had been the "chance" encounter outside Apsley House. Chance or design?

"That is Princess Desirée's cat." What point could there be in avoiding mention of Desirée. He wished she were with him now — so violently did he wish it that sweat broke out on his brow. He prayed this rare girl would be happy, no matter what came their way, but he prayed even harder that the hours would slip fast away until he was able to put his arms around her again. Verbeux had taken away any shred of doubt about the elopement but seemed determined that Adam understand Desirée would be his wife in name only, and not for longer than necessary. Perhaps he would comply . . .

He realized his mother was watching him. "That girl you were so eager to protect when we all met in the street. Princess Desirée. An odd alliance, wouldn't you say — between the two of you? I understand she's illegitimate."

Adam crossed his arms and shook his head. "How stories do get twisted. Why do you care about Desirée and her situation?"

His mother turned solemn eyes on his face. "Because you care about her. I found her delightful. She would have been within her rights to throw my silly coins at me."

"Desirée would never do such a thing. She has a rare gift, she sees a situation from all angles."

Halibut chose that moment to wind himself in Mama's skirts.

"He likes it here," Adam said. "Spends time with me when the Princess has other duties."

"He likes you," she said and laughed. "You always did have a way with children and animals."

He looked up quickly to judge whether she was referring to Desirée as a child but concluded he was being too touchy.

His mother straightened up rapidly and took a backward step. Her cry was muffled and Adam looked closely at Halibut. A torn apart, stringy and partially eaten chicken leg held his mouth in a wide smile. *Dratted cat.*

"He's offering you some of his treat to show how much he likes you."

Clearly unimpressed, Mama's smile didn't convince him one bit. "Adam, do you have time to talk with me. I have a great deal on my mind."

For years he'd rehearsed how, if he were ever face-to-face with this woman again, he would pretend he didn't as much as know her. But he had grown up.

"Of course I have time. Please sit down. Should you like tea, or a sherry perhaps."

"Nothing, thank you," she said and passed up the comfortable couch in favor of a straight-back cane chair. "I will do my best to be brief. Before I start, I want to make it understood that I do not expect you to agree to my request, but I have nowhere else to go and must at least try."

Buying time, Adam took off his smock

and hung it on a hook. He took up an oily rag and removed the worst of the paint from his hands before washing them. And all the time his tension rose.

He sat on the couch and stretched out his legs.

"You aren't going to help me, are you?" Lady Elspeth said. "But why should you? First I want to tell you that I love you with my heart and soul, that I always have, and that my suffering at being separated from you has been beyond all."

He felt he couldn't breathe.

"I know you cannot possibly understand what happened. I just ask you to try to find a little affection for me.

"Now, to Lucas. I understand the two of you are becoming good friends. Lucas has mentioned it and his happiness shows. For the first time in a year or more, I see light-heartedness in his eyes and I thank you for giving him that. He did not treat you well when you were younger."

"Boyish stuff," Adam said, at last able to make his voice work. "Happens all the time."

"I suppose. Adam, I'm in a pretty fix and I don't know a way out of it. I cannot turn to my mother again. Already she has spent too much on me."

"Surely you still get your allowance from Father."

Her mouth trembled and she tried to hold her lips tight together.

"Mama?"

"I have the allowance my father arranged for me. If it weren't for that I should have been unable to do even as much as I have for Lucas. And he lives at Manthy House, which helps him greatly. He is good to his grandmother, who enjoys the attention."

"What has happened to Lucas?" Adam stopped himself from checking his watch. Soon Verbeux would bring Desirée.

"He isn't a bad man," she said. "Rolly used to be a terrible influence, but that has changed and now he is a source of wisdom for your brother."

Adam couldn't bring himself to agree. He still could not like Rolly. "Father provides for Lucas."

She produced a handkerchief and twisted it. The tears had disappeared. "Lucas has squandered considerable sums. He has tried to live far above his station, gambling in high stakes games, engaging in wild and wildly expensive parties. And then — Adam, you won't repeat this to anyone?"

"Not a word."

"He involved himself with a woman who became pregnant and said the child was his. She expected him to marry her. He refused, wouldn't even acknowledge there had ever been anything between them — even though they were known to have been together. She killed herself."

Adam pressed his fingers into his temples. "Where was his honor? Regardless of how he felt, if there was any chance the child was his he should at least have offered financial —"

"I know. When the girl's father realized there was nothing to be had from Lucas, he went to Gilbert and threatened to expose the whole thing. Gilbert paid but he treats Lucas appallingly and has cut off his allowance until he decides Lucas has reformed. Lucas is supposed to live very simply and stay away from any occasion of evil."

"Father is unrealistic," Adam said. "Nevertheless, Lucas should be horsewhipped."

"He's being punished every hour of every day. Now he thinks your father favors you rather than him —"

"And how dreadful that would be," Adam said before he could stop himself. "Why shouldn't father be nice to me rather than Lucas when it's always been the other way around? Oh, forgive me, I am petty. I wish Lucas no harm."

"Are you attempting to get your father to change his will and leave the bulk of his fortune to you — because he's angry with Lucas?"

Adam's mind became blank.

"I know this isn't the case," Mama said, "but your brother believes it's so and I want to help Lucas see the truth."

"My father came to see me," he said. "He wanted to reiterate all the things he blames me for, and to tell me that he's cutting me out of the small inheritance he was leaving me and stopping my allowance. I knew nothing of Father's situation with Lucas. None of this matters because I support myself very well." The thought of a woman killing herself because she had no hope outraged him. "Did the child die with his mother?"

Lady Elspeth shook her head. "I don't know. I was never even allowed to hear the girl's name." Lady Elspeth put her head in her hands and sobbed. Her shoulders heaved. She must have heard Adam move to go to her because she waved him away. "All my fault," she said. "One foolish mistake and I paid a great price, but I could have been stronger afterward. I thought you boys would do well with your father. I was wrong, of course. You needed me, too."

He had so many questions but didn't want to risk her pulling back and never finishing her story at all.

"Adam," she said, "you have a generous income from my dear father. I've been so glad he did that, particularly in light of your father's favoritism toward your brother. I don't know the details but I believe the sums are substantial. What I want to ask of you is that if it will not cause you difficulty, could you help Lucas get out of financial trouble — in the form of a loan, of course — and arrange your repayment with him? I don't like to suggest that you threaten him, but if you said that if he started gambling again you'd stop lending him money, he'd have to behave himself."

Her misery overwhelmed him but she'd shown him she didn't want him to get too close. "I have not accepted grandfather's trust."

Her head snapped up. "What are you saying? Of course you have."

"No, mother. I declined. Of course the trust was set up so that the solicitor and I would be the only ones with any knowledge of the money involved or what I chose to do with it."

Lady Elspeth, her face stark, had shifted to the edge of her chair. "Adam, surely you can access the money whenever you please."

At the moment he wished that were the case. "My wishes are reviewed every six months. I have recently reiterated my decision.

"I do have money of my own. Not a huge estate, but becoming quite satisfactory. I will have that talk with Lucas and arrange to pay him a small amount on a regular basis."

Mama leaped to her feet. "I am proud to be your mother, your undeserving mother, but please say nothing to Lucas. And don't concern yourself with me because I know what to do now. You are too straightforward to imagine the sums I'm talking about so put them out of your mind.

"I do ask you to continue to build a friendship with your brother because I think it will help him find some peace and security."

"I want to do that," Adam said, still wondering how he could help raise the money Lucas needed, even as he questioned if Lucas could possibly give him an excuse for his behavior toward a pregnant girl. "Please have faith that we shall do what must be done."

She tugged at her hat strings and took the thing off. She had changed so little. "I believe I will have that sherry now. Just a small one."

Adam went to the marble-topped cupboard where he kept his liquor and poured sherry into a finely cut crystal glass. He was placing it in his mother's hands when a bellowing voice was heard. A loud man, probably still in the foyer, was demanding, but what he demanded was indecipherable.

Lady Elspeth got out of her chair once more and went to stand behind it.

"Mama," Adam said, "are you all right?"

She nodded, but put down her sherry and replaced her hat. She located her gloves in her reticule and pulled them on. "I'm going to leave you to your work. Adam —" she looked at him in appeal "— your grandmother speaks of you every day. And every day she asks what I know of you and says how much she wants to see you. I don't ask you to make your mind up at once, but will you at least consider it?"

"Desirée says I will be a disgrace if I don't go."

"The girl has spirit. I like that. Let me

know what you decide."

"Tell Grandmama I will be visiting her and soon. Tell her I love her."

Once more tears filmed his mother's eyes and she dabbed at them with her handkerchief. "Thank you, Adam," she mumbled.

The bellowing grew closer, then stopped abruptly, but the owner of the big voice wasn't far away.

"Could you see me out, please?" Lady Elspeth asked in soft tones.

But she was too late to make her escape without encountering whoever had been shouting and backed as far as she could into a corner. A thumping sounded and the voice announced, "I'm coming in, Adam," before its owner threw open the door, marched into the room, and closed them all in. "Have you been keeping things from me? Things I have a right to know? Because if you have, by God you shall suffer for it. You're already above yourself, but if you've still got a notion to marry a daft Princess just to make Lucas look bad, you can forget it."

"What the hell do you mean?" Adam swallowed with difficulty and hoped this didn't mean Gilbert had found out the truth.

"Don't raise your voice to me, my boy. Rolly Spade-Filbert came to me on another matter. He mentioned how you are inseparable from this girl."

"So there we are," Adam said. "Rolly has already spoken for me."

"Well . . ." Gilbert rocked to his heels and curled his lip. "Rolly has been concerned for Lucas. Apparently he feels a bit low. Seeing your success, then getting some ideas about you and the Princess may have made him more depressed."

Why would my brother begrudge me happiness? At least his father had not found out about the elopement, but Adam still intended to find out if Lucas knew Rolly had made his troublemaking little visit.

A slight movement from Elspeth grabbed Gilbert's attention. "Good Lord," he said in a completely changed tone. "Elspeth, dear one, I didn't see you there. Look at you. It is as if not a day has passed since I first saw you."

Abruptly he remembered Adam's presence. "Get out, you. I'll deal with you later. Can't you see your mother and I need to be alone?"

Adam watched his mother's face, saw the fear in her eyes, fear tinged with dislike. "Should you like me to go, Mother?"

"No man has the right to order another out of his home," she said. "I shall leave at once."

Gilbert paled to the lips. "Absolutely not, I have learned what I came to learn."

"You have learned nothing," she said. "You heard a rumor about Adam and, as always, rather than take his part, you came roaring to accuse him. I suggest you look at your son's work. It humbles me, as it should you."

Gilbert glanced at Summerfield's portrait and moved a little closer. "Never understood these things myself but I suppose it's clever. Pay well, does it?"

"Well enough, thank you, Father."

"Aye, well, that's good then. You'll need it." The man turned to his estranged wife and the hunger Adam saw in his eyes rocked him. "How are you, Elspeth?" he asked in a low voice Adam didn't think he'd ever heard before.

"Well, thank you."

Gilbert looked into her eyes and Adam saw him swallow repeatedly. "And your mother?"

Elspeth actually smiled a little. "Her attitude toward life remains positive. She sees everything as possible and that keeps her mind and body healthy."

"I'm delighted," Gilbert said, never breaking his concentration on Lady Elspeth. "Your father was a good man but you inherited your spirit from your mother."

Adam began to feel like a voyeur.

His parents fell silent but it was as if they touched each other, embraced each other passionately without needing to move.

At last Mama said, "And you, Gilbert? How have you been?"

Gilbert raised his arms and let them fall to his sides. Such a handsome, vital man, with such lines of unhappiness around his eyes and mouth. "Good. Thank you very much for asking."

Lady Elspeth smiled again and nodded. "Good. You look vigorous and you haven't changed at all since we last met."

Didn't they say something about love being blind? The thought shook Adam. His parents were older and the years had left marks even if they were marks that only served to make them more handsome in a different way, but he was certain they didn't lie when they said they saw no change, one in the other. They were still in love.

Sadness, sudden and overwhelming, enveloped him.

"I must go down and find my cloak," Mama said. "It's still so cold. The snow is lovely but I'm grateful it isn't falling today."

"I'll come down and help you with your cloak," Gilbert said and Adam felt how desperate he was to prolong the meeting.

"That's not necessary, thank you. The old butler might think we considered him frail and I shouldn't like to shame him."

"No, no, of course not. Why didn't I think of that?"

Because you never would have thought of such things, Father. You have always been too angry.

"Your boots," Gilbert continued, looking down at Mama's feet. "They are lovely but surely not sturdy enough for such weather. The cold will strike at you through such thin soles."

Mama didn't lower her gaze quite quickly enough to hide the glimmer of tears on her lashes. "I don't have far to walk. But thank you for your concern."

"My carriage is outside," Gilbert said. "Allow me to escort you to Manthy House. I shall carry you over the snow."

Adam thought Mama might lose her composure entirely, but she straightened her back and managed a polite but remote smile. "You're too kind. But I have my own coach." She tied her hat ribbons a little tighter, slipped her reticule strings up to her elbow and walked toward the door.

Gilbert make a subtle move toward her. Adam doubted his father knew he'd done so.

Mama hesitated as she passed the man who was still her husband. So quickly a blink might have stolen the moment, she touched Gilbert's arm and bobbed to her toes to place the lightest of kisses on his cheek.

"Be happy," she said. Then she left.

With his fingertips on his face, Father stood where he was. He looked into a distance Adam could not see. "I am a fool," he murmured.

Adam felt sorry — for his parents, for Lucas and for himself. Two people who had loved one another had sacrificed that love for some disagreement — and he had been made the excuse. And those two people still loved each other, only they had dug such a wide ditch between them he doubted they could ever get across it.

Father seemed frozen in place.

"Why do you hate me?" Adam asked and couldn't believe he'd revealed himself so.

Gilbert looked at him, turned to stand in

front of him. He studied his son and Adam saw no sign of bitterness. "Hate you?" he said. "What I've done was all for nothing, but I cannot change the past."

21

Adam had left Desirée in Lady Hester's care. The Princess had not wanted him to go, particularly since he'd been so vague about his reason, but she'd bowed to his wishes. They still had a number of hours before they would leave and their packed bags were ready in Adam's flat. Verbeux had somehow managed to smuggle Desirée's there.

Taking action helped, keeping busy until the two of them could leave. The encounter with his father would never be forgotten and had left Adam wanting to find out his parents' whole story.

Edward, Adam's coachman, was a discreet and devoted man. He drove through the gray afternoon toward St. John's Wood where a neighbor of Rolly Spade-Filbert's had said he and Lucas could probably be found. The man, older, garrulous and apparently lonely for an audience, had produced the address but sworn Adam to secrecy about where he got it. Adam was glad to agree and would not have revealed his source anyway.

St. John's Wood looked graceful, regal even, in its mantle of white. When the coach turned the corner at Circus Road, the area was quiet and there were no other conveyances in sight. It was as if this place where married gentlemen kept their lady-birds, and kept them in high style amid neighbors who were writers and painters, had fallen asleep by the fires that burned brightly inside the pretty semidetached villas.

For the sake of discretion, Adam had Edward wait in nearby Abbey Lane, and went the rest of the way on foot. The only living soul he passed was so swathed against the cold that he resembled a large gray beehive on booted feet.

Adam walked quickly, wanting to keep this encounter short and to return to Desirée as quickly as possible. The address he sought appeared closed up. Not a window was uncovered, but the place was kept in good condition. At the door he rang the bell and waited, deliberately keeping his head down in case someone looked through a window and saw who he was — and decided they didn't want his company.

Adam had rung several times before he saw light and heard rapid footsteps. The door opened a crack and a pale, oval face with dark eyes appeared considerably below the level of his own. Hair with a reddish cast was caught up inside a white linen maid's cap. The girl's apron and brown linen frock were spotless.

Then she opened her mouth and spoiled everything. "Watcha want then? Nobody's expected so don't try nuthin' funny."

Adam plastered on a smile and added a wink for good measure. The wink had the required result since the maid fluttered her lashes and winked back. "My brother and his friend are visiting here," he said. "Mr. Lucas Chillworth and Mr. Rolly Spade-Filbert."

That earned him giggles. "Silly name, ain't it? Makes yer think of diggin' up trees."

It had never made Adam think exactly that, but he agreed on the comical quality of the name. "I'm Adam Chillworth, Lucas's brother and I have important business with him."

"Nice gent," the girl said, opening the door a little wider. "Which is more than I can say about that other cove. Nasty one, he can be, and too sneaky wiv 'is 'ands."

She frowned and said, "Yer card, please. Just to satisfy meself."

Adam produced a card and handed it through the door.

"Ooh, swish," the girl said. "Mayfair Square. Very nice. You follow me." Rather than put the card on a salver for her employer, the girl slipped it into a pocket in her apron and Adam hoped she would not decide to use it one day.

"Upstairs, sir. Me name's Cherry Pick, by the way. You'll be thinking I'm a fine one to laugh at anyone else's name but I've learned to make fun of me moniker. Me mum and dad thought they was clever, choosin' a name like that to go with the season. They 'ad cherry trees, see, and it was pickin' time when I was born. O'course, I'd have been Pick anyway, wouldn't I?"

"Mmm." Adam rather thought that *Picked* might be more appropriate by now.

"All right," Cherry said when they reached the third floor. "This is it. Wait here, please." She slipped inside the room, closed the door behind her and took so long to return that Adam wondered if he should leave. At last she appeared and said, "In you go, now. A word of warning you may already know, but the tree digger's got a temper on 'im. A wild one 'e is, specially when there's been a lot of drink around." This time she winked at him and trotted her shapely body quietly downstairs. Within seconds the front door slammed and he assumed Cherry had left.

Rolly Spade-Filbert's slurred voice was easily recognized, as was feminine laughter. Adam stood, listening, wanting to be as sure as he could be of what awaited him on the other side of the door. That was to be no clearer before he gave a brief knock and walked into the room.

The scent assaulted him first: heavy, stale perfume, liquor and sex. In the semidark room his impression was of slithering among heaps of brilliant silks and satins piled on a bed and scattered in mounds about the room. Gradually he made out a chaise in shades of red, purple, green and black silk. Some of the mounds on the floor were made up of an abundance of fringed and jeweled pillows. In addition to silk, there were furs on the bed.

And the bed? He had seen such things before but not in so-called private homes. Manacles and lengths of leather hung from the tall bedposts. Through openings in the canopy, two pieces of velvet-wrapped chain were bolted to the ceiling and they supported a trapeze some three feet above the mattress. Adam was staring at the trapeze when a somewhat plump woman wearing black lace from neck to ankle, nothing but black lace, emerged from somewhere on the floor and leaped onto the bed. She put her hands on her knees and bent to look at him, her blond hair wild. "Who are you, luscious one?" she said.

"I'm Adam Chillworth. I —"

"Lucas's brother?" Her cultured voice was a surprise. "You must be. Welcome to the show. Take a seat. No, no, absolutely do not take a seat." She grasped the trapeze and flipped herself upside down with ease. "I used to be with the circus, you see. I was a flyer and a contortionist — very useful skills — so I keep myself in practice."

"Bloody get back here, you," Rolly said, his head appearing behind the chaise. "I don't pay you to give it away to anyone who wanders in."

That the man didn't recognize him — even after he'd spoken his name — was no surprise to Adam. Rolly's hair hung over his face, which he repeatedly turned from side to side as if trying to bring the scene into focus. He held a bottle aloft.

"He's no danger," the woman said. "He

couldn't stand up if he wanted to." With that she hooked her knees around the chains and leaned back. If she made a complete drop from the trapeze her head would not clear the mattress. Back and forth she swung and with each pass Adam was given a view of an open crotch in the long, lace things she wore. She released her knees and pulled up into a headstand on the bar. Spreading her legs she dropped them, one forward, one behind, in an unnatural movement that left her completely revealed. He looked away.

Apart from these two, the room was empty, but Lucas could be elsewhere in the house. Adam considered ways in which he might ask his whereabouts without sending Rolly off in some mad tirade.

"Leave your trousers behind, and anything else you can do without," the woman said to Adam. "Come on up. You're a tall one, you can help turn this into some fun, which is more than I can say for some people. Miserable pair. Rolly's all right sometimes, aren't you, my love? Until you get too much hock in you. The other one's always morose. Never joins in."

The other one? "You are as charming as you are inviting, Miss . . ."

"Mrs. Lavender Gay-Pierce. You, my

lovely man, may call me Lavender."

An animal-like roar, and Rolly's stumbling scramble from the cover of the couch put Adam on his guard. The man might be too much in his cups to land a blow even, but taking him too lightly would be a mistake.

"Chillworth," Rolly yelled. "Oportunished. Belay, I say. Pishtols or swords. Second a pick. Oh, gawd." It was the sight of Lavender gently swaying on her trapeze, that stopped him. He ran his tongue around his lips and staggered toward the bed. "I'm coming, sweet handfuls, I'll be there, my bouncy beauty."

Adam all but swallowed his tongue. Laughing now wouldn't be wise.

Bouncy Beauty had talked about a pair of men. He took note of two extra doors, one each side of a fireplace where the coals were dusty and cold. He would just have to start looking for Lucas.

"Oh, yes, yes," Rolly said. "Let 'em out."

Letting them out referred to Lavender Gay-Pierce unbuttoning her sleeveless upper garment and exposing her astonishing breasts. Bountiful and undoubtedly heavy, Adam wondered how their pressure, presently directed at Lavender's neck, allowed her to breath at all.

From the way she used her hands to jiggle them, he decided the position she was in caused no problems at all.

She fascinated, but more repulsed than aroused him.

"Lucash is a sod," Rolly mumbled. He'd landed on his knees and pulled himself slowly onto the bed. It was impossible not to note that he was very well-made and powerfully built. "Tries to spoil my fun every time. Just shits there and pouts."

Adam frowned. "Sits where?" he asked, deciding Rolly was drunk enough not to have any coherent notions as to why Adam might be there.

"Shut up," Rolly said. "Can't you see I'm busy? Wait your turn."

Adam leaned against the wall, crossed one foot over the other, and did as he was told. He didn't want to consider too closely what Rolly meant by *turn*.

Long curtains drawn across a bay window twitched, then parted enough for Adam to see his brother's face. True to what had been said, Lucas just sat there on a chair facing the window and looked grim. He narrowed his eyes at Adam and shook his head. He mouthed the word, "Wait," and turned his chair around so that he could see what was going on in the room while he made sure he could drop the curtains again and effectively disappear.

Adam carried a small but deadly knife strapped inside one of his boots. He prayed he would never have to use it here but was glad he had it.

Rolly, on all fours, had made it onto the mattress where he held his face up and his mouth open, alternating between licking one breast, then the other. With each contact Lavender cried out. From a net attached to a bedpost behind her, she took a little pot from which she scooped something pink and oily. This she massaged onto her breasts before swinging toward Rolly again. This time he slid his hands over her flesh, moaning as he did so. Adam noticed that what had formerly hung between his legs was rising to the occasion. Quite impressive. He was losing all control over the pink oiled breasts. Squeezing them together, he pulled on the nipples with his lips and laughed each time he lost his grip.

Adam looked to Lucas and motioned for him to come out of the room, but Lucas ignored him and continued to observe the display on the bed.

Wavering as he did so, Rolly managed to

hold a bedpost and stand up.

Mrs. Gay-Pierce's laughter soared and she changed positions. With her upper body over the bar and her hair — among other things — hanging, she assumed the posture of an airborne frog getting ready for a mighty leap.

Rolly, who obviously knew the drill, hooted like a foxed owl, managed to walk toward the promised land and grip a chain in each hand. Strong legs clamped around his waist and drew him close. Adam saw Rolly take charge of swinging the trapeze ever so slowly and drop his head first back, then forward as he increased the pace.

There were points when even the unexpected became boring, sickening even, and Adam crossed the room, hauled his brother to his feet, and marched him from the room.

Once the door was closed and they stood on the landing, Lucas crossed his arms on the banister and settled his forehead on his hands.

"I'm taking you to your home," Adam said, not relishing the prospect. "When you're ready, we should talk. You are an unhappy man and if I can do something to change that, I will."

Lucas rolled his head from side to side.

"I'm not going *home* as you call it. I don't have a home. I'm a failed man."

"A hotel, then. Or perhaps there is another friend?"

"I have somewhere to go until I can collect myself. If you want to talk, we'll do it here. Can't imagine what we'd have to say."

Adam looked down the landing at several closed doors. "What's in those rooms, d'you know?"

"No."

"You can be an unhelpful bastard," Adam said.

Lucas grinned and said, "You aren't the first to tell me that."

Adam went to the last door, the one farthest from where Bouncy Beauty and her rubber-legged swain headed for the grand finale on a trapeze.

"We're in luck," Adam said. Lucas was right behind him. "Doesn't look as if this is used."

He walked into a sheet-draped bedroom and pulled the dusty cloths from two floral upholstered chairs set at an angle as if intended for intimate conversation. Exactly the thing. Lucas joined him and they both sat.

When they'd been there, quietly regarding the drab walls or their own finger-nails, for far too long, Adam let out a long breath and said, "How did you let yourself get into such a mess?"

His brother inclined his head and re-garded Adam steadily. "Do beat about the bush, won't you?"

"You're in debt. Father has suspended your allowance." He hesitated before adding, "And you're living with more guilt than most decent men can handle. Under all the swagger, you're a decent man." Adam didn't add that their father had threatened his elder son's ruin if Adam didn't do as he was told.

Every vestige of color seeped from Lucas's face. He wetted his lips and his breathing became more rapid. "I don't have the faintest idea what you mean. There's nothing worse than a little boredom wrong with me. Where have you been getting your so-called information?"

Lucas wasn't stupid. He knew the most likely informant was their mother, al-though it could be possible that Gilbert had spoken to Adam about his brother. He wouldn't mention Rolly's visit to Gilbert yet. That might be more useful later. "You wouldn't believe it if I told you, so forget it. Let's just say that someone who knows a lot about you came and tried to get money out of me." It could work, there had to be more than one or two who fit the description.

The ruse wasn't a total failure. Lucas frowned and his eyes moved rapidly as he thought about what Adam had said. He put a shaky hand to his brow and wiped sweat from his hairline.

"I want to help."

Lucas snorted. "Father just cut you out of his will. You're supporting yourself from *painting,* which can't pay as well as you'd like me to think, and you want to *help* me? You're here because some swine told you my business and you want the pleasure of watching me squirm."

"Right," Adam said, and made to get up. "You obviously see right through me and I shan't get any more fun out of your misery today, so I'll be off."

"Don't go." Lucas didn't have far to reach to stay Adam's hand on the arm of his chair. "For God's sake don't leave me like this. I'm a fool. I'm my own worst enemy and I don't think I can go on as I am."

Adam dropped down into the seat again and put his spare hand on top of Lucas's. "Let me help you, then."

"You can't. I've got to buy time and figure out a way to tell them that if I'm dead, they'll never get anything back. I don't know if there's a chance I can reason with them — I don't even know if they'll cut me down before I can say anything."

Adam's scalp prickled. "You're talking about your creditors." He turned sideways in the chair and looked straight into Lucas's face. "We'll get the money. I want you in hiding until I can finish some business I have in hand, then I'll do what has to be done."

The slightest sign of hope entered Lucas's eyes. "You can do it?"

"Yes. Wait until nightfall, then get to Vauxhall Gardens. Snow or no snow the party will be in full swing. Find a fortune teller who calls herself Crystal. Say this to her: *I stayed too long.* Tell her you are my brother and I told you to come to her. She'll hide you."

"Why would she hide —"

"Because, in a particular way, she loves me. I'll tell you the story one day."

"Thank you," Lucas said, his fingers like an armored glove on Adam's arm.

"Just wait wherever she puts you until I come. There is something else I must ask you before I go. You won't be happy, but I have to do this. You were . . . *close* to a young woman who died. What was her name?"

Lucas's head fell forward as if he'd taken a blow. "Don't ask me this," he said in a hoarse voice that broke. "Let it be."

"You are pained by it?"

"Don't ask."

Adam struggled to decide if he should pursue the question further.

"She wasn't sophisticated. I thought she was and the result was disastrous."

"Lucas —"

"No. Let me think, please. I see her face and it's killing me. There's no way to change the ending now. If I'd known what was happening, I would have saved her."

"She is definitely dead?" Adam asked.

Lucas nodded, yes, and withdrew his hand from Adam's arm. He rested the back of his head on the chair and his eyes closed. "Drowned. She walked into a river until the water was deep enough to cover her if she sat down. That's what she did, she sat down."

Freshly appalled, Adam couldn't speak. Tears streaked his brother's face but he made no sound.

Adam didn't think his mouth would be moist again, or that his throat would ever stop hurting. "And the child died with her?"

Lucas pulled his lips back from his teeth. The awful distortion of his face twisted Adam's heart. "One night she just didn't meet as we'd arranged. It was like that. We met and went to a rooming house. I brought food and we stayed together for hours. Sometimes all we did was talk about things that would seem foolish to anyone else. Parting was unbearable. She was respectably dressed but poor, I was sure of that, and she would never tell me who her people were or where she lived.

"Then like I said, she didn't come one night. She never came again. For months I searched for her but I had no clue where to find her." He looked at Adam. "Her father didn't come to me. He went to our father who turned him away at once and said nothing to me. I can't go on." He leaned forward, lacing his fingers at the back of his neck.

Their mother had told the tale differently but Adam couldn't bring himself to probe further. It would be easier to stop now. Sympathize and let it be. But Adam had to be sure of one thing. "I just want to be certain the baby hadn't already been born, that there isn't a child you sired somewhere."

"I don't know." Lucas glared at him with bloodshot eyes. "She was still alive herself when her father was first turned away by ours. Her father returned within days to tell how Enid had killed herself when she heard I didn't want anything to do with her. Father had told him that. The man threatened to let the world know about me and Father paid him off. That was more than a year ago. I was told about the death shortly after that second visit because Father wanted to punish me and watch me suffer."

"Let it go," Adam said. He would discover the truth of it but not now.

Lucas pointed a finger at him. "You always had your love, your painting. You knew what you wanted and it made you happy enough not to care that the old man favored me. I had nothing but the man's so-called favor until I met Enid but I didn't have the courage to throw everything in to be with her. I could have found a way for us to make a living.

"I've calculated and recalculated — dozens of times — trying to decide how pregnant she might have been when she died, or if there was a chance the child was still alive. Impossible. And pointless. The only woman I shall ever love is dead. And if there should be a child, the only way I'll ever know is when he or she is old enough to settle the debt for Enid."

Only a couple of hours of daylight remained. With a heavy heart, Adam hurried along Circus Road toward his coach. Lucas had promised he would go to Crystal in the Vauxhall Gardens, which gave Adam some relief. She would keep him hidden if anyone could. Later, when the journey to Gretna Green had been made, Adam would set about discovering the identity of Lucas's Enid.

But first there was Desirée.

He was beset on all sides, but just thinking her name caused a hammering in his chest and an excitement that felt like fire in his blood and bones.

The sight of the coach was a relief. Abbey Lane was quiet with few buildings to be seen. Adam marched the last few yards and called out, "Edward."

He wasn't surprised to get no response. Edward had a habit of falling asleep beneath the blankets inside his master's conveyance.

The horses. Adam peered into the coach to find it empty. He took a few more steps and looked in all directions. "Where are the bloody horses?"

Lady Hester Bingham, Desirée decided, could be most devious. There could not be more than an hour or so before she and Adam should leave. She was anxious and had a need to hover by the windows in Lady H.'s newly decorated receiving room where she could watch for the coach. But as if by magic, Sibyl had just arrived from Number 17, "on impulse," she said, which meant Desirée couldn't show any sign of being upset unless she wanted to be questioned about the reason.

Sibyl would probably swoon with glee if she found out an elopement was about to occur, but there must be no risk of word getting to the wrong ears — Jean-Marc's ears.

When Sibyl had removed her very pretty pink bonnet and put it aside, she rubbed her hands before the fire, bobbled on her toes, smoothed her hair and, all the time, aimed smiling glances at Desirée.

"It's good to see you," Desirée said. For no reason, tears filled her eyes and actually overflowed. "I am so blessed in my friends. When I was a child no one took notice of me, except for Jean-Marc but he wasn't there often. I didn't know what it meant to have people who *wanted* to be with me. Now look." She raised her shoulders and sniffed while she found a handkerchief in her reticule.

Immediately Sibyl rushed to hug her, and Lady H. got up from her beautiful plum-colored sofa and joined the exchange of tearful happiness. "Jenny will be here at any moment," she said. "And you know how she loves to cuddle. Such a sweet thing. That Latimer has depths I would never have guessed at. He knew what he was doing when he made that girl his wife."

Desirée had grown rigid. "Jenny? Why is Jenny coming?"

"I lied," Sibyl announced. "I didn't come on impulse, it was arranged. And I am to spend the night here for nostalgia's sake."

Lady Hester clapped her hands. "Isn't that clever? And it was all Sibyl's own idea. She will spend the night with you in 7B —

although you won't really be there — and since girls chatter far too late, they always get up too late. And there will be no cause for anyone to wonder why you don't return to Number 17 to sleep. Meg — poor, poor girl. She will need all of our support when Jean-Marc turns into . . . who was the character that strange Mary Shelley wrote about?"

"Frankenstein," Sibyl said, not looking at all happy.

"That's it, Frankenstein. A really horrible and frightening creature. No matter, we shall be beside her. Your husbands included." She gave Desirée a coy smile. "Your husband, also, of course."

"Actually, Dr. Frankenstein wasn't a monster, he made one," Sibyl, who read a great deal, said.

Desirée breathed deeply and couldn't contain her conviction that with so many knowing what was going on, one of them would lose their nerve and tell Jean-Marc too soon.

"Och, it's a cold night, but at least it's stopped snowing so your drive will be easier." Jenny More, flushed from the cold she spoke of, rushed in. "We've put furs in the carriage. And some libations to warm the cockles of your hearts, not that you'll likely need much help in that department." She smiled and looked openly wicked.

Unable to think of anything to say, Desirée drew farther back into her own plump silk chair and threaded her fingers tightly together. The boots she wore were too warm in here, but she'd need them on the journey.

"I dropped by the greenhouse at Number 8," Sibyl said. "Meg sent things, too, and Lady Hester. Did you find them all?"

Jenny's smile lighted the room. "Of course I did. They're also in the coach. Now don't say any more or you'll give everything away."

"You're darlings," Desirée said, wishing she didn't feel sick. "Do please make sure no one tells a thing to Jean-Marc."

"Not only will nothing be said to him," Sibyl told her, "but tomorrow he has an appointment with the Prime Minister and with a number of statesmen. He'll be gone all day and when he gets home he may well not think about your whereabouts for some time, perhaps not until the following day."

Desirée hoped so. If that were true, then she and Adam would be safely married and there would be nothing Jean-Marc could do about it.

"Oh," she held up a hand. "You put things in the coach for us? But Adam has his coach with him." *Please come back Adam.*

The ladies looked, one at another. Finally Lady Hester sat very straight and looked glowing. "We needed a particularly fast conveyance and we have secured one. And outstanding horses to be sure you have a fine start. Sir Robert Brodie has contacted all the posts along the way and made sure the new horses will be of the most outstanding variety."

"Sir Robert?" Desirée's voice sounded as if a frog had kissed *her.*

Lady Hester pinched her nostrils and produced a lorgnette through which to glare at Desirée. "I have the best of tastes in gentlemen."

They all glanced quickly at one another and just as quickly lowered their eyes. Lady Hester's last gentleman had all but killed Latimer in an attempt to make Jenny his own. Very grisly.

Lady Hester gave off waves of ire. "I know what you are thinking, but I can be forgiven for a small mistake in that case. You all know the circumstances. Sir Robert is a respected surgeon in this city — and we are engaged. Now, don't start twittering about that. The marriage is a long way off and this is Desirée's time."

Of course, there was a fluttering and a twittering, as Lady H. had predicted. And she loved every moment.

Meg was the next to arrive. "Oooh, the male of the species can be very difficult. You may be proud of me. I didn't even get cross when he laughed about hen parties." She looked around. "Where's Adam?"

She earned herself ferocious scowls from everyone but Desirée who promptly burst into tears. "He is either dead or has abandoned me."

All eyes rolled. Meg said, "You'll be on your way very soon, not that I actually know that. In fact I can't think where the words came from, it's —"

"*Meg!*" The ladies scolded.

Jenny said, "Doesn't Sibyl look lovely in that tartan. I love tartan silk. It's rich, all the pinks and blues, the little yellow and red lines."

"Suitable, too," Lady Hester said, "since you're off to Scotland."

Desirée waved them all into seats. She felt serious and that made her unhappy. "There are some things none of you know. Please don't interrupt. I won't discuss the strange trouble Adam and I have encountered, but it means that the only sensible thing is for us to be together at all times so that we can make it as hard as possible for anyone to capture one of us and use that capture against the other. That's all I'll say on that subject for now."

"Nothing to worry about," Meg said. "You are to be together from this night on."

Desirée lowered her eyes. "This is both the happiest and the saddest time of my life. My brother will never accept a marriage between Adam and me. You know what he wants out of my marital alliance. What he will have to accept is the reason for this marriage to Adam — or the reason we will pretend to embrace — and what we have been assured is the only way any of this can work.

"We will be married. We will do our best to find joy in that much. But Verbeux has warned us that Jean-Marc will find a way to end the marriage by annulment and that it will be best for us never to consummate the union. We are to prepare ourselves to announce that we are not truly husband and wife so that a so-called appropriate marriage can still be contracted."

"No," Jenny whispered. "It's unnatural."

"An abomination," Lady Hester added.

"There has to be a way," Sibyl said. "Why should yours have to be a political marriage?"

Desirée shook her head and tried to smile. "Because I have no choice." She wasn't ready to share the truth, that she had thrust this elopement on Adam, who was convinced they would never be allowed to marry under normal circumstances. "Verbeux says this way Adam and I can remain friends as long as my . . . my husband tolerates such a thing. But that is all we may have."

"Oh, my dear," Meg said. "Damn this advantageous alliance nonsense." She blushed and said, "I should not have said that. Forgive me."

"You're right," Sibyl said. "And look how often rich men marry women who are not their social equals. Well, we shall do all we can to make sure you take all the happiness you can, Desirée. I meant to tell you we heard from Finch and Ross. They are planning to come to London fairly soon. They say they cannot bear to be left out when everyone else is here."

Desirée smiled, but could think of nothing but Adam. Another half hour had fled.

"Your packed bags are also in the carriage," Jenny said, sounding troubled. She had a way of knowing how others felt.

Old Coot knocked and entered. Bent so that he must look to the side to see his mistress's face, he held out a salver with two cards on it.

Lady Hester slid off the cards and said, "I don't suppose you've seen Barstow lately? We could certainly use more hot tea and refreshments. In fact, a little sherry all the way around wouldn't go amiss."

The sight of Coot turning red was quite a spectacle, but turn red he did. "Mrs. Barstow is helping a friend. Unexpected, it was. Um, once we've dealt with this," he said, looking at the cards, "I'll pour sherry and get some of Cook's cheese popovers. Fresh from the oven, they are."

The ladies made appreciative noises.

"Why on earth would that scallywag Verbeux send in his card? And who's this? Mr. Anthony FitzDuram."

"M. Verbeux asks that they be allowed to visit for a few minutes," Coot said.

So, Desirée thought, Verbeux was also aware that Adam had not returned, but perhaps he knew why. She hardly dared hope.

Lady H. tapped one of the cards. "Roses in a Ming vase. I recall. What a nuisance.

We'd best get him in and out. Verbeux knows the urgency. He won't allow this to interfere with our plans."

Desirée felt she was borne along on a fast flowing river made up of hands pushing her toward her fate, or whatever part of her fate this would turn out to be.

"Show them in," Lady H. said. "And we should be in your debt for the sherry and the cheese popovers. Don't offer the gentlemen anything, Coot. We would be delighted to see them for a few minutes but we're enjoying a gathering for ladies."

"As you wish." Coot bowed out.

"Anthony FitzDuram must have gone to Number 17. Jean-Marc will be suspicious."

Jenny stroked her hair. "Why should he be?"

The entrance of Verbeux and Anthony FitzDuram closed that subject nicely. Coot went to a delicate, hand-painted chest and took out a bottle of sherry. He lined up glasses on a silver tray.

Cook, the frilly edges of her white cap flapping, came in without warning. Fragrant steam rose from cheese popovers on a large plate. She set this on the chest beside Coot's silver tray and departed without so much as a word. Those who kept the house running didn't approve of being expected to do work that wasn't their own. Cook belonged in the kitchens, not carrying food above stairs.

Verbeux, looking too somber to please Desirée, stood apart from his fellow and his watch came out of its pocket several times within a few minutes.

Desirée's stomach tightened, but it was Anthony FitzDuram who caught and held her attention. He was blond, with eyes of that searing blue shade. In the three years since she'd last seen him, his body and presence had matured. A muscular man of average height, he'd grown a beard and mustache that were more than a little red. She glanced at the other women and smiled at the hints of admiration in their eyes.

She took the sherry Coot offered.

"Nothing for me, thank you," Anthony said, his voice very deep. "I simply wanted to make sure you were well, Princess, and nothing untoward had befallen you." He held her eyes and what she saw in his overwhelmed her. He was most troubled.

"I was taking the air in the gardens when I saw Mr. FitzDuram's coach arrive," Verbeux said. "I ascertained that he was looking for you and had his driver bring him around to Number 7."

In other words there was no need to fear FitzDuram had somehow alerted Jean-Marc.

"Whatever would make you worry about me?" Desirée said. "I'm touched, of course."

The corners of his mouth turned up in a humorless smile. "I see. So you simply forgot we had an engagement today? Please don't look so horrified. I was surprised you could make time for me at all and I'm sure you are so much in demand it's difficult to keep these things straight."

"No," she protested. "Yes, I forgot, but no, not because I am leading a life crowded with engagements. I . . . I forgot. I have no excuse."

His features softened. He looked around and raised his hands. "See? How can a mere mortal man be condemned for being enchanted by such honesty. The Princess has special qualities. She knows how to make a man laugh, and she is honest. She doesn't play games. And I thought she was lost to audacious suitors such as I. I cannot tell you how often I think of you."

"You embarrass me," Desirée said, "but thank you for being so nice. Forgive me for missing our engagement."

"Consider yourself forgiven — for

nothing." He winced a little. "How about giving me another chance, say on Friday?"

"We are going to the country." Desirée disliked lying but saw no option.

"When do you return?"

"That depends on what is decided," she said, horrified at feeling so trapped. "Next week I should think."

"Good. Then I shall check next week. But do not think you have got rid of me. No, no, I cannot give up on you so easily as that."

"Good." *Oh dear.*

"Charming room," he told Lady Hester, who dimpled. "The colors are daring and wonderful together. Be careful or you will find yourself copied."

"Thank you. The entire house is receiving some extra attention. Not that it needs it, of course. But I do like to entertain more than I have in recent years. I intend to start a salon — to encourage discussion of moment. I'm sure you know the type of thing. And, of course, I will be holding an affair for Princess Desirée within a few weeks. I hope you will join us. But it is far too soon to think of such things. I will see to it that you are invited."

Anthony FitzDuram pushed back his coat and put his hands on slim hips. His shoulders and chest seemed to expand with pleasure. "I think I'll take that drink after all," he said. "Make it a little FitzDuram if you've got it. And make sure Verbeux experiences the family elixir, too." He laughed. They all laughed — except Desirée.

Adam's first thoughts had been for Edward's safety. The horses' tack had been cut and the animals let loose from the shafts. What had come to him with force was that his plans to get away with Desirée had been tampered with. Late-afternoon shadows had turned into a deepening gloom. He should be close to Mayfair Square by now, not standing in the snow like a man without a mind, or at least a man with a mind that didn't know what to do next.

He must look for Edward.

Logic told him the animals would bolt straight ahead out of the shafts, he climbed up a bank to get as good a look ahead as possible.

He saw and heard nothing.

Then he heard a rush of movement all about him, but before he could turn around, the crushing force of heavy fists on the back of his head and his shoulders drove him, face first into the snow.

There were at least two of them, perhaps more. He was caught by surprise and out-numbered. But there was a way, there was always a way.

"We sent you a warning," a muffled voice told him. "Don't tell me the girl didn't pass on the warning. We told her you were dangerous to her and you are — or you have been. You won't be dangerous anymore."

He had to push to his feet and hope they didn't use a pistol before he could try to fool them.

The back of his neck throbbed. Letting his head fall forward, he got to his knees, swaying, and very slowly started to get up. The knife was inside his cuff before he was almost on his feet and they started beating him again. He heard more than two voices. At least three and not one of them familiar. He could not risk putting up a fight, even with the knife when they might have pistols and could probably do him enough damage to leave him helpless anyway.

"You big men think you're too strong to die, don't you?" a man said. "You're not. You just die harder." The fists beat into his back again and he cried out, his cries cov-ering his groan when he sliced the knife into the palm of his left hand. He felt the blood pour forth and flexed his fingers to encourage the flow.

Slowly he began to turn his head to the left and was rewarded with a fierce blow to the side of his head and his ear.

"Keep your face down, fool. Not that it matters since you won't be telling anyone what happened here."

Accomplishing a gurgling noise that almost sickened him, Adam leaned forward, inch by inch, letting the knife slip up his sleeve and angling his head so it would be almost impossible to see that he smeared blood over his ear and covered his face with it.

"He's wishing he'd stayed with his pretty paints," a nasal voice said. "In fact, the gentleman doesn't appear to be feeling at all well. He — oh gawd, he's bleeding from his head — from his ear. Look, it's running. He's damaged."

"I thought that was the idea," another voice said. "Damaged enough to make him decide he's not so keen on the Princess after all."

"What if his head's injured inside?"

"He could bleed to death. Or never be the same."

"Gawd."

Might as well see how much of the thespian he had in him. Spreading his arms a little, continuing to gurgle, Adam fell straight forward, the way he'd done as a child showing off with friends, and landed, spread-eagle and facedown. His weight took him several inches into the wet snow.

Muffled, the thin-nosed voice reached him. "You've killed him. Bloody fools. We've got to get away from here fast. If any of us ever gets connected to this, we'll lose the best chance to get filthy stinking rich we're ever going to see. Run!"

Adam didn't move a muscle. He lay there until his clothes were soaked through. At least the snow was keeping the wound in his hand clean.

Darkness fell entirely and a wind picked up, scraping a layer off the snow and tossing icy spicules on his head where they went directly to his scalp, melted and ran in painfully chill rivulets.

At last he heard a voice in the distance, an angry voice. With luck someone benign was about to stumble on him and he'd feel safe to move.

"Brains the size of peas," he heard. "Great big strong bodies with nothing to control them. Hurry up. Come on, pick it up. You're going to cost me my place, damn you."

Adam knew that voice. He turned over

onto his back and saw diamond brilliant stars in the sky. The voice came closer, and the sound of hoofs on beaten-down snow. With care, testing each limb, twisting his head on his neck and feeling bumps on his head, Adam rose to his feet. He took the knife and put it back in his boot. The wound on his hand wasn't pretty.

He saw Edward approach holding the two horses and walked toward him. Edward was too busy yanking on halters and swearing at the poor beasts to hear his master's approach until they were face-to-face and Edward looked up.

Edward looked directly at Adam, let out a horrible yell, and let go of the horses as he tried to scramble away.

Adam threw himself at the cattle and found holds on their tack despite his battered hand.

"The devil," Edward said, on his back where he'd overbalanced. He scuttled on heels and elbows like a crab. "It isn't my time, I tell you."

"Shut up," Adam said. "And get up. Help me find a way to secure these animals. We've got to get back. Now. Later we'll be talking. Much later, but if you don't want to see the devil sooner than you'd like, get us back to Mayfair Square."

23

The front door opened and closed softly.

Sibyl was upstairs sleeping at 7B, Verbeux had returned Meg home, and Latimer had come for Jenny. Lady Hester had long since retired. At her own insistence, Desirée waited alone and had just watched Adam's coach draw up, then pull away again once he had alighted. It was several hours beyond the time when they were to have departed for Scotland and she was convinced he had only come now to tell her he couldn't go through with it.

She was frightened. Frightened about what would happen to them if they took no steps to protect themselves, and frightened about how she would go on if Adam had decided to turn aside from her.

It was entirely possible that she, not he, was the one bringing trouble to them and that without her, his life would return to normal.

The door opened.

Whatever he said, she would not break down and cry, or allow him to see her distress at all.

He stepped into the room and Desirée's hands flew to her face. She felt faint and terrified, yet now was the moment to pull herself together and show him she was a strong woman.

Rapidly, she went to him and urged him across the carpet, struggling to take off his greatcoat as they went. She felt a strength she hadn't known she possessed and pushed him to sit in a chair before hurrying to close the door again.

"Desirée, it's not what —"

"Be quiet. Rest. You need your strength. This will not be comfortable but it is the best way for me to clean your wounds without unsettling the household. I am concerned about that Mr. Lumpit. It would not do for him to discover what is happening."

While she spoke, she selected a bottle of whiskey from the cabinet, gave up on discovering a suitable cloth and tore the ruffle from the bottom of one of her petticoats instead. She tried not to think, but the face of the man before her, her love, her hope, was caked with dried blood. More blood soaked his left sleeve and was still wet; his clothes were wet and filthy.

She soaked a length of the ruffle with whiskey and went to work searching for the source wound. In the process she found lumps and cuts on his scalp and neck.

"Desirée," he said quietly. "I am tired, but not too tired. And apart from losing a little blood — from my hand not my head — I am all right. I made my own face look like this to fool my attackers. Apparently they wanted to frighten me off but they didn't want to kill me. Now they think they have, which could be useful."

Desirée looked into his face, kissed the cleanest spot she could find on his brow, and caught up his hands. Blood seeped slowly from a fierce wound in his left palm. Immediately she soaked it with whiskey and Adam jumped from the chair to caper about, shaking the hand and blowing on it by turns. "Little rogue," he said. "I do believe you enjoyed that."

She shook her head and looked at her toes.

Adam put his good arm around her and pulled her near. "I have put you through a great deal this evening."

She should protest. "You don't know a small part of it," she said, thinking of the rather dear, but very inconvenient Anthony FitzDuram. "Who were your attackers?"

"I never saw them."

She frowned. "What do you intend to do now — other than change into dry clothes?"

"Leave at once."

She closed her eyes and rolled her face against his chest.

"We have time to make up."

"There is a new coach Lady Hester acquired for the occasion," she told him. "It's in the mews with well-rested horses. Apparently it is exceedingly fast. Our bags and provisions are in it already."

"Praise be," Adam said. "All we have to do is get away. I'll be five minutes getting dry clothes, then we'll go through the kitchens where I can wash my face and do what I can in a few minutes — then it's to Scotland with us. I'll change in the coach."

Change in the coach?

"Desirée?"

"Yes, one can do anything in a coach, hmm?" She paused, wishing she could pretend she hadn't just said what she'd said. "It is all an adventure," she said, creeping into the hall with him, and crossing the foyer.

He tucked her into a corner beyond the

staircase and ran upstairs.

Desirée stole out and collected coats from the foyer closet, and in less than the allotted five minutes, Adam returned carrying a roll of clothes.

They descended below stairs. "We shall make this our grand adventure," Desirée whispered.

"That we shall." His eyes met hers and unspoken was what they both knew, that the next few days might be all they had of each other to last two lifetimes. Adam had sounded weary and, even with his face and head sluiced with cold water in the scullery, he could not hide his exhaustion or the lines of pain around his mouth.

Covering up warmly, they let themselves out into the kitchen garden and sped through the darkness to the gate that led to the mews. Once outside, their boots scrunched on the icy snow while they headed for the stable.

Edward awaited them. "We're in luck, Mr. Chillworth," he said. "Best coach I've ever driven. Sturdy. And the horses must be worth a fortune. Get in now, you need to be off your feet. Good evening, Your Highness," he said as if in afterthought.

"Mon Dieu," a familiar deep voice came from the shadows; Verbeux, who strode to

the side of the coach. "Where have you been, Chillworth?"

Adam said, "It would take too long to explain, but our enemies are real. They left me for dead, which apparently wasn't the plan since they thought my demise might cost them the best chance they might ever have at gaining a fortune."

Desirée shivered. "You were here in the cold all this time, Verbeux?"

"My job is to watch over you, Princess — as best I can when you never obey an order."

"We'd best get going," Adam said.

Verbeux grunted. "Do not forget the purpose of this charade. I will never be far away."

"But you will be missed at Number 17," Adam said, frowning.

"I have left on personal business," Verbeux said, and walked into the darkness.

The flight north was made at such a pace as to panic Desirée. Adam soon diverted her. "Kindly look away," he told her. "These clothes are freezing."

Hiding her curiosity, she turned to the windows and thought about covering them — for a moment or so. They made wonderful mirrors — and she was a wicked girl, but she would close her eyes, of course, most of the time.

He removed his greatcoat and threw it on the seat facing where boxes and bags had been piled. His coat and waistcoat followed. The stained shirt tore, in so great a haste was he to get it off. He dropped it, and once he'd removed his boots, his trousers fell on top of the shirt.

Desirée did close her eyes. The size of the man overwhelmed her. His size and his hard flesh that moved smoothly beneath his skin. Wide at the shoulder, narrow at the waist, a flat abdomen with a ripple of muscle and shiny dark hair narrowing from his chest to beneath his navel.

She was very bad.

Opening her eyes a slit, she discovered he'd pulled on dry trousers but appeared to be looking through the window on her side of the coach.

Oh, he was looking at her. Please don't let him know she'd been watching.

He sat down to replace his boots, then used a cloth from a picnic basket to rub himself down. Ooh, she thought she could scrunch herself up like this and watch him for such a long time.

"Almost done," he said. In fact she saw

him pull on his shirt and tuck it into his trousers, don a new waistcoat and jacket, and work at tying a neckcloth without benefit of a mirror — until he used the windows opposite from hers to see what he was doing.

Once more she felt overwarm.

"There," he said, "let's get you settled comfortably."

She turned toward him while he put on a dark green coat over his buff waistcoat. Adam always dressed simply.

He gave her his entire attention, setting her among the fur throws provided by their dear friends and insisting she take a glass of sherry from one of the bottles provided. He placed an assortment of sandwiches and cakes before her but she didn't feel hungry. Adam, on the other hand, ate well and drank half a bottle of Madeira.

Boxes and bags were packed into every space. Desirée's halfhearted attempts to look at one or two of them only showed her tags with instructions for when they were to be opened — mostly after the wedding and when they were alone.

Adam's comment had been, "They really don't understand that this marriage will be a farce and quickly undone again. They mean well."

While Desirée remained awake, turning his sad words in her mind, Adam slept for some hours. When they stopped at a posting station to change the horses Adam took her from the coach to walk around, but they were off again in less than ten minutes.

Settled again and traveling much too fast for safety, Desirée was sure, she snuggled deep into the furs and closed her eyes. She felt Adam sliding sideways toward her and, finally, his head rested on her shoulder. She tried to make him as comfortable as possible, eventually managing to work his head onto her lap and encourage him, through gentle pulling, to fold his long legs up on the seat. He would not be comfortable when he awoke.

The coach swayed and when Desirée looked through a window she saw the lamplights wavering as they swung from their hooks.

Adam muttered from time to time. At one point he squirmed around until his knees were jackknifed up and his sleeping face was hers to watch. Perhaps the greatest gift would be for this journey to go on forever like some mythical story. She gently smoothed back his hair and rested a hand on his brow. Fortunately he remained cool and his sleep had become untroubled.

She smiled at his stubbly chin and bent over him to touch her cheek experimentally to his. The sensation prickled, and made her prickle in a most tantalizing fashion. In repose his mouth was more beautiful than ever and it was only with difficulty that she restrained herself from resting her lips on his.

He'd loosened his neckcloth. Desirée finished untying it, millimeter by millimeter, and undid the buttons on his shirt. A fur throw would be softer and more comfortable on his skin.

Desirée softly stroked the base of his strong neck. She became bolder, and folded his shirt back so that she could comb the hair on his chest with her fingertips. With a throw resting over his shoulders and another over his knees, he looked comfortable enough, and warm.

She passed a fingertip over a flat nipple and held still when he drew back his lips and dragged air in through his teeth. Little by little she was learning what pleased him.

Waking and sleeping, they moved in the confines of the carriage. Through daylight and another dusk they drove, talking little, watching each other a great deal. Desirée's hair fell down but when she tried to put it back up, he stayed her hands. "It looks so pretty. And it makes me feel things I like to feel." Her hair remained down, just as Adam's shirt remained open and now he occasionally carried one of her hands there and closed his eyes while she explored him.

Once he sighed and said, "This will not make the inevitable any easier on us."

Desirée looked away and kept her thoughts to herself.

From time to time they ate, usually with Desirée sitting on Adam's lap.

It was late on the second night when she dozed, and felt him flatten her hand on his belly and hold it there. She felt him watching her, and then she felt him lean over her and nuzzle her cheek. He played his tongue at the corners of her mouth and finally settled his lips on hers.

Desirée opened her eyes and looked into his. Then she opened her mouth and strained her head up to kiss him. Adam slid a hand behind her neck and took charge. They kissed until she could scarce draw a breath.

Adam stopped the kiss as abruptly as it had started and Desirée tried to read his expression as he looked straight ahead.

Once more he held her hand to his chest.

"We will be there soon," he said. "According to the instructions Verbeux left, we are to stay in a private home near the village. The family rents rooms. We can wash and change there before meeting with the marriage officiator — and with Finch and Ross. If you've changed your mind about this, just tell me, Desirée."

"I haven't."

"I will take great care of you for as long as you need me."

"We're going to work together to discover what it is these people want and how they intend to get it. They have tried to frighten each of us away from the other," Desirée said.

He took her hand to his mouth. "I should not have agreed to take this course."

Her stomach turned. "What choices did we have?"

"I had the choice to deal with my own problems and allow your brother to look after yours."

"We can still do that."

He shook his head and captured her face in his hands. "No, we can't and we both know it. I've allowed things to go too far. Believe it or not, I would never sleep another peaceful hour if I were strong enough to turn aside from you. It might have been the better, safer way to proceed, but it would mean that I would miss even the fleeting pleasure of calling you my wife."

24

Spivey here:

And I have never, ever, been more flummoxed.

I suppose you think it funny that my so-called worldly assistant is beyond my control. Where is he whenever I need him? — well, we certainly know where he spends a good deal of his time, perverted fiend that he is.

It's all well and good for him to be obsessed with his own pleasures. I knew he was and planned to use all that business going on in his brain to mask my own activities — when I slipped in a request for action.

The FitzDuram incident ended well enough, no thanks to Spade-Filbert who was supposed to drop by Number 7 on the pretext of looking for Lucas, then "remember" FitzDuram and lure him away somewhere quiet where he could find out exactly why the man is pursuing the Princess after showing little interest for years. These things can blossom into dangerous complications if one doesn't watch them.

How did FitzDuram know Desirée was in London just now? Tell me that. She's arrived very early for the Season and doesn't go about enough for there to be gossip about her presence.

I need a reliable assistant.

Lucas could become a problem. Lady Elspeth could become a problem. Gilbert Chillworth is a problem and he'd like to do his younger son harm, though don't ask me why.

Well, look who is coming in my direction. Old Will himself — blasted nuisance.

Well, well. Look, concentrate while I can still get a word in without interruption. I've come to a conclusion that rattles my bones: Women have a cunning that might almost pass for intelligence in the area of accomplishing necessary maneuvers. That gathering at Number 7 tonight was little short of amazing. What have any of the men actually come up with in the way of a plan? Nothing. In fact they mostly wait around for the women to tell them what to do, then, if not supervised, make a mess of things.

What's the matter with me? Complimenting females? Overworked, I shouldn't be surprised.

"Evening to you, Will." Damn him.

My friends, do we trust Verbeux? What does he get out of all this, that's what I'd like to know. Or should I say I'd like to know what he's planning to get out of this?

"It is a nice evening, Will — You think it would be polite if I called you, Mr. Shake-speare. Absolutely, Will. Oops, slipped. I'll try to do better — Will."

Listen, you lot, because I've got to whisper. Something's afoot with Larch Lumpit, the wretch. I suppose I'm the only one who has noticed he isn't around. One wonders why, but I won't give any hints to make a solution easier for you.

Also, that attack on Chillworth. Never saw those fellows before in my life . . . afterlife. They have to be working for someone, but who? Think about it. Try to be helpful for once.

"No, Mr. Shakespeare, I can't say I do know any Hamlet. Odd name that. Someone you met in that common scribblers' circle where all your ilk fight for time to spout off on the open air plinth, is he?"

The way the man looks at me — really, one would think he had some grudge against me.

"He's the son of the King of Norway, you say? Of course he is Willy boy. Try not to bump into anyone while you're hopping — I mean, flying out."

25

"It's so cold," Desirée said as Adam lifted her down from the coach to the yard at the inn where they were to meet Ross and Finch before going to the rooming house.

He reached back inside for a fur throw and this he wrapped around her. "I should have taken more care about what you brought to wear," he said. In fact it had never crossed his mind to think about her clothes at all.

"Is that better?" he asked. This was one more sign of the difference between caring only for oneself, and having another to consider.

"I am wonderful," she told him and he looked down into her brilliant smile. "Wonderful. So much excitement. So much happiness."

And all so fleeting. "Yes," he said and found it impossible not to smile back at her, and to drop a kiss on her nose. She had wound her hair up again and replaced her bonnet. He put his mouth to her ear and whispered, "You sparkle, lovely one."

"I know." Her voice was warm and naughty, and filled with good humor. "I sparkle and shine and I know it. And you, sir, are the most sparkle and shine-making man on earth. There. We are both very perceptive people."

The hour was about three in the morning and the activity slow enough to allow post boys and relief drivers for the Mail to sit around drinking and laughing. Ripe-scented steam rose through the inn lights, and jingling tack vied for attention with the scrape of hoofs.

Edward busied himself tending his own horses and Adam eyed the man, knowing how exhausted he must be, but Edward was of a hardy breed and moved efficiently. Tobacco smoke and the smell of strong beer splashed on straw-strewn cobbles tickled the nose. Adam held Desirée close and kept a watchful eye on all comers and goers, looking for Ross, Viscount Kilrood and his wife. It seemed a long time since Finch had lived at 7A with her brother Latimer, but Adam did not forget the open, caring woman he'd known since they met in Mayfair Square.

"Verbeux said he would never be far away," Desirée said. "Do you suppose he's here now?"

"Yes," Adam said. "But I won't waste energy looking for him. There is a man who won't be found unless he wants to be found. Ah, I think I see a Kilrood coach."

Adam's stomach clenched. He did indeed see Ross's Coat of Arms on the door of a gleaming coach that swept into the yard. Two coachmen rode the box and at the rear, where the tigers might have been, two more men stood back to back with pistols at the ready.

The precautions pleased Adam.

Desirée let out a frightened, "Oh," and huddled close enough to slide her arms around his waist.

"Ross is a man of the world," Adam told her. "He is traveling with his wife and you know what she means to him. He takes no risks." *Any more than I shall take risks with you.*

"I have been privileged to see some wonderful love affairs — of the enduring kind," Desirée said. "My brother was an unapproachable man before Meg came into his life and now he is a completely happy man — except when he has to deal with me. Sibyl and Hunter — a difficult path to bliss but an inevitable one, and I hear Latimer More used to be likened to an absentminded professor before Jenny. He also had quite the reputation, you know." She made sure he couldn't see her face. "Sought after by adventurous ladies, as was, of all people, Sir Hunter Lloyd. And look at them all now."

Amused and a trifle abashed, Adam said, "Indeed," while he considered his own less than lily-white past. She was right, though, it was amazing how love could change men, and women, he supposed.

"There's Ross." Desirée squealed and left Adam's side to trot over the cobbles. Adam followed more slowly.

A solidly mature figure, no hat, light playing on his dark hair, Ross reached to help Finch get down and, before that lady's feet touched the ground, Desirée hugged her and Adam heard her lapse into French at which Finch laughed and said, "Ah, ah, ah, you know what Meg would say. *English,* remember."

They laughed together. When the Princess was seventeen and a sullen girl about to make her Season, she had tormented Meg, who was then her companion and tutor, by pretending she spoke no English. The episode became a joke.

Finch, a diminutive woman with hair so red it glinted, embraced Desirée and made angry faces at Ross over her shoulder.

The Viscount stood a few feet distant, his arms crossed and his chin set high. Not a happy man. Adam tossed the throw back inside the coach and made his way to join Desirée and the Kilroods.

Finch saw him coming and cried, "Adam," before launching herself at him. "The world is a very strange place that we should meet here like this — and for such a reason."

He held her hands and said, loudly enough for Ross to hear, "Indeed. And a serious reason not arrived at lightly."

"Let's get inside," Ross said, extending a hand to Finch who joined him at once. "We are all hungry. I've arranged a private room where we can talk."

Desirée joined Adam, her face anxious. "I thought we were to go and change before the ceremony," she said.

"So did I," Adam said, scarcely parting his lips. "Leave everything to me."

"I love them," she said, "but they cannot change my mind about what we intend to do here."

Adam marked her words and entered the Three Thistles by the door Ross and Finch had taken. These two waited for them inside, with an obsequious landlord hovering. As soon as Ross gave him the word, he showed them to a small, warm room where a fire burned bright. A table had been set and there were pewter plates piled high with bread and jugs of beer waited. Butter glistened in a heaped dish.

The landlord seated them and asked the ladies if they'd care for a little mulled wine. Both accepted.

Uneasiness clawed at Adam. Ross had yet to say a word to him directly.

"I feel so dirty," Desirée said. "The journey was long. I thought we were to go to a rooming house where we could change."

Finch patted the Princess's hand. "Plenty of time for that later. Ross . . . we decided it would be best to talk together first."

The arrival of a serving girl with a creaking board of cheese and slabs of cold beef gave Adam time to prepare himself for the worst. He didn't want Desirée put through a bad time, though.

"Look," Ross said. "Might as well get straight to the point. I don't think that your plan is wise."

Desirée pinched her lips together and

Adam saw how upset she was. He feared he might use a fist imprudently and set about putting cheese on a dark piece of bread instead.

Ross pushed his own plate away. "Jean-Marc is my very close friend. We don't have secrets from each other."

"Oh dear," Finch said quietly.

"A good friend is a fine thing," Adam said, unable now to look away from Desirée. Her hands were clasped on the edge of the table and she concentrated on them, when she wasn't concentrating on him so hard he felt she was trying to make him read her thoughts.

Ross coughed. "After hearing the true reason for the marriage — in a letter from Jean-Marc's man, Verbeux — I have devised an alternate plan, which should satisfy all of us."

"We should all eat first," Finch said. In better light, the pale brown of her eyes and the fact that her eyelashes were as red as her hair, showed clearly.

"How are the children?" Desirée asked, her complexion ashen now. "And Oswin."

"Well," Finch said, "all of them. I actually believe Oswin is becoming fat!"

Oswin was the dog who belonged to Hayden, the boy Ross and Finch had rescued from the backstreets of London and adopted.

All four of them grew silent.

"The point is to make people believe you are married and that it is perfectly in order for you to be, er, intimate. That is, not exactly intimate but living in the same quarters. Not that it won't be assumed that you are intimate. It will require some careful politics to change that opinion, but as long as what we say is the truth, patience will be our shield."

Rather than fill with tears, as Adam would have expected, Desirée's eyes glittered with anger.

Adam waited until Ross continued. "I will go this far. I will tell Jean-Marc that you are married so that he will not try to stop you from being together, but you don't have to *actually* get married. Then, when the trouble passes, and if you decide you do really want to be husband and wife, try to get Jean-Marc to agree. He would be demolished if he were not to see you married before God."

Desirée had tried to pick up her wine but her hand shook so badly she slopped red stains onto the cloth. She looked at Adam with such misery that he longed more than ever to land a fist in Ross's face.

"It's no good," Finch said abruptly, her voice high. "We cannot interfere with love, my dear, and these two are in love. Can't you see that?"

"They have no right," Ross mumbled.

"Every right," Finch said and sounded beside herself.

Ross stood. "May I have a quiet word with you, Chillworth?"

If this was going to get nasty, Adam would prefer to shelter the women. "Certainly," he told Ross and got up to follow the other man outside the door.

Finch felt positively light-headed. Her husband's honor shaded every move he made. A staunch friend, he never betrayed friendship, and she knew he was unlikely to be swayed by someone he considered an enemy to one of his friends.

"Finch," Desirée said in an alarmingly small voice. "What is Ross saying to Adam out there?"

"I don't know," Finch said honestly. "I can guess that he is trying to make Adam see his point of view, but I may be wrong."

"You love the Viscount. You have loved him for years."

"Yes." Finch felt a welcome rush of warmth at the thought.

"He has a beautiful heart, Finch, and

seeks always to do the right thing. Unfortunately he is only a man and sometimes he's horribly wrong." She smiled a little and was grateful when Finch did the same thing.

"I want to be married to Adam. We have decided that whatever we can have together, for however long, is worth any sacrifice. And we *need* each other as we never have before. We have both suffered vicious attacks, Finch — when we were alone. And we know these things are because someone is desperate to keep us apart. Two reasons come to my mind. I was warned to stay away from Adam and it could be because someone has designs on marrying me himself. Or Adam could be a danger to someone who has decided to kill him. For us to be together does not suit them, so —" she turned up her palms "— once we are wed it will be too late for the villains. It only makes sense for us to be together all the time, don't you think?"

Finch thought that she was looking at a woman so in love she would concoct any reason to be with Adam.

"I should do for you what your mother won't," Finch said hurriedly. "First, please be truthful and tell me if you have . . . are you still . . . do you?"

Desirée chuckled. "You didn't used to be so shy," she said.

"Don't play with me, young lady." Finch shook a finger at Desirée and found the courage to say, "Have you and Adam already been intimate?"

"No."

"Oh," Finch said, and felt a little disappointed for the pair of them. She cleared her throat. "Well, that's very honorable of you. Now listen carefully. I'll get through as quickly as I can.

"The days and weeks before the marriage are the best part of the whole thing because the man is more attentive than he will ever be once you are formally his and he doesn't have to pretend he dwells on your every word anymore."

Desirée frowned and pursed her lips.

"It is important to try to set some standards whilst courting. The only way a marriage truly works is for the woman to have the upper hand."

"Absolutely," Desirée said with gusto and promptly pressed her lips together again.

"The woman decides the pace of the relationship, what she expects from the man who is to be her husband," Finch said. "She lets him know that a peaceful household, *their* peaceful household cannot be built around a man who reads the newspaper at every meal where there are no guests. Harmony is not reached by forgetting the subtle art of conversation. When a lady asks her husband, 'Do you like my gown,' he may not say, 'Humph, or yes, or very much,' without looking at the gown. He is to learn the enjoyment of his own children. This means he will hold them, play with them, and allow them to sleep upon his chest — regularly. They will consider him a friend, as well as a firm disciplinarian and a protector." Finch ran out of breath.

"Bravo," Desirée said, clapping her hands. "Most excellent."

"Thank you."

"You have a very clear and clever mind," Desirée remarked.

"Hmm." Finch knew she had arrived at The Subject, that which she must not botch if she were to help the Princess as much as possible. "Conjugal bliss. If courting is crowning bliss, the wedding night is hell. Oh, sorry for that. I got a little passionate."

Princess Desirée looked at her with bright, inquisitive eyes. "Was your wedding night hell?"

Finch recalled her own somewhat unconventional courtship — and an interlude on a bench in Ross's museum. Determinedly she turned her mind to her wedding night. "Not hell, dear one, heaven. It was such heaven."

"And yet you warn me of the dangers."

"All men are not Ross." She refused to admit that the lovemaking she shared with her husband was a wild and drugging thing, or that their trysts were not confined either to the night, or to the bedroom. "It is quite the routine for a bridegroom to enter his new wife's chamber, to order her into bed, where he joins her — dressed in his nightshirt, of course — and to perform his husbandly duties in a manner intended to obtain only his own satisfaction. Then the tendency is for the oaf to leave without as much as a kiss or a word of endearment. Well, my dear, that is just not on."

Desirée appeared to digest what Finch had said. Then she said, "Rather like a horse in a night rail."

Finch felt her mouth fall open.

"Well, if a man tried to do that to me, I should reward him with terrible surprises."

"What terrible surprises?" Finch found Desirée's spirit irresistible.

"I should bite him. Hard," Desirée said.

Finch looked for men's shadows near the

glass windows in the door but saw none. She whispered, "Where?"

"In bed, I should think."

"No, no, I mean *what* would you bite? His ear?"

Desirée let out a long sigh and said, "Why, I would bite him *there* of course. Right on the Pinnacle of his Pride."

"Desirée." Finch held her stomach and laughed aloud. "You would do no such thing. For all you know you might manage to inflame the creature's passion even further and he would set upon you. He could be so out of control that he would hurt you with his violent assault."

"You mean he might like what I'd done," Desirée said. "It might turn him into a sexual *animal.* A horse — have you ever seen the size of a horse's —"

"Yes, and I don't want to discuss that now. I am trying to guide you and it isn't easy as long as you can't keep your mind off horses."

"Was Ross ever an animal with you."

"Good heavens, *no,* Desirée."

"Do you enjoy it when he comes to you — or perhaps when you go to him?"

This was not at all the way the discussion should have gone. "I enjoy being with Ross."

"Do you imagine that Adam would all but attack me — with a nightshirt on — and not bother to as much as kiss me?"

"Of course not. Adam is gentle."

"He is rather large, though," Desirée said with a thoughtful expression on her face. "He could have his way with me if he wanted to."

"He would never do such a thing," Finch insisted.

"What if I got carried away and bit him — just for fun. Would he punish me for it?"

"I rather think he might make you pay, but you would each get equal pleasure out of the price."

"So why should I be worried about my wedding night?"

Finch stared at Desirée and realized the girl had neatly bamboozled her into defending Adam and what his behavior was likely to be once they were married. "You are well able to care for yourself," Finch told the girl. "And I'm going to do my best to make sure this wedding takes place."

26

Finally Adam couldn't take it anymore. He landed a punch on Viscount Kilrood's handsome jaw, knocked him backward over a crate, and stood ready to hit him again when he got up.

Ross wiped the back of a gloved hand over his chin and rested on his elbows in the mingled straw and snow in an alley leading from the side of the inn to the stables. They had been there, disagreeing, for ten minutes.

"Feel better?" Ross said.

"Not much."

"You aren't a violent man by nature."

"Neither are you," Adam said. "But you could be if you or someone you love were insulted to your face."

Ross grunted and held out a hand. Adam hauled the man to his feet.

"Was that necessary, d'you think?" Ross asked. "Did it make any of this easier?"

"You just listed all the reasons why I should not be allowed to marry Desirée, even in name only. I'm inconsequential, have a peculiar family background, I don't have enough money, my social skills make me an impossible match for someone like Desirée since I would embarrass her whenever we were with all the important people her family knows. She is too shallow for me and I should quickly tire of her. Jean-Marc would behave like my father rather than my brother-in-law. Desirée would grow tired of me and seek diversion elsewhere because that is the way of her class. And last, and most, the comment that required the punch, and I quote: 'Have you already had her?' Nothing I can imagine will make Desirée's and my own plight easier, but the punch was absolutely necessary."

Ross narrowed his eyes.

"Punch me back if it'll make you feel better." Adam touched his head and winced. "On the other hand, I'm not sure it's fair play to hit an already injured man."

"We'd best get back to the ladies," Ross said, and gave the crate he'd fallen over a kick.

Side by side, they made their way back, but paused outside the door to the private room.

Ross looked at Adam and raised his brows in question.

Adam shook his head — no they would not reveal what they'd been discussing — and opened the door.

"Brrr, what a night," Ross said from behind Adam. "But I doubt there's anything like a wedding to warm one up. I'll send a messenger ahead to the Spring-field Inn to awaken the officiating man and we'd best get the business over with — just in case Adam and Desirée are being pursued."

The appraisal Desirée gave her pretty but creased clothes almost made Adam say they should change first, but his own sense of urgency caused him to keep his mouth shut.

Perhaps they might one day have a celebration of what they were about to do, and even repeat their vows — if the plans made for them went awry and they remained together.

Spring-field lay less than a mile from the Three Thistles and the little party was shown hastily into a shabby room and told to wait there.

Desirée stood a little apart, her mouth firmly set, while she seemed lost in

369

thought. Ross paced while Finch waited beside Adam, her gloved hand tucked beneath his elbow. From time to time she smiled at Adam as if they were accomplices in some wonderful conspiracy.

At last an immensely rotund gentleman entered the room with a rolling gait, tugging at his neckcloth as he came. "A happy day," he said in a gruff voice. "You'll want to make the most of it so we'd best get this done."

Adam extended a hand to Desirée and she held it firmly. He could feel her resolve. Standing in front of the officiator with Ross at Adam's shoulder and Finch beside Desirée, they listened to the man — who had demanded fifty guineas for his services — mumble his way rapidly through the Church of England wedding service, pausing for Adam and Desirée to respond, but often continuing before they'd finished speaking.

When Adam produced a ring from his pocket and put it on Desirée's finger, tears stood in her eyes, tears of surprise he rather thought. Lady Hester had assisted him in finding what pleased him by having a jeweler bring him a selection. Her Ladyship had *made suggestions,* but he saw the simple band with its crest of turquoise, diamonds and pearls and knew it was the right one.

"Inowpronounceyoumanandwife — kissthe-bride."

Desirée giggled and raised her face.

Ignoring Ross's cough, Adam kissed her lightly and gave her a hug. And now he'd best be very careful what physical contact he had with her. How little it might take to strip away his resolve not to touch her — really touch her.

"I thought we should see Verbeux at the Spring-field Inn," Desirée said while the coach rocked along rough lanes on the way from Spring-field to Mrs. MacFlake's rooming house to the northeast of Gretna Green.

Adam thought about Verbeux and not with a great deal of comfort. "Perhaps he was there, watching. We must be careful not to mention his traveling with us. Wouldn't want him in trouble with Jean-Marc."

They took a sharp curve in the lane and Desirée craned her neck to look back at the Kilroods' following coach. "Why are they coming with us?"

A question he had asked himself. "I think Ross has slipped into Jean-Marc's shoes and become your guardian and brother in absentia. I've little doubt he wants to see that you will be in a safe place for the night." He ground his teeth when he closed his mouth.

Desirée sat very upright and crossed her arms. "If I were in need of protection, I would turn to —" she breathed a sharp breath and looked startled "— I would turn to my husband."

She sat beside him and Adam's attention was caught by the way she repeatedly rubbed a finger over the stones in the ring he'd given her.

"And if I need a champion, I shall turn to my wife," he said. "I think I shall need her . . . a great deal."

A rising sun, a beaten gold streak in the deep purple and navy-blue sky, stretched just above scattered housetops and shone through trees. Thick ice ringed with frost-covered grass, covered every puddle. Adam looked at the girl he had married, at the reflection of the early sun in her eyes, and felt in an extraordinary way, changed forever. He would never be the same, of that he was sure.

He felt alive as he never had, and numbed at the same time. His jaw stiffened. What he wanted more than anything was to say, "I love you," but he must not, not yet if ever.

Desirée's clear gray eyes never left his face. She didn't smile. In her pale throat a vein pulsed visibly. The corners of her mouth trembled. This moment, looking at her, seeing her vulnerability and her trust as she looked at him, wouldn't be such a bad moment to die.

Adam shook his head. Dammit that he should think such a thing at such a time. If he didn't fear punishing her by changing her station in life forever, he'd bide his time and they'd make it away together — and their marriage would be consummated. He smiled a little. Oh, *yes*, the marriage would be consummated.

"That smile, Adam Chillworth, makes you appear wicked. Incredibly happy, but wicked just the same."

He bent forward and braced his forearms on his knees. With his long fingers, he snared hers and brought them to his lips. His kiss wasn't fleeting and Desirée gasped a little. "You are very observant," he told her. "I am happy. I've taken happiness, decided I have a right to it, and called it my own. And have a care, my girl, because I am definitely a wicked man."

She leaned a little closer. "A shy, quiet

man. Keeps to himself. Doesn't need other people. That's what everyone thinks, you know. I used to think it myself."

"Very astute of you." He tried, but failed, to be serious now.

"Very silly of me," she said. "Certainly you are a deep man, but you are not really shy, nor are you always happy to be solitary. In fact, I think you like being with me very much — especially now."

He laughed at her.

"Laugh on. We shall see how much you hate lying in the same bed with me and sleeping. We shall have to sleep before we can start to enjoy our short time of peace together."

Adam said, "Hmm," but thought that although he would not hate lying with her at all, he was most unlikely to get much sleep and he would never be at peace as long as she was his only in name.

"I think I see the rooming house," he said, leaning toward the window. "I do see it. Praise be. Now, my dear, listen to me carefully. I foresee some nonsense from Viscount Kilrood. Overbearing stuff. Unless I ask you a question, just let me take care of things."

She widened her eyes and managed to look pinched. "You'll have to do better than that, Adam. Ordering me about will never do."

He frowned and thought a moment before he said, "Didn't you agree to love, honor and obey —"

"I mumbled the last word," she told him. "Now trust me to be judicious, if you please."

Henpecked already. He sniffed, but found he enjoyed a woman with a strong mind and will. "What a pretty place," he said, changing the subject as Edward drove into the courtyard of an Elizabethan country house with mullioned windows that winked in the early sunlight. Holly bushes flanked the door and were covered with so many shiny red berries the leaves appeared to have been forgotten.

A row of animals lined the two front steps, an assortment of dogs and cats warming themselves in the unexpected rays from the sun.

Edward pulled to a stop and jumped from his box with the kind of agility that should have been impossible after so much exertion. He opened the door and put down steps. "It's a very good morning, Mr. Chillworth, Mrs. Chillworth. That is Princess, Mrs. Chillworth, I suppose. Or perhaps not. I can smell smoke from the fires that must be alight inside, and cinnamon — no doubt because a fine pie is baking. As soon as you are settled, I'll away to the Three Thistles and see about a room."

"You'll away nowhere," Desirée said. "You will be staying here, won't he, Adam?"

He nodded. "Of course." As a matter of fact that was exactly what he'd planned.

Adam hopped to the slippery gravel and handed Desirée down. And the burgundy Kilrood coach swept into the forecourt, tassels flying from polished brass rails surrounding the roof. Ross and Finch joined them, although Finch hung back somewhat, and in addition to the driver and the two men who had ridden on the back of the equipage, several more with expressionless faces arrived in a cart.

"I say, Ross," Adam said. "Why the army?"

"Don't give them a thought," Ross said. "I take my responsibilities seriously. We must be sure Desirée is safe."

"My husband will keep me safe," Desirée said, so sharp and snappy as to catch Adam unawares.

"Of course he will," Finch said quickly. "Isn't it a lovely feeling, to know you have someone to care for you forever."

"Female dreaming is all well and good," Ross said, "as long as the truth of this event isn't forgotten."

"I think that's enough," Adam told the other man. "We're tired, and so must you be. We'll make sure we send word to you before we leave Scotland."

He basked in the brilliance of Desirée's adoring smile.

"You fellows," Ross called to the men in the cart. "Kindly assemble over there —" He pointed to a white stone statue of a small boy feeding cherries to a small girl. "Martin and Martin — one each side of the door. They're brothers," he remarked.

Once the men were all at their stations, Adam took particular notice of the menagerie, which appeared as some sort of welcoming committee. Not one of them had left the steps. They watched the proceedings, their heads moving from one direction to another, almost in unison. An English sheepdog overflowed one end of the lower step and balanced with two paws, one front, one back, on the step and the other two on the gravel. He appeared quite comfortable.

Edward unpacked their coach and piled valises, boxes and bags in a tidy heap.

Ross had developed a fascination with his boots but Finch's eyes darted from face to face and she looked miserable. Eventually she went to the steps and picked up a small, scruffy white dog with black rings around his eyes.

"Have a care, my love," Ross called, sounding worried. "One never knows whether a strange dog may bite."

Finch held the animal close to her neck and got a licking interspersed with intimate nuzzling to her face.

"Did anybody ring?" Adam said.

The front door flew open as if on springs and operated by Adam's question. A lady of younger old age stepped out and made her way carefully between her pets, patting and bending to kiss them on her way. She picked up a particularly small orange cat and popped him into her pocket.

In a white cap, blue kerseymere dress and her starched apron, with sturdy laced boots on her feet, she stood in front of the four-footed gallery and clapped. "Helloo Mr. and Mrs. Chillworth," she cried. "Welcome to Mrs. MacFlake's. That would be me. And I'm honored ye've chosen to start married life at my humble home. Oh, Blossom —" she took the cat from her pocket and held its nose to hers "— we've a brand-new Mr. and Mrs. with us. Ye'll be nice t'them. Ye'll all be welcoming," she said gruffly, casting a military eye over the gathered troops. "Come along in wi' ye," she told Adam and Desirée.

She winked, but both eyes closed and spoiled the conspiratorial effect. When she started to lead the way, she saw Martin and Martin — together with their pistols, and stopped at once. Her back became very straight. "Who are ye?" she asked. "What d'ye think ye're doin' here wi' those blunderbusses? I'll thank ye t'be on your way."

Ross came forward and said, "Excuse me please, Mrs. MacFlake. I'm Ross, Viscount Kilrood and the lady over there is my wife. We are friends of Mr. and, er, Mrs. Chillworth. We'd like to make sure they're well settled. And those are not blunderbusses."

"No armaments on my property," she told him and waved Martin and Martin imperiously away. They lowered their pistols and their eyes and walked to the back of the Kilrood coach.

Mrs. MacFlake caught Finch's smile and offered a two-eyed wink. "Ye're my only guests and I'll have plenty of time to make sure ye have everythin' ye need."

When she looked at Ross, her face was smooth, like a young girl's, and might never have been used at all. No smiles. No winks. "I dinna think a grown man like Mr. Chillworth — and he's verra grown —" She looked Adam up and down, pulled her elbows tight to her body, and gave a little shiver, which did not mean she was cold, "I dinna think he's in need of being *well settled* by ye. He's verra grown indeed, and quite in command of whatever he's about, I'm sure. And he and his lady will want to go to their bed at once."

The look on Ross's face was priceless. Small giggles erupted from Desirée and he tried to look severe. He failed.

Mrs. MacFlake accomplished an almost perfect wink at Desirée. The second eyelid didn't immediately sink. "That's the lassie. A lusty one. Maybe we'll make ye an honorary Scot. Come along in."

"Let me help you with the bags," Adam told Edward and loaded up with boxes before indicating that Desirée should go ahead of him into the house.

Edward followed, then the ragtag MacFlake brigade. Ross followed but Adam noted that Finch remained outside. The men who had ridden in the cart brought up the rear.

They walked through a warm and fragrant kitchen where a boy peeled potatoes over a large yellow bowl with a pot of water beside him, and a girl washed dishes and pans in a deep sink.

"Will ye want baths?" Mrs. MacFlake asked. "Or would ye prefer plenty o' hot water brought t'your room. There's a big fire alight in there. A perfect place for a man and a girl to learn more about each other."

Adam couldn't have missed Desirée's blush. He felt a little warm himself.

"We'll be happy with hot water in the room," Desirée said and Adam found one more reason to love her; she was sensible and could overcome small difficulties.

Ross caught up and made the passage through the lower floor and upstairs to a landing where frost still clung to the windows, difficult at best.

Every few feet, the lady of the house turned around, slowing enough to all but bring the rest of the entourage to a halt and frowning at Ross who looked sheepish.

"This is it," she said, flinging open a crookedly hung and heavy oak door. "Take everything inside, then we'll show ye where ye're t'sleep," she told Edward. To her pets she said, "No babies, my wee beauties, not you, you can visit later. And if the Viscount has a word or two of wisdom I'm sure we'd all love t'hear them."

Adam almost felt sorry for the other man.

"I hope you know," Ross told Adam, "that I have known and loved this girl for a long time. Her brother and I have been like brothers. He would do anything for me and in return, I would never knowingly fail him. You are honorable. I know you understand me."

"Thank you, Ross," Desirée said. "You are one of the loves of my life, even if you can be a ninnyhammer sometimes. Mrs. MacFlake, do you suppose you could give his Lordship and his lady a cup of tea before they leave. It's been such a tiring night."

"O'course I can." Mrs. MacFlake's voice and expression softened. "I know how it is to worry about friends, and to feel responsible for helping to take care of what matters to them most. Off t'the kitchen with ye m'lord. And get your lady. There's apple crumble just out of the oven. A fine breakfast it'll make and your men can have some, too."

Ross's eyes were sad when he said, "Thank you. You're very understanding."

He turned to the men who accompanied him. "You and you, one at each end of this corridor. No one comes or goes without proving who they are and what their business is. Williams, at the foot of the stairs to relay any alarm to Martin or Martin."

All Adam wanted was to be with Desirée, alone, and to fall asleep with her while the whole world was about its business and without interest in them. At least, that's all he had the energy to want this morning.

Two dark wood, highly polished steps led down to the bedroom. Adam took Desirée's hand and helped her into the room. She made a gleeful sound and he smiled himself. Mrs. MacFlake knew how to turn an ordinary room into the kind of bower dreams were made of.

"This is one of my most trusted employees," Ross said, blithely following along into the bedroom. "Come along, Gus. Gus has worked on our estates here in Scotland for years. He's almost part of the family. He won't take up much room. Use the sofa by the commode, Gus, and no falling asleep, mind."

Short, broad of shoulder, with sturdy legs, Gus's gray hair stood on end and he had a kind round face with sharp eyes. He took a few steps toward the sofa before Adam caught him by the collar.

"You're out of your mind," he told Ross. "What is this man supposed to do?"

"He'll make himself comfortable there and make sure all's well with the two of you." At least Ross couldn't look at Adam.

Adam released Gus and saw the amused look on his face.

"I shall have something to say to my brother about this," Desirée said. "We are insulted, aren't we, Adam?"

"If ye aren't," Mrs. MacFlake said, "I'm insulted enough for both o' ye. It's mad ye are, Your Lordship. Does this person sit in your own chamber while ye lie in your wife's arms?"

"Don't be impertinent," Ross told her. "Very well, Gus. Get a chair and sit outside the door."

"Get on a bloody horse and ride out of here," Adam said. "And the rest of your friends can go with you."

"I'll just have to take the duty myself," Ross said, and then, "Not again," as Adam's fist landed on his chin and he tripped backward on the steps to sit on the landing floor. He massaged his jaw. "I've got a wonderful idea. Would you please pack up and go back to London — and leave me in peace. I will do what I have promised to do when the time comes. I will help make your way smoother with Jean-Marc. But please just go. If you want to talk to me, if you want to ask my advice or to discuss matters with me, I shall be at your disposal. I like you, Chillworth — despite your damnable fists — and you, Desirée are a spirited girl and admirable. Who could blame a man for falling in love with you?"

Adam felt uncomfortable. Again he hauled Ross to his feet, and this time suffered a solid blow to the midsection that left him gasping for breath. "There *will* be guards around the property," Ross said with a look that dared Mrs. MacFlake to challenge him. "I must get Finch home. This is a delicate time for her and she has already overexerted herself."

"She's increasing again?" Desirée squealed. "Oh, I'm so happy for you. This is going to be a wonderful year for babies."

Adam aimed a hard look at her but added his congratulations to Ross.

At last the crowd dispersed, all but the sheepdog whom Adam hadn't noticed was in the room. He raised an eyebrow to Desirée who pointed to the immensely furry gray and white animal who appeared to move on tippytoes, on his claws, in fact. And he grinned and tilted his head in the most winning way before he leaped onto the bed and arranged himself in the middle.

Adam threw up his hands. "Foiled in the end. The wretch must belong to Ross."

27

The pitcher on the commode was empty. Desirée looked into it and wondered what to do. She had no idea how one sent for such things as hot water in an establishment like this.

She glanced at Adam who was pulling heavy, rose-colored draperies over the window. Without firelight and a candle by the bed, the room would be in darkness.

He removed his coat and began to unpack the valises. Her mouth fell open when she realized he was taking the clothes from hers and hanging them up. While she watched, her two dresses were whisked into the wardrobe, her intimate clothes were set carefully inside a drawer, and her toiletries appeared in a tidy array on the commode beside her.

Adam smiled at her distractedly and returned to deal with his own possessions. Next he checked inside the two picnic baskets they hadn't as much as opened. He placed a bottle of red wine and one of champagne on a dressing table with a pink chintz skirt to match the pink chintz feather-filled quilt and bed hangings. The baskets he placed in the recesses of a corner, close to a dressing screen, the very sight of which raised goose bumps all over Desirée's body.

"These appear to be wedding gifts," he said of the boxes. "It would probably be best not to open them at all. They'd be easier to transport back to London that way."

She turned her back on him. "And easier to return to those who gave them when it's revealed that our marriage is a sham."

Stillness settled. Adam must have stopped moving around, which meant that he was standing somewhere behind her trying to decide what to say.

"None of this is your fault," she told him. "In fact, I'm ashamed of myself. It's true that there are those who want to keep us apart and who have tried to harm us, but I should not have pressured you into a situation such as this. I have upset everyone. The way you have seen Ross behave is not at all like him. He is a man who is kind, somewhat distant because he had a solitary life until he fell in love with Finch, but generous and concerned for others. I caused him to behave like a villain."

"That doesn't matter," Adam said. "The predicament we're in does. So far we've kept . . . no, I will not speak of it now. We need water. I'll go down for it."

"So far, Adam? What have we *kept* so far?"

"Let me think it all through. Nothing must be done in haste." He came to stand behind her and rub her shoulders. "I have become the impediment. You decided you cared for me and didn't want to be with another man. But there *is* another man who is determined to make you his. First he tried to frighten you away from me. And what happened to me was for the same reason. Either of us could have been killed. Having us walk away from each other would present less difficulties than the course we've taken."

"There is a very simple way to end all of this," Desirée told him. She faced him, looked up into his tired face. "We can ignore what my family wants from me and go away from them. We can decide that instead of putting off a decision we'll have to make anyway, we'll make it now. We'll decide to stay together always. I don't know how my inheritance is set out. If I do still inherit, then we have no problems. If I don't, we'll learn to live as quietly as we must. I want you, Adam, only you. There are not enough gowns or shoes, or pieces of jewelry to make up for the loss of you —"

"The loss of you will be like the end of my life," Adam said and pressed his fingers against her lips. "But don't be so impulsive. Don't you think I want to take what you offer? I do, but I fear, as I have since I knew I wanted you as a man wants a woman, that when you are a little older and your wit and grace are attracting every man in London, you will become bored with me. There is nothing unusual about a man being some years older than the woman he marries, but ours would be as much a marriage of the minds as of the bodies. How could I bear to watch you gradually slip away from me? We would not be poor, in fact we would be comfortable, but very often we would be quiet, just the two of us — or more if God granted us children — living for each other, to be with each other.

"How long do you think you could be happy as the wife of a reclusive man who finds his pleasure in talking by the fire, or under the trees in a park, or painting while you listen to my silence? My world is different from yours."

Her throat tightened so much it hurt. "I have never liked parties or a lot of fuss."

"People would say I took advantage of an impressionable girl because I wanted to become part of her elevated world — and to get my hands into deep pockets."

"Adam!" Her heart pounded. "You care more for the opinions of others than for mine? I know those things are not true."

He shook his head. "I know you do. But I have to be the wise one now, I have to think of your future."

"Then don't send me into the darkness, and that's where I'll be without you."

Adam put more coals on the fire and went to stroke the dog's massive head. The creature all but purred. "We lied to ourselves and to each other," he told Desirée.

She would be sensible, otherwise she placed too heavy a burden on him. "We did it because we wanted so badly to be together that we used what happened and turned it into an excuse to run off together."

"Yes," Adam said, and his shoulders slumped. "I even pretended I could live with you until our enemies were caught and not make you my wife in every sense. Fool that I am."

She swallowed and swallowed. "We have not been truthful."

"Not at all." Adam touched her face lightly. "We'll have to give it up. As soon as we return to London tomorrow — obviously we cannot prolong this misery — we'll confess our duplicity to Jean-Marc and get it all over with. But he must see the wisdom of dealing with our enemies before the marriage is annulled."

A single knock made only a dull thump on the thick, old door and Adam went to unlock and open it.

Desirée let out a little cry.

"The devil take me!" Adam fell back a step and Verbeux, dressed in what looked like a butler's garb, walked in with two steaming buckets. He nodded to Adam and to Desirée and proceeded to fill the jug on the commode with hot water. He set the buckets down on the hearth.

"Verbeux," Desirée said, delighted to see a friend. "You enjoy shocking people, don't you?" She ran to throw her arms around his shoulders, and kissed his cheek.

He stood as still as a gravestone, although he was warmer, and made no attempt to touch her. When she released him, he ahemed and said, "I told you I should be watching and I have been. It's my duty."

She laughed. "Have I shocked you by kissing your cheek? Oh, Verbeux, we have known each other since I was a little girl."

"Princess, I did not touch you then, nor do I touch you now. It isn't seemly. Mr. Chillworth, I do have some concerns. You handled the Viscounts' men well. Just the right thing. But I've been told there was a man, a lone rider, asking questions about the two of you at the Three Thistles. Fortunately the landlord had been well paid to insist he knew nothing, but I don't like it. I shall be keeping watch in the entrance hall. I suggest you remain alert — just in case."

"I understand," Adam said. "But how did you come into this house? And doing the duties of an upstairs maid?"

Verbeux actually smiled a little. "All arranged ahead of time. When you begin the journey home, Chillworth, don't be surprised to find you have escorts. I have retained two men — riders — who will be on lookout. I must head to London as quickly as I can — to separate myself. I'm sure you understand." He collected the dressing screen and spread it open before the commode.

Desirée felt cross, and embarrassed.

"Thank you for helping us," Adam said. "Rest as much as you can, Princess.

Plenty of sleep is what you need." Verbeux studied the dog on the bed. "Hmm. An animal like that makes a good deterrent for any unwanted advances. Shouldn't be surprised if he's got a good set of teeth on him."

"You mean if someone tries to break in?" Adam asked and, although his expression was serious, his eyes laughed.

"Of course," Verbeux said, preparing to leave. Abruptly he turned back and returned behind the screen to emerge with the wall mirror. "Best be safe," he said, and left with the mirror under his arm.

"Dammit all." Adam put his fists on his hips. "Why would he take the mirror?"

Desirée fell into a chair and laughed so hard that tears squeezed from her eyes. "I thought I was supposed to be the naive one. He did it so we should not somehow see a reflection, one of the other, less than fully clothed. I think poor Verbeux is the one with a problem. We should find him another wife."

"You amaze me," Adam said, shaking his head. "Please go ahead and do whatever will make you feel comfortable before you sleep."

"I should feel awkward going first. Please do it, Adam. I'll make friends with this terribly ferocious dog and find out just how long his teeth are."

"Very well." Adam gathered his needs quickly and went behind the screen. Soon Desirée heard water splashing and had to fight an urge to pop her head around the screen to say "boo." Adam was right, she was still a child in too many ways.

Truth told, she was also a woman in the important ways and mostly she wanted to watch him wash. The dog didn't react to her overtures and she wandered to the boxes they were apparently not to open. There were far too many for the number of people who had known their plans, which meant they had sent more than one each. She smiled fondly at the thought of them all. Most of her friends wanted her with Adam. All she had to do was work on Jean-Marc. *All* she had to do.

One box, wrapped in white paper and tied with a silver ribbon, caught her fancy. The envelope bore only her name and said, Open When You Are Alone. She was alone and slipped out the card. "I had this made especially for you. I was naughty and arranged for your companion to help me with the size. I think it will be perfect and I'm sure Adam will think so. Wear this in happiness — but take it off when you're too hot. Affectionately, Lady Hester Bingham." Desirée pressed her fingertips into a flimsy heap of white silk and lace, a nightgown with the weight of gossamer.

Desirée looked at Adam's shadow moving behind the screen. He might not be too much longer. She made up her mind, rolled Lady H.'s gift inside a towel and put it on the bed beside her. She pushed the empty box under the bed.

With her hands in her lap, she waited, and studied the shape of Adam. Such a pleasing shape. He cut off an annoyed exclamation, but Desirée couldn't stop herself from smiling. He was pulling some garment over his head. This, she assumed, was the joked-about nightshirt and she doubted Mr. Chillworth was accustomed to sleeping in such things.

He reached from inside the screen to lift a bucket from the hearth. Water gurgled into the jug, then he emptied the bowl into the bucket and set it on the other side of the commode.

"If you need more water than this," he said, filling the bowl from the jug, "tell me and I'll deal with it for you."

Her, "Thank you," was lost in his whirlwind exit from the scant hiding place and his forceful dive beneath the bed covers.

But he wasn't fast enough for Desirée not to see that the nightshirt had a plain band at the neck, with several buttons — which he'd firmly closed — full sleeves loose at the wrist, and that the thing flapped about his knees.

He settled in, lying on his back with his face turned away from her. The dog had inched higher on the bed and looked sleepily into Adam's eyes.

Determined that he should not have time to feign sleep before she was beside him — more or less — Desirée got out of her clothes as quickly as the awkward things would allow and tossed them over the screen. Her gown, her many petticoats, her chemise, the daring peach-colored silk drawers Meg had given her and her fine embroidered stockings. Perhaps terrible experiences could come of what she was trying to do, but at the moment she felt wonderfully excited.

The water had cooled and goose bumps sprang up as she washed. She had a bar of rose-scented soap Anne had made and it smelled so sweet and clean. She also had a rose perfume, which soon warmed in the spots where she placed it. Once her hair was down, she brushed it until it shone and rather thought she'd like to walk out to

Adam wearing nothing but the fair ringlets that covered her shoulders and slid across her breasts.

He would think her forward.

She would be forward, but the idea of shocking him thrilled her.

But she would behave. Lady Hester's silk nightgown slipped over Desirée's head like snow sliding down a windowpane. Over her skin it glided, chill, smooth, awaking every nerve in its path. And when the gown fell to froth about her feet she saw that it fitted like a sleeveless shift as far as her hips, then grew wider so that the skirt swirled at the slightest move. She'd been able to put the garment on without fastenings but it did have a row of silk-covered buttons on each shoulder.

When she looked down at herself and realized that the bands of lace were wide and without backing, all but transparent, she longed for the mirror Verbeux had removed. Perhaps she should have put on one of her own, much more modest night rails.

Carefully, wondering just how much the lace revealed, Desirée emptied her water into the bucket, threw back her hair and went forth with what felt like duelling butterflies in her stomach.

One pace past the screen and she looked into Adam's eyes. He glanced down at her body, then back to her face. Muscles in his jaw jerked. "Into bed with you and go to sleep," he said in the most odd voice. He sounded angry with her. And he averted his face to the dog again.

Desirée breathed through her mouth and tilted up her face so that tears couldn't fall. Fine, he preferred the company of a dog, so be it.

A sound in her head jarred her. She looked at Adam to see if he could have howled out in frustration, but he hadn't moved. The noise sounded again and it was a howl, a man's furious yell but very far away and apparently only in her head.

Adam shifted a little, and without warning rolled out of bed to slam on the floor. He was checking the legs of the bed when Desirée decided she shouldn't watch.

In moments there was silence again and she looked over her shoulder to find him back in bed, the covers pulled up to his chin.

She felt a presence in the room, one she couldn't see and she hugged herself.

The yell didn't sound again, only a noise as if someone strained to move something.

There were several noises the same. The dog opened his eyes, then lifted his head — he whined a little and tried to settle. But he must have changed his mind because he twirled onto his back, arched to rest on his head and rump, and catapulted from the bed to the floor.

"Dogs," Adam muttered. He got out of bed and walked to the door with a hand shielding the sight of Desirée from his eyes. "Out," he said, waving the dog onto the landing before shutting and locking the door yet again.

"That wasn't normal," Desirée said.

"The animal needed to go out." Adam leaned his back against the door and studied Desirée. Evidently his need to look was stronger than his need to be strong. "If I didn't fear for you, I'd leave," he said.

"Verbeux is downstairs," she said, raising her chin. "You may tell him I'll be traveling back to London alone. Make sure the men he's hired suit you."

"I don't trust anyone —" He shut his mouth.

She took a step toward him but he waved for her to stop. "You don't trust anyone else with me?" she said. "Is that it? I wonder why."

"Because one moment you are sensible,

the next you allow passion to bear you along. I understand you because I've watched you mature and I've seen how you are a dragonfly caught in your own sunbeam. No, no, I cannot help fearing for you."

"If we made our marriage real they couldn't do a thing about it." She trembled and rubbed her bare arms. "I'm cold."

"Get into bed. If I didn't need sleep, also, I'd lie on that wretched little sofa."

"Adam, if we decided to be married — I mean, really married — nothing would be a lie anymore. We'd be looking after each other and I'd be loving the life you described to me before. Not everyone will turn from us. You know how we've been encouraged to be together."

"Get yourself into that bed," he said, pointing with one long finger. "And sleep. I can't play the fool anymore."

He got in and this time stretched out on his back with his eyes closed.

Desirée muttered, "bully," slipped between the covers and curled up in a ball on her side. Her misery was abject and it was all her fault for preying on Adam's natural instincts while she forgot he had the kind of willpower and honor that would always make him do the right thing in the end.

He moved and she heard him blow out the candle.

"Don't you wonder who the man was who rode alone to the Three Thistles and asked about us?"

He took so long to answer she thought he never would.

"Aye, of course I wonder," he said, just when she'd given up. "I'll find out who he is but not *now*. Now I'm going to sleep and so are you."

She pulled the covers all the way over her head.

"Where did you get that thing?" His voice was muffled.

Desirée made a little space to hear and speak through and said, "What thing?"

"That, that, *thing* you've almost got on. You can see through it. Did you know that?"

"Of course." She was furious now. "I am an expert in seduction and I acquired this nightgown especially for the moment when I took advantage of you."

"Don't speak to me like that, Desirée. Respect is a sign of maturity."

She shot out from beneath the covers and sat on the edge of the bed. "*Don't* say the word maturity to me again. Lady Hester sent this gown as a wedding gift — for both of us."

He sighed a long, long sigh. "Get back into bed and relax until you sleep."

"You don't want me."

"Please don't do this, Desirée. Just . . . *don't*. And I do want you."

"No you don't." She sniffed repeatedly.

He rolled over and touched her back. "You aren't yourself. This seems romantic now but wait until you face Jean-Marc. He is your brother and you love him."

It was more than she could bear, begging this man to love her enough to face whatever came their way, only to have him refuse her. She went to the couch and sat there with her eyes closed.

"Very well," Adam said, and there was a rustling loud enough to fill the room. "I can't take it anymore. I'm a strong man, some have even suggested I'm so controlled because I don't have any feelings. Well, they're wrong, as you are about to find out."

Desirée's eyes opened in time to see Adam pulling off the nightshirt in the darkness. The white thing sailed through the air and landed near her feet. She shrank back and her eyes opened so wide she thought they might never close again.

"Changed your mind yet?" he asked.

"I certainly have not."

He loomed over her and she knew he was naked. She bit her bottom lip and made herself sit still. His hand, closing on her left wrist, might even leave a bruise there. Adam pulled her up and across the room. "Stand there and don't move a muscle," he said, and lit the candle again.

He most certainly was naked. Adam Chillworth wore absolutely no clothing and that included shoes because she checked.

"Now let us see what we have here," he said. He pulled a bench from the dressing table, positioned it in front of the fire and lifted Desirée to stand on it.

So, he thought he would mortify her into backing off. She held out her arms and turned a slow circle. The way he moaned and let his eyelids slowly droop brought her satisfaction. There was no question of his moaning because he didn't like what he saw because she could see him in detail and from her reading she knew that in this situation his bodily reaction would be entirely different if he were not aroused.

Adam was aroused. She frowned down at her body and had one wild, frightening thought: How would so much of him go into so little of her?

"Your breasts might as well be bare,"

Adam said. "And your waist — it's very small, isn't it? Then we have windows on what you insist should be mine. By the way, when you turned around, your bottom was a delight. I am close to sexual frenzy. In that state, I may do anything. Still want to continue?"

"I want you to stop talking and do it. I want you to do everything there is to be done. Make a good job of it so there can't be any questions afterward."

Adam didn't say another word. He blew the candle out again and returned to lift her, to wrap his arms around her thighs and press his mouth against her stomach. He kissed her there, again and again until the silk and lace were wet, and he turned with her, around he turned humming some soft piece of music deep in his throat.

Desirée bent over him, spread her hands on his back and felt his muscles bunched there. She caught her fingers in his hair. He sucked her stomach gently, pulled the taut flesh in and kept his mouth wide-open, blowing a little, and pulling her in again, and she wanted him to touch her everywhere. Inside, her belly stung. His cunning mouth sent a current of bees to work. The stinging started between her legs and she became so wet she blushed at the possibility that he might know.

Adam needed only one arm to hold her. He righted her and with his other hand he worked the gown upward, baring her legs. She wound them about him and she felt the hair on his chest against the insides of her thighs. Desirée shuddered. Cupping her bottom he lowered her until he could look at her breasts through the lace. And with the very tip of his tongue, he made her feel as if a hot needle jabbed at the end of each nipple.

He didn't tire, didn't stop. Inch by inch he slid her down his body until she felt him, fully distended, resting along her sensitive flesh, pulsing there while she panted and was helpless to stop herself from trying to urge him closer.

He undid the buttons at her shoulders, buttons of slippery silk intended to slip free easily. The bodice fell until it was held up by her breasts and Adam put her on the floor, abruptly, and stood back to look at her. By the firelight she saw veins at his temples pulse, and the way his lips parted as he took his time looking at each part of her.

She thought she heard him whisper, "Careful," but couldn't be sure.

He offered her his hand and she took it,

and he led her to the bed. Swiftly, he sat cross-legged in the middle of the mattress and stood her before him. "Tell me you are not afraid of anything I might do," he said.

Desirée shook her head, "Nothing. The way you make me feel is sweet and wild. Don't stop."

First he bared her breasts and, while she clung to his shoulders, covered the tender flesh and squeezed. He squeezed, made circles over her nipples with his palms, kissed her stomach again and all at a leisurely pace that made Desirée want to scream. Her legs threatened to buckle.

He abandoned her breasts to lift her gown into a bunch around her waist. He moved her so quickly she cried out and Adam promptly clamped a hand over her mouth. "I should enjoy having you heard if I didn't fear it might be Verbeux who is listening." She had landed on her knees and Adam bent her backward over a pillow.

"Adam!"

His mouth closed over the center of her and again he used his tongue in a way that had never occurred to Desirée. He flicked it hard, paused to pull a little part of her between his teeth and repeated the maddening process again, and again, while she clawed at his hair and writhed.

A sound escaped her, but Adam's mouth covered hers while his thumbs went where his lips had been — and a flooding heat shot through her. She rocked from side to side, urging him to press harder. Like ripples on a lake when a stone broke the surface, ripples of pleasure widened through Desirée.

Sweat coated Adam's body and his hair was damp. Desirée might not know how it would work, but she knew what must happen, and she would do it. She pulled herself up and sat astride his thighs. With only a small hesitation she took him into her hand, and suffered the same amazement as before, yet it must be possible because that's how the mystery of babies was accomplished.

"Desirée," he said quietly against her neck. "I cannot stop now."

She rose up and positioned the head of his manhood at the opening to her body.

"If there is pain," he said, "it will not last. But lie down so I may enter you carefully."

Carefully. No, she didn't think she wanted this thing that would change her forever to be done carefully. She wanted to feel it all. At first she sank enough to bury an inch of him inside her. So he was too big for her, but she liked feeling him there.

"Desirée —"

"Be quiet," she whispered and took another inch of him into her body.

His moans were incoherent but she heard how he sucked air through his teeth.

Downward she pressed again, covering more hard, slick flesh. He started to move in her and she wanted all of him.

Plunging him into her, she felt stretched, she felt on fire all over again and it still wasn't enough. Wrapping her legs around him, crossing her ankles behind him, she pushed him deeper. She panted and tried to move, but couldn't make that happen.

"Hold onto me," Adam said. He sat on the edge of the bed, leaned back on his arms and bounced with her, creating a space between them for a moment, only to push into her again and make their bodies one.

Her teeth jarred together and her breasts bounced with each jolt. Beneath her bottom, Adam's thighs were hard and straining. Faster, with each thrust more violent than the last, he filled her.

Too soon, Adam cried out and she felt a rush of warm moisture inside. He moved several more times and stopped, breathing heavily.

The end was a longing, a longing for this not to be over. Still inside her with his pulse beating in her flesh, he turned her on her back on the bed and lay on top of her. He curved over and around her as if taking her into himself and cutting her off from the world.

Adam didn't say a word.

Desirée couldn't speak.

They panted together until Adam's breathing slowed, and he became heavy. Desirée stared at the beamed ceiling. She stroked him, kissed his cheek where it rested beside hers, and all the time tension built in her again. Tension and need.

She moved and when he didn't, she moved again. He'd fallen asleep. Just like that! She filled a hand with his thick hair and shook his head until his eyes opened a fraction, then quickly opened all the way. "What is it?" he asked, his voice slurred. "Something's wrong. Have I hurt you badly. Just tell me. Don't hold back."

"Nothing hurts," she fibbed. She didn't care about the soreness, he could make it go away. "Forgive me if that was hard on you, though."

"Hard on me?" He peered at her. "Of course it wasn't hard on me. It was wonderful. You're wonderful. You're amazing."

"Good." Desirée squirmed from beneath him, lay flat on the mattress with her arms and legs outflung and said, "Do it again."

28

Spivey here:

Yes, yes, yes!

That's accomplished and now I can concentrate on you for a moment. You aren't hanging around for the second show. That was rather titillatin' though, wasn't it?

That's enough from you lot. You can't flatten my victory tonight.

What? How would you know? — and, by the way, my temper wears thin over your remarks about cheap tricks. Dogs jump off beds all the time. No, well . . . no, I decline to answer that, too. But falling out of bed might agitate a man into action, I suppose.

I'm late for school, but I'm getting my house back, tra-la.

29

Those at the late afternoon gathering in Lady Hester's beloved green and plum receiving room smiled a great deal but what conversation there was consisted mostly of whispers.

Desirée sat near the fire and Adam stood beside her. The journey back from Scotland had exhausted her and he was worried about her health — and the sadness he knew she was feeling now that they were in London again.

"See how perfect this will be for soirées and salons?" Lady Hester said suddenly and rather too loudly. "There are enough of us for such an occasion right now."

"Absolutely," Sibyl said from the padded windowseat where she sat with Jenny and little Birdie, Lady Hester's adopted daughter, who spent a great deal of time with the Lloyds.

Latimer and Hunter hovered near the

drinks cabinet, each of them drinking Madeira, and not their first glasses.

"And what do the rest of you think?" Lady Hester demanded. Her face was strained.

"I think this entire thing is a bloody mess and Jean-Marc is a fool. Forgive me for being blunt," Hunter said.

"Hunter," Sibyl said. "Little ears present."

He grunted but didn't look particularly contrite.

"What hurts me so is that dear, sweet Meg is sufferin'," Jenny said. "Miss Anne came t'me and said the Count's no' speakin' t'his wife. He's no' speakin' at all. But we're celebratin' wi' ye, Adam and Desirée. We think it's a wonderful thing that ye're married and so in love. Gi' Jean-Marc a wee while and he'll celebrate, too."

"Before or after he calls me out?" Adam said, but he smiled to take the edge off his remark.

"Well," Latimer said, "You've already got your seconds. Make it pistols, will you? Swords can make such a mess and besides, Jean-Marc is a whiz with a sword and I doubt you've ever touched one, Adam."

Desirée found a handkerchief in her reticule and pressed it to her lips. She was far too pale and sad-eyed. Adam could kick himself for his careless tongue.

"I never expected to be blessed with a wife who would bring me so much pleasure," he said, and meant it. "I'm not unaware of Jean-Marc's disappointment. I don't exactly bring marvelous connections to his family, but I'll love his sister enough to make up for it, or I hope that will be enough for him."

In the breathless pause that followed, Adam saw that every eye in the room was suspiciously moist. So much emotion made him uncomfortable.

"It will be more than enough for me," Desirée said, "and that's what matters in marriage. That the husband and wife find joy in each other. I did not know there could be such love."

Sniffles were added to the moist eyes but Adam found he didn't care. "I do love you, Desirée."

"Damn fool, Jean-Marc," Hunter said.

"Yes, damn fool," Latimer said.

"Well," Sibyl got to her feet. "He won't get away with making my sister unhappy, I can tell you that. He'll have to deal with me first."

"Poor fellow," Hunter said, pretending not to notice his wife's narrowed eyes.

Old Coot came in and, if he'd knocked, Adam hadn't heard. "More bad news," the butler said, casting a gloomy look around the room. "More company. The Fitz-Duram fellow."

Adam looked at Desirée and she grimaced.

"I wish Barstow were here," Lady Hester said. "I can't imagine why she felt she needed a holiday right now."

"She told me she hasn't had one for ten years," Birdie said in her high voice. "That's as long as I've been alive, Mama."

Lady Hester beamed at the wispy child in her billow of flocked yellow muslin with yellow rosettes pinned in her unraveling ringlets. Birdie had only to say, "Mama" for Lady H. to forget the rules of polite behavior for little girls at grown-up events.

"Shall I show this other one in then?" Coot asked. "I'd better tell Cook she'll have to put a maid or two to work and have them bring up refreshments. Cook won't like that."

"Thank you," Lady Hester said. "Do show the gentleman in."

Coot backed from the room and said, "Good riddance to that Reverend Lumpit or whatever he is. Seems to have taken himself off."

Adam knew this was all too much for Desirée who had already received a message from Verbeux, writing on Jean-Marc's behalf, to say she wasn't welcome at Number 17. At the first possible excuse he'd take her to the attic where she could rest.

When Anthony FitzDuram came into the room, Adam felt a pang of sympathy. The vibrancy had gone out of the man and, although he kept a warm countenance, his eyes were empty and his shoulders sagged. He handed Desirée a box and said, "Something for a beautiful bride. Adam's gift will be to look at it on you."

"You aren't the first to come up with that notion," Adam said and winced at Desirée's raised eyebrows.

Lady Hester chuckled, obviously pleased with herself.

The box from FitzDuram contained another box, this one of black velvet. Desirée frowned as she opened it to reveal a creamy satin lining, a bed for a delicate and exquisite parure. Pearls and diamonds, set like small flowers, had been strung together to make the necklace and bracelet. The earrings were diamond and pearl clusters with a single pearl drop.

Desirée had already been pale, now she

became white to the lips. "I can't take this," she said. "It's too much."

Adam was just as glad she didn't say that it was inappropriate.

FitzDuram accepted a glass of whiskey from Hunter and looked thoughtful. "Those belonged to my great grandmother. They came from France. When they were passed to me I was told to use them for something and someone really special. I decided your marriage to Adam, and you, were really special enough. I am happy for you to have them."

Desirée looked to Adam questioningly. If the three of them were alone, Adam would give the valuable jewels back to Fitz-Duram, but with such a crowd around, he could not bring himself to embarrass the man further. He said, "Perhaps Desirée shall borrow them, then give them back when you take a wife of your own. You'll want them then."

"I'll never want them," FitzDuram said and Adam didn't know how much more awkwardness he could allow Desirée to go through today.

Lady Hester bobbed to her feet and shook out apple-green skirts. "My first event of the year is to be a party for Adam and Desirée. It will be held within the month and I hope you will all come. Invitations will be sent out, of course."

Sibyl looked grim and said, "A good idea, Lady Hester. I hope I may help with the planning."

"I'd like to, as well," Jenny said.

Lady Hester had no chance to answer before Sibyl said, "Meg will be here — she'd never get over it if she weren't."

Desirée turned the corners of her mouth up and said, "Anne is at Number 8, you know. I'm sad to say she's had a difficult time while I've been gone. Something else I must deal with."

Jenny leaned forward and said, "Dinna worry, Princess. We'll take good care o' Anne and she'll be free to carry out her duties as your maid."

"Princess, you appear tired," Anthony FitzDuram said. Adam had noted how the other man's attention remained on Desirée. "You must take care of yourself, dear lady. And please know that you have good friends to turn to should you ever be in need."

And who, Adam wondered, should he turn to in such circumstances.

Coot returned with a letter for Adam on his salver. Adam opened the envelope and unfolded a single sheet of paper. "I understand your father is still hanging around London. Your grandmother says he's been pestering your mother. You may be sure your father will have dire warnings about your marriage."

Adam was already prepared for something of the sort and muttered, "I'll be ready for him."

The note was from Rolly who added, "I need to speak with you about Lucas. Haven't seen him for days."

People prepared to leave and filed out, kissing Desirée and shaking Adam's hand. He rubbed the space between his brows and rested his other hand on the back of Desirée's neck. "I'm going to put you to bed," he said.

"Only if you come."

He winked at her. "Perhaps I am a little tired, too."

Lady Hester, clearing her throat, caught his attention. She nodded toward the door and Adam looked over his shoulder. Jean-Marc Count Etranger stood there.

30

"You're sure you wouldn't rather use this room?" Lady Hester asked from behind them as Desirée and Adam left the receiving room with Jean-Marc.

Desirée said, "It's time to start enjoying our home together." If Jean-Marc's reason for being so quick to accept Adam's invitation to the attic was so that her brother could look down his too-handsome nose at the place, so be it. She liked it there.

She ran back and kissed Lady Hester's cheek and said in her ear, "Thank you, darling. You are a champion, but don't worry so. I'll let you know how this turns out."

Sir Robert Brodie, fresh faced from the cold outside, arrived and Desirée noted he had a key to the house. He said, "Wonderful to see you, Your Highness," but had eyes only for Lady Hester.

Desirée slipped away and ran upstairs,

anxious not to leave Adam to the accomplished chop of Jean-Marc's tongue. She needn't have worried; the two men waited for her at the top of the first flight of stairs. A glance at Adam's smile, the warmth in his eyes when he looked at her, and she set her back straighter. She led the way to 7C but waited for Adam to let them in.

The instant the door opened, Halibut rushed from other parts and threw himself into the attic. He gave Desirée a disgruntled glare and made directly for the bed where he curled in as tight a ball as possible for a cat his size, and narrowed his eyes to slits.

Desirée was grateful that they had arrived the previous night and that the rolled carpet was once more on the floor.

Adam went directly to freshen the fire and light two lamps on the mantel. He drew curtains over the windows, closing out the start of a gunmetal night.

"Please sit down," Desirée said to Jean-Marc.

"I prefer to stand."

He could be so irritating. "Will you have a drink?"

Adam said, "Yes, please have a drink."

Jean-Marc's mouth was open and Desirée knew he would refuse. Instead he said, "Brandy, please," and Adam left the fireplace to gather glasses and select a decanter.

"Would you like a little sherry, Desirée?"

She refused. Waiting for Jean-Marc to say whatever he'd come to say was an agony.

Adam had worked on the painting of the splendid young soldier for a few hours earlier in the day and the canvas was still uncovered. Jean-Marc stood before it and crossed his arms. "You're good," he said to Adam. "I find I have seen several of your portraits without knowing they were yours. How did you make your start without connections — or none you'd apparently care to use?" Usually his French accent was less marked than Desirée's but it didn't seem so this evening.

"I was lucky," Adam said. If his mother had played a part in his success he would simply have to accept that her intentions were kind and move on. "Art's like that. Talent without luck is a poor combination. Then, of course, there was word-of-mouth."

Jean-Marc shook his head. "Amazing nevertheless. From nothing to painting the rich and famous."

Desirée prepared to tell Jean-Marc that

Adam wasn't and never could have been *nothing,* but she caught Adam's eye and he shook his head slightly.

Desirée expected him to ask how Jean-Marc knew about his commissions. He didn't.

"Come, Desirée," Adam said, holding the back of a chair and indicating she should sit. As soon as she did so, he told Jean-Marc, "If you insist on standing, I shall have to stand also."

As if Adam hadn't spoken, Jean-Marc said, "This is a conversation you and I need to have. Man to man. I'm sure Lady Hester would be glad to have you join her again, Desirée."

Too amazed at his arrogance to consider prudence, she said, "If it were not for me, you wouldn't be here at all. I'm not a child to be dismissed when grownups talk — especially when they intend to talk about me."

"I am your guardian —"

"Not anymore," Adam said, cutting him off. "She is my wife, this is her home, and she leaves if and when she wants to leave. It is our hope that you will come to be happy for us."

Jean-Marc's eyes took on the expressionless quality that had the power to subdue.

Tall, dark-haired, somberly dressed and with a presence that could usually overshadow any gathering, his struggle to dominate was palpable. But he had confronted a man who might not have a grand title or royal blood in his veins, but who was intimidated by no man.

Adam draped the painting as if he didn't want anyone to look at it.

"My own wife deceived me," Jean-Marc said. "She is a romantic and a dear creature to her soul, but what you have done has made her life difficult."

"Because Meg didn't betray me and that meant you couldn't stop me from leaving London," Desirée said. "She has known how I love Adam and that I would never be happy with any other man and she did not wish me to remain a spinster."

Jean-Marc swirled his brandy and drank from the glass. He spoke to Adam, "There was no need to go to these foolish lengths to make sure Desirée was safe and you know it."

"Or Adam?" she said, seething. "Doesn't his safety matter, too? What man would you have had with me all the time to ensure my safety. I hardly think Anne was a likely candidate as a bodyguard. Verbeux is wonderful, but he must sleep sometimes and, again, he cannot be in my presence at all times. Adam was in danger because of me, because there is someone who wanted me for himself and who wanted to get rid of him. You know what happened to me when I was snatched into that dreadful house. The answer was for us to be together as man and wife. I am no longer available and, therefore, no longer a threat to anyone."

"I am aware of the dilemma," Jean-Marc said. "Your champion Verbeux has taken a great deal of time telling me all about the so-called wisdom of your decision. I sometimes think he forgets he is in my employ. You two made a problem into an excuse to get God knows how much of what you wanted anyway."

"That's very true," Desirée said. She felt on fire with defiance.

"Desirée's right," Adam said, catching her eye and smiling slightly.

Jean-Marc stared from one to the other of them. "What the *hell* does that mean? Verbeux assured me you were going to manage . . ." He threw up his hands. "You let it be known that you would be married in name only — so what are you telling me? Ross also assured me that would be the case. He should have stopped the so-called ceremony. I'm going to set about getting this ridiculousness annulled at once. Any threat to safety will be dealt with."

"You said God knows our actions and you're correct," Adam said.

"I repeat, what the hell do you mean?" Jean-Marc strode to refill his own brandy glass.

"God knows our every move." Adam sent Desirée an intimate little glance. "And he also knows that as you've suggested, we used a dilemma as an excuse to be together. We will remain together."

There now, Desirée thought, there would be no more artifice. The thought made her giddy with happiness; watching Jean-Marc drink as she'd never seen him drink before did not ease her mind at all.

He flung around toward her. "You little fool. You think this is a game? You were not born an ordinary girl. You have responsibilities to your family and one of those responsibilities is to make an extremely advantageous marriage."

"Responsibilities to a family, which doesn't as much as consider me an individual? A family whose members abandoned me emotionally? I think not. You are the only one who ever cared for me.

Anyway, it's a little late for me to make this *advantageous* marriage now, isn't it, since I've already made the best possible marriage in the world?"

"Desirée," Adam said, rubbing the back of her neck, "please don't upset yourself so, my love."

"*Mon Dieu,*" Jean-Marc said. "Are you telling me — yes, you are. You're telling me you have gone ahead and, and —" He waved his free hand.

"We are man and wife in the true sense," Adam finished for him. "And why shouldn't we be? I want to care for Desirée for the rest of my life."

"And have her take care of you, no doubt," Jean-Marc said. His high cheekbones were slashed with red. "You don't mind living off her money, I suppose."

"Don't you dare speak to my husband so," Desirée said. The injustice of it all paralyzed her.

"Child," Jean-Marc said. "A child playing a game in this — this *hovel*. Pretending. How soon will you come to your senses and realize there is nothing wrong with being privileged. As a young child you had a house, a small one built for your play, that was more comfortable than this. Adam is not a bad fellow, but who can blame him for jumping at the opportunity to become part of a society he would never otherwise have a chance to enter?"

Adam passed her in a blur and Desirée closed her eyes. Nevertheless, she heard the "oomph" of air being knocked from a stomach, and the sound of bone on bone. She opened her eyes again and jumped to her feet. "Stop it at once before you hurt each other."

The two men rolled together on the floor, landing blows at every opportunity. Jean-Marc took a fist to the nose. Blood flowed instantly but he ignored it and punched Adam hard enough in the belly to bend him double.

"That's enough." She rushed into the space created by Jean-Marc's blow, fell to her knees and grabbed a handful of each man's hair. "I had better never hear myself called a child again. I am dealing with children now. Two hulking children who still want to settle differences with fisticuffs."

Jean-Marc wiped the back of a hand over his face and spread the blood seeping from his nose. Adam, still short of breath, grasped Desirée by the waist as if she weren't pulling his hair and lifted her. He carried her back to her chair and plunked her down. "Don't ever interfere like that again. You could be seriously hurt."

"And you oafs can't be?" she said.

Jean-Marc had also got to his feet. He'd found a handkerchief and was mopping his face.

"My wife," Adam said, "will not be required to go without anything and she will not need money from your family."

"You understand nothing," Jean-Marc said. "She has an allowance, a very large allowance, and when she is thirty or married, whichever comes first, she automatically comes into a legacy. Naturally, as a married woman none of those funds are hers. They go instead to her husband. Those are not things that will be changed by any wild words from you, Chillworth."

"We are married," Adam said. "I have my own funds — ample funds. I will not touch a penny of hers."

His voice had changed and Desirée looked at him with concern. He appeared different, with a different light in his eyes. It was as if he'd thought of something that brought him pain.

"No doubt." Jean-Marc picked up the glass, which, for some reason, had not broken, returned to the decanters and poured more over-large measures. One of these he gave to Adam. "I see I am faced with a disaster and might as well do the best I can to put a good face on it. It will take a long time for me to forgive this."

Desirée frowned. She reached for Adam's brandy and tasted that liquor for the first time in her life. But she did not cough and found the taste pleasant and the after-heat exhilarating.

She was running her tongue around her lips when she realized her husband and her brother were watching her. "What is it?" she asked.

Adam shook his head. "You never cease to surprise me. And that, of course, is another part of your charm. Brandy is not considered a lady's drink, however."

"We are agreed on something," Jean-Marc said.

"How nice." Desirée still held the glass and took another goodly taste before handing it back. "I'm so glad you two have found common ground."

The two men had sat on the couch and both showed signs of their scuffle.

"We have to be practical, and quickly," Jean-Marc said. "It won't be long before our father learns of this debacle. Verbeux thinks we can hide it from the old man, but he's wrong. Since I was given full guardianship of you, I could have given permission for the marriage. That I would never have done but since you have taken matters into your own hands, I shall shield you from our father and tell him I did agree. Father will recover when it suits him.

"Of course, Verbeux believes that you are existing like a nun and a monk and intend to stay together simply until any danger to either of you can be disposed of. He is more gullible than I thought."

"He is a special person," Desirée said. "You are lucky to have him."

Jean-Marc sniffed, then said, "I am aware of that. Now, to business. This will not do." He indicated the attic. When he looked toward the bed, Halibut got up, stretched, jumped down and made his leisurely way to join the party.

"This is where we live," Desirée said. "It has been good enough for Adam and now it is also good enough for both of us."

"And Anne? Where will you put her?"

The threat wasn't subtle and it saddened Desirée. "If you would be kind enough to have her remain in your household for a day or so, I'll talk to Lady Hester about an arrangement here."

"Preposterous," Jean-Marc said. He stroked Halibut who flopped down on his boots. "Naturally I would never put Anne out. We have a responsibility to her. But I will not take argument from either of you and I will have my own way. A suitable residence will be purchased at once. My wedding gift to you."

"No!" Desirée slapped her hands down on the arms of her chair.

Adam confused her by laughing. "Your sister is a firebrand, m'lord. And as usual, we are agreed, there can be no question of our accepting such a gift, but we thank you for your generosity. We will remain where we are."

_____ 31 _____

It's . . . me. Spivey:
  Noooooooo!

32

Latimer heard Jenny wish one of the maids a good morning and thrust Finch's letter into his pocket. Of late, his dear wife had been given to easy tears and he thought it was the situation with Adam and Desirée that made her feel so low. Now was not the moment to let her know that in the week since Adam and Desirée had returned from Scotland, Jean-Marc had contacted Ross and told him their friendship was over — or that Finch was desolate at the impossible strain placed on any future encounters with their old Mayfair Square friends.

Jenny entered the library, followed closely by a new maid, Gretta, who carried a hot chocolate pot and cups on an enameled tray. Taking chocolate with Jenny late in the morning had become a ritual in recent weeks and, although the rich drink wouldn't have been his choice at such a time of day, he did love to be with her under whatever pretext.

As usual, the tray was placed at one end of the long map table and the maid left.

Latimer caught Jenny about the waist and kissed her soundly. In fact he kissed her so long and so thoroughly that he had to raise his face and rest his chin on top of her head — otherwise, he was not sure he could contain his always ready drive to make love to her.

She snuggled into him . . . and started to cry softly.

Alarmed, Latimer looked at her closely. "You're crying again, love. Won't you please tell me why? Is it because of all this unpleasantness among our friends."

"Oh, Latimer, I am ridiculous." She wiped away tears. "I am desperate about our friends, o'course, and I canna bear feelin' angry with Jean-Marc even though it is he who has taken all the joy out o' somethin' wonderful. But these are tears for a different reason. I'll pour chocolate."

He subdued his desire to stop her from doing anything until she'd explained herself, but then he realized that something else was different about his wife and it unnerved him. "I am particularly fond of that dressing robe, Jenny," he said. Until recently it had been her habit to get up before him and dress before coming downstairs.

With a pink floral cup and saucer in each hand, she turned around and went to a sofa near the fire. Jenny held a cup out to him and he took it before joining her on the couch.

She smoothed a hand down the lace panel on the front of her yellow and cream striped robe. "Forgive me for not dressing before I came down. It look me much longer than usual t'get up today and I didna want t'miss the opportunity for our time together before ye're away to the warehouses."

Something was wrong with her. She was sick. Latimer breathed deeply through his nose and tried to calm himself. "We will always have our special times together, no matter what."

Jenny looked to the tall windows where a strong, cold wind threw the naked branches of a willow tree across the panes. The hollow, scraping sound they made cast Latimer lower and he only retained his pleasant expression with great effort. What could be wrong with Jenny? Would she tell him if he didn't press her?

She set her cup aside. "These are happy tears."

"Happy tears," he repeated, disposing of his own chocolate in one scalding swallow. He coughed and put the empty cup down.

"In a few months, there will be three members of our family, Latimer."

He inclined his head. "Three?" His smile must make him appear foolish. "Three." The reality of what she meant flooded him. "We are going to have a child?"

Jenny nodded. She was, he noted, pale and her face was thinner than usual. "But dinna worry, I'll no take t'wearin' night-clothes all through the days. It's just tha' —"

"You may wear whatever makes you feel most happy, comfortable and calm," he told her. "And you will think happy thoughts and do things that make you happy. Otherwise it won't be fair."

She frowned at him.

"Because I'm going to be outrageously happy so you shouldn't let yourself be less so." He closed his eyes and swallowed. Damned if he wasn't close to tears himself.

He felt Jenny's fingers on his cheek. "Are ye cryin', too?"

With great care, he scooped her onto his lap and cradled her. "I think I may be. I thought I already had more good fortune than I should ever have hoped for."

"No, no, that was me. I already had more than I should have hoped for."

"You look thin. Have you been seen by a medical man yet?"

She took his hand and pressed it to her belly. "Thin?" she said and laughed. "If I'm thin in some parts it's because I'm not feelin' like eatin' so much. But there are parts that are far from thin."

How could he not have noticed how the shape of her stomach had changed? "It's wonderful. I'd like you to feel like this all the time."

"Well, I wouldna', sir, if ye dinna mind. But I'll enjoy each moment while we wait. And then I'll pray for more — but not all o' the time." She kissed his cheek.

Latimer leaned back and held her close. "Now we won't be the childless ones anymore. I can hardly wait to tell our friends."

Jenny's giggle wasn't like her, but it was something else Latimer fell in love with. "There's somethin' so funny, Latimer. Sibyl's increasin' and so is Meg. And Finnie, too. What d'ye think o' that?"

"They aren't having this baby," he said touching her belly again, "but I suppose they'll have to be happy with the babies they do get . . . Finnie?"

"Yes, Finnie, too. She wrote t'me about it."

"She never said a word in her letter to me." He knew his mistake as soon as the words were spoken. "But I suppose she wouldn't since it was all about the business." Finch still owned a part of the import business they'd started together.

"No doubt," Jenny said, still smiling and looking softly distant.

He expected her to say something more about the letter at any moment, but Jennings knocked and announced that Miss Anne Williams hoped to speak with Mrs. More.

"Bring her in at once," Jenny said, and to Latimer, "It's such an unhappy time for so many. Nothin's been said about what's t'happen t'Anne."

Anne Williams brought a breath of cool morning air with her. Strands of blond hair had blown free to trail at her neck and the sides of her face. Latimer liked her determined posture and unassuming air.

"Good mornin' t'ye, Anne," Jenny said. "There's hot chocolate in the pot. Take some. It'll warm ye up."

Anne smiled and murmured her thanks — and poured a cup for herself.

"A busy time for everyone," Latimer

said, almost at a loss for anything at all to say.

"Very busy," Anne said. Her mouth and chin were firmly set and she made a pretty picture in a red pelisse and dress with a simple matching bonnet. "And confusing. I came to you because you are sensible and I think you will do me a small service."

"O'course," Jenny said at once.

Latimer would prefer to wait and find out what Anne wanted before agreeing so readily.

She didn't sit down, but wandered about the room, slowly sipping her chocolate and glancing at Latimer and Jenny. At the windows she inclined her head and said, "This isn't a day for sitting in the park."

"Too cold," Latimer said, but her manner puzzled him. "There's someone out there?" He went to take a look himself.

"Poor man," Anne said. "I think he's sick with love for the Princess — or, if he's lucky, it's the idea of being in love with her that's got him so sad."

"Anthony FitzDuram?" Jenny said.

"Yes." Latimer glanced back at her and smiled. "Poor fellow is sitting on a bench with his chin on his chest. Hardly seems the thing to do under the circumstances."

"Hopelessness can make a person stop

caring what others think," Anne said, sniffing the chocolate. "When there seems to be no one who cares and no reason to go on." She looked quickly at Latimer and turned away from the window.

Latimer watched FitzDuram, hat tilted forward, hands pushed into the pockets of his greatcoat. The man disturbed him.

"Would you please give a message to Princess Desirée for me," Anne said.

Curious, Latimer left the window and picked up a book he'd left on the desk. He took it to the shelf where it belonged, glancing at Anne from time to time.

"I'm going to leave London," she said, and her chin rose even higher. "It's time for me to —" She swallowed and coughed before going on, "It's time for me to go elsewhere."

Alarm tightened Jenny's expression. "Ye canna. Ye've no relatives or friends. I know because I asked Desirée. Ye're tryin' t'do this because of her marryin' and the trouble with that mutton-headed brother o'hers."

Rather than rebuke her, Latimer grinned.

"Would you please tell Desirée I know I'm a coward but I can't bear to look at her and say I'll never see her again, but I'm going because it's the right thing to do."

"It is not, so." Jenny stood up. "I know ye're t'stay at Number 17 until a place can be . . . well, Desirée said Jean-Marc said ye'd always have a place there."

Anne looked at the floor. "They're trying to work it out for me to be at Number 7. Lady Hester will take me in but I don't think it's right. There's not enough for me to do and the Princess has Mr. Chillworth now — I'm happy to say."

"She's going to need you for so many things," Jenny said. "As a new wife wi' no experience, she'll be askin' ye all sorts o' things about keepin' her house."

"Her attic," Anne said, and shook her head. "I think it's lovely up there, but she doesn't need me to help her. She doesn't even have more than a handful of her dresses with her. They're all at Number 17. There's nothing for me to look after, nothing to do."

She was right, but Latimer would not stand by and see a young woman, alone, head off with nowhere to go. "What's wrong with remaining where you are and helping the Princess from there?" he asked.

"I don't like it at Number 17," Anne said loudly. Her face paled and she covered her mouth.

"Why not?"

She shook her head again.

Latimer drew closer to her and said, "Anne, if something's amiss, tell me about it."

Anne put down her cup and saucer. "I just don't feel right there. There's no reason other than that."

"Would you feel right here?" Jenny asked in a rush, her eyes wide and on Latimer's face. "I don't have a personal maid because I don't —"

"Wonderful idea," Latimer said before Jenny could both invite Anne to work for her and tell her she didn't need her in the same breath. "Anne, you're an answer to our dreams. We're going to . . . we need as good a girl as we can find and we were about to start looking for someone suitable. Anne's suitable, wouldn't you say, Jenny, dear?"

"Aye." Jenny's green eyes sparkled. "Aye, verra suitable. Perfect. Can ye believe we're . . ." She stopped speaking and Latimer knew she'd been about to blurt out that she was increasing.

"Jenny and I can hardly wait to share our news," he said, with a wink at Jenny. "We're to have a child and before long Jenny will need you, Anne. The sooner you start getting used to each other, the better.

And, of course, at least until the baby comes, you'll be able to help the Princess."

Sadness was the last emotion Latimer expected to see in Anne Williams's eyes, but for a moment there it was. Immediately she smiled and said, "I'm so glad for you, and if you mean it, I'd like to come to you. I'll have to give . . . well, I'll have to explain it to the Princess and let the Count and Countess know my plans, but that shouldn't take long." For a moment she seemed unsure what to do, but then her smile broadened and she took a breath as if it were the first for some time. "*Thank you.* Oh, yes, oh, thank you. If you're sure there is a place for me."

"There's a place," Jenny said.

"You're not just making it for me?"

"Noo," Jenny said. "Are we, Latimer?"

His mind was moving on to the Egyptian pieces he expected today. "No, we aren't. Jenny needs a personal maid, and another female to speak with whenever she pleases. Will you go to the Princess now, Anne? She'll be happy for you."

She thought, but not for long. "I think I'll go to Number 17 first and put my things to rights so I'll be ready to go."

He saw then that this woman had a deep need to leave her present surroundings.

Her anxiety was obvious.

"If it were suitable, I should speak to Mr. FitzDuram on the way," she said, attempting to straighten her hair. "I can at least wish him a good day."

"Latimer's leavin'," Jenny said. "Cross the square wi' Anne, my love. Then it'll be appropriate t'stop awhile."

There was no arguing with Jenny once she'd made up her mind on one of her humanitarian adventures.

Mr. FitzDuram didn't hear them approach. He must have caught a flash of her red dress and pelisse, Anne decided, because he glanced up suddenly and almost leaped to his feet. He took off his hat and said, "Good morning, Latimer, Miss Williams."

" 'Morning," Latimer said sounding, Anne decided, a little too hearty. "Bracing, hmm. Good day for a walk in the park."

"Is it?" Mr. FitzDuram asked, vaguely surveying the square. "I suppose it is."

"I love the cold," Anne said with honesty. "I grew up in Dorset, on the coast, and the wind could be bitter but I relished it. Sometimes I had to lean against it to stop from being thrown down."

FitzDuram looked away. "I spent most

of my growing years in Scotland. It was always wild, or so it seems in my memory. Even in summer."

"I expect you still live there sometimes," she said. "With your family's whiskey-making."

"No. I've never been interested in that, apart from an occasional drink of the stuff."

Latimer stamped his feet and flapped his arms and Anne was embarrassed when she realized she'd forgotten he was standing there. "Well, I'd best see Miss Williams home and get on to Whitechapel," he said. She was certain he had one of the nicest faces and dispositions ever. He was handsome, of course, but that wouldn't be what she would notice about Latimer first.

FitzDuram caught Anne off guard by offering her his arm. "Why not allow me the pleasure of walking the lady back, Latimer? I can tell you're a man with things to do." He grimaced. "Which is more than I can say for myself."

Latimer looked uncertain and appeared about to refuse when Anne spoke up and said, "I don't really need an escort, but thank you, Mr. FitzDuram. I've already taken too much of Mr. More's time."

After the slightest shuffling of his feet,

Latimer tipped his hat and made his farewells before striding away across the park.

"A nice fellow," Mr. FitzDuram said. "Solid."

"Yes," she agreed, rather wishing she could go on her own way now.

"Of course, he has every reason to be pleasant with all he has in his life."

Anne fiddled with the strings of her reticule. It was most unsuitable but she said, "I do believe you are sad, Mr. FitzDuram."

His regard from bright blue eyes was sharp. "How would you know if I am sad?"

Flustered, she said, "Forgive my forwardness, please. Of course, I don't know. That was presumptuous of me."

He continued to look into her eyes. In a quiet voice he said, "Are you too cold to sit with me a little."

Anne glanced around.

"It will be all right. We are in the open with houses all around us. No one can think badly of us."

"Then I'll sit down," she said, feeling impetuous. In fact she was chilled, but once she sat on the bench she threaded her gloved hands into her sleeves and tucked her booted feet well under the bench.

He joined her. "I am sad, y'know," he said. "This is the last place I should have come but there are good people here, people I wish were really part of my life, and my feet brought me to Mayfair Square."

Anne didn't know how to answer him.

"I've failed at everything I've touched."

She frowned and looked sideways at him. How could what he said be true? He was well-to-do, educated, had a future in politics and was a very personable man to boot. "The Princess is a special lady," she said. "And you fell for her. That's not a sin."

Once more she got the full force of Mr. FitzDuram's blue stare. "And I failed with her, too. Not that my suit was long or well-thought-out. You see before you a lonely man, Miss Williams, and I hope you will forgive me for revealing myself to you so."

Anne turned sideways on the bench to look at him. "There is nothing to forgive. We all have our troubles."

"I hope yours aren't like mine. I think I loved the idea of having the Princess more than anything else. Please don't misunderstand me. I first met her when she was seventeen and thought her irresistible then, and when I heard she had returned to Town preparatory to another Season I decided I must pursue her, but she isn't for me and never was. There isn't a woman who is. Do you think she'll be happy with Chillworth?"

Anne almost told him how much his gift had embarrassed the Princess but thought better of it. "Very happy." Adam intended to return it later anyway.

"You'll freeze to death," Mr. FitzDuram said, "I'd best get you home." But he didn't get up.

"I went to Mont Nuages as a governess," Anne said, feeling strange to be sharing a part of her life she never mentioned. "I considered myself fortunate to be offered the position because I had recently lost my mother and spent almost everything from the sale of her things to pay bills. My father died some years back. But, after little more than a year in Mont Nuages my services were no longer needed so I was told I must leave. Then I had the fortune to meet the Princess." She raised her shoulders and smiled.

"And now she doesn't need you," he said with candor, not malice. "You have been cast adrift by the acts of others, while I have managed to scuttle myself at every turn."

"I'm sorry," she told him. "Actually, I have had the most extraordinary fortune today. I am to become Mrs More's maid. That means I shall be able to keep on seeing the Princess. I do love her."

"Good," he said and there was no doubt he was pleased for her. "You deserve good luck. A great deal of it. Come, I shall walk with you to Number 17 and be on my way." She stood and took his arm for the short walk. "I am trained to practice law," he told her while they dawdled. "But I cannot abide the law. My father is a judge and has had dreams of my following in his footsteps. He is a fine man whom I respect, yet I am a disappointment to him. I thought I wanted to be involved with politics, but I don't. I hate the self-serving wrangling. The posturing, the *lying*. These men lie for personal gain and the people they supposedly serve be damned . . . oh, do forgive me. I'm so sorry."

"Are you giving up politics, too?" Anne asked. Best to pretend you hadn't heard a thing in these circumstances.

"Yes." He sighed. "I resigned early this morning, which is why I wandered here like a homeless waif drawn to a place where he might find succor. I can't bear to tell my father. He already thinks me a complete failure."

She raised her eyebrows. "Because you

do not want to do the things he believes would be good for you? Of course I should not say so, but that is selfish."

"Perhaps, perhaps not. I am trying to convince myself that I could indeed take over the distilleries. Perhaps, given a little time to find my feet, I will find solace in returning to my heritage, and to the moors and the silent land of my birth."

"What should you like to do?" she asked him.

He became edgy and didn't seem disposed to answer. Then he blurted out, "I should like to write," in a manner that didn't invite discussion.

They reached Number 17 and Anne's disappointment surprised her. "I wish you the best of everything, Mr. FitzDuram," she said, shaking the hand he proffered. "I should think Scotland could be wonderful if you've a tight home and a good living. And soon enough there would be a loving wife and children to surround you. I feel a free spirit in you. You should let it fly."

He studied her as if he'd never seen her before, then said, "I'll watch you go in."

When she had opened the front door and stepped inside, she turned back to wave, but he had turned away.

33

"Go to Lady Elspeth," Desirée said. "You can't delay a moment longer. Lucas may be there."

"If I go to my mother and grandmother, they will be frightened."

"And you don't think they're already frightened if they believe Lucas has disappeared? They will be frantic that he hasn't returned home after so many days." Really, Adam was a most intelligent man but the male just seemed to . . . *miss* some things. "According to what you've told me, it is a week and a half since you sent him to this flower garden to hide."

Adam dropped a quick kiss on her lips, but didn't hide the exasperated breath he exhaled. "You show how you have been protected, my sweet. The Vauxhall Gardens are pleasure gardens, not *flower gardens*. All manner of *things* take place there — many of them unsavory. But I

know a fortune teller named Crystal —
from my much younger days, of course —
and I sent Lucas to her. I knew she would
hide him."

Desirée felt suspicious. "Why would she
do that?"

"Because I asked her and because I once
did her a favor." He tapped her nose.
"There, Mrs. Curiosity. You know the way
of that."

"But he isn't there so where is he? When
did you last see this Crystal?"

He crossed his arms and thought — and
looked annoyed at her probing. "Perhaps a
year."

"She has probably moved on. And Lucas
has gone back to Manthy House, I tell
you."

"You're wrong. He went to Crystal."

"And you've had Rolly try to find her
every night since we returned from Scotland. She isn't there, Adam. She probably
wasn't there when Lucas went to seek her
help."

"You don't know what you're talking
about. I should go to Vauxhall myself." She
knew the reason he hadn't done so already
was that he wouldn't leave her. "Others
near the place where she has her caravan
told Rolly she rarely leaves — yet she's

been gone a week or so as far as they can remember. That would mean she disappeared about the time when Lucas went to her. I should go."

"So you said, not a moment ago," she told him. "We shall go together tonight. Don't argue. I mean it, Adam. I must be sure you are safe."

"We're all right now, my love. Nothing has happened since we were married. Anyway, I have made arrangements for Verbeux to be here within the hour and he shall make you laugh while I'm gone."

"Make me laugh?" She rolled her eyes. "You know how fond I am of him, but he almost never as much as smiles. And if you believe we are no longer in danger, why must Verbeux guard me in your absence? You patronize me, Adam. No, I will not stay here without you."

"Not even if I tell you I intend to stop at Manthy House on the way, just to see if Lucas has been there — and to make arrangements to take you to meet my mother and grandmother?"

She threw her arms around his neck. "Thank you, Adam. Oh, thank you. I have worried so that you were estranged from your family."

He remained estranged, of course, but

this would be a start.

Desirée went to look at herself in the only mirror Adam owned. "But I shall be coming with you regardless."

The summons to Number 7 to assist the Princess, together with instructions to bring certain of her things, had surprised Anne in the nicest way. Too long had passed since she'd fussed over Princess Desirée and they'd chattered together like girls about so many things.

Back at Number 17, she had taken her supper in the kitchens with the servants, who were kindly and accepted her into their midst.

But all that lay ahead now was another night of her own company while she worried about what was to become of her and how she would cope with her responsibilities. She left the jolly group in the kitchens and climbed upstairs.

She continued to sleep in the room adjoining what had been the Princess's chamber. Since *he* had entered her bed, and she could not bring herself to give him a face or a name, even though she knew them, but since then she had found little peace in a place that used to bring her comfort.

He had returned several times, always with the same threats but never a repeat of the crude sexual advances of the first occasion. He had mentioned that night and told her he would not touch her again as long as she obeyed him.

The Princess had not been quick enough to hide disappointment at Anne's announcement that she was to move to Number 8. Anne had explained that she didn't feel right about staying at Number 17 and she didn't think it a good idea to add more to Lady Hester's burden. And she'd been proud of herself when she held fast against the Princess's argument that Lady Hester loved being surrounded by people and there were no longer as many as she liked to have.

Anne had heard how Lady Hester intended to turn Number 7 into a social "must" and pointed out that Her Ladyship wouldn't want strays all over her house — particularly since Barstow had failed to return, even though she had sent a message to say she was having a lovely time in Brighton and would return "when she could."

"In you come and not a word."

A whispery voice caused her to jump, but she had no time to run before she was pulled into a dark closet where she knew shelves of linens lined each wall. She hadn't noticed the door opening and he'd timed it to capture her from behind just as she'd passed by.

"Let me go," she whispered. She'd learned the rules. He had kept his promise that if she was very quiet and docile nothing would happen to her.

He pushed his arms beneath hers and pulled her sharply back against him. "Don't tell me what to do. I don't like that — particularly from women. I told you that if you behaved, you would be treated with more respect than you deserve. You are not behaving." He crossed his forearms over her body and pulled her bodice beneath her breasts. When he plucked at her nipples there was no stopping the dart of pleasure between her legs, or the arch of her back so that she rested the back of her head on his shoulder.

"Stop it," she told him.

He laughed softly in her ear and replaced her bodice. "You are wasted, my dear, a passionate creature like you. We must see if we can work something out. Now." He pushed her forward into a corner and stood close behind her. "Where have you been? And I don't mean, for supper."

Her body continued to throb and she took deep breaths. She must be very careful not to annoy him. "I went across the square to Lady Hester's house, to Princess Desirée who needed some more of her things there." She knew it was dangerous, but she could not be completely crushed by this man. "You will be caught if you continue as you are. How do you get —"

His hand, clamped over her mouth, stopped her. "That is none of your business. Don't forget how much I know about you, how you would be sent from this or any other decent house if even a whisper of your past were heard. Then what would you do?"

Anne closed her eyes and wished she could sleep and forget.

"Did you talk with the Princess?"

She hesitated, then quickly said, "Yes. I helped her change and do her hair because she and Mr. Chillworth were going to visit his mother and grandmother."

"Charming," he said, and she could almost hear his leer. "When will they be back?"

"I don't know." That much was honest.

"They return to Mayfair Square on leaving St. James?"

"I . . . no. They plan to visit Vauxhall

Gardens." Surely there could be no harm in telling him. The Princess had been so excited when she spoke of going to that place.

"You," he said, "are a very good girl. Count to a hundred before you leave this closet. Then go directly to your bed. Sleep will be good for you."

With that he left her alone in the darkness.

Anne didn't count, she didn't want to leave the dark, silent place. She wanted to live, to hope for a new beginning, but she was a danger to others.

Perhaps the time she'd feared had arrived, the time to sleep forever.

34

Manthy House had been built just off St. James Square and bore the unmistakable stamp of Robert Adam. Desirée hardly dared look at the man beside her in their coach when they drew up before the impressive building. Adam Chillworth lived in an attic in Mayfair Square whilst his mother and grandmother — and his brother — resided in a mansion where a graceful driveway curved before a grand facade rising four stories with a half-columned wall to the west where a dozen statues stood in oval recesses. More columns rose from the second floor to the stone balustrades fronting the roofs.

By the time Edward pulled up the horses, the front doors to the house were opened and a butler, followed by an entourage of servants, filed out to line the steps. At Desirée's insistence, a message had been sent ahead to tell the Countess and

Lady Elspeth they might expect Adam — and his new wife.

"It is a beautiful place," Desirée said but she detested the hard and closed expression on her husband's face.

"It has nothing to do with me," he said. "I grew up in a fine home, too, and although I'll always be a northcountryman and proud of it, my father's estate there has nothing to do with me. Now, my darling, I must ask you to allow me to lead the conversation. We shall not be here long. I have work to do this night."

This dutiful wife convention might not be easy to follow. "Very well, Adam." There were times to fight and times to be docile.

Rolly Spade-Filbert would arrive within the hour and wait for them several streets distant. After they left Manthy House he would accompany them to Vauxhall Gardens.

Edward opened the door of the coach, put down the steps and stood back while Adam got out. Adam handed Desirée down and she saw the pride in his eyes when he looked at her. She had deliberately asked Anne to come and help her dress — this was not the moment to ask Anne to reconsider her plans to move into

Number 8 — and had chosen a gown and cloak of Calamanco worsted in mulberry with dark fur edging the hooded cape. She also carried a muff but was cold despite the heavy outfit. Her teeth chattered, but she was not so foolish as to blame that on the temperature.

The butler, whom Adam said he had never seen before, came to meet them with an air of a man welcoming a long lost hero home and said, "Good afternoon, Mr. Chillworth, Princess. I'm Cripps. The Countess and Lady Elspeth are expecting you."

"Gawd," Adam said under his breath. "Nothing changes except the faces and some of those are the same."

They had barely mounted the bottom step when a very old and very frail lady appeared in the doorway. Once tall, but stooped now, she wore widow's black, which became her thick white hair. She smiled down upon Adam and her face became as lined as a crazed plate, a beautifully aged and crafted piece. She had blue-veined, transparent skin and light gray eyes that watered in the wind. A heavy cape enveloped her and a servant stood solicitously by whispering to her.

Countess Manthy leaned on a stick with

a shiny wooden ball at its crown. She leaned on it with both hands, but managed to wave an arm and flutter long, bejeweled fingers at her grandson.

"Forgive me," Adam said in the strangest of voices. "She's not strong. I should go to her. Attend my wife please, Cripps." With that he ran to meet the old lady, taking the steps two at a time, and hardly hesitated before wrapping her in his arms. He turned and led her into the house with Desirée walking beside Cripps.

Countess Manthy stood in the middle of a towering foyer that rose through all the stories of the house and was crowned by a domed, stained-glass window. She pointed a wavering finger at Cripps and said, "I hope there is a good fire in my sitting room, my boy."

Cripps, chunky, balding, and never to see fifty again, assured his mistress that everything was just as she liked it.

"Lovely," the Countess said, making Desirée the focus of her pointing finger this time. "A lovely girl, Adam. Strong, too, I see it in her face. Welcome to our family, Your Highness." A lace handkerchief trailed from the hand that held the stick and from time to time she pulled it free to dab her eyes.

The sitting room was an old-lady's sitting room, one packed with treasures: glass-fronted cabinets filled with seashells, some exotic, some the simple kind so common on local beaches, china dolls in a row along the windowsills, porcelain statues crowding surface after surface. Miniatures covered so much of the walls that only inches of turquoise silk were visible between. The fires of fifty years had clouded a fluted, gold-etched mirror over the fireplace and Desirée was certain the comfortable old furniture had been there just as long.

The countess wanted little more than to sit in a favorite armchair and look silently at Adam. From time to time she looked at Desirée. When she beckoned her closer, a bony arm extended and Desirée smiled while her face was patted and examined. "You're a good girl, Your Highness," the Countess said in a voice like a breeze through dried grasses. "I know because Adam is good. Look after him."

"Please call me Desirée." Perhaps she was truly to become part of a real family.

"Desirée," the lady said.

Adam looked anything but comfortable and glanced around repeatedly, looking for his mother no doubt or, quite probably,

Lucas whom he must wish would materialize.

"Have I let you have them to yourself for long enough, Mama?" Lady Elspeth came into the room. "Aren't they beautiful?"

"Beautiful and far too scarce for this old woman's likes," Countess Manthy said, surprising Desirée. She flapped her handkerchief at Adam. "All that nonsense is over now. And don't tell me things can't be mended just like that. If I say they can, they can. Poof. Over. There has never been a bad word between us, boy, and your grandfather loved you dearly. He would love your bride dearly." She gave a dry chuckle. "My spies tell me your brother doesn't consider my grandson good enough for you, my dear. We knew of your marriage some days since but could not approach you until you were ready. I intend to invite the Count and his lady to tea and make sure he understands how wrong he is."

"I should enjoy seeing that," Desirée said and laughed aloud before she remembered herself. "I mean —"

"You mean that you would enjoy seeing your brother taken down a peg or two. Don't blame you. I had a brother myself — stuffed shirt."

"Cook is promising to outdo herself for dinner this evening," Lady Elspeth said. "The staff is delighted. It is too quiet for them here."

Desirée looked at Adam who shook his head. "Mother, I came to see both of you and to ask how you are. I see Grandmama couldn't be better."

"That's what you think," Countess Manthy said, settling her chin against her thin neck. "Wait until you're my age and we'll see if you think you've never been better."

"Mama is well now," Lady Elspeth said. "Now that you have come. We understand if you were not prepared to stay but please say you will come again." After a pause she added, "I'm blackmailing you, but then, you knew that."

"You blackmail so charmingly," Adam said. "How is Lucas?"

Desirée held her breath.

"Very well, I think," Lady Elspeth said, beaming. "He has gone to York to visit friends. He's been gone almost two weeks. Before he left he was excited and I am so happy to know his spirits are lifted." She gave Adam a knowing look from behind her mother's back.

"Good," Adam said, unsmiling.

In other words, Lucas had made an excuse for going away so that he wouldn't worry his mother and grandmother. Desirée hoped she would get to know her brother-in-law better.

"I am beside myself," Adam said, "but this has to be a very short visit. Desirée insisted we must not delay longer before coming to see you, but now we must leave. We already had a prior engagement."

Lady Elspeth looked away but her mother never took her eyes from Adam's face. "Tuesday evening? Will that suit? There will be dinner and some musicians. Your brother should have returned by then. We shall have a proper family reunion."

"We would love to come," Desirée said, giving Adam no chance to waffle.

"Good. I hope your brother and his wife will also agree to be here."

Desirée stopped smiling. "I'm not sure he'll —"

"He will come," the old lady said. "Now, before you go I want to give you something."

"No, no, please."

Ignoring her, Countess Manthy worked a ring of deep yellow-gold over the enlarged knuckles of the first finger on her left hand. She glanced at Lady Elspeth who nodded and showed delight. "This has been in the Manthy family for generations. It has been passed down to the wives of the first sons to marry. It's yours now. Put it on."

Desirée looked to Adam who said, "Grandmama, you have always worn it. This is not the time —"

"It *is* the time." Countess Manthy gave her grandson a stern stare. "My husband's mother gave it to me when I married. We had no sons, but we have you and Lucas. You married first. Put this on your bride, please and I'll tell you about it."

"I am not a Manthy," Adam said.

"There are no more Manthys. You are the only male heir we have." She pushed the ring into his hand. "It cannot be made either larger or smaller. If it is too big for any of her fingers, the back may be wrapped with soft cloth."

Still Adam hesitated, but then he made up his mind and took Desirée's right hand in his. The heavy piece fitted the middle finger perfectly.

"When your own son marries you'll pass it on," the Countess said. "It is said to have belonged to Cleopatra. Look at the inscription on the dome. Translated it reads,

Follow me. The dome may be lifted by inserting this tiny rod into the hole you see on one side." She took a worn leather bag from a pocket that hung from her waist. "Keep it safe. Supposedly the ring has never been opened and a legend that once existed is long since lost. By some it has been said that there is a fantastic jewel inside. Others say there is or was a potent poison intended for the wife to take on the death of her husband."

"Good Lord," Adam said, reaching to take the thing from Desirée.

She put her hand behind her back and both the Countess and Lady Elspeth laughed. "You note that I appear to be alive," Countess Manthy said. "Despite the loss of my dear husband. It is just a rather wonderful ritual and fun to think of all the women who have worn it — not one of whom followed instructions."

35

Spivey here:

And all this frittering away of time on people being nice has got to stop.

I have been at fault, but — no, of course I'm not at fault, I have been taking my studies seriously and expecting a certain person to act on the suggestions I've made. Rolly Spade-Filbert has been hopeless, a perfect example of a completely selfish man. I had thought to stop using him entirely but he and that feckless Lucas are too much involved with Adam and Desirée and I have no choice but to come up with some brilliant solution.

Hmm.

Oh save me. Anne Hathaway, no less, and doubtless looking for me because she's decided I'm her champion against Willful Willy. I am in no mood to listen to stories of his transgressions as a faithless husband. Give me a moment to relocate and I shall continue to ponder the problem.

Oh, she's changed her mind. Praise be. Hah, she saw her swain and has taken off in pursuit. I almost feel sorry for the man — almost.

If Adam could become kindly disposed toward Jean-Marc, he would be inclined to accept the gift of a home.

Oh! Excuse me while I calm myself. It could all be so perfect if that pesky painter would behave like a normal man and show gratitude for such largesse.

I've got it! Spade-Filbert shall redeem himself yet. If Jean-Marc were responsible for rescuing Lucas from his debtors, Adam would change his tune toward his wife's brother.

This is perfect. I am saved. Off I go to set things in motion.

36

So much for wives being submissive to their husbands, Adam thought. He had made arrangements for Desirée to be taken home in Rolly's coach while the men went on in search of Lucas.

As so often happened, Adam's plans for Desirée had gone awry. He would never consider himself a weak man, apart from where his wily wife was concerned. He and Rolly had arrived at Vauxhall Gardens and Desirée walked between them. At least she was too overwhelmed to speak.

An unexpected fog had settled in heavy banks over the city, not that the revelers in the gardens were daunted by it, rather they used its cover to get up to even more daring high jinks. Women were heard shrieking and men laughing. The chases were on and culminating in stolen kisses that often led to other things.

Strings of colored lanterns hung between

trees. Jugglers, acrobats, singers, bands, players on rough stages acting out their tales to crowds that alternately laughed and jeered.

The ground remained icy and many slipped, some saved from falling by companions, others descending in heaps, alone, or often with members of the opposite sex with whom they rolled around. Adam cursed himself for not insisting Desirée return to Mayfair Square. He didn't want her to witness the bawdy, often lewd behavior of those who came there for just that purpose.

Without warning, Rolly stopped walking.

"What is it?" Adam asked, impatient to get on.

Rolly held up a hand to silence him and gazed into the glowing coals of a nearby brazier belonging to a costermonger selling roasted chestnuts. He had abandoned any attempt at conservative dress and wore blue and gold striped trousers, a gold brocade coat and a purple waistcoat embroidered with gold roses. He carried a cane with a silver snake as its handle and had been sauntering in a manner that embarrassed Adam. He had known the other man as a dandy but, with the exception of his appetite for excessive quantities of lace, Rolly had seemed more conservative recently — until tonight. The events Adam had witnessed in St. John's Wood had never been mentioned again.

Desirée cast Adam a worried look and he put a finger to his lips.

"Rolly," he said clearly, "something's on your mind. Can't you share it?"

"Oh." He seemed to notice his surroundings as if for the first time. "Forgive me. I was lost there for a moment thinking about Lucas. I fear for him and I had this . . . *vision*."

Adam shivered a little. "What vision?"

Rolly shook his head and turned his eyes in Desirée's direction as if he didn't want to speak in front of her. He minced to Adam's side and spoke into his ear. "You already know there are those who are making demands on him. I looked into the fire and saw him there. He was burning. And those men, those to whom he owes so much money, were laughing and pushing him back each time he tried to escape."

Adam felt sick. "Imaginings," he said. "You drank too much while you were waiting for me. This way, this is where Crystal's caravan has always been."

"It's not there anymore," Rolly said.

Adam was not to be easily diverted. Holding Desirée's hand tight beneath his arm, he took a small path between gypsy caravans, most of which offered readings or potions, or lucky amulets. He hadn't reached the spot where he hoped to start making enquiries about Crystal when a wild-looking yet striking man with black curly hair that reached below his shoulders emerged from the darkness and approached Adam directly. He could have been a pirate on shore to create mischief.

With a hand on the pistol in his pocket, Adam said, "Off with you. We have no business together."

"You Adam?" the fellow asked.

"What do you want with me?"

"I mean you no 'arm," the man said. "Crystal told me to watch for you."

Adam stiffened. Hope flared but he was afraid to embrace it. "Where is she? Hurry, man, take me to her."

"I'm to speak with you. Only with you." He glanced significantly at Desirée then stared at Rolly. "Not in front of them. That one come 'ere every night but 'e wasn't the one she told me about. You are. Just step away a bit."

"I won't let anything happen to her," Rolly said, offering Desirée an arm. "He may tell you where Lucas is."

Reluctantly Adam let go of Desirée and moved closer to the fellow who pulled him to the side of the path and began to whisper.

"Princess," Rolly said. The most he could hope for was a minute or two alone with her. "May I speak with you? Confidentially?"

She turned her face up to his and he was overwhelmed, yet again, by her loveliness. Too bad he had not been in Adam's position when her vulnerable teenage heart was ready to fall for a mature man, a man who would know how to make the most of that little windfall.

"What is it?" The Princess frowned and glanced repeatedly at her husband.

"You know that Adam and I are beside ourselves with worry about Lucas. I doubt you know all because Adam is honorable and a gentleman and would not want to burden you with his problems."

Her eyes flashed. "I should hope he knows that I couldn't be burdened by anything that troubles him."

Was that true, Rolly wondered. He supposed it could be but he still believed he had come up with the only plan that could save Lucas — and himself. "You know that money is needed to pay Lucas's creditors, a lot of money, and it's doubtful we can raise it between us. Gilbert Chillworth turned me down and Lucas would not hear of approaching his grandmother." He must be careful here. "I understand the Countess has been most generous in the past and I cannot blame Lucas for being unwilling to approach her again."

"How much money?"

He had her complete attention and interest. "A fortune. Fifty thousand pounds."

"And you think these people would leave Lucas alone if the money were paid?"

"They would have no reason not to. He would owe them nothing." Neither of them would owe anything. Life could start afresh with the shadows removed from every alley and quiet place. He looked at the ground. "I am embarrassed to ask you this. Please, just don't answer me if I am overstepping my bounds too badly to be tolerated."

"Go on," she said. "Quickly."

She already knew her husband well, knew that his pride would not accept charity. Rolly's heart lifted a little. If she helped, Adam need never know.

"Rolly?" She sounded impatient.

"Your brother. He is angry about your

marriage but he will accept it. He's probably just looking for a way to mend the differences between the two of you and still save face. If you went to him and explained the trouble Lucas is in, do you think he would do it — for you? Give you the money, I mean."

"Hush," she said. "Adam's coming back."

Adam put an arm around Desirée's shoulders and, with Rolly still holding one of her hands in the crook of his elbow, they started back the way they'd come.

"Hurry," Adam said. "I'm to return to Mayfair Square and await word."

"From whom?" Desirée asked, her voice unnaturally high. He detested all she had been through because of him.

"From someone Crystal knows." He took off his hat and wiped a forearm over his sweating brow. "They'll tell me how to find Lucas."

"I don't like it," Desirée said. "I don't want to wait to go and help him."

"I don't like it, either, but what choice do I have?"

Adam noticed that Rolly was unusually quiet. The man must deal with his own troublesome thoughts.

"I told you I had to get back to Mayfair Square to await instructions," he said to Desirée. "I can't go anywhere yet. Two men arrived to see Crystal. She was getting ready to leave on a journey and they decided to go partway with her. They asked our long-haired helper back there to find me and tell me they'd be in touch about Lucas. He didn't bother to look for me because Crystal had already said I'd show up."

"I'm frightened for Lucas," Desirée said.

Adam agreed but held his tongue.

Rolly made a desperate sound and started to run so that they all ran together. "Ransom," he said, his breath coming in gasps. "They'll be in touch all right — and if we ever want to see Lucas again — alive — they'll want all the money he owes and more on top."

They found Edward and piled into the coach.

"I'll drop you at your carriage," Adam told Rolly. "I'll let you know as soon as I hear something, but they want me to be alone when they arrive. For the sake of anonymity, they say. Desirée, my love, I must ask you to let me leave you at Number 17. You'll be safe there. And do not argue with me."

"That's right, Princess," Rolly said. "You'll be safe at Number 17. The Count will make sure of your comfort."

37

At first Adam would be cross that she had returned to him before he came for her, but Jean-Marc himself had escorted her to the door and seen her safely inside Number 7. Adam would soon forget to be angry when he discovered what she'd done.

She ran up each flight of stairs with light steps and rushed into 7C. Adam sat in his chair with a drink in his hand. He looked so worried, she could hardly wait to tell him her news.

"Adam —"

"My love, you cannot be here. I told you — asked you to remain under your brother's roof until I came for you." But a little of the worry eased from his face and he smiled at her. "It's getting late. Perhaps they will not come tonight."

"Perhaps not," she said. "But it is not so very late and I hope they do."

He beckoned for her to sit on his lap and

when she settled there, he began kissing her, each kiss more ardent than the last. He paused to look at her. "I hope they come, too. You are truly my helpmate. You know what is most important to me, and what is right. I love you, Desirée."

Adam had told her he loved her before but usually in the wild heat of their lovemaking. Tonight he looked at her with such intensity she quaked. Whatever happened she would always crave that look.

Turning in his embrace, she put her arms around his neck and did some kissing of her own. It was amazing how the sensation of his lips moving on hers only became more exciting.

She took her mouth from his. "Adam, I can't wait another moment to tell you. Our troubles are over. Lucas's troubles are over. We have the money."

Adam regarded her blankly.

"I have the money to pay Lucas's debts," she told him, and got to her feet. She took off her cloak and from a pocket inside she withdrew a thick, heavy envelope. This she gave to Adam. "Fifty thousand pounds."

His silence touched her. She had overwhelmed him by lifting his burdens. "Fifty thousand pounds," he said, opening the envelope and staring in at the contents.

"How did you know this was the sum needed? I didn't."

She smoothed back her hair and pulled a little stool near his feet to sit on. "Rolly told me when you were talking to that man at the gardens. I was so flattered that he would trust me and come to me."

"Were you?"

"Yes." She waited, expecting him to take out the money, but he didn't.

Eventually he raised his eyes a little to look into her face. He wasn't happy and she didn't understand why. Those eyes turned almost black might have been a stranger's, a stranger who found her baffling. There was hurt there, too. And he'd grown so pale that the flamboyant bones of his face cast the darkest shadows.

"What is it?" she asked him. "Why aren't you glad?"

"Where did you get this?" he said.

Her heart beat faster and faster. Halibut approached and jumped onto Adam's lap. He rested a hand on the cat's back but the animal looked up at him, gave a high whine, and fled.

"I asked you a question," Adam said.

"From Jean-Marc," she said, barely able to get the words out. "I asked him to loan it to us and he got it at once. Within half an hour it was in my hands. Jean-Marc didn't even ask what it was for. It was just the way Rolly said it would be. My brother was glad to be able to do something for us. Adam, I think he regrets being so angry with us and wants to make amends."

"By giving us money as if I were incapable of taking care of you and your needs?"

Her limbs trembled and felt weak. "No. He didn't ask me why I needed the money but I told him it was to help Lucas who has some problems. I said he would get it back, but he told me he'd be offended if we tried to repay him."

Adam raised a hand and Desirée flinched. He laughed and the sound was awful. "You know so little about me that you think I would strike you?" He tossed the money on the floor and stood up. "I was right all along. You and I were not meant for each other. Our backgrounds are too different. I should have listened to my instincts, no, I must be more fair than that — I should have found a way to stop wanting you and moved where I would never see you again."

"Adam, please —"

"No, don't beg me. Begging isn't becoming of your station. You are too young,

I should have listened to my instincts there, too. If you were more mature you would understand that to do what you have done is to question my manhood. You have confirmed your brother's opinions of me. And you have betrayed my trust by going behind my back."

She got to her feet and reached for him, but he backed away. "I wanted to make you happy and I wanted to save Lucas," she told him.

"Pick that up." He pointed at the envelope. "You will take it back, thank your brother, and tell him I don't need his help, which is true. Today I did what I had never intended to do. I sent word to the Manthy solicitors, telling them I've changed my mind and will take the inheritance my grandfather left me. I had decided I was being foolish and selfish when Lucas needed money and when I wanted to provide you with a beautiful home that would bring you pleasure."

"This place brings me pleasure." She spread her arms. Her hands felt like ice and she shivered all over. "I never wanted more than to be with you wherever you are."

"I believe you think that's all you wanted. But that was easy enough as long as you could always run to your family for those things you thought I couldn't provide. I was not a poor man when we married. I am about to become an exceedingly wealthy man, only the thought is like a stone in my heart.

"You are not for me. I had come to believe you were, but I have been more wrong than I could have imagined. Please God this marriage can be annulled somehow and you can marry one of your own kind."

Her eyes stung but she couldn't cry, even as she couldn't stop the burning in her throat. "There will never be anyone but you. If one of us has been wrong, it is me, but my motives were the best. I wanted to do good. And anyway, you are also wrong for being too proud." Once more she reached for him and once more he stepped back. "I am desolate," she told him, not caring how she pleaded. "You are my life."

He pressed his eyes shut and she saw his lashes were moist. "And I have wanted you to be mine."

A rap on the door caused Desirée to jump and she heard Adam curse under his breath. He threw open the door and said, "Yes," into the face of Evans, the under-butler.

"You've got visitors," Masters said, showing no sign of being disturbed by Adam's sharpness. "Mr. Lucas Chillworth wants to know if he can bring his wife up to meet you."

38

Spivey here:

Well? Help me, please. How shall I avert complete disaster?

That poor, poor, girl — Princess Desirée. She is young, Chillworth is right about that, but there is neither malice nor avarice in her. If he destroys the marriage it will be a tragedy. For me, of course, although it is possible the man will do as he says and leave Number 7 anyway, but it is also a blow from which neither of them will ever recover. Certainly I no longer have the ridiculous feelings that plague the living, but I remember them.

Adam will be a bitter man for as long as he lives and . . . oh, my word, when he eventually comes here to higher places and some twit talks out of turn about my activities at Number 7, and we all know who that will be, well then, my existence will hardly be worth not living.

So I can't give up. See, it works so often that when I come to you for help, which you never give, just talking things through helps me.

I suppose I should thank you for that.

Mmm.

I can't go into what that silly woman Barstow is up to or how she has interfered with my plans for Hester's new venture. Hester is so upset she cannot seem to keep her mind on the arrangements she should make, but that, too, shall change. I can't decide what I think about Sir Robert Brodie hanging around, not that I think that will come to anything. Her flings never do.

But you wonder how I intend to deal with the current debacle. First, I take Spade-Filbert off the case. My idea to impress Jean-Marc with Adam's connection to the Manthys worked by having Lucas reveal the truth. It no longer matters, but my hope that Rolly would press Lucas to pursue the Princess just enough and have her find him just amusing enough to make Adam jealous — didn't work. That was because Spade-Filbert has been too busy looking for ways to feather his own nest. I believe he needs that money as much as Lucas does.

Glad that one's back, by the way. I rather thought we might never see him again. Back and with a wife, no less. These Chillworths are impetuous.

With Rolly gone, I shall have to do all the

work myself, of course, starting with finding a way to divert Adam from his present course.

My, I have an idea! It's a risk, a gamble, but it might just do. I shall have to be most careful because if I misjudge by even a small degree and there is an accident, the results could be — deadly.

39

Lucas and his new wife, Enid, sat on the green sofa. Adam didn't remember seeing his brother as excited as he was tonight. Enid was his long lost love who apparently had not only never sat on a riverbed to drown, but who had unfortunately lost their child quite early in the pregnancy. Having discovered her affair with Lucas, her father decided to turn her transgressions to his own advantage by spinning tales and squeezing money from Gilbert Chillworth. The man convinced Enid he had gone to the Chillworths only to plead with Lucas to make her an honest woman. Lucas, he said, had refused and said he never wanted to see her again.

"You all but took the entire blame upon yourself when you told our mother," Adam said. "Why? To take away Gilbert's guilt in her eyes."

Lucas looked at the floor. "It's all over

now. I only wish I had made a better search for Enid, or that she had come back to me."

"I couldn't go to you, Lucas, because I was told you didn't want me," she said. Brown-haired with blue eyes, she was pretty and plump and completely different from any of the women Adam had known from his brother's past. "If you hadn't come for me when you did, I would never have left the farm again. I'd have stayed there looking after my father forever."

Lucas watched her as if he were afraid to miss a word she spoke or any fleeting emotion on her face.

"We're so happy for both of you," Desirée said and Adam saw how she was able to put herself aside to celebrate this news and this wonderful homecoming. But he suffered each time he looked at this girl who was both his heaven and his hell.

"Lucas," Enid said, leaning closer to him, "did you forget the men outside?"

Lucas slapped his forehead with the heel of a hand. "Two fellows. They approached as Enid and I got out of the carriage. It was so strange, Adam. They asked if I was you and when I said I was your brother and on my way to visit you, they looked at each other, then walked away without another word. Does that mean anything to you?"

"Yes," Adam said. "But it doesn't matter anymore." His awaited messengers rightly realized they weren't needed.

"Crystal took me to Bradford, y'know. A strange one, indeed, but generous. She said she'd decided to visit relatives in the Cotswolds and she'd take me where I needed to go. I had asked her how I could find Enid. In the end I told her everything and she said her people could find anyone. And they did. Crystal told me she would have died once if it weren't for you."

Adam waved the comment aside. "That's history. What are your plans?"

Lucas's smile faded and Adam knew why. He didn't want to speak out of turn in front of Enid. "You will be well received at Manthy house," Adam said. "And you will soon have nothing else to worry about."

He met Lucas's eyes, saw the question there, and the hope. It would have to be enough for now.

Lucas stood and drew Enid up beside him. Her simple dress and pelisse were of dark rose wool and she wore black shoes that laced and were not new. Nevertheless, she looked lovely.

"We'll leave the two of you now, then,"

Lucas said. His brow furrowed when he looked from Adam to Desirée. Adam supposed it would be impossible not to sense that something was amiss between them. "Rolly will be worrying himself about my absence. I'll get to him tomorrow."

Adam had pushed the envelope of money into a drawer before Evans showed up with Lucas and Enid. Desirée stood where she'd been when he went to see them out and wondered if he would march across to Number 17 and return Jean-Marc's gift at once. She quaked at the thought but would go with him gladly if that were his decision, and hope that by supporting him she could make him see that she wanted only to help him.

Surely it was too late to go to Number 17 tonight.

She heard Adam's boots meet each stair as he returned. Twirling around, Desirée let her hair down and picked up a bucket to get hot water for both of them. Last evening they had bathed together. How she loved the intimacy of their bodies sliding against each other, and how she responded to the sensation of Adam's soapy hands carefully washing every inch of her before she washed him. And afterward — making love in the warm water, and again as soon as they were dry but before they reached the bed, and, finally, when they were curled together beneath the covers.

She met Adam at the door and he glanced at the bucket before taking it from her and setting it down outside the door. He walked into the attic, closed the door behind him, and she stood aside, rubbing damp palms on her skirts.

He went directly to retrieve the money and give it to her. "Here, let me help you with your cloak. I would go with you myself, but I think it's best if I don't. Toby has gone across to get Verbeux. He will take you home."

"This is my home," she told him, her own temper rising.

"Look at it." He did so himself. "You would grow tired of living a game soon enough."

"I like it. I keep telling you I like it. And anyway, you said you intend to buy a house for us. Sibyl and Hunter are buying Number 12 Mayfair Square because they think they crowd Lady Hester when they come here. Isn't that lovely?"

"Lovely," he agreed but she knew he was not changing his silly, stubborn, man's mind. Well, she would not give up.

"Verbeux will be here shortly." He picked up her cloak again and held it for her.

Desirée didn't turn so that he could swathe her shoulders. Instead she looked into his face and tried to see his heart. What she saw was despair, grief — and determination. The foolish man actually thought he could send her to Jean-Marc and go away, absolutely miserable, and then everything would be put right.

Do you think I will get over you, Adam?

Well, she never would and the way to prove it was by shocking her husband back into his senses. "Very well," she said, allowing him to help her on with her cloak after all. "I'll bring in the bucket before I go, if you don't mind."

He shrugged, and she left the room. She left and began to run. Down the stairs with her cloak billowing about her, she ran and she was already in the foyer when she heard Adam thundering down behind her.

She had left her muff behind but at least she hadn't removed her boots. With both hands, she tore open the front door, praying she wouldn't confront Verbeux and Toby. No one was there and she fled down the front steps, turned left on the hardpacked and icy residue of snow, and dashed recklessly onward.

The cold whipped at her face and made her ears ache, but she kept running. Foolish, foolish, to come out in the cold and the darkness without a complete plan. But it didn't matter, she would not allow Adam to ruin what was already wonderful. She would make him see that he could never make her return to her brother's house like a child because she would not leave the man she'd married. If shocking him didn't work, well then, she'd follow him around until he gave up and took her back.

"Desirée!"

Adam's yell turned her stomach. Faster she went, sliding around on rock hard clumps of frozen snow. Several times she stumbled but righted herself.

"Stop, *now*," he said, obviously gaining on her.

She panicked, paused to gasp in air, and took off down one of the passages leading to the mews behind the houses.

When he caught her, one of Adam's large hands cut off her scream. "After what you've seen, after what's happened — to both of us — you run away, alone, in the night." His voice rasped in her ear. "When will you learn to do as you're told?"

"I won't," she told him. "Never. I will

never simper and bob and say, yes, Adam, when I want to refuse. And you shall not stop me from doing what I want to do now, do you hear me?" Going limp, she managed to slip through his arms and fall to the hard, cold cobbles. Instantly she scrambled away.

She didn't make more than a yard or so before he caught her again and this time they went down together. Adam managed to take the brunt of the fall but was quickly on top of her.

"Listen to me," he said, grappling with her.

She would not stay still. She would show him she was not like any other woman he'd been able to control.

"What are you doing?" He had caught her wrists but she squirmed, kicking at him until she managed to land a toe on his shin. "Stop it at once, dammit. Desirée, *stop.*"

At last tears started but she made no sound. She pulled up her knees and wrapped her legs around his hips.

"For God's sake, woman, cover yourself. Oh, damn, oh, please do as I tell you. You don't know what could happen here."

She thought she did and the idea excited her beyond reason. Adam released one of her wrists and tried to pull her legs down. In the front, her skirts had risen to her waist and when he encountered her bare skin he groaned.

Desirée wasted not a bit of her opportunity and began loosening his trousers. He made a grab for her hand but she was too quick for him and got inside before he snatched her wrist again. She also took advantage of the small freedom he gave her to slither over his hip. He turned and landed on his back with his wife astride his most vulnerable parts.

"You little devil," he said through his teeth. "I taught you too well, and you like what I taught you too well. You are wild."

She moved on top of him, rocked her hips back and forth and bent over to kiss him. Her tongue entered his mouth and rather than make more attempts to deny her, he burst into activity. His kisses were hard enough to make her lips swell instantly. He released her hands entirely and pushed beneath her cloak to undo her bodice.

Desirée swallowed her own cries when his mouth fastened on a breast. With each of her rocking parodies of having him inside her, his hips rose from the cobbles. The hardness of their bed only inflamed her more. Later she would be bruised, Adam would be bruised, and they would both know the source of their pain.

"No," he said against her breasts when she pulled him free of his trousers. "Not here."

"Yes, yes, yes," she said, mounting him and driving him where she wanted him to be. *"Yes."*

Somewhere in her mind she marveled that the night was hot, not cold, that coils of white heat sprang tight in her breasts and belly, and deep inside her where Adam drove into her with a kind of madness that inflamed her.

Sensation exploded. She contracted around him but he kept pushing deeper and deeper until he buried his face in her neck and she felt the rush of wet warmth inside. "I love you, Adam," she whispered. "I love you so."

"He probably loves you, too, at the minute, lady," a man's thin voice said, making to pull her away. "Sorry to break up a stirring scene."

"Don't touch her!" Adam caught her in one arm and surged to his knees.

A dark figure, no more than a blur, appeared. A thud brought a moan from Adam and he slipped away from Desirée.

While she struggled with the man who held her, she saw Adam lifted over the man's shoulder and borne away toward the mews. The assailant staggered under the weight but he didn't stop.

The instant Adam had been carried from the alley, the remaining man spun Desirée around and slapped her face so hard she crumpled to the ground, holding out her hands to ward off more blows.

No more blows came. The man ran from her and after his accomplice.

She hurt all over but that was of no importance. Awkwardly regaining her footing, she stumbled forward, moving as fast as her protesting body would allow, until she reached the end of the passageway.

The sounds of activity were muted but plain.

Flattened to the wall, edging closer inch by inch, Desirée could finally peer into the mews. What she saw almost made her scream — an old black carriage, its doors open while Adam's limp body was pulled by a man inside and pushed by another outside. His sheer stature and his dead weight brought loud grunts and panting.

Desperate for the help of strong friends, Desirée told herself she was alone and that alone she would rescue Adam.

How, she had no idea.

At last they had Adam bundled into the carriage. One man stayed with him while the other checked the horses and jumped onto the box.

Barely able to breathe without wanting to be sick, Desirée had already left her hiding place. If she were to be of use, she must risk being seen.

She was within inches of the coach.

It rolled forward.

She threw her arms out, running as hard as she could, but the distance between her and her goal widened. The coach gathered speed, but she still ran behind.

Hoofs sounded as someone must have ridden a horse from one of the stables, then pounded in front of the carriage and away.

The vehicle had slowed for a moment, just long enough. Desirée's fingers curled around one of the metal handholds intended to help someone mount and she flung herself from the ground onto the narrow rear platform.

With her skirts trailing and her hair plastered across her eyes, she pressed herself against the carriage and gladly accepted the trouncing of her bones, the jarring of her teeth, the grinding of skin from her hands.

She was where she belonged, with her friend and lover. If she couldn't save him, she'd die with him.

Unconcerned that she wore her nightgown and robe in the middle of the foyer at Number 17, Meg put an arm around Jean-Marc's waist. He had already surrounded her shoulders and pulled her against him.

A ruffian, a big grimy creature in some sort of theatrical clothing and with a mane of hair curling down his back, lay on the floor with his hands pulled up behind his back by Evans, the under-butler at Number 7, and by Sir Robert Brodie. Hunter sat on the man's feet. Latimer dashed through the door with Ross, Viscount Kilrood to hover with Meg and Jean-Marc.

After an amazed glance at Ross, Jean-Marc pointed at the intruder and demanded, "What the devil is happening here? Who is this man and why is he in my house?"

Toby danced around the group on the

ground. " 'E stopped me when I was on my way 'ere and wanted to know where I was goin'. I said the truth, like Jenny always told me I should, that I was coming after Mr. Verbeux. 'E wanted to know where Mr. Verbeux was. Said they 'ad an appointment and Mr. Verbeux owed 'im money. I said I couldn't 'elp with that and 'e cuffed me."

Meg took strength from Jean-Marc who had apologized to her earlier in the evening and accepted her tongue-lashing for bad behavior like a man. He'd also accepted the lovemaking that followed like a man.

"And you subdued the villain on your own and brought him here?" Ross said, smiling slightly. He and Jean-Marc eyed each other from time to time and Meg could tell there would be a great deal to discuss between them later — as long as Jean-Marc didn't regress into idiot mode. Ross added, "Finnie and I arrived at Number 8 late this afternoon. Seemed best to come to Town and clear the air."

Jean-Marc grunted, but at least he didn't order his old friend from the house and Meg considered that a victory.

Toby stepped from foot to foot waiting for the men to finish, then said, "I leaves this one and comes to get Mr. Verbeux like

Mr. Chillworth said, only this cove was still in the park and 'e steps out and starts shoutin' at Mr. Verbeux. Mr. Verbeux didn't 'alf wop 'im one. So I runs ahead to get Mr. Chillworth only 'e and the Princess is gone. That's when Sir Robert come with me. 'E said 'e seen Adam and Desirée leave Number 7. Or he seen her runnin' away and Adam runnin' after 'er."

Meg noted that in his excitement, Toby forgot all formality and lapsed into the speech of his cockney roots. At any other time she might have chuckled.

"Brodie?" Jean-Marc said, sharply enough to make Meg cringe. "What's all this?"

"Adam and Desirée? Lovers' tiff, I'd say," Sir Robert said. "Perhaps we need the law for this one."

"Not until we know what brought him to the square," Hunter said, fighting with the fellow's kicking feet. "Where's Verbeux?"

The man laughed and squirmed with more vigor. "That's who you want. Verbeux, the scoundrel. Doesn't pay his debts."

"I've got to talk to you, please." Anne Williams, coming slowly down the stairs, her eyes huge and with high color along the cheekbones of her otherwise white face, captured everyone's attention. "Your Lordship, My Lady, could we talk alone."

Jean-Marc looked irritated and surveyed the mayhem in his foyer.

"This isn't a good time," Meg said. "In the morning, perhaps? *Later* in the morning?"

Anne's jaw set. She blinked slowly. "What I'm going to tell you will endanger the person I love most in the world, my daughter, but I don't have a choice anymore. Verbeux isn't here, is he?"

"He run off after he got what he wanted from me."

Anne looked at the unkempt man with horror. "Ran off where?"

"Why should I tell any of you?"

"You'd better find Verbeux," Anne said. "He knew about the child I had in Mont Nuages, and my shame, and how the man who took advantage of me turned away when I was increasing, then allowed his wife to take my baby and send me away."

Meg's knees felt weak. She pulled apart from Jean-Marc, sat on the stairs and motioned for Anne to join her. "This is true?" she asked her. "Does Desirée know?"

"Only that I lost my place, nothing more, but Verbeux knew it all, and he's been threatening to reveal the truth and ruin my daughter's life if I didn't tell him everything about the Princess's plans and what she does and where and who with. I don't understand why he wanted to know, but he did and he wouldn't leave me alone. My little girl will grow up with a good home and never know what really happened. That's best and I don't want it changed."

"You're safe now," Meg said. "We'll keep you safe."

A sleepy Sibyl wandered down and sat on the other side of Meg from Anne. "What is this?" she said and yawned. Then she saw the prisoner and yelped.

"Hush, darling," Hunter told her. "We have everything under control. Go back to bed."

" 'Course you do," the man said. "That bleedin' maniac's probably killed the big man by now and made off with the girl. That's what he was anglin' for. I knew it as soon as I saw 'em in Vauxhall Gardens and thought about Verbeux saying he couldn't have had her if she was a virgin, but if she was a widow, he had a chance to marry her."

First there was silence, then everyone spoke and demanded information at once.

"You don't get a word more out of me if

you don't promise to set me free afterward. I didn't do nothing to those two, only did what I was told."

"What Mr. Verbeux paid you for, you mean," Toby said. "Or didn't even pay you for. You don't care if you're helping him 'urt people."

"Hurt who?" Jenny entered the house in a rush with both Finch and Lady Hester Bingham behind her. "Who's hurt? Who did it?"

"Please," Latimer said, shaking his head. "Will all of you ladies go to your beds. There's nothing you can accomplish here. This man has something to do with ill befalling Adam and Desirée but we intend to get them back."

"Intend?" Jenny's voice rose. *"Intend?* Preserve me from men. There's no choice but to get them back."

Before anyone could stop her, she bent over the man and grabbed a handful of his hair, which she twisted until he squealed. "Tell whatever we need to know to find Adam and Desirée. *Now.*" And she twisted his hair tighter, lifted his head back as she did so. *"Now."*

"Get 'er off me!"

"*Now,* or I shall find other ways of torturing you and they will be even worse."

"Jenny," Latimer said.

"I know where they are," the man blurted out. Tears ran down his cheeks. "I think so anyway because Verbeux does all his nasties there. He took me there when he wanted to make sure I'd do what he wanted me to do. It's a bit of a way, but not too far."

The door stood open and Gilbert Chillworth walked in. He looked at the assembled crowd with what appeared to be a victim in their midst and his mouth hung open.

"Can I help you?" Jean-Marc said, with heavy sarcasm. "Or do you just want to come to the party?"

"I'm Gilbert Chillworth, Adam's father. I'm looking for my son and a rude old butler at Number 7 told me to come here."

The coach had taken so many turns that
Desirée had no idea where they were. There
were still houses, but they were growing
more scattered.

A wild swerve to the right and the horses
set up a racket, complaining at the whip on
their flanks. Desirée's arms were afire, her
shoulders and back strained beyond endurance, and her icy, bleeding hands felt
fused where they clung to the metal rungs.
The coach swayed as if it might turn over
and Desirée closed her eyes. She couldn't
give in to fear and pain now.

Between open gates they jangled and
screeched. There were outbuildings like those
on a farm and as they went farther, she
saw that a high fence enclosed the property.

Men's shouting voices reached her. The
horses were reined in and she heard heavy
scraping sounds and more yelling. At peril
of falling off, she crawled to peer around

the side of the coach and almost let go. The scraping had been the doors of a big barn being opened and she could see yellow light shining inside. The vehicle and its cargo were to be taken in there and away from the eyes of the world — away from anyone who might help Desirée to save her husband.

She could not go inside with him.

Crouched on the platform, she waited. The coachman thumped aboard again and the coach sagged. He urged the horses to move, and Desirée let go. She slipped to the ground, curled into a ball, and made no attempt to run away. Her only hope was that in the poor light and confusion she wouldn't be noticed.

Adam listened to the same, high, droning voice he'd heard in St. John's Wood when he was beaten and left for dead. The man seemed to think his prisoner remained unconscious but entertained himself by heaping insults upon him anyway.

The coach had stopped and men shouted. They had arrived at some important location.

Adam watched through slitted eyes from behind his arms where they rested in front of his face. Too bad the oaf had a pistol trained on him or he would have taken him already.

"I do hope you've been a good boy," the man said. "You're about to meet your maker and he'll be deciding what to do with you. Of course, if you like it warm there's a chap in another place who is always on the look out for recruits . . ." He fell silent and practiced looking down the barrel of the pistol when he leveled it at Adam's head.

Adam had never seen the man's forgettable face before, but he'd always remember that nasal voice.

What a fool he was, Adam thought. The most lovely girl in the world had shamed him, not deliberately or maliciously, but because she loved him and wanted to help him. But he wasn't big enough to be gentle with her and teach her more about the importance of a man's honor. No, instead he had told her to leave him.

She hadn't given up easily. He thought of her all but taking him on those icy cobbles and barely stopped a purely sexual shudder at the memory. Why not admit that she had taken him? His wife fascinated him and titillated him with all the power of a practiced courtesan.

What had the other fellow done to her?

He felt leaden and his head pounded. The blow he'd taken had knocked him out — he didn't know for how long. Might he be forgiven for failing Desirée, even though he would never forgive himself?

The coach bounced forward, then ran smoothly before stopping again. First one crash, then another followed. If he had to guess he'd say the coach had been taken inside somewhere — probably into a coach house. And he hadn't been brought here to be entertained.

Desirée.

"Whoa," the coachman hollered at his jostling horses. "Easy does it. Whoa!"

"Out with him," a familiar voice called. Adam frowned. "Then get out of here. And don't look for me. I'm paying you handsomely now but if I see you again . . . make sure I don't see any of you again. And you can take this one with you."

A woman whined but Adam couldn't make out what she said.

Someone yanked the door open and grabbed the back of his jacket to drag him out. That didn't accomplish much and amid curses, the man inside the coach helped deposit Adam on the floor of what smelled like a barn. He sniffed and hay prickled his nose.

It was a barn.

"Here you are." In the pause that followed, Adam heard the dull jingle of heavy coins in a bag. "There's a bonus here for a job well done. Now disappear."

The woman spoke again. "I'll be waitin' for you so you better not be long."

"Fear not, sweetness, it won't be long before you see me again."

Once more Adam used the shelter of his arms to look around him with slitted eyes. He located the owner of the familiar voice and felt a rush of hatred, and trepidation. Verbeux was likely to be a worthy enemy and he had surprise, and knowledge, on his side. Adam also assumed the man had done his share of fighting.

Suffering the torment, Adam swung to sit up. Every move was costly and his bound wrists and ankles caused his hands and feet to tingle. He met Verbeux's enigmatic gaze and felt sick to his stomach. He saw not one shred of remorse in the other man.

Verbeux didn't speak to him. "I want you men to take this one with you and see her home." Still he didn't say anything to Adam, but he pushed Cherry Pick, the voluptuous maid from St. John's Wood, in front of him and poked at her until she walked to the two men who stood beside the coach. One of them held the bag of money Verbeux had given him.

"You said if I did like you asked, you'd make me 'appy," the girl said. "I did everythin'. I delivered the message when that one showed up at Lavender's 'ouse. That was dangerous, that was. I could've got caught. Ought to be worth something extra."

"Oh, you shall have lots of things that are extra, my dear, including your own little house in St. John's Wood if that's what you'd like."

Cherry squealed, "Ooh," and got into the coach. She pulled the door shut and stuck her head out the window to flutter her fingers at Verbeux and blow him kisses. "Hurry up, Verby, I'll want to see you quickly."

The commotion started again while the two men opened the place to the night once more and boarded, both on the box this time, and backed the carriage from the barn. And it was a barn, a huge one. Straw loaded a loft and more bales stood ready to feed horses although, apart from one, all the stalls were empty.

Once they were alone, Verbeux closed and bolted the doors before walking in a slow circle around the barn. Adam didn't expect Verbeux's next move. Never looking away from Adam, he sank to the straw-littered floor and crossed his legs. He took out a knife with a thin blade some eight or so inches long and held it up, almost reverently, to allow light to flash on steel, then placed it carefully in front of him, handle toward his hands.

"This is how I wanted this to be," Verbeux said, "how I planned it. There should be a time for disclosure between the hunter and the hunted. I have known since I left Mont Nuages for the last time that you and I would be together, alone, and that I would tell you things you could never have guessed."

Adam didn't speak for fear of setting the man off on some mad rampage. He already sensed that Verbeux looked at the world through a prism that distorted truth.

"Do you know what it's like to be a cultured man from a fine old family, yet forced by circumstance to become a servant to others?" Inflection had all but left Verbeux's voice. "You have masqueraded as a man of few means, yet that was never the truth, and you have never had to call another, master."

The cold ground didn't soothe Adam's cramped limbs, or lessen the ache in his head. He wanted to look around, to weigh his options and decide what he would do, and he *would* do something. Giving up without fighting could be another man's way, but not his. Unfortunately instinct told him not to move at all.

"Nothing to say?" Verbeux asked. "No, I don't suppose you have. I have suffered. You cannot begin to imagine how I have suffered. I thought my marriage to Ila would at least soften my burden and it might have had she not died and taken the child with her.

"Do you know what it is like to love and know you can never hope to be loved in return?"

Verbeux's raised voice jolted Adam. He shook his head. Now wasn't the moment to say that he had and still did love a father who detested him.

"No. No, of course you don't. I am a man deeply in love. Not in the manner men such as you think of love, not carnal love, the urge to defile, to imprint yourself on an innocent body and soul that should never be touched in such a base manner. My love is as pure as the creature who owns my heart, yet I had no choice but to allow — no, to encourage you to take the Princess as your wife.

"I wanted to keep her untouched but, no

matter, she is young and not to blame. And it is your fault she is not as she was. If you had done as you were told and kept her virginity intact, I would never have to imagine what you've done to her."

He lifted the knife with both hands, turned the blade this way and that to send bursts of light darting. Studying Adam, he experimented until that white light hit his captive's eyes.

Adam turned his head aside and blinked.

His temper grew thin. He wanted to ask the man to say what he had to say and be done with it.

"I have wanted her, and waited to find my time to make her mine, but she doesn't love me — yet — and I would never be considered while she was suitable to become some nobleman's lady anyway. But she already loved you. A childish love you have encouraged for years. She saw you as her poetic hero with whom she would one day ride away.

"I despaired until at last I saw how I could use you to stop her making the Season and undoubtedly being spoken for by some pink of the *ton* who would be much more difficult to get rid of later. A temporary sham marriage to you was perfect. I made certain it happened because you are easy to deal with.

"Soon, when you're gone and she's a widow, it will be my turn. She thinks of me as almost a brother and when she is in need of a shoulder to cry on, of someone who does not criticize what she did, I shall be there.

"You have nothing to fear for her future because I shall always be with her and she will learn to love me. Jean-Marc trusts me and he will see how good I am for his heartbroken sister. When I ask for her hand, he will grant it gladly."

Dark, shifting spaces caused by light from the blade gradually faded from Adam's vision and he looked at Verbeux. "And then you will be no man's servant," he said, quickly adding, "neither should you be. To answer to another as you have must have been like salt on raw flesh."

Verbeux nodded. "I see you understand. I am going to be their peer and there will be little ways to make them pay. I shall have a grand home and nothing but the best of everything."

"And children?" Adam asked, even as he felt like puking at the thought. "You'll have children, of course."

"*No!*" Those dark, dark eyes widened to show white all around each iris. "Never.

That perfect body shall never be misshapen by that filth. I told you my intentions are not carnal. I have ways of dealing with such needs elsewhere."

Behind Verbeux's head, hooked over a nail, a scythe hung against a wooden pillar. If there were a distraction, something to get Verbeux out of the barn for a few minutes, perhaps the great curved blade could be used to cut Adam's bonds.

"It pains me to have to kill you."

"Then don't," Adam said with an engaging smile. "Why don't we work together to make the world a better place." When with a rattle, one might as well rattle along.

"Don't toy with me," Verbeux said. Without warning, he lifted the knife and aimed it as only a man who has done so many times before could do. He aimed the knife at Adam, and threw it.

Adam tried not to flinch, but failed.

Blood hammered in his ears.

He heard the blade split the air as it passed not more than inches from his left ear. There was a thump and a whine. He whipped his head around to see the knife vibrating, its point sunk deep into another wooden pillar.

Verbeux turned the corners of his mouth up and went to retrieve his weapon. He returned to his former spot and repositioned the knife on the floor. "Believe it when I say I can hit whatever I choose to hit. If I'd learned your grubby little family secret earlier, it might have been amusing to use it in some way, but even so, perhaps I would not have chosen to sink to such depths."

"Good of you," Adam said, with no idea what the bounder meant. Damn but he wished his wrists were tied at his back where he would have at least some chance of working them free.

"Think nothing of it," Verbeux said, "after all, which of us doesn't have a glass window or two. You do know what I'm talking about, don't you?"

He didn't, but he wasn't about to tell Verbeux as much.

"Damn me, you don't."

Adam had thought he hid his feelings better than that.

"You know your mother was having a child when she married your father?"

If his legs would cooperate, he'd throw himself on the man and get this over with.

"I'll be . . . You know nothing. Oh, yes, the Earl of Manthy's beautiful only child married Gilbert Chillworth, a wealthy but inconsequential farmer, because he loved her enough to claim her child as his own."

"Stop!"

"We have to be brave about these things, unpleasant as they are. I can't believe this has all been kept from you. Elspeth was swept off her feet by a handsome rake who took advantage of her, then asked another girl to marry him. Chillworth — I know how he felt of course — he would have done anything to get her and so it was. Lucas Chillworth isn't really Lucas Chillworth at all."

"This is all lies." Just for an instant, he thought there was a movement in the loft but didn't dare look more closely in case someone was hiding there and would be in danger if discovered.

"No, no, I have it on the best authority. That's why old Gilbert behaves as if he can't stand you. Foolish man, to take it so far. He — but, I'm sure you don't want to talk to me about it."

True enough, but Verbeux could not invent all this. "Talk away," Adam said, feigning a yawn. "Not a bad tale."

"I shall always know you died bravely," Verbeux said. "And I shall be proud of you for that.

"There were already whispers about your mother and then, when the baby was born so soon after the marriage, well you can imagine. Your father would not have your mother's reputation questioned so he has spent all these years pretending Lucas is his most beloved son. He has appeared to dote on him, to favor him — and when your mother left him because she could no longer bear the way he treated you, well, it was too late for Gilbert to do much but keep up the charade. No wonder poor Lucas has been so undone by the change in the wind there. Gilbert has cut off the ready funds. And exactly when Lucas needs to get his hands on a large amount of money, too."

Adam sat straighter. "None of this is true."

"You know it is. Your father finally sees that the loss of his wife is his own fault and he still has hopes he may reclaim her. He always doubted she cared for him at all, you see, but in the years since she left him there has not been another man and he must see his error in not trusting her fidelity."

Adam opened his mouth to breathe. How could he protest? For all he knew the story was indeed the truth. His throat was so dry he coughed and it took time for him to stop. In the guise of gasping for more air, Adam raised his chin and lowered his eyelids — and took a careful look at the loft.

A hand, not a very big hand, waved from the cover of a bale and for an instant he saw a mulberry-colored sleeve — and the suggestion of an eye peering at him.

He did choke then. Desirée was here, here in the loft and, given her outrageous conviction that she could accomplish whatever she pleased, he had no doubt she thought she could save him.

Save him. This was beyond all. She was alive and that's all that should matter, but if she tangled with Verbeux, if she got in the middle of things, how long would she live then? At the very least she could be seriously wounded.

He caught his breath. "I need to relieve myself."

"Be my guest."

Adam fell silent but his mind tumbled, tried to catch at first one idea, then another, only to have them dissipate. *His hands and feet were tied.*

"Don't you want to know how I found all this out and why?"

"No."

"Of course you do. I didn't set out to dig up nasty secrets. Someone who also didn't want you to succeed with the Princess told me."

Adam raised his face to look at the other man. "My father?"

"We won't play guessing games," Verbeux said. "This person thought to discredit you — the story would have been twisted, of course, making you the by-blow. I wouldn't go for it. After all, even if it did make it near impossible for you to get close to the Princess once it was revealed, someone was bound to remember the Count's own less than salubrious history. I would never hurt the Princess by stirring up the past."

To Adam's horror, at the outer edge of his vision, he saw Desirée leave the cover of the bale of hay. She did lie on her stomach but would still be easily enough seen by Verbeux if he turned around.

"No questions at all?" Verbeux asked.

"None."

"Very well," Verbeux said. "I wanted to give you a chance to discuss anything you wanted to discuss with me. Now I grow weary and since I don't relish my task I would prefer it behind me."

Standing up, the knife held loosely in his right hand, Verbeux regarded Adam. "I should prefer to cut your bonds first so that you could die trying to live, but I don't underestimate your strength. I'm going to blindfold you."

"No!" No, he didn't want his eyes covered and no, he didn't want Verbeux moving behind him where he might see Desirée.

By the heavens, she began to climb down a ladder. Very cautious to make no sound, she took the rungs slowly and, intelligent as always, kept her eyes ahead rather than try to see what was happening behind her. She reached the ground and threw herself behind several bales.

The rustle caught Verbeux's attention and he swung around, crouching as he did so, aiming the knife in one direction after another.

"Rats," Verbeux said. "Can't stand the things. Where would you prefer me to stab you?"

"Let me think about that." Bizarre as the question might be, his answer must be useful to him, and to Desirée, not flippant. "Perhaps you wouldn't like me to stand, but I would prefer to die on my feet."

Verbeux motioned with the knife for Adam to get up and he did so only to find his balance impaired by the position he'd been in and by his ankles still being strapped. He swayed but managed to remain standing. Another purpose for the scythe had occurred to him. If he could knock Verbeux down and manage to release even his hands, he could use the scythe against the would-be killer.

Desirée, holding her pelisse before her, tiptoed from her hiding place and Adam wanted to yell at her to go, to run, to hide, to scream — and none of it would be of any help.

"Where?" Verbeux said. "The eye may be fairly quick if my aim is good and my thrust deep enough. I'd advise against the stomach. Painful and takes too long to finish you. The heart? A good, clean wound to the heart might be your best choice. But it's up to you."

Desirée was moving. He must not, Adam knew, panic and cry out. "You give me a difficult decision, Verbeux," he said, deliberately raising his voice. "Do you have a preference."

She crouched and came toward them.

"Choose," Verbeux demanded.

The pelisse Desirée held landed over Verbeux's head. She tightened it around his neck and jumped onto his back. The man bellowed and tossed around.

"Stop it at once, Verbeux," she said. "You are a wicked, evil man but I shall put in a word to have you spared. That is if you drop that knife now."

Adam had already made his way to the scythe. The instant he began to cut at his bonds, the tool fell to the floor and he went down after it, scrabbling to position his wrists, one each side of the curved blade.

"Princess!" Verbeux wailed, the sound desperate. "I have come to save you. You have been led astray."

The scythe wasn't sharp but gradually the ropes frayed and began to fall away.

"Stop it," Verbeux yelled.

Adam glanced up to see Desirée pummeling his head, but then she reached for his face, found his eyes, and drove her fingers through the pelisse and deep into the sockets. Verbeux screamed. He also dropped the knife.

The last piece of rope parted and with a single slash, Adam freed his feet and held the scythe at the level of his shoulders.

Verbeux had flung Desirée from his shoulders, swept her in front of him and managed to retrieve the dagger. The pelisse had fallen away.

"Let her go," Adam said, advancing. "Do as I say and things will go better for you."

The sound of hoofs and wheels and

shouting voices approaching the barn didn't cheer him. If Verbeux's friends had returned, he and Desirée were done for.

Someone rattled the doors. The voices were too muffled to make out.

"I will speak for you if you let her go free," Adam said, willing to promise anything to gain his wife's freedom.

Verbeux behaved as if he hadn't heard the offer.

A shot sounded, and another and another. With each one, sparks shot through a small space between the doors, but the bolt didn't budge.

Quiet followed, interrupted by scuffling, then by grunting, and the doors burst wide, and in rushed a band of men holding a battering ram.

"Have a care," Adam said to Jean-Marc who was in the lead. "This is delicate."

The Count took in the situation at once. "We will talk," he said, beckoning his fellows forward.

Verbeux retreated, dragging Desirée with him, the blade actually drawing a thin line of blood at the base of her neck. Adam could not throw himself at them, he couldn't do anything but remain calm, at least on the outside.

Ross was at Jean-Marc's side. Hunter

and Latimer stood, shoulder-to-shoulder, a short way distant from them. Sir Robert and Evans were there and behind them came Adam's father. One look at the man's face showed that he didn't hate his son. Gray-faced, he appeared suddenly older, but when he looked at Verbeux, wrath made his stance vigorous.

"You are all going to do as I tell you," Verbeux said. He kept his voice steady and must have felt Desirée's blood on his hand because his face twisted and he said, "*No, my love*. I have cut you. Forgive me. You men are going to leave this place, you will leave the Princess and me. We will contact you in good time. And I promise she will be safe. Say you forgive me, Princess."

Adam's brave wife had lost her fire. She leaned against Verbeux, staring only at Adam. "I forgive you," she murmured. "You have cut my throat."

"I know." Aghast, Verbeux held the knife away from her skin.

"You cannot escape," she said, so very quietly. "There are nine of us and you are only one. We will win."

"You are with me, not with them," Verbeux said. He captured Desirée's right hand and he worked off the domed ring Countess Manthy had given her. "Anne told me about this. A delightful idea. I know all about such things and this would be worth a pretty penny. A poison ring."

"It's empty," Desirée said, her voice growing even fainter.

"Let's see, shall we?" Verbeux said and pushed the point of his dagger into the hole at the side of the ring. The top popped open and he snared a tiny fold of paper between his fingers before letting the ring fall. He unfolded the paper enough to see what was inside and a look of resolve settled on his face. "Poison, you see. Just as I told you. Undoubtedly very strong poison so that death would come quickly."

Relief almost sent Adam to his knees. He glanced at Jean-Marc who nodded slightly. Verbeux knew he would never get out of here alive and was going to poison himself.

Collectively they all held their breath while he tipped the powder into his palm and began to raise it to his mouth.

He paused long enough to say, "As the ring instructs, follow me, my sweet," as he relinquished the knife to force some of the stuff into Desirée's mouth before swallowing the rest himself.

Adam ran at them. Too late.

Verbeux fell to the floor, and Desirée fell with him.

42

"Dead? My God — *dead?*" Rolly Spade-Filbert had dashed into the barn and forced himself between the other men. "The ladies at Number 17 told me where you were. How could this happen?"

Adam stumbled to his knees. He had to drag Verbeux aside to get to Desirée. Other hands came to his aid but he neither knew nor cared who they belonged to. He pushed them all away and gathered her into his arms.

"Adam," she said. "I fell because he fell and knocked me down."

He touched her face, brushed back her still-loose hair and looked at her closely. "You . . . You're hurting, my love." Her face twisted. The wound on her neck was nothing, a scratch that would heal — if only she lived.

Sir Robert would not be forced aside. He felt Desirée's pulse and put his ear to her chest.

"I say." Spade-Filbert bent over Verbeux and poked his back. "From what Lady Hester said — granted she was hysterical — but I thought this one came with the rest of you. What's happened to him?"

Verbeux moaned.

"Best thing is to make them cast up their accounts," Sir Robert said. "Could be the stuff's so old it's lost its potency."

Verbeux rolled onto his back and raised a hand in the air. "Too late. Let us be. The Egyptians . . . They knew their poisons. I can't see properly."

"Can you open your eyes, old chap?" Rolly asked.

Adam kissed Desirée's cheek and said, "How do you feel? Is the pain bad."

"No," she said. "He got a lot more of it than me."

Verbeux had opened his eyes and Rolly said, "How about now? Can you see now?"

Dark eyes rested on him. "Through a film," Verbeux said. "I'm fading."

Adam and Sir Robert reached for the fallen paper at the same time.

"Watch out for this one," Verbeux said, pointing at Rolly with a finger that wavered. "He didn't care how he did it, but he wanted to be accepted by the Etrangers. He wanted to move in their circles and have access to their money. He's in more trouble than Lucas Chillworth. He thought he'd get what he wanted by helping me. It's too late to get me, Chillworth, but he's still alive. He's the one who carried the Princess into that house. He paid the boy to lie about the cat."

"He's delirious," Rolly said, standing back. "You can see that. He doesn't know what he's saying."

Adam licked his finger, touched it to the residue of powder on the paper and tasted it — and wrinkled his nose. Sir Robert did the same and they both looked at Desirée. Her own nose was still wrinkled but she managed to grin at the same time.

Without a word, Jean-Marc took a few grains and passed the paper to Ross. It didn't take long for each man to rest a finger on the end of his tongue.

Verbeux had thrown himself to his back again and writhed in earnest now.

There was a yell, and Adam saw that Evans had caught Rolly on his way to the door and doubled him up with a punch to the belly. The under-butler folded Rolly's arms behind his back, snatched up some of the rope Adam had discarded and used the longer pieces to lash Spade-Filbert's thumbs together with knots that grew tighter each time the man tried to yank his hands apart. Such a howling followed as Adam had never before heard from a grown man.

The assembled men closed into a circle around Verbeux. Adam pushed to the center and landed the first punch. He picked the man up by the shoulders and threw him down again with enough force to raise dust.

Desirée's laughter brought a smile to every mouth but Verbeux's and Rolly's. "It's salt, Verbeux," she said through her chuckles. "Salt, much more valuable a long time ago than it is now."

43

Lady Hester would hear of nothing but that she be allowed to host what she called the "wedding breakfast" for Adam and Desirée. After all, she had insisted, it was at Number 7 that all these wonderful *tendres* had begun. Not entirely true, but Jean-Marc and Meg had agreed as long as they were allowed to oversee the details.

"Stop staring at me," Desirée told Adam. "Everyone will see you."

A day and a night had passed since the horrors of Verbeux and Rolly Spade-Filbert. Both had been arrested. And little more than an hour earlier, with help from friends in high places, a bishop had blessed the marriage of Adam and Princess Desirée.

"Stop," Desirée said. Adam had manoeuvered her into a corner of the small ballroom where they were to eat, and placed himself between his wife and the guests who crowded about the flower-

festooned room drinking champagne and chattering. "You're embarrassing me. What will everyone think?"

His smile had the expected result. Her legs, her stomach, her breasts, all of her most sensitive places tingled or ached. "They all think the truth. I want you all to myself. You and I have been through a great deal but now we are together and I don't want to share you."

She couldn't stop the corners of her mouth from twitching. "And I don't want to share you, but I shall manage for a little while before I bear you away and ravage you."

Adam actually turned a little pink. "You are beyond all, madam. I think I may take you right here. What have you to say about that?"

Making a little show of fussing with his neckcloth, she said, "I say that I have nothing to fear from the man who was embarrassed when I took *him* in a deserted passageway."

He closed his eyes and shook his head, and when he kissed her it was so sudden she couldn't get her breath. She leaned against the wall and he opened her mouth, thrust his tongue inside, rocked their faces together.

Desirée didn't care that all of their friends must be watching them. Adam's hands at her waist, stroking her sides, her back, pressed the rosettes of pearls on her ivory satin gown into her skin and she loved the heat of him.

Adam paused and rested his forehead on hers. "I love you," he said. "I always will. You are my miracle."

Tears filled her eyes and she whispered, "You are my everything."

The room had grown silent but for a cleared throat or two and the odd sniffle. Adam looked into Desirée's face. "I suppose we should join them so that they can eat."

"But we don't really want to, do we?"

He raised his brows. "I have another meal in mind and very soon. Come."

Adam turned and pulled her beside him. Immediately she hid her face. Standing in a semicircle, the gathering watched them. More than a few handkerchiefs were in sight and there was a collective, "Ah."

Lady Hester, her eyes red despite a wide smile, ushered them to their seats at a very long table procured for the event but, that lady reminded them, soon to be used for many more grand affairs. The others took their places and Old Coot signalled for service to begin.

"A moment." Jean-Marc stood with his champagne glass in his hand. "One toast before we eat." He raised the glass high. "To a couple who have proved the strength of their love and commitment to each other. Thank you for bringing such joy to Meg and me, and to our family — including our next little one, I'm sure."

"Bravo," the cry went up.

"And to Finch and myself," Ross said, jumping to his feet. "You brought me closer to my grave in Scotland, but all is forgiven. We should tell you that we are also looking forward to a new family addition."

Latimer rose and pulled Jenny up with him. "My wife tells me I should assure you that you have our love always, and I do assure you of that. We love you. Including the little More who is not yet with us."

Laughter and applause followed before Hunter stood, "Sibyl and I wish you as much happiness as we have found." He indicated a second table where the children sat, trying to behave, with teenage Hayden — Finch and Ross's adopted boy — Birdie, and Toby attempting to keep order. "I speak for all the children, too — including the one we await."

Sir Robert beckoned Lady Hester to his

side, gave her a glass and raised his own. "Lady Hester is not increasing," he announced amid laughter. "But in May we shall marry."

"And live here," Lady Hester said, looking like a rosy girl. "Robert understands how attached I am to this house. I can never explain exactly what each of you means to me, and to see Adam married — to Desirée of course — is more than I could ever have hoped for."

Desirée could scarcely bear the burning in her throat. She turned to Adam, only to discover his attention elsewhere. He stared from his father to his mother, seated side by side probably for the first time in some years. The former's regard was steadily on his wife while her head was bowed, her face not visible.

Abruptly, Lady Elspeth stood up. She had no glass but she said, "I wish great happiness to my wonderful son and his bride. Thank you for allowing me to share in your lives." She turned to Gilbert and offered him her hand. "My husband and I both wish you a wonderful life and hope you will visit us often when we return to the farm."

Desirée watched her husband. He and Lucas exchanged a long glance. There was too much to absorb, almost too much emotion to absorb. Lucas put an arm around Enid's shoulders and clearly could not form words.

"Everything is getting cold," Lady Hester said, dabbing away at her eyes and nose with her handkerchief. "Coot?"

The staff set to work at once while Adam and Desirée held hands tightly under the table. She put her mouth to his ear and said, "Everyone is to have a new child. Except Lucas and Enid as far as we know."

"And us," he said, kissing her cheek. "But we'll see if we can't change that very soon."

Desirée refused the soup and reached for a sugarplum instead. This she held close to her lips but before she popped it in, she said, "We already have changed it."

Adam's eyes widened. "How?"

"Dear, dear, I had no idea how little you understand about these things," she told him. "I'll explain later, but I do believe it happened on our wedding night."

"Minx," he said. "Wonderful minx. How am I supposed to sit here? I will not share you, or this moment."

Desirée squeezed his thigh and said, "I think you should eat. You need your strength."

Evans came into the room and bent to talk to Lady Hester. She nodded and continued eating her soup.

"Where's Barstow?" Jenny asked, obviously savoring her soup.

"In Brighton," Lady Hester said, offhanded. "She and Mr. Lumpit were married there several days ago. She wrote that they preferred a quiet affair and time alone. But they will return to live at Number 7."

Chuckles ensued but Lady Hester said, rather loudly, "I'm very pleased for Mr. and Mrs. Lumpit. Everyone deserves someone to love."

Without warning, sugarplums, fruit and nuts began to cascade from the exquisite silver epergne at the center of the table. Gardenias floated from their decorative dishes. Desirée opened her mouth to exclaim but no sound emerged. Apparently of its own volition, the epergne fell to its side and rolled back and forth until Lucas stopped it.

Old Coot waved a maid forward to clear up the mess.

Everyone continued eating as if each of them had decided the less said about toppling delicacies, the better.

Evans came in again, this time with a

somewhat awkward Anthony FitzDuram. "I'm sorry I couldn't make the blessing," he said, and Desirée felt badly for him. "Thought I should pay my respects as soon as I could, though. All the best to the bride and groom."

Desirée and Adam said, "Thank you," a little too heartily.

Anthony made to leave but Lady Hester told him to stay and a chair was brought for him, and a place set.

"Are you sure you want to go to the attic?" Adam whispered to Desirée. "Sibyl and Hunter offered us their rooms until we decide on a new place of our own."

"The attic," Desirée responded. "That's where we first lay on a bed together. Today that bed shall discover that there is always more to learn about the art of making love."

He kissed her neck — in front of everyone. "I've got to get you out of here."

"Mmm," she said, doubting he wanted to go more than she did.

"Before our bride and groom leave," Lady Hester said knowingly, raising titters around the table. "I should let you know that when they have chosen their new home — and I know it is to be in Mayfair Square — then Mr. FitzDuram will join us here. He has decided to do what he has always wanted to do. He will write wonderful poetry and considers the attic just the place. So you see, my tradition of giving refuge to worthy protégées continues."

With a yowl, Halibut, who must have been under the table, shot into view, hissing and snarling as Desirée had never seen him do before.

She could have sworn she heard feet thumping and she definitely felt a heavy breeze whirl about them. Glasses blew over, spilling champagne.

"I say," Hunter remarked, grabbing for glasses with the rest of them.

Halibut, his eyes crossed, drew himself up and seemed to walk on the tips of his claws, or stalk rather.

"Look at him," Adam said. "He is annoyed."

"Very annoyed," Desirée agreed. "But we are going now."

They stood up.

Halibut took off for the door but pulled up before he reached it. Thumping sounded and the cat backed off, only to sniff about suspiciously before sitting down with a disgruntled look on his face.

"If I were given to fancy," Finch said,

"I'd wonder if some spirit is angry with us."

Jean-Marc got up and opened the door. "Off with you two," he said, grinning. "You've had a tiring day and need your sleep."

From downstairs came a crashing noise.

Desirée and Adam ignored it and followed Halibut up to the attic.

Epilogue — Part 1

7 Mayfair Square
London
February 1824

My good friends:

Yes, although you have misunderstood me, maligned me, laughed at me, you are my friends.

Stop at once! What happened at that celebration is a result of my once being human. I remain an artist, a passionate, talented artist and my behavior is supposed to be flamboyant.

No, sorry to disappoint you but I will not discuss either Lumpit or Anthony FitzDuram. I won't, won't, won't. That's that so don't try to irritate me further.

What? What did you say? Dash it all no, magic tricks have nothing to do with it. How many times must I tell you so? Skill is everything. And I have made great progress in that department. The cat? Vicious creature — surely he will never enter this house again once Adam and the Princess are on their way.

I can't dwell on that.

You are amazed, aren't you, and that disrespectful scribbler is amazed? She may even think me foiled and about to be forgotten.

We shall see.

Hold your tongues. I'm not going to tell you my intentions but I will say that I have worked too long and too hard to allow Hester to waste all my efforts.

A poet in the attic? What a cliché. Foolish woman. Absolutely I lost my temper, wouldn't you?

I need a rest. I need a long rest without any distractions from my problems at Number 7 Mayfair Square, or from the likes of Willy boy or any other nuisances.

There's a chance I may become a teacher's helper at school. I knew my skills and possibilities would eventually be noted.

But first, rest, and then we'll see where my afterlife takes me.

Be assured that I shall be watching and that I shall never desert my post.

Spivey

PS: Never allow others to embarrass you out of taking chances. If you should be in a likely house — on one of those dreadful house tours, say — and something reminds you of me (perhaps a marvelously carved you-know-what), lean close and ask for Sir Septimus.

Epilogue — Part 2

Frog Crossing
Watersville
Out West

Dearest Friends:

I doubt if Spivey's invitation included me.

He has improved, though. Or he improves in some areas if not in others. He wouldn't thank me for saying so, but he seems almost human.

If he'd allow me to give him one piece of advice, I'd suggest he rethink this whole earthly helper thing. The man is a rotten judge of character. What he knows about character . . . well, he doesn't know anything. Empty minds? Selfishly busy minds? Why not be straightforward and look for a willing representative who would do a good job for good pay. Advertise the position like this: WANTED: An ordinary mind with average curiosity and an advanced ability to follow instructions, no matter how ridiculous. Good benefits. Generous vacations. Counseling always available. No ministers, lawyers, law enforcement officers, scientists, clairvoyants, scribblers — or cats need apply.

Oh dear. What am I saying?

The man has finally worn me out. I'm off to find my own post.

Until we meet again, I am, as ever, your undaunted and devoted scribbler.

Stella Cameron